HIS LAST COMMAND

IT IS THE twenty-first year of the Sabbat Worlds Crusade and Warmaster Macaroth's main battle-groups are making large gains against the Chaos forces of Urlock Gaur. Against all odds, Colonel-Commissar Ibram Gaunt returns from a long mission behind enemy lines, only to find his regiment, the Tanith First-and-Only, has been redeployed under a charismatic new commander. Gaunt faces his most difficult battle yet as he fights to reclaim his command before the evil forces of Chaos counter-attack.

A WARHAMMER 40,000 NOVEL

HIS LAST COMMAND

Dan Abnett

For Matt Farrer

A BLACK LIBRARY PUBLICATION

First published in Great Britain in 2005.
Paperback edition published in 2006 by BL Publishing,
Games Workshop Ltd.,
Willow Road, Nottingham,
NG7 2WS, UK.

10 9 8 7 6 5 4

Cover by Alex Boyd
Map by Nuala Kinrade

A CIP record for this book is available from the British Library.

ISBN 13: 978 1 84416 239 0
ISBN 10: 1 84416 239 7

Distributed in the US by Simon & Schuster
1230 Avenue of the Americas, New York, NY 10020, US.

See the Black Library on the Internet at
www.blacklibrary.com

Find out more about Games Workshop
and the world of Warhammer 40,000 at
www.games-workshop.com

IT IS THE 41st millennium. For more than a hundred centuries the Emperor has sat immobile on the Golden Throne of Earth. He is the master of mankind by the will of the gods, and master of a million worlds by the might of his inexhaustible armies. He is a rotting carcass writhing invisibly with power from the Dark Age of Technology. He is the Carrion Lord of the Imperium for whom a thousand souls are sacrificed every day, so that he may never truly die.

YET EVEN IN his deathless state, the Emperor continues his eternal vigilance. Mighty battlefleets cross the daemon-infested miasma of the warp, the only route between distant stars, their way lit by the Astronomican, the psychic manifestation of the Emperor's will. Vast armies give battle in his name on uncounted worlds. Greatest amongst his soldiers are the Adeptus Astartes, the Space Marines, bio-engineered super-warriors. Their comrades in arms are legion: the Imperial Guard and countless planetary defence forces, the ever-vigilant Inquisition and the tech-priests of the Adeptus Mechanicus to name only a few. But for all their multitudes, they are barely enough to hold off the ever-present threat from aliens, heretics, mutants – and worse.

TO BE A man in such times is to be one amongst untold billions. It is to live in the cruellest and most bloody regime imaginable. These are the tales of those times. Forget the power of technology and science, for so much has been forgotten, never to be re-learned. Forget the promise of progress and understanding, for in the grim dark future there is only war. There is no peace amongst the stars, only an eternity of carnage and slaughter, and the laughter of thirsting gods.

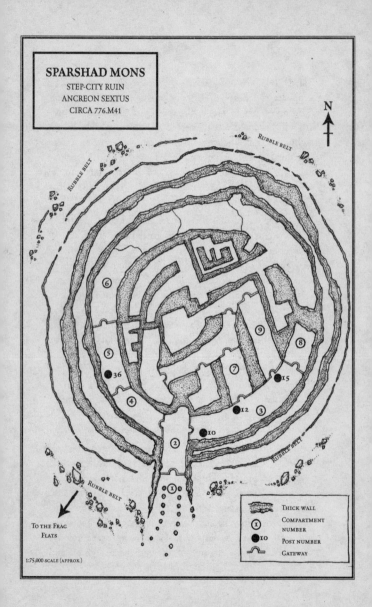

'BY THE MIDDLE of 776.M41, the twenty-first year of the Sabbat Worlds Crusade, War-master Macaroth's main battle-groups had penetrated extensively into the Carcaradon Cluster, and had become locked in full-scale war against the main dispositions of the archenemy overlord, ('Archon'), Urlock Gaur.

However, to Macaroth's coreward flank, an equally savage war front was being prosecuted by the War-master's secondary battle-groups – the Fifth, Eighth and Ninth Crusade Armies – as they attempted to oust the forces of Magister Anakwanar Sek, one of Gaur's most ferocious warlord lieutenants, from the margins of the Khan Group.

The theatres of that campaign read as a roll call of Imperial heroism and endeavour: the glass beaches of Korazon, the black glaciers of Lysander, the high sierra forests of Khan Nobilis, the step-cities of Ancreon Sextus…'

– from A History of the Later Imperial
Crusades

PROLOGUE

23.45 hrs, 185.776.M41
Imperial Internment Camp 917 'Xeno'
Southern Polar Plateau, Ancreon Sextus

'Are you sure about this, sir?' Ludd yelled above the storm as they crossed the yard, heads down into the knifing gale.

The wind was full of ice crystals that flashed like glass dust in the beams of the blockhouse stab-lights. Kanow had no intention of opening his mouth to reply.

They reached the iron porch of the assessment block, and pulled the cold metal hatches shut behind them. The wind-howl subsided slightly.

'I said–' Ludd began.

'I heard,' Kanow replied, brushing powder-ice off his leather coat. 'Sure about what?'

Junior Commissar Nahum Ludd shrugged. 'I was only wondering, sir, if we should wait.'

'For what?'

'Corroboration?'

Kanow snorted. 'This camp's at full capacity, Ludd. We must process, process, process.' With each repetition of

9

the word, he slapped his hands together quickly. 'If I waste time checking each and every tall story these deserters and heretics spin, we'll be overrun. What's my motto, Ludd?'

'Fast appraisal, fast despatch, sir.'

'Fast appraisal, that's right. And in this case, are you in any doubt?'

The junior commissar hesitated.

'Well, I'm not,' Kanow said. 'Deserters and heretics. You can see that just by looking at them, and smell it just from the stink of their bodies. And that story? It doesn't deserve corroboration, Ludd. It's patently mendacious.'

'Yes, sir,' said Ludd.

'What are they?'

'Deserters and heretics, sir.'

'That's right. Did you actually think we should get this verified?'

Ludd looked at his feet. Pools of ice-melt were forming on the metal floor around his boots and coat-hem. 'There were certain aspects which I felt to be compelling and worth–'

'Shut up, Ludd,' Commissar Kanow said.

Kanow pushed through the inner hatch into the main hallway of the assessment block. Ludd followed. There was an animal warmth in the air, a cattle-bower stink. Laced with metal walkways and staircases, eight storeys of prison containment rose up on either side of the gloomy hall space, and from the shuttered rockcrete pens all around them, Ludd and Kanow could hear moans and murmurs issuing from thousands of incarcerated men. Dirty, degenerate wretches with ragged clothes peered out at them through the serried wire gates of the sorting cages on the ground floor.

'Please, sir! By the grace of the Throne, please!' one man called out, reaching a filthy hand out through the bars.

Kanow unholstered his bolt pistol and racked the slide. The wretch drew back immediately, and inmates in the nearby pens shrank away to the far walls with a muted wailing, like reprimanded dogs.

A nearby blast-hatch whined open and let in a fierce gust of icy air. The commissar and his junior both shielded their faces from the cold. Yelling and waving shock mauls, a gang of armoured troopers began herding in another batch of new arrivals from Outer Processing.

'Pen one seventeen!' a voice shouted, and a buzzer sounded as the electric cage door on one seventeen unlocked with a clack. The troopers drove the newcomers inside, enthusiastically beating the slowest or most reluctant amongst them.

Once the cage was locked again, the gang of troopers began to disperse to other duties.

'Trouble, commissar?' asked Troop Sergeant Maskar, noticing the drawn bolt pistol as he came over.

'Not yet, Maskar,' Kanow grunted. 'But I need you and an armed detail, if you've got a moment.'

'At your command, sir,' Maskar nodded, and turned. 'Squad six, with me!'

Maskar was a big man, shaven-headed and fleshy. Like all the Camp Xeno troopers, he wore leather-jacked steel armour that was articulated around his body and limbs in interlocking segments, so as to give the impression of well-developed but flayed musculature. He slid his shock maul into its belt loop and unlimbered his cut-down autorifle. The five troopers with him did the same.

Kanow ejected the magazine from his bolt pistol. The afternoon's round of executions had left it almost spent. He slammed home a fresh one.

'Pen three twenty-eight,' Kanow said, and the troopers fell into step behind him, arming their rifles.

'Summary kills, sir?' Maskar asked.

'I'll have the paperwork done by the morning, sergeant. The warrants too. But this can't wait. Follow my lead.'

'Sir, I–'

Kanow looked round at Ludd.

'What? What now?'

'Nothing, sir,' Ludd said.

The party clattered up two flights of metal stairs, their heavy tread shaking the steps, then turned right along the third deck gallery.

They reached the cage door of three twenty-eight. The chamber within looked empty.

'Pen three twenty-eight!' Maskar yelled, and the automated bolts shot open as the buzzer sounded.

Kanow entered. The third deck pens were larger holding tanks reserved for groups of up to thirty inmates. Several of the wall lights in three twenty-eight had apparently malfunctioned. Kanow could just make out some dark figures, a dozen or so, cowering in the shadows at the back of the pen.

'Were they armed?' asked Maskar.

'They were when they arrived,' Ludd replied. 'But they surrendered their weapons without protest.'

Kanow ignored his junior's pointed emphasis.

'Where is the leader here?' he called.

A figure walked towards him out of the shadows: tall, lean, feral. The man's clothes were a dirty patchwork of leather and canvas, stained almost black with dirt and dust. A vagabond. His angular face was masked behind a thick, grey beard of matted dreadlocks, but where it could be seen, it was lined with scars, and seemed to have a discoloured, grey cast, as if the dirt was ingrained. His hair was shaggy and long, and also matted grey. His eyes were piercing.

'Commissar,' he said, with a formal nod that was strangely at odds with his matted, shaggy appearance. His voice was dry, with a peculiar, alien inflection. 'I trust you have reviewed my statement and have made contact with–'

Kanow raised his pistol. 'You are a heretic and a deserter. You now face the justice of the Imperial Throne and–'

An immense and sudden force tore the pistol painfully out of Kanow's hand. Simultaneously, a knuckle-punch struck him in the throat and he fell back, gasping.

A vicing arm locked around his neck in a throttle-hold. Kanow felt himself being dragged back tightly against his assailant's body. Then he felt the cold muzzle of his own pistol brush gently against his temple.

'No one move,' said the man behind him, with that same, dry, curious inflection.

Maskar and all the other troopers were aiming their autorifles directly at Kanow and his captor. Ludd stood in the middle of them, bewildered.

'Put the gun down. Now,' Maskar snarled over his shouldered weapon.

'So you can shoot me?' replied the voice behind Kanow's head. 'I don't think so. But I'm a reasonable man. Look, sergeant. I had the stone drop on you just then, and yet no one's dead so far. Is that the act of a heretic or a deserter?'

'Drop the gun!'

'Put up your weapons, sergeant,' Ludd urged.

'That young man's got the right idea,' said the man with the gun to Kanow's skull.

'Not in a million years, you bastard,' Maskar replied.

'That's a shame,' the man choking Kanow said. Then, quietly, he added, 'Dercius.'

Figures moved out of the shadows. Either that, or shadows moved out and became figures, Ludd wasn't sure. All he knew was that in a heartbeat, Maskar and his men had been crippled and dropped by swift phantoms, their rifles ripped out of their hands.

Maskar and his men writhed on the deck, clutching bloody faces, snapped arms and broken noses. The shadows, now armed with the troopers' weapons, surrounded Ludd.

'What do you want?' Ludd asked quietly.

'Shut up, Ludd! Don't give them anything!' Kanow yelled. The choke-hold tightened.

'You were saying, Ludd?' said one of the shadows.

Ludd swallowed. 'What… what is it that you want?'

'What I asked for in the first place,' replied Ibram Gaunt, his arm locked around Commissar Kanow's neck. 'I want to talk to Lord General Barthol Van Voytz, and I want to do it *now*.'

ONE

HE HAD BEEN expecting to get a view of the infamous Sparshad Mons as they dropped into their shallow approach, but all he could see via his relay screen was a flat expanse of endless dust dunes baked bone-white in the merciless glare.

He fiddled with the screen's magnification, and zoomed in on the desert floor, glimpsing dark dots and tiny litters of black specks. The white flats were not so spotless as the distance had suggested. There were thousands of square kilometres of wreckage down below: the twisted shells of war machines, burned-out ruins, human bones, a dead city, the legacy of the previous year's fighting. The debris was covered with a coating of white dust, smoothing it into the flatness of the desert. Once, the entire zone had been the site of the mighty prefecture city of Sparshad Celsior. War had transmuted it into Frag Flats.

15

'Where's the Mons?' he asked.

'Directly ahead, sir,' the pilot's voice crackled over the intervox.

'I can't see… oh.' He still couldn't see the Mons, but he could now tell where it was. Where the flat, white land ended and the pitiless blue sky began, a vast bank of orange cloud covered the horizon, directly ahead. It looked like a natural weather pattern, or the haze of a gathering dust storm, rising like a cliff-face above the desert.

But it was smoke. A gigantic slab of smoke lifting from the battlefront and veiling the bulk of the Mons. He dialled up to maximum magnification and was able to detect tiny flashes in the base of the fume-bank, like sparks. Laser artillery, heavy ordnance, earthshakers, all assaulting the hidden edifice.

'Escort peeling off,' the vox reported.

He looked round, squinting out of the tiny window port, and caught a glint in the sunlight as the Lightning escort turned away, leaving the Commissariat Valkyrie alone for its final approach.

'Two minutes,' the pilot reported.

'Thank you,' he replied. He adjusted his viewer again, and lined up on the rapidly approaching HQ. It squatted like a reptile on the bleak, white landscape. Four Command Leviathans docked together in a cross, surrounded by the vast, regimented lines of ranked fighting vehicles, gun-platforms, extensive habi-tent camps, fuel and munition depots, and parked fliers. A vast assembly of Imperial Guard power, a mobile city: each Leviathan alone was an armoured crawler the size of a small town.

He switched off the viewer, and looked at his own face reflected in the blank plate. He put on his cap and adjusted the set of it, but despite the cap, and despite his splendid formal uniform, he still looked like a pale-faced youth. And a frightened one, too.

Junior Commissar Nahum Ludd sat back in his restraint web, closed his eyes, and tried to calm his nerves. He was the only occupant of the passenger section, and the vacant seating all around troubled him more than he cared to admit. The transport rocked slightly as it applied thrusters to decelerate hard. Ludd felt his stomach flop as they began to drop vertically.

'Thirty seconds to touchdown,' the pilot reported, his voice calm and expressionless.

Ludd swallowed. *My lord general*, he rehearsed for the umpteenth time, *I extend a cordial greeting from my commanding officer, Commissar Kanow, who apologises that he could not come here himself…*

THERE WAS A thump, a hard vibration, then all sense of motion fell away. The internal lighting flickered on, and the red runes on the bulkhead switched to green.

'Sparshad Zone HQ, sir,' the vox crackled.

'Thank you, pilot,' Ludd replied, unclasping his harness and rising to his feet. The cabin's air-scrubbers had switched to external circulation, and the slightly stale air blew fresher from the vents. Ludd walked over to the hatch, past the rows of empty seats. Since boarding at Camp Xeno, he'd not seen another human face. That fact continued to bother him.

There was a hand-written notice pasted to the inside of the hatch. It read 'GLARE-SHADES!'. Ludd smiled, took his glare-shades out of his coat pocket and put them on.

'Hatch, please.'

With a slight pop of decompression that hurt his ears, the hatch disengaged and began to slide away and out on its hydraulic arms.

Light flooded in, and heat too. Ludd gasped at the hard bite of the atmosphere outside. The light was as white and fierce as a laser. Without his glare-shades, he'd have been blinded.

Ludd looked out into the radiant world awaiting him. Then, with his data-case under his arm, he walked down the ramp.

The Valkyrie had set down on a landing pad on the hunched back of one of the vast Leviathans. Service crews in full sun-shrouds were hurrying forward into the shadow of the big transport to couple it up and attach fuelling lines. The landing pad was a flat disc of pale green metal, coated with a thin dusting of fine, wind-blown white sand, so that the crews' progress was recorded in smudged footprints and the smears left by trailing hoses.

Ludd wandered a few paces away from the Valkyrie. The dust-caked back of the Leviathan spread out around him in all directions, a grim vista of cooling vents, gun-turrets and sensor domes. Ludd had not been aboard a Leviathan before. It was immense. Turning, he could see the other three crawlers, docked with it, a vast cruciform of dirt-swathed steel.

There was a loud bang and a doppler scream of passing jet-wash as a pack of Imperial Interceptors streaked overhead. Ludd watched them as they turned north, jockeying into attack formation.

Ludd walked over to the guard-rail. On the Leviathan's back, he was as high up as if he'd been standing on the roof of a hive stack. It was a giddying drop to the desert below, but not so distant as it had been from the air. He could see the extent of the HQ encampment clearly now, the huge, marshalled assemblies of men and machines spread out around the Command crawlers. Brigades of fighting vehicles waited in the sunlight for deployment orders, tenders and armoury loaders moving amongst them. Vast forests of troop tents covered the desert like infestations of domed fungi, surrounding the large prefab modules of infirmaries, mess-halls and training barns. To the west, beyond the heavily defended mass of the supply dumps and the temporary hangars, lay a massive stretch of rolled-down hardstand matting lined with parked fighter-bombers and their smaller escorts. At the camp's northern perimeter, he could see a column of armour, kicking up dust as it moved out towards the front. Dozens of black vox masts sprouted from the camp all around, like spears planted into the ground.

The heat was amazing. There was no shade. The sun was so hot it seemed to crackle and buzz in the sky. Ludd felt his exposed skin tingle. A tan, he thought. It would be good to go back to the camp with a tan, after all those months of polar night.

He looked north, at the towering smoke bank, at Sparshad Mons. Now he was outside, Ludd could distinctly smell the reek of fyceline   bardment. And the Mons was a good fifty, sixty kilometres away.

He could just make out the battery flashes, but he wanted a better look. He raised his hand to his glare-shades.

'I really wouldn't, if you're fond of your ability to see.'

Ludd turned. A man was approaching him across the landing pad. He was tall and straight-backed, and wore the dress uniform of an Imperial commissar.

Ludd made the sign of the aquila and saluted.

'Junior Commissar Nahum Ludd, Camp 917,' he said.

The man mirrored the sign and the salute, and then offered his hand. 'Commissar Hadrian Faragut. Welcome to Frag Flats, Ludd.'

Ludd shook the proffered hand.

Faragut had a commanding manner, but appeared only a few years older than Ludd. He evidently hadn't been a full commissar for long. What little Ludd could see of Faragut's face was lean, tanned and clean-shaven. But the black lenses of his glare-shades hid his eyes, and therefore his character and temperament. There was a slight crook to his lips, as if Faragut was amused by something.

'I'm the welcoming committee,' Faragut said. 'The commissar-general was going to greet you personally, but it was felt that might be too intimidating.'

'Indeed. I'm glad it's you.'

'First time at the Flats?'

Ludd nodded. 'First time on a Leviathan, too.'

'Throne, they have kept you locked away, haven't they? Xeno. That's a polar station, isn't it?'

'Yes. Deliberately removed from the war zones. It's pretty bleak.'

'Count yourself lucky. The zones are… demanding.' Faragut spoke with an increasing curve of smile, as if to suggest he had seen many things and, more importantly, done many things. Heroic, glorious things.

Ludd nodded. 'I often wish for something demanding,' he said.

'Careful what you wish for, Ludd,' Faragut replied, his smile disappearing. 'The Sextus Zones are hell. There's not a single man of my rank doesn't pray for a soft posting like yours.'

Ludd bridled slightly. Not only was Faragut teasing him for being out of the fight-zones, he was teasing him for landing an easy option. Camp Xeno wasn't easy. It was a bastard, bitter job. Thankless, punishing, relentless–

Ludd decided not to say anything.

'You were admiring the Big Smoke?' Faragut said.

'Excuse me?'

Faragut gestured towards the orange roil rising off the horizon.

'Oh, I just wanted to get a look at the Mons,' Ludd said.

'Not from here. The Big Smoke's been a permanent fixture since the assault began three months ago.'

'It's what… sixty kilometres away?'

Faragut chuckled. 'Try *two hundred* and sixty. Have you any idea how big the Mons is?'

'No,' Ludd replied.

'Shame you won't get to see it,' Faragut said, in a tone that suggested he enjoyed meaning the opposite. 'Sparshad Mons is so wonderfully impressive.'

They turned as they heard a clank and hiss behind them. A deck hatch had opened directly under the Valkyrie, and the entire cargo pod was lowering away on power hoists, disengaging from the transport and sliding down into the hull of the Leviathan.

'You're handling them like freight,' Ludd said, disapprovingly. 'It was bad enough they had to be transported that way. Won't you even let them disembark on foot?'

'That's not appropriate,' Faragut said. 'Not until we've had them checked out.'

'You do know who they are?' Ludd asked.

Faragut looked at him, his eyes unreadable behind his black glare-shades. 'I know who they want us to think they are, Ludd. That's not quite the same.'

'You've read my report, though?'

Faragut frowned. 'Yes, Ludd. And we've read your commanding officer's report too. Commissar Kanow, isn't it?'

'Yes.'

'So… you will allow us to be cautious, I hope? Kanow was quite specific. What was his last command to you?'

'To bring the prisoners to the person of the lord general,' Ludd said.

Faragut nodded, solemnly. 'Just so. Because we do want to handle this according to Commissariat rules.'

'Absolutely,' Ludd replied. He didn't like the way Faragut had emphasised the 'do' in his last sentence. The man was condescending, patronising. And Ludd didn't like the way Faragut was suggesting he was anything less than a true commissar because he didn't have a warzone posting.

Ludd decided he didn't actually like Faragut all that much.

All of which became academic when Faragut said, 'Well, let's not keep him waiting.'

'Who?'

'Why, the lord general, Ludd. Who else?'

Ludd's stomach turned to water at the idea he was keeping such a great man waiting even for a moment.

He followed Faragut to the deck-stairs, his pulse elevated.

TWO

'WAIT HERE,' FARAGUT instructed him, and Ludd did as he was told. They had descended together through the Leviathan's vast interior and, after almost fifteen minutes' brisk walk along armoured, air-cooled hallways and heavy, bulkheaded companionways, had come to a halt in a gallery that overlooked one of the main tactical command centres.

Ludd looked down through tinted and slightly inclined panels of glass into a massive, tiered chamber where scores of intelligence officers, Imperial tacticians and high-order servitors manned display consoles and logic engines. In the centre of the chamber, a strategium pit cast a large, pulsing hololithic display up into the air. A huddle of senior officers surrounded the pit display; evidently a briefing was just coming to an end. Ludd saw the uniforms of a dozen different divisions, including Navy Wing and Guard Armour. There was

23

intense bustle down in the chamber, but the glass was soundproofed. Ludd could only imagine the constant racket of reports and data-chatter.

Faragut appeared in the room below, and dutifully approached a tall, striking man who wore the plain, dove-grey day-dress of a lord general. That would be Van Voytz, no doubt, Ludd thought. Lord General of the Fifth Crusade Army, commander in chief of this war-zone operation, master of this theatre. Everyone in the strategium was deferring to him. Ludd had never antic-ipated having to meet with a man of such staggering seniority. It was one step away from meeting Warmaster Macaroth himself.

His mouth went dry and cottony. He tried to remem-ber his rehearsed words.

Faragut spoke to the lord general, and got a brief nod and a pat on the arm for his trouble. *Oh, to enjoy such informality in those lofty circles,* Ludd thought. Van Voytz finished his conversation with two Navy squadron lead-ers, shared the knowing laughter of old comrades, then turned and followed Faragut from the chamber.

Half a minute later, Lord General Barthol Van Voytz was standing in front of Ludd on the gallery.

'Junior Commissar Nahum Ludd,' Faragut introduced. Ludd snapped to attention and made his salute.

The lord general was flanked by Faragut and a short, stern man wearing the black-and-red uniform of a senior Imperial tactician. Behind them waited an hon-our guard of six veteran soldiers in full ballistic plate.

'Van Voytz,' the lord general said, as if there were some doubt as to his identity. His voice was surpris-ingly soft and amiable, and there was the rumour of a smile on his lips. He stepped forward and offered Ludd his hand.

Surprised, Ludd hesitated, then shook it. 'Welcome, Ludd,' Van Voytz said. Then, still clasping Ludd's hand, he leaned closer and whispered in Ludd's ear.

'You're trembling, young man. Don't. I'm not a man to be afraid of. And besides, you don't want to show fear in front of that arse-kisser Faragut, or he'll never let you live it down.'

Ludd felt a little easier immediately. He nodded and smiled back. Van Voytz seemed to be in no hurry to let his hand go.

'As I understand it,' Van Voytz said aloud, 'I owe you a great deal, Ludd.'

'Sir?'

'I've read the reports, Ludd. Yours, and that of your commanding officer. Today, I will take great pleasure in welcoming back friends I had long since given up as dead. I cannot begin to imagine what they've been through, but it would have been a supremely tragic irony if they had been executed by mistake at Camp 917.'

'Yes, sir.'

'And I've you to thank for that.'

'I'm not sure about that, sir,' Ludd said.

'You listened. You listened when others did not. Kanow will hear from me about this. Later on, I'd like you to tell me all the details, the things you left unsaid in your report.'

'I wouldn't wish to betray Commissar Kanow's authority, sir,' Ludd said.

'That was an order, Junior Commissar Ludd.'

'Yes, sir.'

'Kanow clearly overstepped the mark. That much is evident even from your very diplomatic account. I won't have behaviour like that in my army, Ludd.'

'With respect, lord general,' said a voice from nearby, 'if Kanow needs to be reprimanded, that office will fall to me.'

A figure had joined them on the gallery deck, a woman of medium height and build who possessed quite the most austere face Ludd had ever seen. Her skin was white and drawn tight around her high cheekbones, her mouth a prim slit with a thin top lip. Her right eye was violet and keen, her left a compact augmetic embedded into a snow-drift smooth fold of scar-tissue that ran down across her brow onto her alabaster cheek. She wore the long black leather robes and cap of a commissar-general.

'Hello, Balshin,' Van Voytz sighed.

Ludd hadn't needed the name to know who this was: Viktoria Balshin, Lady Commissar-General of the Second Front theatre, one of the few women ever to ascend to such a rank in the Commissariat. She was a legend and, if the stories were true, a scourge to friend and foe alike. It was said that in order to thrive in such a male-dominated service, she had compensated for her gender by being the most ferociously hard-line political officer and disciplinarian imaginable. If Ludd had realised who Faragut meant when he'd referred to the 'commissar-general' he'd probably have just got straight back aboard the Valkyrie and fled.

'We will see for ourselves if Kanow overstepped the mark,' Balshin said. 'Personally, having reviewed the intelligence, I don't believe he did. You're fooling yourself, my lord general, if you believe that the individuals escorted here by this young man are… how did you put it? Your friends.'

'I know who they are, Balshin,' Van Voytz retorted, bristling slightly. 'I've known Ibram and his boys for years. I sent them off on this damn mission personally, and by the Throne, they have done me proud. I won't have them coming home to mistrust and accusation. They're heroes of the Imperium.'

Balshin smiled. 'Barthol, I don't refute any of what you say. Fine soldiers, yes. Brave souls who undertook a vital and thankless mission, yes. Heroes, why yes, that too. But precisely because of what they have endured, they may no longer be the soldiers you knew. I advise caution.'

'Noted,' Van Voytz said.

'And I advise you dispense with fond sentiment. You must think with your head, not your heart.'

'In that, Balshin, I'll follow your example,' Van Voytz said. 'How is your heart, these days? Still in a drawer somewhere, gathering dust?'

Balshin snorted.

'I'm not going to let you spoil this moment, Viktoria,' Van Voytz said. 'A great hour of victory has just been reported by the senior commanders. The fifth compartment of Sparshad Mons has just been breached, and we are advancing to the gates of the sixth.'

'Praise be the God-Emperor,' Balshin nodded. 'That is wonderful news.'

'Indeed,' Van Voytz said. 'And to top it off, a courageous friend of mine has just come back from the dead, when all hope was gone. So don't you go pissing on my parade, lady commissar-general.'

There was a frosty moment. Ludd dearly wished he was somewhere else. Then the Imperial tactician stepped forward and said, 'Senior staff in forty-five minutes, my lord.'

Van Voytz nodded. 'Indeed, Biota. Then let's get on with this. Ludd? Take me to greet your charges, please.'

***

THE FREIGHT SILO, deep in the bowels of the Command Leviathan, was unnaturally cold. Vapour from the landing jets was still swirling out of the overhead extractor vents. The cargo-pod from the Valkyrie sat quiet and still in its hoist supports.

'If you please, Ludd,' Van Voytz said.

Ludd hurried forward to the pod's hatch. Faragut went with him. The commissar eased his laspistol out of its holster.

'There's no need for that,' Ludd said.

'Do your job, Junior Ludd, and I'll do mine.' Like Ludd, Faragut had removed his glare-shades upon entering the command crawler, and now Ludd saw his eyes clearly for the first time. Cold, white-blue, uncompromising.

Ludd glanced nervously back at the lord general, Balshin, the Imperial tactician, and the veteran escort waiting on the deckway behind them. Van Voytz nodded, encouragingly. Ludd tapped the numeric code into the hatch lock.

Nothing happened.

He tapped it in again.

Still nothing.

'Do it right, for Throne's sake!' Faragut hissed. 'This is embarrassing!'

'I am doing it right!' Ludd whispered back. 'There's something wrong with the lock.'

He tapped a third time. The readout remained blank.

'Stand aside,' Faragut said. 'You must be making a mistake. What's the code?'

'Ten-four-oh-two-nine,' Ludd replied.

Faragut pounded the numerals in with the index finger of his left hand. Still nothing.

Faragut reached out and tugged at the heavy hatch. It swung open, free, unlocked.

'What the hell?'

The veteran guards immediately raised their weapons and prowled forward.

Pistol braced, Faragut peered into the open pod.

'Lights!' he commanded, and the bank of glow strips along the pod's ceiling flickered on, bathing the interior with a hard white glare.

The pod was empty.

'Oh, God-Emperor...' Ludd murmured.

'Sound general quarters!' Balshin yelled. 'Full security lock down, my authority! Now!'

The Leviathan's internal klaxons began to whoop.

THREE

'You CHECKED THE pod was sealed when you departed Camp Xeno?' Balshin demanded as she strode along.

'Yes, ma'am,' Ludd replied, struggling to keep up with her pace. 'The security detail locked the container, but I double-checked it before it was stowed on the transport.'

'And it was locked?' Balshin asked dubiously.

'It was, ma'am. On my life it was.'

'Bad choice of words,' Faragut muttered privately to Ludd. 'Your head's going to roll for this.'

They were rushing down one of the inner companionways behind Van Voytz and Balshin. As security squads swept the Leviathan deck by deck, Balshin's priority was to get the lord general safely sequestered in his private quarters.

'We didn't even have time to bio-scan them,' Ludd heard Balshin say over the noise of the blaring alarms.

'The intruders could be anyone, posing as the missing guard team to gain entry.'

Ludd was sweating. This was down to him, just as Faragut had taken pleasure in noting. Not only had Ludd been in charge of the transfer, he'd also been the one to advocate trusting the prisoners.

Had he just facilitated getting a team of archenemy assassins into the lord general's central command post? *Everything will be all right*, he tried to assure himself. The Leviathan was swarming with armed, vigilant troopers. Everywhere he looked, he saw fireteams running point-and-cover searches down hallways and along through-deck walks, or conducting stop-and-search examinations of passing crew members. No intruder, no matter how determined, was going to get far under these conditions.

The hurrying party reached the heavy blast hatch of Van Voytz's quarters. 'Stay with his lordship,' Balshin told Faragut, and then marched away to take direct charge of the manhunt. Faragut followed Van Voytz and Tactician Biota in through the blast hatch.

'Come on,' he said, beckoning impatiently at Ludd. Ludd hurried after them. The guard escort took up station outside, and the heavy hatch sealed and locked. The air pressure changed immediately. Amber runes lit up to show that the lord general's chamber, a virtual bunker at the heart of the huge crawler, was locked down and running on its own independent systems.

They were in an ante-room, well-appointed with seating and a table for debriefing sessions. An inner hatch led into Van Voytz's office, and they followed the lord general in that direction. The office was functional and service-issue, but piled with books, pictures and trophies from Van Voytz's worthy career. There was a desk with a high-backed chair at the far end, a couple of couches, and a side door into the sleeping pod.

'Dammit,' Van Voytz muttered. 'Dammit all.' He glanced at Ludd. 'Locked, you said?'

'Yes, sir.'

Van Voytz shook his head. He seemed to bear no particular anger towards Ludd. It seemed more as if he were puzzled, disappointed.

Faragut was listening to the security channel traffic on his earpiece. 'Sweep has now reached deck six and seven. Internal scanners still show no sign of the intruders.'

Biota muted the alarm blaring in the office. The hazard light panels continued to flash. Van Voytz was pacing.

'Sir,' said Ludd, suddenly and very quietly.

'What?' Van Voytz replied, looking round at him.

'I think you should remain very still, sir,' Ludd said, his voice trembling.

Ibram Gaunt, bearded, thin and dishevelled, had slowly risen to his feet from behind the high-backed chair. He was holding a chrome and silver ceremonial laspistol. It was aimed at Faragut, the only one of them with a drawn weapon.

'Lose your sidearms,' Gaunt said. 'Onto that couch. Now.'

Ludd unholstered his laspistol and tossed it onto the couch. Biota took out his small service auto and threw it down too.

'I said lose them,' Gaunt told Faragut, his aim not wavering. Faragut's gun was pointed at Gaunt.

'Don't be a fool,' Gaunt said. 'Do you really want to start a firefight in the presence of the lord general?'

Faragut slowly lowered his weapon and slung it onto the couch cushions.

Van Voytz took a step towards Gaunt.

'Ibram.'

'My lord general. Not quite the reunion I was hoping for.' The more Gaunt spoke, the more they could all detect the odd, alien cadence in his accent.

Van Voytz stared at Gaunt, bewildered. 'Throne, man. What happened to you?'

'I followed your orders, sir. That's what happened to me.'

'And those orders included holding me hostage with my own sidearm?'

'It was all I could find.'

'Ibram, for the love of Terra, put the gun down.'

'Only when I'm assured of my safety, and the safety of my team.'

'How could you doubt that?' Van Voytz said. He sounded hurt.

'Being herded up for summary execution at that processing camp didn't help,' Gaunt replied. 'Neither did having my honour and loyalty ignored. That boy there was the only one who had any faith at all.' Gaunt indicated Ludd with a nod of his head. 'But I'm not sure I can even trust him now. We were put into a cargo pod, *locked* into a cargo pod, and brought here like animals.'

'There were security issues, colonel-commissar,' Biota said. 'You must understand. You were brought here for formal identification and debrief.'

'Like animals, Antonid,' Gaunt replied. 'By the time we were being unloaded, I didn't feel I could trust anything or anybody. I had to make provisions for the good of my troops.'

'How did you get out of the pod?' Ludd asked.

'Does it matter?'

'It's a fair question,' said Van Voytz.

'My men developed many skills on Gereon. Resistance tactics. I don't think there's a lock made that can beat either Feygor or Mkoll.'

'Where are your men?' Faragut demanded.

Gaunt seemed to smile, but the expression was obscured behind the caked, grey mass of his beard. His wary aim still favoured Faragut. 'Hidden. Where no security sweep will find them. Hiding's something else we've got very good at.'

'How can we resolve this, Ibram?' Van Voytz asked.

'Your word, sir. An assurance of safety for me and my team. I think you owe us that.'

Van Voytz nodded. 'My word. You have it, unconditionally.'

There was a long moment of stillness, then Gaunt lowered the weapon, flipped it over neatly in his hand, and held it out to the lord general, grip-first.

Van Voytz took the pistol and put it down on the desk. Faragut hurled himself forward to tackle Gaunt.

'No!' Van Voytz bellowed. Faragut stopped in his tracks.

'I gave this man my word!' Van Voytz roared at him.

Faragut stammered. 'Sir, I–'

Van Voytz slapped Faragut hard across the face and knocked him to his knees.

'I'm going to send a signal, Gaunt. All right?' Van Voytz said. Gaunt nodded. The lord general crossed to his intercom.

'This is Van Voytz on the command channel. Stand down general quarters and cancel the search.'

'Balshin here. Please clarify.'

'The situation is contained, commissar-general. Follow my orders.'

There was a pause. Then the vox crackled. 'My lord, are you under duress?'

'No, Balshin. I am not.'

'Please, sir. I need the clearance.'

'Clearance is "Andromache".'

'Understood. Thank you, sir.'

The hazard lights stopped flashing, and the distant howl of klaxons outside faded. Heavy bolts automatically retracted and the outer hatch of the general's quarters opened. The escort detail stationed outside hurried in. Gaunt stiffened.

'Shoulder arms!' Van Voytz ordered, and the men did so immediately. Van Voytz pointed at Gaunt.

'Now salute him, damn you!'

THEY FOLLOWED GAUNT down to the huge enginarium in the belly of the Leviathan. In every hallway they passed through, personnel turned to stare, some so bemused by what they saw, they quite forgot to salute the lord general. A tall, shaggy, filthy man in ragged, leather clothes, wrapped in the torn remnants of a camo-cloak, leading the supreme imperial commander, two commissars, an Imperial tactician and a vanguard of troopers.

The turbine hall of the enginarium was cavernous and gloomy, dominated by the vast whirring powerplants that drove the Leviathan's systems. The air smelled of promethium and lubricants. Van Voytz ordered the tech-adepts and engineers out of the chamber.

'Here?' he asked, raising his voice above the machine noise.

'The heat and machine activity mask bio-traces,' Gaunt said. 'The best interference you can get when it comes to beating internal sensors. We learned that taking out a jehgenesh at the Lectica hydroelectric dam.'

'I don't know what that means,' Van Voytz said. 'I trust you'll debrief fully.'

'Of course, sir,' Gaunt said, as if surprised there might be any doubt. He walked over to a wall-set vox, adjusted the dial to speaker, and said, 'silver.' His amplified voice echoed along the engineering bay.

The Ghosts came out of hiding. It was unnerving to have them appear, one by one, out of shadowed cavities that didn't seem deep enough to conceal a human being. The Tanith troopers didn't so much emerge as materialise.

All of them were as underfed, grubby and ragged as their commander. Their eyes were bright, wary, cautious. Their beards and long hair were caked into dreadlocks with what looked like grey mud.

'Holy Throne,' Van Voytz said. 'Major Rawne.'

'Sir,' Rawne replied, making an awkward salute as he came out into the light.

'And Sergeant Varl. Sergeant Mkoll.'

The two men also saluted as they came forward, Mkoll unwilling to look the lord general in the eye. The others approached. Van Voytz greeted each one as they appeared.

'Trooper Brostin. Sergeant Criid. Trooper Feygor. Vox-officer Beltayn. Scout-trooper Bonin. Marksman Larkin.'

Gaunt looked at Van Voytz, quietly impressed. 'You… you know their names, sir.'

'I sent you and these soldiers on a mission we both thought you'd never come back from, Ibram. What kind of lord general would I be if I couldn't be bothered to remember a handful of names?'

Van Voytz turned to face the group of tattered Ghosts. 'Welcome, all of you. Welcome home.'

Two more figures emerged from the shadows.

'And these I don't know,' Van Voytz said.

'Major Sabbatine Cirk,' Gaunt said. The tall, dark-haired woman stepped forward and bowed to the lord general.

'Cirk was a principal leader of the Gereon Resistance. She's come with us to supply High Command with full intelligence concerning the situation on Gereon.'

'Welcome, major,' Van Voytz said. 'The Emperor protects.'

'And Gereon resists,' Cirk replied sardonically.

The other figure was abnormally tall and slender: a disturbingly tribal, grey shape in a long, feathered cloak, who seemed more uneasy than any of them.

'Eszrah ap Niht,' Gaunt said. 'A warrior of the Untill Nihtganes, a Sleepwalker.'

'Welcome, sir,' Van Voytz said. The Sleepwalker made no movement or response. The skin of his thin, moustachioed face seemed to have been stained with grey clay, and oval patches of iridescent mosaics surrounded his deep-set, apprehensive eyes. Van Voytz glanced at Gaunt. 'And he's here because?'

'Because I own him and he refused to remain behind.'

Van Voytz raised his eyebrows. 'Two are missing. Scout-trooper Mkvenner and Medicae Curth.'

'Last I knew, both lived,' Gaunt said. 'But Mkvenner and Curth elected to stay behind on Gereon in support of the Resistance. Ana Curth's medical skills were proving invaluable, and Mkvenner... Well, let me say briefly that Ven and the Sleepwalker partisans have become the elite commandos of the Gereon Underground.'

'You'll make a full report?' Van Voytz said.

'Again, as I said, of course, sir.'

'Good.' Van Voytz stepped towards the Ghosts and shook each one by the hand, though he didn't even attempt to take the hand of the mysterious tribesman. 'I understand that your mission was accomplished... and more besides. The Emperor will never forget your efforts, and neither will I.' He glanced round. 'Balshin?'

Lady Commissar-General Balshin came out of a nearby access, flanked by armed Commissariat troopers. More troopers, rifles levelled, surged in through the enginarium hatchways on all sides and formed a ring around the battered Ghosts.

'No…' Ludd gasped. Faragut began to snigger, despite his bruised cheek.

'Take them into custody,' Balshin said.

Gaunt stared at Van Voytz in furious disbelief. 'You bastard. You gave me your word!'

'And it stands. And it will not be broken. I assure the safety of you and your team. But that is all. I attested to nothing more than that, Ibram. You threatened my life, the security of this HQ, and the very core of Imperial Command here on Ancreon Sextus. Take them to detention.'

The troopers closed in and began to manhandle the Ghosts away.

FOUR

09.01 hrs, 189.776.M41
Frag Flats HQ
Sparshad Combat Zone, Ancreon Sextus

LUDD WALKED INTO the small interview cell and heard the hatch lock up behind him. The cell was crude and stark: just scuffed bare metal and rivets, glow-globes recessed in cages, a small steel chair and table in front of the wire screen cage. Pict units mounted high in the corners of the cell recorded the scene from multiple angles. The air was stale and stuffy. On the far side of the wire screen stood another empty steel chair.

Ludd put the plastek sack he was holding down on the deck, took off his gloves, and laid them on the small table along with his data-case. Then he sat down, opened the case, and took out two paper dossiers and a dataslate.

A buzzer sounded and the door inside the cage opened. Ludd rose to his feet.

Gaunt entered, and the door closed automatically behind him. He glanced briefly at Ludd and then sat down on the empty chair.

'Commissar Gaunt,' Ludd said, and took his seat again so he was face to face with Gaunt through the wire screen.

'I'd like to begin by apologising,' Ludd said.

'For what?'

'You said yesterday, during the altercation in the lord general's quarters, that you didn't believe you could trust me any more. I want to assure you that you can. If I gave you any cause that provoked yesterday's incident, I apologise.'

Gaunt's hard gaze flickered up and down Ludd. 'You locked us up in a cargo pod,' he said.

'In order to placate Kanow, who would have had you shot. Besides, can we start to be realistic, sir? You have served the best part of your career as a commissar and a discipline officer. Given the circumstances, would you have handled it differently?'

Gaunt shrugged.

'Let me put it more plainly. You encounter a dozen armed renegades. No idents, no warrants. Their story is difficult to believe. They are... not attired to regulations. Indeed, they are shabby. Barbaric. At the very least they have suffered hardships. Perhaps they have gone native. It is also entirely possible that they are tainted and corrupt. And they demand a personal audience with the most senior ranking Imperial officer in the quadrant. Do you not agree that any Imperial commissar would be duty-bound to exercise the utmost caution in dealing with them?'

There was a long silence. Gaunt shrugged again, and stared at the floor behind Ludd as if bored.

Ludd was about to continue when Gaunt spoke. 'Let me put it plainly, then. You are a unit commander. Your team has been sent on a high priority mission behind enemy lines on the personal request of the lord general commander. The secrecy of the mission is paramount. Against the odds, after the best part of two years in the field, you get your team out again. Whole, alive, mission accomplished. But you are treated like pariahs, like soldiers of the enemy, mistrusted, abused, threatened with execution. Do you not agree that any Imperial officer would be duty-bound to do everything to safeguard his men under such circumstances?'

Ludd pursed his lips. 'Yes, sir,' he said. 'Within the letter of regulation law. Threatening the person of the lord general–'

Gaunt shook his head sadly. 'I didn't threaten him.'

'Please, sir–'

'I did not aim the weapon directly at him, nor make any personal threat against his life.'

'Semantics, sir. Regulation law–'

'I've fought wars in the name of the God-Emperor most of my adult life, Ludd. Sometimes regulation law gets bent or snapped in the name of victory and honour. I've never known the God-Emperor object to that. He protects those who rise above the petty inhibitions of life and code and combat to serve what is true and correct. I don't much care about myself, but my men, my team… they deserve better. They have given everything except their lives. I will not permit the blunt ignorance of the Commissariat to take those from them too. I am a true servant of the Throne, Ludd. I resent very much being treated as anything else.'

Ludd sighed. 'Candidly, sir?'

Gaunt nodded.

'You don't have to convince me. But therein lies your problem. I'm not the one you have to convince.'

Gaunt leaned back in his seat, stroked his long, dirty fingers down through his heavy, woaded beard and then folded his hands across his chest, almost forming the sign of the aquila. 'So what are you doing here, Ludd?' he asked.

Ludd opened one of the dossiers on the table in front of him, and weighed down the corner of the spread card cover with the dataslate. 'There is to be a tribunal,' he said. 'You, and each member of your team, will be examined by the Office of the Commissariat. Individually. It is being called a debrief, but there is a lot at stake.'

'For me?'

'For all of you. Lady Commissar-General Balshin suspects taint.'

'Does she?'

'Sir, it would be suspected of any individual or unit exposed for such a length of time on an enemy-occupied world. You know that. Chaos taint is a very real possibility. It may be in you and you don't even know it. It might also–'

'What?'

Ludd shook his head. 'Nothing.'

'Say what you were going to say.'

'I prefer not to, sir.'

Gaunt smiled. There was something predatory about the way the expression changed his face. Like a fox, Ludd thought.

'You'd prefer not to. Because you fear what you have to say might enrage me. Or at the very least piss me off.'

'That would be a fair assessment, yes, sir.'

Gaunt leaned forward. 'You know what a wirewolf is, son?'

'No, sir, I do not.'

'Lucky you. I've killed six of them personally. Say what you have to say. I'm big enough to take it.'

Ludd cleared his throat. 'All right. You might be tainted with the mark of Chaos and not even know it. Furthermore, a subconscious taint like that might also explain your paranoia and your volatile, desperate behaviour.'

'Like waving a gun in Van Voytz's face, you mean?'

'Yes, sir.'

Gaunt leaned forward a little further, and hooked his grubby fingers through the mesh of the wire screen. He glared at Ludd. His voice became a tiny, dry crackle. 'So you think my mind might have been poisoned by the enemy, corrupted without me even knowing about it, and that's why I'm a… what? A loose cannon?'

Ludd shrank back slightly. 'You asked me to be frank…'

'You fething little–!' Gaunt snarled, and threw himself at the wire screen, his teeth bared.

Ludd leapt up so fast his chair toppled over. Then he realised that Gaunt was sitting back, laughing.

'Ludd, you're too easy. Throne, your face just then. Want to go change your underwear?'

Ludd righted the fallen chair and sat back down. 'That sort of display isn't going to help,' he said.

'Can't take a joke?' Gaunt asked, still amused with himself. 'A little gallows humour?'

'No, sir,' said Ludd. Gaunt nodded and folded his arms, his amusement subsiding.

'And if I can't,' Ludd added, 'you can be sure as hell Lady Balshin won't. Pull a stunt like that during the tribunal and she'll have you ten-ninety-six in a flash.'

'I have no doubt. It was clear to me the woman had a little too much starch in her drawers.'

'Again–' Ludd began.

Gaunt waved a hand dismissively and looked away. 'Ludd, you're talking to me like you're coaching me. Are you coaching me?'

'I'm trying to prep you for the examination, sir. Understand, the examination will be both verbal and medical. You will have to submit to all manner of analysis scans and investigative procedures. All of you will. Balshin will be thorough. The merest hint, be it verbal or physiological, that any of you are unsound… she will declare Commissariat Edict ten-ninety-six on all of you.'

Gaunt looked at the deck.

'I take it you recall what that edict is?'

'Of course I do. Do you intend to prepare every one of my team for the hearings?'

'Provided I have the time, yes. I'd appreciate it if you passed the word along to your team members to cooperate with me.'

Gaunt looked up. 'I'll recommend it. It's up to them. Be advised, you'll have trouble with Cirk, Feygor, Mkoll and Eszrah especially. In fact, I'd like to be present when you handle Eszrah. He's… not Guard. He's not like anything you or this tribunal will have ever handled.'

Ludd made a note on the dossier with a steel stylus. 'So noted. I'll see what I can do.'

'So why do we get you as an advocate, Ludd?' Gaunt asked.

'You're permitted one under the rules of the tribunal, sir,' Ludd replied.

'And we don't get to pick?' Gaunt asked.

Ludd put his stylus down and looked squarely through the cage at Gaunt. 'No, sir. It's a voluntary thing. The tribunal appoints an advocate if no one volunteers, of course. No one did besides me.'

'Feth,' said Gaunt, with a sad shake of his head. 'How old are you, Ludd?'

'Twenty-three, sir.'

'So a twenty-three year-old junior is the only friend we've got?'

'I could stand aside, allow the tribunal to appoint. You'd probably get Faragut. I didn't think you'd want that, so I put my name forward.'

'Thank you,' said Ibram Gaunt.

Ludd turned a few pages in the open dossier and replaced the dataslate to weight them down. 'I need to clarify a few points, sir. So I'm up to speed for the hearing. I will be a greater asset if I'm not taken by surprise.'

'Go on.'

'This mission you refer to. You mentioned it back at Camp Xeno too. But without specifics. It was on Gereon, right?'

'That's right.'

'What were the parameters?'

'The parameters were encoded vermillion, Ludd. Between me and the lord general. I can't divulge them to you.'

'Then that makes it hard for me to–'

'Go to Van Voytz. If he gives you written clearance, I'll tell you. If he comes and gives me a direct order, I'll tell you. Otherwise, my lips are sealed… to you and the tribunal.'

'I'll do that,' said Ludd. He closed the dossiers and put them away. 'The hearings begin tomorrow at 16.00 hours. As mission commander, you'll be called first. Your testimony may take a day or two to hear. I'll be back at 18.00 hours, sooner if I can get the waiver from the lord general. We may be prepping into the night.'

'If that's what it takes.'

'One last thing,' Ludd said, picking up the plastek sack from the floor beside his chair and dropping it into the hopper basket built into the wire screen at knee height. 'I need you to shower and put on this change of clothes. Your team will have to do the same. I'll provide kit for them as necessary.'

Gaunt looked dubiously at the sack of clothes. 'What I'm wearing,' he said firmly, 'I've been wearing through it all. It's my uniform, though I don't suppose you'd recognise it any more. Patched, repaired, sewn back together, it's been on me from start to finish. It's like my skin, Ludd.'

'That's exactly the problem. You're filthy. Ragged. You smell. I can smell you from here, and I can tell you, the smell isn't pleasant. I'm not talking dirt, sir, I'm talking a sweet, sickly stench. Like corruption, like taint. And that grey hue to your skin.'

'That won't come off easily.'

'Try. Scrub. And shave, for Throne's sake. Don't give the commissar-general any reason to suspect you more than she does.'

Gaunt took the plastek sack out of the hopper.

'So I stink?'

'Like a bastard, sir. Like a daemon of the archenemy.'

THE COMMISSARIAT GUARDS led Gaunt back along the cellblock of the Leviathan's detention deck. Grim bars of lumin strip made a ladder of light along the low ceiling. The air was damp and musty. Patches of green-white corrosion mottled the iron walls.

They were walking past a row of individual cages. Each one contained a Ghost. Young Dughan Beltayn was in the first cage, sitting close to the bars. He nodded to Gaunt, a little eager, a little hopeful, and Gaunt tried to put some reassurance into the half-smile he sent back to his adjutant as he passed. Next in line was Cirk. She simply followed Gaunt with her caustic gaze as he went by, then looked away as he tried to make eye contact.

Flame-trooper Aongus Brostin, thuggish and hairy, was in the next cage. He was standing at the back, leaning against the far wall, with his meaty, tattooed arms folded and his eyes closed. Dreaming of lho-sticks, no doubt. Then came Ceglan Varl, sitting on his cell's folddown cot. The sergeant was stripped to the waist, displaying his dirty, lean torso and his battered augmetic shoulder. He flipped Gaunt a laconic salute.

'Just keep walking,' said one of the guards.

In the next cell sat Hlaine Larkin, huddled in a corner, looking more like a tanned leather bag of bones and nerves than ever. He watched Gaunt pass with a sniper's unblinking stare. Larkin's neighbour was Simen Urwin Macharius Bonin, Mach Bonin, the darkly-handsome and preternaturally fortunate scout-trooper. Bonin was standing at the cage front, leaning forward and clutching the bars with raised hands.

'Any luck?' he asked.

'Shut up,' one of the guards said.

'Screw you too,' Bonin called after them.

Gaunt passed the cell holding Tona Criid. She'd not cut her hair since the start of the mission, and it had grown out long and straight, returning to its original, brick-brown colour, stained with Untill grey. She'd taken to wearing it loose, swept down to veil the left side of her face. Gaunt knew why. As he passed her cage, she made the quick Tanith code-gesture that was Ghost shorthand for 'everything all right?'

Gaunt managed to reply with a quick nod before he was marched on out of sight.

Eszrah ap Niht, or Eszrah Night as they had all come to know the Untill partisan, stood in the next cell, silent and staring, his mosaic-edged eyes hidden behind the old, battered pair of sunshades Varl had given him so long ago.

'Histye seolfor, soule Eszrah,' Gaunt called out quickly in the Sleepwalker's ancient tongue

'Be quiet!' the guard behind him cried, and prodded Gaunt between the shoulder-blades with his maul.

Gaunt stopped in his tracks and looked round at the three armoured guards. 'Do that again,' he began, 'and you'll–'

'What?' taunted the guard, patting his maul into the palm of his glove.

Gaunt bit back, tried to counsel his temper, tried to remember what Ludd had told him.

He turned round and continued to walk. The next cage in the line held Scout-Sergeant Oan Mkoll. The grizzled, older man remained staring at the floor as Gaunt went by.

Murtan Feygor lay on the cot in the next cell. He sat up as Gaunt passed and called out 'We dead yet, Ghost-maker?' His voice had a rasping, monotonous quality thanks to the augmetic larynx in his corded throat, the legacy of an old war wound.

One of the guards kicked the bars of Feygor's cage as they went by.

'Oh, you think so? You think so?' Feygor called after them. 'Come back here, you feth-wipe, come back here and I'll make your momma weep.' The threat was curiously dry and flat uttered in that monotone. It was almost comical.

Rawne was in the final cage they passed. He was sitting on the floor, near the front, his back against the left-hand cell partition. He didn't even bother to look up.

At the last cage on the block, the guards slid the barred gate open. Gaunt looked at them.

'Shower pen?' he asked.

'We'll be back in twenty minutes,' one of the guards replied. Gaunt nodded, and stepped into the empty cell. The guards slammed the cage shut with a reverberating clang of metal on metal, locked it, and walked away.

Gaunt dropped the plastek sack onto the cell floor, then walked across to the right hand partition and slithered down, his back to it, near the cage mouth.

'So what's the story, Bram?' Rawne asked quietly from the other side of the wall.

'We're in it up to our necks, Eli,' Gaunt replied. 'My bad call, I think. I pushed them way too far.'

There was a long pause.

'Don't beat yourself up,' Rawne said. 'We all knew why you called it like you did. They were treating us like shit. You couldn't take chances.'

'Maybe I should have. We're facing a tribunal. Balshin's in charge. Van Voytz may not be on side any more, after what I did.'

'Combat necessity, Bram,' Rawne replied, stoically. 'If we'd stayed in that fething pod…'

'We might be all right now. Or in a better situation. I should have trusted Ludd.'

'That feth?'

'We're all going to have to trust him now, Elim. That feth's our only friend. Pass the word along. We have to comply with his every instruction and recommendation, or we're blindfolded with our backs to a wall.'

'Why?'

Gaunt sighed. 'The accusation is Chaos taint.'

'Hard to prove.'

'Harder to disprove. Eli, as a commissar, I'd always err on the side of caution.'

'Shoot first, you mean?'

'Shoot first.'

'Feth.'

'Ludd's in our corner, and I may be able to swing Van Voytz round, if I can get any time with him. But make sure the Ghosts cooperate with Ludd. Whether you like him or not, he's the only decent card in our hand.'

'That an order?'

'More than any other I've ever given you.'

'Consider it done.'

Gaunt looked over at the sagging plastek sack nearby. 'Ludd wants us to shower and clean ourselves up. Get new fatigues on. Get fresh, shaved and scrubbed for the hearings.'

'I'm fine as I am.'

'Rawne, I'm not kidding. We stink of filth and corruption. We reek of what they think is taint. Everyone does this, or they'll answer to me.'

'Eszrah won't like it.'

'I know.'

'And Cirk…'

'I know. Leave her to me.'

'You gonna follow my advice?' Rawne asked.

Gaunt shook his head. Rawne's advice, repeated two dozen times through the last few days, had been to sell Cirk out, to give her to the Commissariat in exchange for the Ghosts' lives. He'd never liked her. And that was crazy, because in the last ten months she'd given Rawne so many reasons to do so. Sabbatine Cirk was a brave, driven officer. But there was just something about her that was inherently untrustworthy. On Gereon, she'd suffered under the archenemy occupation too long. She'd learned that essential skill of the die-hard resistance fighter, that quality that was both a blessing and curse: no one, not a friend, not a family member, not even a life-partner, was beyond betrayal if it benefitted the cause. That made her as mercurial and unpredictable as a razor-snake.

Cirk had been Elim Rawne's lover for the past eight months. Rawne desired her, but he still didn't like her much, or trust her even slightly.

'So what happens now?' Rawne asked.

'They'll start with me. You'll be next, I'm guessing. Stick to the facts. And observe our clearance unless I tell you otherwise.'

'Got it. Feth, I can't believe I'm thinking this, but… we'd have been safer staying on Gereon.'

Gaunt grinned. 'Yes, maybe. But we had our chance and we took it. We had to get off-world with the news about Sturm. And about the Sons. Demands of duty, Eli.'

'And this is how they thank us,' Rawne said bitterly. Gaunt heard him slide closer to the edge of the wall. Rawne's dirty hand appeared through the bars.

'I never wanted to go to Gereon,' Gaunt heard him say. 'I thought it was madness, I thought it was suicide, and it so nearly was. But I did what you ordered and what the God-Emperor deserved. And by feth, I never expected it to turn out like this. We're loyal soldiers of the Imperium, Bram. After all we did, and all we sacrificed, where the hell did justice go?'

Gaunt reached his own hand out through the bars and clasped Rawne's.

'It's coming, Eli. On my life, it's coming.'

***

'I WANT THIS quashed,' Van Voytz said.

'After what they did?' Balshin replied.

Van Voytz waved his hands as if brushing crumbs away from his lap. 'We treated them badly. I owe them–'

'Nothing, sir. You owe them nothing if they are tainted. That's the bottom line. Whatever mission they accomplished, whatever great service they did for you and the Crusade, if they've come back tainted, it's the end. We can take no chances. We would be derelict in our duty to the Golden Throne if we did.'

'You're such a bitch, Balshin,' Van Voytz said.

'Thank you, Barthol. I try.'

Seated at the long debrief table in his chambers, Van Voytz looked sidelong at Biota. 'Are they tainted, Antonid?' he asked.

Biota keyed open a dataslate. 'Medical scans say no, though there is a significant degree of obscurity. For all their filth and organic corruption, they seemed to have survived exposure to what we might think of as actual taint–'

Balshin raised her hand. 'Point of order, lord general. Master Biota, with respect, is a member of the Departmento Tacticae Imperialis. Since when did he get to render psycho-biological evidence? It's not his field.'

Van Voytz got to his feet and went to the sideboard to pour himself an amasec. As an afterthought – and a silent gesture of solidarity – he filled a thimble glass with sacra instead.

'Antonid is my right hand man. He also knows Gaunt and the Ghosts of old. I've asked him to bring his close scrutiny and eye for detail to their case. Go on, Biota.'

Biota cleared his throat. 'I am not an advocate or a specialist martial lawyer, madam commissar-general, as you indicate. But my mind is trained to a superior level in the processing of evidence and intelligence. As far as I can determine from the medicae and psychologicae reports, Gaunt and his men are not tainted. They are genuinely damaged in many ways: they are tired, scared, traumatised, unappreciated. But there is no sign of actual taint. Medicae and toxicological scans agree. They are physically infested... lice, worms, bacteria... and they show perplexing registers of some kind of toxin or venom that they have built up a resistance to. They are scarred, they are battered, they are strung out, and they may never again be the fine warriors we once knew. But they are not tainted.'

Balshin nodded. 'I don't agree. At least, I'm not convinced. Lord general, you trusted your man Biota here to process the data on your behalf. I saw fit to call upon the services of another expert.'

'Did you?' Van Voytz asked.

Balshin turned and gestured to Faragut, who was waiting by the door.

Faragut opened the hatch and a short, thickset figure walked in. He was wearing a dark brown leather coat reinforced with patches of chainmail. His greying hair was receding, but a tight black goatee covered the chin of a face that was pugnacious, almost sunken in aspect. His eyes were entirely dark blue, without a hint of white.

'Lord General Van Voytz,' Balshin began, 'may I present–'

'Lornas Welt,' Van Voytz finished. 'Lornas and I know each other of old, Balshin. How fare you, master inquisitor?'

'Very well, my lord general,' Welt replied in soft, clipped tones.

Van Voytz turned to Biota. 'Inform Junior Ludd that the Inquisition is now involved.'

Biota got to his feet.

'I don't believe that's necessary, my lord,' Balshin said.

'I do, Viktoria,' Van Voytz snapped. 'You've just upped the ante. Ludd needs to know that. Throne, Gaunt needs to know that.'

'This is acceptable,' Welt said, politely.

Biota left the room. Welt took a seat at the table beside Balshin.

'I've reviewed the data,' the inquisitor said. 'It's a tough call. These people have served the Imperium creditably. They have given their all. However, for the safety of us all, I believe they should be put to death quickly and quietly.'

Van Voytz glared at the inquisitor. 'That is a brutal–'

'It is the price you pay, my lord. The price of the mission you had them undertake. They did what you ordered them to do, and for that, they should be celebrated. But there is no way they could have come out of that nightmare untouched. It would have been better for them if they had died on Gereon. You sent them to their deaths, after all. The only nagging problem is that they've come back and now you're faced with doing the dirty work Chaos failed to do for you. You must execute them.'

'If they survived the hell I sent them into,' Van Voytz said, 'then I'll give them a chance.'

Welt nodded. 'Hence the hearings. We will be compassionate.'

'I hope so,' said the lord general.

Faragut approached Balshin and handed her a slip of paper.

'My lord, I am called away briefly.'

Van Voytz nodded.

Following Faragut out of the hatchway, Balshin asked quietly. 'Is this true?'

'Yes, ma'am.'

THE CAGE-HATCH of the detention deck slid open and Balshin walked down the block, Faragut tailing her. The lady commissar-general stopped at one of the cages.

'You wanted to see me?' she asked.

Sabbatine Cirk got to her feet and walked to the cage-front. 'Yes. I want to cut a deal.'

FIVE

16.03 hrs, 190.776.M41
Frag Flats HQ
Sparshad Combat Zone, Ancreon Sextus

THE GUARDS STATIONED around the hearing chamber
came to attention with a rattle of armour, and the eight
senior Commissariat officers seated around the semicir-
cular dais rose to their feet. Commissar-General Balshin
swept in through the main hatch, her long gown bil-
lowing out behind her, accompanied by Faragut,
Inquisitor Welt, and an Imperial Guard colonel in a
dark blue dress uniform. The four of them marched to
their seats at the centre of the curved dais.

'Be seated,' the colonel said. 'This hearing is called to
order on the one hundred and ninetieth day of 776, by
the grace of the God-Emperor. Let us commence without delay.'

The main hatch opened again, long enough to allow
Ludd and Gaunt to enter, side by side. They strode
smartly across to the small desk facing the half-circle of
the dais, came to a halt beside it, and stood at attention.

'Junior Commissar Nahum Ludd, advocating for the defendant,' Ludd announced.

'So noted,' replied the colonel. 'Have a seat, junior commissar. The defendant will remain standing.'

Ludd glanced at Gaunt, who was ramrod stiff, staring down the tribunal, then sat down behind the small desk.

'The defendant will identify himself,' the colonel called.

'Ibram Gaunt, colonel-commissar, Tanith First, serial number–'

'Your name is sufficient, Gaunt,' the colonel cut in. 'At this stage, you have no recognised rank in the eyes of this tribunal. I am Colonel Gerrod Kaessen, and I will be presiding over the hearing today.'

'Was the lord general too ashamed to face me?' Gaunt asked.

Ludd jumped to his feet. 'The defendant withdraws that remark, sir.'

Kaessen raised an eyebrow. 'Do you, Gaunt?'

'If that's what my advocate advises, sir.'

'For your information, Gaunt,' Kaessen said, flipping through some papers in front of him, 'Lord General Van Voytz is unavoidably occupied at this hour, and has asked me to represent High Command interests in his stead. It would be unusual, don't you think, for the supreme commander of this theatre to be directly involved in a comparatively minor tribunal hearing?'

'It depends what you mean by "comparatively minor", sir,' Gaunt replied.

'Well, let's see,' the colonel shot back. 'Compared to… the ongoing prosecution of this war, for example?'

'The point is taken, sir,' Ludd replied.

'The point is also that Lord General Van Voytz is the sole reason I'm standing here today,' Gaunt said.

'How so?'

'Because he personally sent me on the Gereon mission, and only on his word have I not been executed for accomplishing said mission and returning alive.'

'Please!' Ludd hissed at Gaunt.

'I withdraw my last remark,' Gaunt said.

Colonel Kaessen pursed his lips. 'Gaunt, do you recognise the authority of this tribunal?'

'I think, colonel,' said Inquisitor Welt quietly, 'that is essentially what we're here to establish.' Several of the commissars around the dais chuckled. Balshin leant over to whisper to Faragut.

'Very well,' said Kaessen. 'The defendant may be seated. Junior Commissar Ludd, you may begin with your opening remarks.'

Gaunt crossed to the desk and sat down beside Ludd. Gaunt was dressed in high black boots, black breeches and a simple black vest, all unadorned by rank pins or insignia. The cut sleeves of the tight vest showed the lean, corded power of his arms and upper body, and also the dozens of old scars, large and small, that decorated his flesh. He'd showered three times since his first meeting with Ludd, but still the dark grey stain of the Nihtganes' camouflage paste lingered in his pale skin, like a faint, all-over bruise. He'd also shaved. The thick, stiff dreadlocks of his beard and long hair were gone, leaving a severe crewcut and a neatly trimmed goatee. The hair on his head and chin were a pale, dirty blond, like faded, slightly stale straw.

Ludd stood up with a dossier in his hand and cleared his throat. 'If it please the tribunal, I would like to begin by reading a transcript record of the colonel-commissar's career to date, making reference to the many meritorious–'

Faragut got up quickly. 'Objection, colonel. Copies of the transcript record have been circulated to all the members of the tribunal. We are all perfectly familiar with it. Reading it aloud will simply occupy valuable time.'

'Colonel,' said Ludd. 'The record attests to the past character of the defendant.'

'The defendant's past character is not in question,' Balshin put in.

'Duly noted,' said Kaessen. 'The objection is sustained. Move along, please, junior commissar.'

Ludd frowned and put the dossier back on the desk. He selected another. 'In that case, colonel, I should like to read the defendant's own, detailed statement regarding his mission to Gereon.'

Immediately, Faragut was on his feet once more. 'Again, colonel. Cause as before. We have all been copied with this statement, and we have all read it.'

'Duly noted,' Kaessen repeated.

'With respect, sir,' Ludd insisted, 'the matter of the Gereon mission underpins the entire nature of the hearing today. It cannot be glossed over.'

'The statement runs to one hundred and forty-seven pages,' Faragut said. 'I must object to a simple recitation of–'

'Colonel?' Inquisitor Welt put in softly. 'I have read Gaunt's statement in full, as have, I'm sure, my worthy fellows. I've really no wish to hear such prepared material repeated out loud. However, I believe Junior Ludd's point to be well taken. Perhaps, as a compromise, and pursuant to the interests of fairness, the defendant might be permitted to make a brief summary of the salient facts in his own words?'

'That sounds fair and practical, inquisitor,' Kaessen replied. He looked at Balshin. 'Objections?'

'None, colonel.'

'Junior Ludd?'

Ludd bent and exchanged a few whispered comments with Gaunt before rising again to face the dais.

'The defendant is happy to comply with the inquisitor's suggestion.'

Ludd sat down. Gaunt rose to his feet and began to speak.

'In the latter part of 774, my unit arrived here on Ancreon Sextus as part of the Fifth Army's liberation contingent. We'd shipped in from Herodor after the scrap there. Shortly after our arrival, I was contacted by the office of the lord general, and summoned to meet with him. He told me he had a high-category mission that needed to be undertaken immediately. It was classified vermillion, and was on a volunteer-only basis. It involved the covert deployment of a specialist mission team onto the enemy-occupied world of Gereon. I agreed to lead the mission.'

'Just like that?' asked one of the ranking commissars.

'Naturally, I reviewed the requirements first,' Gaunt replied sardonically.

'Once you had, you accepted?'

Gaunt nodded. 'It was clear the matter was potentially vital to the continued success of the Crusade on this front. Besides, I felt the lord general was asking a personal favour of me.'

'Why was that?' Faragut asked.

'The nature of the mission suited the skills of my regiment. The Tanith are experts at stealth infiltration.'

'Wasn't there another reason?' Faragut pressed.

Gaunt shrugged slightly. 'I believe it's possible the lord general had a decent regard for my abilities, and the abilities of my soldiers. I'd like to think he asked me because he trusted me.'

'You had worked directly with the lord general before, isn't that right?' Ludd put in.

'Yes,' said Gaunt. 'Most particularly on Phantine in 772, and a year later on Aexe Cardinal.'

'In both instances, you served him well?'

'As far as I know, he was satisfied.'

'It's fair to say then,' Ludd continued, 'that you had become one of the lord general's favoured commanders? He regarded you highly, and counted on your expertise during special circumstances?'

'I was honoured to enjoy the favour and friendship of Lord General Van Voytz,' Gaunt said.

Balshin rose. 'None of that is disputed. General Van Voytz has imparted to me on several occasions that he considers the defendant both a close comrade and a friend. However, I believe Commissar Faragut was pressing at something else.'

'Such as, my lady?' Kaessen asked.

Balshin looked down at Gaunt on the main floor below her. 'Perhaps the defendant might describe the specific parameters of his mission?'

'I was just getting to that,' Gaunt said, totally at ease. 'The mission was to infiltrate the occupied planet Gereon, broker contact with the local pro-Throne resistance, and then locate and eliminate with extreme prejudice an individual held in custody by the archenemy forces.'

'And that individual was?' Balshin asked.

'The Imperial traitor General Noches Sturm.'

'Why was this important?' Balshin added.

'Sturm had been disgraced and was awaiting court martial when the archenemy captured him. He had been carefully mindlocked, so that the information in his brain could be reopened during the trial. It was a distinct possibility that the enemy might penetrate that mindlock and recover all manner of sensitive information from Sturm. Fleet codes, ciphers, deployments, tactics. If he could be opened up, he would surely betray significant Crusade strengths to the archenemy, resulting in catastrophe for our cause.'

'Indeed,' said Balshin. 'Tell the tribunal, if you would, why General Sturm was facing court martial?'

'For dereliction of duty during the siege of Vervunhive,' Gaunt said.

'Who found him so wanting at that time?'

Gaunt coughed slightly. 'I did, ma'am.'

'You were the one who placed Noches Sturm under arrest and saw that he was charged?'

'Yes.'

'You were a colonel and he was a militant general?'

'Yes. I found him wanting in my capacity as an Imperial commissar, and removed him from command.'

'I see,' said Balshin. 'And in your capacity as an Imperial commissar, were the charges against him valid?'

'Absolutely.'

'Let me get this straight,' Balshin smiled. 'In the middle of a quite notorious siege, in the extreme heat of combat, you removed General Sturm from command... in your capacity as a commissar?'

'Yes, as I just said.'

'Under such intense circumstances, Gaunt, did you not consider that summary execution was more appropriate? In your capacity as a commissar, I mean? '

'I did not.'

'But it was quite within your power. Instead, you stretched vital reserves of manpower to keep him a prisoner.'

'An objection to the commissar-general's tone and inference!' Ludd called out.

'Overruled,' said Kaessen.

'Gaunt?'

'It was also quite within my power to order his internment,' Gaunt said quietly. 'I do not shrink from execution where it is needed, but I felt that Sturm deserved to face full court martial because of his status and rank.'

'So he was alive because of your judgement?' Balshin said. 'Let me rephrase that... Noches Sturm was only alive *to be captured by the enemy* because you had let him live?'

'Yes.'

'The entire jeopardy he represented when he fell into enemy hands was *your* fault?'

'Another objection!' Ludd cried.

'I made no error,' Gaunt growled. 'Perhaps the fault lies with the office of the Commissariat for guarding him so unsuccessfully.'

'But isn't it true that you undertook the Gereon mission because you felt it a personal failing that he had got away?'

'Objection!'

'Isn't it true,' Balshin urged, 'that Van Voytz asked you to undertake the Gereon mission because he wanted to give you the opportunity to clean up your own mess?'

'Objection! Colonel, please!'

'My last remark is withdrawn,' Balshin said, and resumed her seat.

Ludd had been on his feet throughout the last exchange. 'Sir,' he said to Gaunt. 'Who won the battle at Vervunhive?'

'The forces of the God-Emperor,' Gaunt said.

'And who was in command of them?'

'I was.'

'If you would,' Ludd said, 'remind the tribunal of the official rating the Departmento Tacticae gave to the Gereon mission.'

'The status was *EZ*.'

'Which is?'

'I believe the definition is *"extremely hazardous/suicidal"*.'

'There were twelve mission specialists on the team including yourself,' Ludd said. 'How many did you lose?'

'None.'

'And was the mission successful?'

'Yes. We eliminated Noches Sturm at the Lectica Bastion. A confirmed kill.'

Ludd looked back at the tribunal panel. 'Perhaps the defendant might resume his account of the mission?'

'So requested,' Kaessen said, with a nod to Gaunt.

'My stalwart advocate has rather ruined the ending, colonel,' Gaunt smiled. Despite themselves, several of the senior commissars on the dais smiled. So did Welt.

'That wasn't the end of it, though, was it?' Faragut asked. 'Once Sturm was dead, I mean.'

'No, commissar,' Gaunt said softly. 'Before we set off, Lord General Van Voytz had made it plain to me that there was very little chance of extraction. It had been hard enough getting us in. Even if we survived, it was likely to be a one-way mission.'

'So you were stuck there?' Faragut pressed.

'Yes. Most of us were injured–'

'In what way?'

'The usual way. Enemy fire. Some of my team were severely hurt. We had also expended most of our munitions and supplies. We had little choice but to throw in our lot with the Gereon underground and serve the Imperial cause by adding our abilities to the resistance efforts. But we did this, I think, gladly. We had seen much of the privation levied on the planet. The Gereon underground was a proud, defiant, valiant force. We were honoured to help.'

'Isn't it true you did more than help?' Ludd asked.

Gaunt shrugged.

'This is not a moment for modesty, Gaunt,' Inquisitor Welt called out.

'Very well, sir. The Gereon underground – which, I might add, had sacrificed great portions of itself to help us achieve our mission – was principally an under-equipped force of local citizens, reinforced by the military skills of a few surviving PDF officers. My team and I were able to spread our knowledge and our combat abilities. We restructured the underground in the Lectica area, and also in neighbouring provinces. We trained them in stealth warfare. For that, I would especially commend my scouts Mkoll, Bonin and Mkvenner. Trooper Brostin supervised the steady manufacture of makeshift flamer weapons. Sergeants Criid and Varl, along with myself, taught them cadre and fireteam drills. Major Rawne and Trooper Feygor travelled the cells, instructing them on demolition and explosives know-how. Vox-officer Beltayn, my adjutant, pretty much rebuilt the underground's communication network. Trooper Larkin hand-trained a school of marksmen using captured las-locks, teaching them how to make the one, sure killshot you need with single-action weapons like that. Medicae Curth's training became utterly indispensable to the underground's needs. I would also, before this hearing, commend Gerome Landerson and Sabbatine Cirk, officers of the resistance, for their courage and determination at all times.'

'You paint a heroic picture,' Welt said.

'What about the partisans?' Ludd nudged.

'The Nihtganes, or Sleepwalkers, of the Untill region–' Gaunt began.

'The what?' asked Kaessen.

'The Untill, colonel,' Gaunt explained. 'The untill-able or un-navigable regions of Gereon, deep marshes mostly. The Sleepwalkers are surviving communities of the original colonists. Infamously separatist, they had been the bane of Imperial authority for many years. But Chaos was a common foe. A tribe of Niht-ganes assisted us in our initial actions on Gereon, and later, principally through the work of Scout Mkvenner, we were able to enlist them in the resistance as elite troops. Without the Sleepwalkers, we would have failed on Gereon, both in our attempt on Sturm, and in the guerilla war that followed.'

'I've seen your pet Nihtgane,' Faragut said. 'Eszrah, isn't it? Not the model Imperial citizen.'

'I would ask that you take that slur back, commissar,' Gaunt replied. 'Eszrah ap Niht is the most loyal soldier of the Throne I have ever met.'

'Why do you say that, Gaunt?' asked Kaessen.

'Because he is loyal to me, sir.'

'This period of operation with the Gereon resistance, it was hard, wasn't it?' Faragut asked.

'Yes,' said Gaunt.

'Demanding, I mean,' Faragut continued. 'From your appearance alone, on your return… you were under-nourished.'

'Food was in short supply. For everyone.'

'And you were deprived of many things. Soap, for example.'

'I won't dignify that with a response.'

'Your clothing too, ragged…'

'As far as I'm aware, the nearest functioning Guard quartermaster was eight light years away.'

'Colonel,' Ludd said. 'Please, is the defendant under scrutiny here because of his dishevelled appearance? That length of time behind enemy lines, it's hardly surprising he was not parade muster.'

'A fair point,' Kaessen said. 'Where are you going, Commissar Faragut?'

'There's more to it, sir,' Faragut said. 'There is the question of taint. We all know that's the heart of the matter. Dirty, bearded, ragged… that's one thing. Gaunt and his team were living rough with the resistance. In many ways, the fact that they seem to… how shall I put it best? The fact that they seem to have *gone native* is understandable.'

'Under the circumstances,' said Gaunt, 'it was vital.'

'But there are other, more concerning matters. The grey staining to your skin and hair–'

'We all adopted the Nihtgane practice of using *wode*. That's their word for it. Essentially, it's a skin-dye paste ground from the wing-cases of the swamp moths. It's excellent for camouflage. Not only visually, but it masks scents too. We would treat our hair, clothes and skin with it. It has other prophylactic properties too.'

Gaunt noticed that Welt was making some hasty notes.

'But it's difficult to get out. Even by scrubbing with carbolic.' Gaunt paused and looked at Welt.

'Does it explain the elevated toxin levels found in your bloodstream and in the systems of your fellows?' the inquisitor asked.

'The moths are venomous, sir, yes,' Gaunt said. 'The paste allowed us to build up a tolerance to local poisons.'

'And anything else?' Welt asked.

Gaunt shrugged. 'The Nihtgane believed that a more concentrated form of the paste could actually fight off Chaos-related infections. I wouldn't know about that.'

'Did you see that done?'

Gaunt nodded. 'Yes, with Trooper Feygor. To startling effect.'

'But "you wouldn't know about that"?' Faragut asked.

'I'm no medicae,' Gaunt said. 'I know what I saw. I know what it was like. Maybe the paste helped Feygor, all of us perhaps. But it may also have been a placebo. I believe the best way to fight Chaos taint is to be sound and determined of mind.'

'Are you saying,' said Faragut, 'that you and your team came off Gereon untainted because you mentally refused to allow yourselves to become so?'

Gaunt looked at Ludd, who shrugged.

'Answer the question please,' Kaessen called.

'Yes,' Gaunt said. 'That's an oversimplification, but I think it's essentially correct. Though we suffered, and we were sorely tested, we rejected the corruption of the Ruinous Powers by force of will.'

Faragut glanced at Welt, who shook his head. Balshin rose instead. 'If you were sitting in judgement here, Gaunt,' she asked, 'would you believe a word of what you just stated to the hearing?'

'Knowing it to be the truth, lady commissar-general, I'd like to think I would.'

'And supposing you didn't?'

'I don't know. It's an aspirational idea. One based on the notion of the essential incorruptibility of true Imperial souls.'

'Indeed. And that is how you see yourself and your team?'

'Yes,' said Gaunt.

'It's interesting,' Welt said, rising as Balshin resumed her seat. 'As you say, Gaunt, an aspirational idea. But isn't it true that even the greatest and purest of men have, through the course of our history, been corrupted by the warp despite their soundness of heart?'

'History speaks of such things. But I think I'm right in saying that Urbilenk wrote that: "Chaos merely unfetters the dark quarters of the mind, unlocking that which was always there. True, pure minds have nothing that curse may use".'

'You quote him well.'

'One of my favourites, inquisitor. I would also cite Ravenor, who said in *The Spheres of Longing:* "Chaos claims the unwary or the incomplete. A true man may flinch away its embrace, if he is stalwart, and he girds his soul with the armour of contempt."'

'Fine words,' said Welt.

'I think so,' Gaunt replied.

'Even so, statistically–'

'My team and I were not tainted.'

'Because you and your team are somehow special? Exempt?'

'I believe the Ghosts of Tanith have been blessed by their interaction with the Saint,' Gaunt said.

'On Herodor, you mean?'

'Then, and before. I think perhaps... we're especially hard to taint.'

Welt smiled. 'You took inhibitors with you?'

'A fair supply. They ran out.'

'Before you left on the mission,' Welt said, consulting a dataslate, 'is it not true that you consulted Tactician Biota for information as to how long you might reasonably last on a Chaos-held world before taint became inevitable?'

'Yes, inquisitor.'

'And to answer that, Biota referred himself to the Ordo Malleus, correct?'

'I believe so.'

'And what was the answer?'

'About a month,' said Gaunt.

'About a month. And how long were you and your team on Gereon?'

'Sixteen months.'

'It's evident that your accent has changed, Gaunt. It has a timbre. A quality.'

'It's the same for all my team. Living amongst the Nihtgane inevitably caused some alterations.'

'Do you acknowledge that the change in your accent is disconcerting?'

Gaunt shrugged.

'Do you acknowledge that it makes you sound like the archenemy?'

'No,' said Gaunt. 'Though we all speak Low Gothic, the accents of the Imperium are many and varied. Ever spoken to a Vitrian, inquisitor? '

'I have.'

'What about a Kolstec? A Cadian? A Hyrkan? Ever heard the burr of a Phantine voice? The wood talk of the Tanith in full, mellow flow?'

'Your point?'

'Accents prove nothing. Would you execute us for a twang in our voices?'

Welt put the dataslate down. 'Voi shet, ecchr setriketan.'

'Hyeth, voi magir, elketa anvie shokol,' Gaunt replied.

An ugly murmur ran around the room. Ludd stared at Gaunt with a queasy look on his face.

'You speak the language of the Ruinous Powers,' Welt said.

'One of them.'

'Fluently and naturally, it seems.'

'How long do you suppose the underground would have lasted if it didn't learn the language of the enemy, sir?' Gaunt asked. 'It was a vital tool of resistance.'

'Even so–' Balshin began.

Gaunt stared up at Inquisitor Welt. 'You speak it well,' he said. 'Why aren't you down here with me?'

Welt laughed heartily. 'Touché, Gaunt,' he said. He sat back down.

Immediately, Faragut stood again, opening his dossier. 'You were embedded with the resistance for a considerable time,' he said.

'As I said, we were resigned to our situation.'

'Why, then, did you leave?'

'Because we had the opportunity to do so.'

'For what purpose, if you were performing such a vital service leading the underground?'

'I felt it was necessary to get the intelligence concerning Sturm off-world as soon as the chance arose. I also wanted to communicate other information to High Command.'

'Such as?'

'Such as the fact that the foul Magister Sek was using Gereon as a proving ground for his own elite shock troops. They are modelled on the Blood Pact. If anything, they are more vicious.'

'You know this how?'

'From fighting them and killing them,' said Gaunt.

'You think they present a tangible threat to the crusade?'

'How tangible is the Blood Pact, Faragut? If the Sons of Sek, as they are known, are marshalled into a proper fighting force, we will be in a shit-storm of trouble.'

Faragut paused, lost for another question. From his seat, Kaessen said 'Tell us about your evacuation from Gereon, Gaunt.'

'Gladly, sir. We had been planet-side and dug in for about sixteen months,' Gaunt said. 'By then, the arch-enemy hold on Gereon had fractured a little. Not much, but enough to allow independent and rogue traders access to remote portions of the planet, conducting black-market runs. Also, they extracted civilian refugees who could pay. Beltayn and Rawne had developed this connection, in order to supply the underground with munitions, but the trade grew, even though the occupying forces dealt harshly with any traders they captured. I've seen more than one far trader ignite in orbit. However, it became possible for people to leave Gereon, if they were prepared to take the risks.'

'And you chose to take that route?' Faragut asked.

'I felt I owed it to my mission team. As I said, I felt I needed to bring word of Sturm's death to High Command. Most particularly, I felt the Crusade forces needed to know about the Sons of Sek before it was too late.'

'So you left Gereon?'

'It was hazardous. We procured a rogue trader, who then let us down five nights running. On the sixth evening, we managed extraction, but it was compromised. Enemy warships pursued us to the limits of the system.'

'And then?'

'Then a month's transit to Beshun. The trader deposited us there, unwilling to risk the Imperial blockade at Khan Nobilis. We had no access to astropath communications, but I knew we needed to reach Ancreon Sextus.'

'Why?'

'We needed to reach Van Voytz. He was the only one who could vouch for us.'

'And what happened?'

'Liberty ships were coming in to Beshun, carrying refugees and survivors fleeing Urdesh and Frenghold. We got passage to Ancreon Sextus as part of a host of Guardsmen trying to rejoin the Crusade main force. On arrival, we were transported to the internment camp for processing. No one I spoke to would believe our story, or allow us contact with Van Voytz. We were told that the opportunity would arise at Camp Xeno, during processing.'

'Did that happen?' asked Ludd.

'It did not. But for the extremis actions of my team... and the interjection of my advocate here, we would have been executed without hesitation.'

'An objection!' Faragut cried.

'Withdrawn,' said Balshin.

An aide had entered the hearing room, climbed the dais and whispered into Inquisitor Welt's ear. Welt looked at Colonel Kaessen.

Kaessen nodded. 'That's enough for now. We'll resume at oh-eight hundred tomorrow. Hearing is in recess.'

SIX

08.10 hrs, 191.776.M41
Frag Flats HQ
Sparshad Combat Zone, Ancreon Sextus

THE FOLLOWING MORNING, Balshin and Welt were late. Kaessen himself arrived almost ten minutes after the appointed start time, and apologised to the waiting commissars. 'An unavoidable hold-up,' he said. 'We will begin shortly.'

Gaunt and Ludd had been sitting at the defendant's desk since just before eight. Ludd was sorting through various papers from his document case, and seemed ill at ease.

'Do you know what this delay is about?' Gaunt whispered to him.

'No,' said Ludd, a little too firmly. 'They choose not to tell me anything.'

Gaunt raised his eyebrows thoughtfully. He could tell Ludd was tense. For his own part, Ludd was trying to maintain a veneer of calm. He didn't want his own edginess to rile Gaunt into further outbursts. But the night had not passed well. Three times he'd been summoned to see Balshin, each time quizzed on various aspects of Gaunt's testimony. He'd spent half an hour alone reviewing the medical records. Something was going on, but the defence advocate was being kept out of the loop.

'When they put me back in the tank last night,' Gaunt said quietly, 'I saw that Cirk had been removed. She wasn't back this morning, either. Any idea what that means?'

Ludd shook his head. 'I'm sorry. I asked, and was told she'd been removed for questioning by Balshin.'

'Isn't that counter to the terms of the tribunal, Ludd? They said they'd be starting with me.'

'I know. It's frustrating.'

'This is increasingly feeling like a scam to me,' Gaunt said. 'Is there something you're not telling me, Ludd?'

'No,' Ludd replied. 'Except that there's something they're not telling either of us.'

Behind them, the heavy door of the hearing chamber drew open with a scrape of metal, and Commissar-General Balshin entered, escorted by Inquisitor Welt. Ludd and Gaunt rose to their feet, and the chamber guards came to formal attention.

'My apologies to the tribunal,' Balshin said as she stepped onto the dais. Then she turned aside and engaged Kaessen in a quiet, intense conversation. Welt took his seat. He was staring at Gaunt, and when Gaunt met his eyes, nodded briefly.

Balshin handed Kaessen a dataslate and then sat down. The colonel reviewed the slate's contents and remained standing to address the hearing.

'I'll keep this brief and simple,' he said. 'I'd like to bring to the tribunal's attention this edict.' Kaessen indicated the dataslate. 'It was issued by the Commissariat at oh-seven forty-five this morning, and personally ratified by Inquisitor Welt on behalf of the Holy Ordos. It states that all charges and suspicions against Gaunt and his mission team are to be dropped with immediate effect.'

There was a chatter from the commissars around the dais. Ludd looked at Gaunt.

'The defendants will be released shortly into the hands of the Munitorum for dispersal. The members of the tribunal are thanked for their time and attention.'

'Sir?' Ludd said. 'Are there terms to this edict?'

Kaessen nodded. 'Gaunt and his team must submit to a full round of psychometric tests and interviews to assess mental health and combat readiness, and they must all make themselves available for thorough debriefings with Military Intelligence. There will then be a probationary period at the discretion of the Commissariat. Other than that, no. Junior Ludd, perhaps you'd stay with Gaunt until he's been issued with appropriate credentials for this HQ.'

'Yes, sir.'

'By the grace of the God-Emperor, this hearing is closed.' Kaessen declared, and the commissars on the dais immediately rose and started talking in huddles as they left the chamber.

'I wanted to ask why the sudden change of heart,' Ludd confided to Gaunt, 'but I didn't want to tempt fate.'

'I know what you mean,' Gaunt replied. 'But I think I'll find out in due course.'

Colonel Kaessen approached. He saluted and held out his hand to Gaunt. 'A good result, if unexpected,' he said as Gaunt shook his hand. 'I'd not have been happy to be the man presiding over your demise, colonel-commissar.'

'Thank you, colonel. Any idea what happened to change events?'

Kaessen smiled. 'I think you have a good deal of influence, sir. Powerful allies.'

'I see,' Gaunt replied. He looked past the colonel, but Balshin and the inquisitor had already left the chamber.

'The lord general's waiting to see you,' Kaessen said.

LUDD LOCATED A watch officer, and had him issue a pass warrant for Gaunt. Gaunt fixed the small plastek badge to the front of his vest and then allowed Ludd to accompany him as far as the outer hatch of the lord general's quarters.

Ludd paused at the doorway, anticipating – or at least hoping – that Gaunt might offer him some acknowledgement, perhaps even thanks. Gaunt merely glanced at him, a brief, almost dismissive look, and then walked on through the hatch without a word, leaving Ludd alone in the hallway.

Ludd looked down at the deck, ran his tongue around the front of his upper teeth thoughtfully, and turned to leave.

'Junior commissar?'

Ludd looked round. It was Balshin.

She beckoned to him with a curt hook of her fingers. 'A word with you, please.'

VAN VOYTZ WAS at his desk in the inner office of his quarters, reviewing reports. As Gaunt entered, Van Voytz dismissed the group of aides and servitors and got to his feet as soon as they had left the room.

He walked around the desk until he was face to face with Gaunt.

'Shall we start again?' he said.

'I'd appreciate the chance, sir,' Gaunt replied.

'Any weapons you'd especially like to threaten me with?' Van Voytz asked.

'My lord, I never threatened you directly. I–'

Van Voytz held up his hand. 'Lighten up. I'm joking. It's over, Ibram. Done with.' The lord general gestured, and they sat down on the battered leather couches beside the desk.

'This is how it should have been,' Van Voytz mused. 'Mission over and done, you reporting back to me, a quiet moment to savour your success.'

'Events conspired against that,' said Gaunt.

'They did. Look, if I could have spared you any part of that tribunal, I would have done. I have authority, Ibram, extraordinary amounts of it, in some areas. But not in others. Discipline and security are not in my remit. You know how it works.'

'I remember how it used to work,' Gaunt said.

'Once you'd pulled that stunt in here, Ibram, it was out of my hands. I had no choice but to give you to Balshin. There would have been hell to pay, otherwise. I had to give you to Balshin, and while she was busy with you, find ways to get you cleared.'

'You did that?'

'I pulled some strings, called in a few favours. My last few favours, probably. Viktoria Balshin is possibly the most fanatical person I've ever met where it comes to issues of Imperial purity. She's devoted her career to the suppression of taint, and won't even let the slightest rumour of it pass her by. Admirable, of course, and understandable given the way things have gone this last year. But even she has a price. I had to give her something to make her drop the case.'

'What was that?' Gaunt asked, uncomfortable.

Van Voytz shrugged. 'It doesn't matter. You'll be better off not knowing. All you need to know is… I made her a proposition. I contacted the office of the Warmaster himself, and got his personal endorsement for my proposal. Inquisitor Welt also supported it, which helped a great deal. I think Welt likes you, Ibram. Admires you.'

Gaunt frowned. 'I don't know why, sir.'

'Neither do I,' replied Van Voytz. 'Who knows how the curious minds of Inquisitorial servants operate? He has his own agenda. Whatever, with the Inquisition and the Warmaster himself backing me, I had the sort of leverage that Balshin couldn't ignore.'

'Are you saying the Warmaster himself vouched for my case?' Gaunt asked.

'On my recommendation. You look surprised.'

'I didn't think he was even aware who I was,' Gaunt said.

'You've met him?'

'A handful of times, but I'm not senior staff, and I–'

'You'd be surprised what he remembers,' Van Voytz said. 'Macaroth might be a very different animal to old Slaydo, but he's still a Warmaster. He has the same skills, the same eye for detail, the same memory for those who serve the cause well, whoever they are. He remembers you all right, and he was fully appraised of the Gereon mission.'

'I see,' said Gaunt.

'About the Gereon mission,' Van Voytz said. 'With Macaroth's approval, I have requested citation for you and your team. A special honour or decoration may be approved eventually. Throne knows, you deserve it. But the matter's knotted up in larger, political issues, and these things take time anyway. In a few months, there might be an official recognition. I'm telling you this because for now, and perhaps for always, you'll receive only private thanks.'

'I didn't do it for the glory,' said Gaunt. 'The Emperor knows there was precious little in it anyway. I'd simply like to get back to active line duties as soon as possible.'

'That was my next question. It's in my power to retire you from the front for the duration. A little soft duty in the rear echelons might do you the power of good. But I expected that wouldn't appeal, knowing how you're made. As soon as you're cleared fit, I can get you into the field again, if that's what you want.'

'It is, sir,' Gaunt nodded.

'Well, then…' Van Voytz began. Gaunt could see that the lord general seemed unsettled. Van Voytz had changed too, from the man who had sent the Ghosts off on their mission. The change was perhaps not as dramatically obvious as the alterations hardship had wrought upon Gaunt and his men on Gereon. But it was there, nevertheless. Van Voytz was older, more haggard, more worn than Gaunt remembered him. He'd lost weight too, so his crisp day uniform hung limply from his frame. The stress of command seemed to have eroded his robust physique.

'Sir,' Gaunt said. 'May I ask what you meant when you said "the way things have gone this last year"?'

Van Voytz shrugged. 'Tough times, Ibram. The Second Front's facing especially bitter resistance from Sek's forces, right across the coreward Khans. Macaroth expects results, but they're just not coming fast enough. Here alone, we should have been done six months ago.'

'Particular problems?'

'Enemy fanaticism is especially high. Plus the special terrain here and on a couple of other key worlds. That's a killer. Here, it's the damn step-cities. Clearing them is a nightmare. There's also the issue of taint.'

'That again?'

'In the last twelve months, the Second Front has lost thirty-two per cent more to taint or suspected taint than during the previous phase. Whole units are deserting the field. Some are even changing sides.'

'Hence the commissar-general's particular obsession with that heresy?'

'Indeed. It's endemic. Oh, there are reasons, I'm sure. Men break easier when the going's hard, and it's certainly hard here. We're making nothing like the palpable inroads the Main Front's achieving in the Carcaradon System. It also doesn't help that the majority of troop units in the Second Front armies are fresh and inexperienced. Most of them are new-founded regiments sent to us from the rear to replace lost strengths. Macaroth took most of the veteran regiments with him for the main push. I'm left with boys, Ibram. Untried, innocent, naive. Their first experiences of real combat are against ferocious cult units lousy with corruption, heresy and the marks of the Ruinous Powers. Suicide is up, mental collapse, desertion…'

'Is the enemy using psykers to magnify the effect?'

'Jury's out on that one, Ibram. Possibly. All we know is, the corruption of the foe is sweeping through our ranks like a plague, right across the Second Front. Morale is at an all time low, and that can only lead one way.'

'The collapse of the Second Front.'

'Unless Second Front Command can turn the tide. Or unless the Warmaster decides we are not leading and inspiring the men in a manner appropriate to our authority, and replaces us.'

'Is that a real possibility?' Gaunt asked.

Van Voytz did not reply. Clearly it was. Clearly he was under immense pressure to dig his command out of a deep, dark hole.

'So, your field posting,' Van Voytz said, at length. 'It'll be good to have another experienced officer on the line.'

'I am anxious to return to the Tanith First,' Gaunt said. He'd deliberately not thought of that possibility for a long time. In the dark days on Gereon, it had been too much to hope for, too painful a hope to cling to. Gaunt allowed himself the pleasure of anticipation for the first time in months.

It was short lived.

'That… look, I'm sorry, Ibram. There's no easy way into this. That's not going to happen.'

'What? Why?'

'There are two reasons, really.' Van Voytz got to his feet and helped himself to a small amasec. He didn't offer one to Gaunt. 'The first is you. I've moved heaven and earth to get you reinstated, Ibram. Called in favours, like I said… and, like I said, I'm down to my last few. Particularly with Macaroth regarding my performance with mounting displeasure. I had to compromise. It was a condition demanded by Balshin and the senior Commissariat. You may return to the line in the capacity of commissar, with a purview to reinforce and support unit discipline. They don't want you given a command posting again.'

'I can't believe this,' Gaunt said.

'I don't like it. Not at all. But it's the hand we're dealt. You must come around to the idea that the future of your career lies with the Commissariat, not with command. A separation of powers. I'm sorry. New duties await you, new challenges. The Tanith First was your last command.'

'Can I file a protest?' Gaunt asked.

'To whom?' Van Voytz laughed, mirthlessly.

'Then… then what was the second reason, sir?'

Van Voytz cleared his throat. 'Simple enough, Ibram. You can't go back to commanding the Tanith First, because the Tanith First doesn't exist any more.'

SEVEN

ONCE THEY HAD made him, they named him Crook-shank. Crookshank Thrice-wrought, in honour of his twisted form and the complexity of his making. It was a name he could recognise – sometimes – but could not say. In the barking cant of the wrought, he was known simply by the depth and timbre of a particular throat-roar.

The sun was rising, but no daylight had yet penetrated the vast black gulf of the fifth compartment. High over-head, the visible sky was blue-white, suffused with smoky light, and the rays of the sun were illuminating the faces of the towering stepped walls of the inner Mons to the east. Where the sunlight touched the stone, far away and high above, it glowed like amber.

The deep floor of the colossal fifth compartment was a blind, cold place, trapped in the shadow of the west-ern wall. The pre-dawn temperature was minus three, and a chill mist shrouded the jumbles of wet, black stones and deep crater pools. It was quiet and still: just the occasional skitter of vermin in the rubble, or the distant grumbling roars of other wrought ones echoing down the compartment's long canyon.

Crookshank Thrice-wrought was hunting. The urge to do so was knotting his omnivorous stomach and needling at the tiny, primitive lump of his brain. Quietly, he clambered his great bulk along a ridge of broken ruby quartz. The only sounds he made were the slight clicks of his thick claws against the quartz, the low wheeze of his phlegmy lungs.

The end of the ridge overlooked a sunken watercourse. He could see it clearly, despite the blackness. His eyes resolved the details of the world as pink phantoms, and he could smell and taste the shapes of it too. He snorted twice, pulling rushes of cold air in through the blood-rich olfactory passageways of his long skull. He smelled the texture of stone, the feeble flow of the shallow water in the sunken course, the damp lichen clinging to the underside of granite boulders.

There were two wrought ones behind him. He'd been well aware of them for the last fifteen minutes, but had made no show of acknowledging them. They were little, once-wrought, immature things, lacking the display decoration of a mature bull, their lank black hair plastered damply over their pink, sutured scalps. They were following him unbidden, hoping he'd lead them to a kill, hoping to share in his success. The once-wrought often did that. They tailed the elders to learn skills from them and benefit from their protection.

Crookshank ignored them. They were making too much noise. One was panting hard as the adrenaline rose, and it was causing his throat tubes to hoot involuntarily.

Crookshank moved forward. His massive hands and feet read every notch and crevice of the rock, but he felt no scratch or graze or pain, just as his body registered it was cold but knew no discomfort. He could smell something new now. He could smell meat.

There was a sudden bang. The thump of it echoed down through the darkness, and made distant voices hoot and bark. Five minutes run ahead of him, Crookshank saw flames. A fierce spot of fire, bright like a star in the darkness, painfully bright to his straining dark-sight.

His blood began to course. Engorged, the fighting spines of his hackles rose up. Crookshank did not choose this reaction. It was bonded into the flesh of him, wired into his bones. The killing instinct that motivated him to do the things for which he had been made. Already, his dark-sight had clouded from pink to red. He felt the flush on his skin, the wetness as his throat tubes distended and vibrated with the rapid gusts of his exhalations.

He stood upright, swung his huge arms back and then forward, and pulled that momentum into a great forward leap which carried him down into the watercourse. He landed in the mud, and began to hurtle along the littered shore on his feet and his knuckles, bounding like a giant simian.

His two followers came after him eagerly. Both leapt off the promontory and landed in the shallow water itself, splashing after him on all fours. One left the water and began to chase Crookshank down the muddy shore, but the other -- which was now hooting loudly with every overexcited breath -- continued to crash and spray through the shallows.

Crookshank slid to a halt and turned suddenly. The once-wrought on the bank quailed back in alarm, but the other one came on, whooping and splashing. Crookshank ploughed into the stream and swung for him. The blow connected with the once-wrought's head and neck, and lifted him clean out of the water. He landed on the far side of the watercourse, twitching and convulsing, black blood pumping from the lacerations Crookshank's claws had left in his throat. But the throat wound wasn't the killer. The convulsions were just nerve-spasms. The immense force of Crookshank's blow had crushed the once-wrought's skull.

Crookshank turned and resumed his charge. He saw only red now. Red, and the bright white star of the flames. He shredded his way through a stand of stiff black thorn-rushes, snapping their stems, came in over a low ridge, and saw the prey. Little meat figures, struggling around a burning metal box. One of them saw him coming and screamed. Darts of light flickered at him.

Crookshank unleashed the full fury of his roar through his throat tubes, shaking the world. As he pounced, throwing all eight hundred kilos of himself forward into the air, arms outstretched, his massive jaws opened on their hinges and the steel daggers of his teeth slid out and locked in place.

'CONTACT!' THE COMPANY vox-officer was yelling, but that much was obvious. A kilometre ahead, the pre-dawn dark in the compartment was lighting up with flashes and flame-light. They could hear the chatter of weapons, and another sound. A roaring sound.

Wilder ran across the ice-clagged track to where Major Baskevyl crouched beside the vox-officer.

'Report!'

'It's not entirely clear, sir,' Baskevyl replied, making dragon breath. He was pressing the vox-set phones to his left ear. 'Sounds like the Hauberkan push has found a mined zone. At least one vehicle crippled. Now they seem to be under attack.'

'Oh, for Throne's sake!' Wilder said. 'I thought the area had been swept?'

'Last night, before dark,' Baskevyl shrugged.

'What are the Hauberkan doing?'

'Their commander's just signalled a halt, citing danger of mines.'

Wilder cursed again. 'Patch me through,' he said to the vox-officer. The man nodded and handed Wilder the horn.

'This is Wilder, Eighty-First Bellad–' He paused, and corrected himself. 'Wilder, Eighty-First First. Request confirmation. Are you moving?'

'Uh, negative on that, Wilder.'

'In the Emperor's name, Gadovin, if you sit still, they'll find you and gut you. Tank or no tank.'

'The zone is mined. We are holding as of now.'

Wilder tossed the horn back to the vox-man. 'What the hell's wrong with these idiots?' he asked Baskevyl. 'Didn't they have this explained to them?'

'The Hauberkan just got here, sir. I don't think they yet appreciate the jeopardy.'

'Did they think we were explaining it because we like the sound of our own voices?' Wilder asked.

'I think that's exactly what it was, sir.'

'Here's what we're going to do,' Wilder said, adjusting the gain of his low-light goggles so he could study a plastek-sheathed chart. 'We're going to move forward in a broad line and come up in support of these morons.'

'The order was to hold these trackways for the second wave,' Baskevyl advised.

'A second wave is going to be as effective as quick piss through a furnace grate if the forward line remains stalled. We'll leave six companies here on the trackways. The rest go forward. Tell the commissars I'll need them with me when we reach the Hauberkan command section. Tell them to bring sharp, pointy sticks.'

'Yes, sir.'

'That's if the Hauberkan are still alive when we get there. Bask, if we advance in the current disposition, which company's going to make that contact point first?'

'Best guess, E Company.'

Wilder nodded. 'Let's get to it,' he said.

Baskevyl saluted and crunched down the frosty track, ordering the men of the Eighty-First First up out of their cover. In their black camo, the troops flooded like shadows down the trackway and up across the open ground to the left.

'Get those support weapons moving!' Wilder heard Baskevyl shouting. 'Slog it! Look alive now!'

Wilder watched the fast deploy for a moment, and was satisfied. Moving together, no shirking. Still, blessedly, no sign of an enthusiasm problem in this newly alloyed force. There hadn't been a single serious issue of morale since the mix. He wasn't sure if he should feel flattered or simply lucky.

He adjusted his microbead link. 'Wilder to E Company lead. Talk to me.'

'Receiving. Go ahead, sir.'

'Chances are your first troop are going to reach that contact, captain. I'm relying on you to deal with it.'

'Understood, colonel. No problem,' the voice of the young captain crackled back.

'Thank you, Meryn. See you on the far side.'

THE FIRST SPEARS of intrusive daylight were stabbing down over the high, black crest of the western wall. A sort of twilight gathered in the depths of the compartment.

This was a bad time of day. Too dark for eyes, too light for goggles. Meryn removed his goggles anyway. According to scout philosophy, the sooner you got your eyes adjusted, the better.

The forward elements of E Company were pushing ahead through stands of black rushes thriving on a strip of wetland between the line of a trackway and a low water-course. They were following the crushed and trampled pathways left by the Hauberkan armour. Ahead, all sounds of fighting had ceased, but they could still see fire, lifting into the air beyond the sticky, black undergrowth. The sight of the flames seemed to emphasise how cold it was.

Dark shapes loomed up ahead. Three Hauberkan treads, parked and immobile. Meryn heard the voice of his adjutant Fargher rising angrily.

'What's the problem?' Meryn demanded as he came up.

Fargher gestured to the vehicle commander in the open hatch.

'He won't budge, captain,' he said.

'I've got orders,' the armour officer said.

'Feth your orders,' Meryn told him. 'Those are your boys in trouble up there.'

'I was told not to move,' the man protested.

'Feth you too, then,' Meryn spat. 'Fargher, take a note of this tread's stencil plate. Put it in the book.'

'Sir.'

'Let's close it up!' Meryn called, turning to the advancing troopers. 'Sergeant?'

Caffran jogged over to him. 'Sir?'

'Move your troop around to the right,' Meryn pointed. 'Come in along those rocks. I'll sweep in from the left, with Arlton's mob at the flank.'

Caffran nodded. It was still as strange to be taking orders from Meryn as it was to be wearing the silver badge with 81/1(r) on it. Times change, war didn't. Neither did men. Flyn Meryn was as fond of giving orders now as he had been as a lowly squad leader. In Caffran's opinion, Wilder hadn't made many mistakes during the mix, but Meryn's promotion was surely one.

They ranged forward, moving fast and low through the rushes. Caffran kept an eye on his troop. Five of them were Belladon, but they'd got the hang of the camo-capes pretty well. Besides, they had their own rep to uphold.

Crossing the rocks, they reached the contact.

A Hauberkan Chimera had churned out of the rushes onto a stretch of shingle and mud, and gone right over a mine. The blast had burst it wide open, scattering the mud with debris and fragments of armour. Fire was boiling fiercely from the machine's exposed guts. Two other Chimeras, moving in just behind, had evidently halted. Open hatches showed where the crews had exited in an effort to help the stricken tread.

Then something else had happened. The ground around the vehicles was littered with torn remains that steamed in the cold air. Caffran swallowed. They'd been hit hard, slaughtered. He knew what must have done this. The deep, terrifying roars of the spooks had echoed down the compartment valley all night.

Lasrifle raised, Caffran edged down onto the mud. Leyr and Wheln followed, then Raydee and Mkard. Caffran waved the others out into firing positions along the edge of the rocks, then gestured Neskon up. The flametrooper slithered down the rocks to join them, gently pumping the stirrup of his burner. The little naked trigger light hissed blue in the gloom.

The state of the bodies was chilling. None of them was intact. Limbs had been stripped of flesh, torsos emptied. Bloody stumps of ribcage poked through torn, soaked cloth.

Leyr made a quick hand signal for stillness. Caffran moved up close to his scout until he could hear what Leyr had heard. A snuffling, a wet crackling. Until now it had been indistinguishable from the pop and crack of the burning Chimera.

Round there, Leyr indicated. They raised their weapons to their shoulders, and edged on. Deftly, silently, Wheln and Neskon followed them. Mkard, and the Belladon, Raydee, moved around to cover the other side of the burning wreck.

The once-wrought had not learned from the example set by the mature bull he had followed. Crookshank had attacked, slaughtered, fed quickly and savagely, and then vanished into the dark again. The once-wrought had killed nothing. He had whooped and roared plenty as he charged in, but Crookshank had already finished the work. Hungry, and twitching with the huge adrenaline rush, the once-wrought had lingered to feed on the parts of the kill Crookshank had spurned and left behind.

He was sucking on the marrow of a Hauberkan officer. Vaguely humanoid, with stunted legs and vast arms and shoulders, the once-wrought weighed around four hundred kilos. The raw, pink flesh of his broad chest was smeared with blood, and tatters of meat dangled from his huge, under-biting snout. Patches of long, black hair trailed from a flat, almost indented scalp that still showed the healing scars of surgery, and hung down across tiny, pig-eyes that glinted behind an implanted iron visor. He raised his massive head as he detected movement.

'Holy feth!' Caffran gasped. He and Leyr began firing immediately, full auto bursts of las from their mark III carbines. The stalker was already coming for them, powering forward on knuckles like tree-roots, jaws opening. It roared a wet, choking roar, gusting a mist of blood and saliva from its slack throat tubes.

Caffran and Leyr saw their shots cutting into the spook's hide, but it didn't even flinch. Blood streaked down it from the multiple puncture wounds.

They feel no pain, Caffran thought. *How do you stop a thing like–*

It was just three metres from them when Neskon caught it in a long, howling spear of flame. The beast fell back, thrashing at the living fire that engulfed it. Neskon kept the pressure on.

Wild, demented, the once-wrought turned and lurched away around the other side of the wreck. Raydee and Mkard met it head on.

Raydee almost managed to get out of the way. He went sprawling, and the once-wrought trampled him, crushing his left foot into the mud and snapping his ankle. The monster grabbed Mkard around the body with its gigantic left hand and slammed him back against the rear-end of the burning Chimera so hard it pulped the Tanith-born's torso.

The flames had died down. The once-wrought's hair was burned off, and his skin bubbled with fat blisters. He roared, his throat sacs vibrating.

A hot-shot round exploded his cranium. The shot had been aimed right down the once-wrought's yawning gullet. There was a stringy burst of gore that left nothing behind except the heavy lower jaw, and the nightmare pitched over dead.

'Move in! Move in and secure the area!' Caffran yelled.

Meryn's troop began to emerge from the rushes. In cover, Jessi Banda lowered her long-las and ejected the spent hot-shot pack.

'Nice shot,' Meryn said, and kissed her roughly on the mouth. Their faces were cold against each other.

'I aim to please,' she smiled.

Meryn grinned and hurried forward to join the others.

DAWN WAS COMING up fast. Light was creeping down the eastern wall of the compartment. The wind was picking up too.

Wilder felt the breeze against his face, like the cool decompression rush of a flooding airgate. No one in Guard Logistics or Intel had yet been able to explain why the winds picked up in daylight, though Wilder had sat through three or four lengthy briefings filled with talk about ambient cooling, rapid-rise solar heating, pressure change and inter-compartment windshear effects.

In the grey light, Wilder saw the stands of thorn-rush and lime swaying and hissing. The landscape ahead, split by outcrops of granite and a quartzy rock, looked like wet hair. Through it, the black figures of his men advanced in a wide fan.

Good spacing, good unit protocol, Wilder thought. *Excellent noise discipline*. Mongrel or not, he was growing proud of the Eighty-First First (recon), with its proud battle-song of–

Well, that was the sort of area where things weren't perfect. He doubted any of the influx would be happy learning the words to 'Belladon, Belladon, world of my fathers', and he couldn't blame them. Likewise, he was sure, the Tanith and Verghastites had songs of their own that would not easily swell the breast of a true-blood

Bel-boy. Where it was relatively easy to combine regimental titles, things became clumsy when it came to songs and traditions. And warcry mottos. 'Fury of Belladon, for Tanith, for the Emperor, and, by the way, remember Vervunhive!' Full marks for effort, but still dead in a slit-trench before you'd said it all and actually started fighting.

Things would come, evolve, but it would take time, and it certainly wouldn't be forced. Braden Baskevyl, Wilder's number two and a keen promoter of esprit de corps, had spent most of the last evening in camp encouraging a little improvisation between the regimental musicians. Belladon fifes and Tanith pipes. It sounded like a disenchanted cat being elaborately stabbed in a sack.

Wilder smiled to himself, but it was not smiling weather.

'Coming up on the Hauberkan line,' Captain Callide reported over the vox. 'Got them in sight, fifty metres.'

'Pull in slow,' Wilder ordered on the wide channel. 'Make yourselves known. The tankers are going to be jumpy. Anyone touch off a black cross, I'll kick their arse. Even if they are dead.'

Black cross. The mark made in Munitorum ledgers to indicate a Guard-on-Guard firing accident.

Major Baskevyl hurried up out of the gloom. He'd pushed his low-light goggles up onto the brim of his helmet.

'How can you see?' Wilder asked.

'It's an accustomisation thing, sir,' Baskevyl said. 'The Tanith scouts reckon it's best to let your eyes adjust as soon as possible.'

Wilder frowned, then took of his own goggles, blinking hard. It had been his experience so far that the

Tanith knew what they were talking about, especially the ghostly scouts.

'Got a signal from E Company,' Baskevyl said. 'Meryn's secured the contact. A spook had ambushed some treads that had been stopped by a stray mine.'

'They get the bastard thing?'

'Yes, sir.'

'Casualties?'

'No details yet.'

The officers turned as they heard a flutter of polite, whispered greetings from the men behind them. The commissars were approaching, and as they moved up the line, the troops were greeting them with formal respect.

'Over here,' Wilder called.

Commissar Genadey Novobazky had been with Wilder and the Belladon for five years. Grizzled and lithe, he was a stern man, a fair man, and one disapproving glance from his grim demeanour was usually all that was needed. When it wasn't, Novobazky really came into his own. He was the best talker Wilder had ever met, the best rabble-rouser, a real burning det-tape when it came to igniting battlefield spirit: funny, loquacious and inspirational. His predecessor, Causkon, had been a real sap, which hadn't mattered much as the Belladon had never needed much field discipline, but Wilder had counted himself lucky to have an asset like Novobazky assigned.

The other commissar, Viktor Hark, he'd inherited from the Tanith. Bulky, heavy-set and impassive, Hark seemed a decent sort, and his augmetic arm spoke of heroic effort on the field of war. Hark had proved good at sorting out matters of petty theft, uniform code violations and mess-hall spats, but he'd yet to reveal any true potency as a commissar. There were the odd hints that Hark had some subterranean strengths, but he seemed to Wilder to be curiously reserved and hesitant, as if used to a subtler style of command. A legacy of the Great Lost Commander, Wilder supposed. Big boots to fill, and Wilder's own boots were quite tight enough, thank you. He pitied the Tanith First for the body-blows it had taken on Herodor and afterwards, but sometimes he was secretly a little glad the other guy was dead. His job would have been so much harder if any hope had remained.

'I want to get the armour moving,' Wilder told them.

'And they're not moving why?' Novobazky asked.

'Mines,' said Baskevyl.

'Nerves,' Wilder corrected. 'They've had a little hiccup, and now they've frozen up.'

'We can impress them with orders,' Novobazky said. 'It was perfectly clear last night. Ridge eighteen is the objective, with an open, covered corridor for the second wave. We're a long way short of that, and Gadovin knows it.'

'He's saying the orders are void because the orders supposed the zone had been cleared of mines,' Baskevyl said.

'Mine. Singular,' Wilder said. 'Boo hoo, that's war. Gadovin is overreacting. And if he sits there much longer, he'll be inviting all sorts of hurt.'

'And you're not happy about that?' Novobazky asked.

'How do I sound?'

'Let's have a word with him then,' Hark said. Hark didn't say much, and when he did, it was low-key, but this was one of those hints that Wilder had learned to pick up on. A muted suggestion that Hark was quietly polishing something large and spiky.

Wilder nodded. 'This they then do,' he said. He turned to Baskevyl. 'Get F Company moving onto that rise around the right flank. And tell Varaine to pick up L's pace before we leave them behind.'

A vox-officer ran up. 'Colonel Wilder, sir. Signal from Frag HQ.'

Wilder took the message wafer and started to read it. Some business about a personnel transfer.

There was the sudden suck-hiss of an inbound ballistic object. A hot, hard fireball burst amongst the line of stationary tanks. Two, three more fell, then a sustained salvo, ground-bursts erupting furiously along the Hauberkan position, throwing soil up into the air. The wind blew the grit back across Wilder's advance.

'Shit!' Wilder cried. He started to run forward. 'Into it! Into it!'

As he ran up through his scrambling troops, Wilder shoved the wafer, half-read, into his coat pocket.

EIGHT

07.56 hrs, 193.776.M41
Fifth Compartment
Sparshad Mons, Ancreon Sextus

WILDER LED THE charge up the slope, through the rushes and the sickly limes, into the wind, into the concussion of the falling shells. He saw at least three Hauberkan vehicles on fire. The quivered air was full of blown soil, dust and fragments of rush-stem. None of the tanks had begun firing, but at least some were restarting their engines. Wilder heard starter-motors whining and coughing. They'd been sitting in the cold for forty, fifty minutes. Some of these old treads would need a lot of nursing and blessing to get going again.

The shells continued to drop – brief shrill whistles, followed by heavy, splattery detonations. Some of the Eighty-First First had reached the spaced formation of tanks and got in between them, firing down across the brow of the slope into mist and shell-vapour.

'Auspex!' Wilder yelled over his link, panting as he struggled through the wet undergrowth.

'No fix yet, working.'

'Faster!' Wilder barked.

He was coming up behind a Chimera that had its turbines running. It was snorting plumes of blue vapour out of its exhausts. An Exterminator, three vehicles to his left, took a direct hit, and went up in a prickling sheet of flame. The concussion jarred Wilder's innards against his ribs. He almost fell.

'Open fire!' he yelled up at the Chimera. 'Open fire, damn you!'

For a second, Wilder thought his shout had actually penetrated the machine's thick armour and made some sense. The Chimera revved its engines hard.

And started to reverse.

Wilder was so amazed, it nearly ran him down. He threw himself out of the way.

'Scatter! Scatter!' he yelled at the men nearby. Other Hauberkan tanks were starting to back violently down the shallow gradient. The men of the Eighty-First First, drawn up between and behind the fighting machines, struggled to avoid them, some falling, some crying out.

Wilder heard a high-pitched scream that could only mean one of his men had been caught under treads.

Colonel Lucien Wilder, Belladon born, proud and decorated commander of the Belladon Eighty-First since Balhaut, was known as a genial, humorous soldier: a soldier's soldier. He had an infectious wit that often earned the disapproval of his superiors, and a track record that had won him nothing but plaudits. Well-made, dark haired, clean-shaven, he had a wry, handsome face and a sort of permanent, knowing, ladykiller squint. When he raised his voice, it was so orders could be understood, or so that the troopers at the back of the mess-hall could hear the punchline.

And, occasionally, when fury drove him. Like now.

As the Chimera reversed past him, splashing him with cold mud and twigs of reed, he hammered against its sponsons and track guards with the butt of his autopistol and screamed 'Halt! Halt, you bastard! Halt!'

It did not.

Raging, Wilder grabbed a netting hawser and scaled the side of the moving vehicle. Up on top, rolling with the lurch of the Chimera, he kicked at the squat turret. A shell went off nearby and threw dirt and debris across him.

'Halt! Halt!' His voice had become a scream. He saw that the top-hatch cover was loose. Wilder yanked the hatch wide open, let it fall with a clang, and lunged inside. In the dim, instrument-lit interior, the pale face of the vehicle commander looked up at him in dismay, and reached for a sidearm.

'Bastard!' Wilder shouted and slapped the gun away. Then he grabbed the tanker by the hair and slammed his head repeatedly against the metal bars of the roll-cage. 'Bastard! Bastard! Tell your driver to halt now! Now!'

'Do it! Do it!' the commander yelled, wincing at the tearing grip on his scalp. The Chimera bounced to a stop.

'Vox-link!' Wilder demanded, and ripped the headset out of the man's hands. Then he smacked him in the mouth for good measure.

The headset was crazy with nonsense traffic, panic-calls, hysteria. The Hauberkan had broken completely.

'Gadovin! Gadovin! This is Wilder! Cease your retreat now! Now, Throne damn it! Gadovin!'

The squealing nonsense was all that answered.

'Gadovin, so help me, stop your line moving and throw down some fire or, by the Emperor, I will hunt

you to the ends of everywhere and shoot you a new
arsehole! Gadovin! Respond!'

Nothing. Wilder threw the headset back at the dazed
commander. 'Use your pintle mounts,' Wilder told him.
'Fire into that mist bank. I have a gun and, so far, you
look like the enemy to me.'

The tanker nodded furiously. He activated turret
power, wound up the autoloader, and then the heavy
linked bolters in the low-profile turret began to blaze
away, gouting flame-flash from the muzzle baffles.

Wilder switched his commlink to the wide channel.
'Wilder to troop leaders. Be advised that the
Hauberkan should now be regarded as without line
of command. I am assuming control. Their orders are
to hold and fire. Do whatever you can to impart that
order. Any refusal must be considered a failure to follow officer directions.'

The shells were still raining down. More than a dozen
armour units were ablaze, destroyed, and the undergrowth at the crest of the rise was burning too. From his
raised vantage point, Wilder saw that half a dozen tanks
had already retreated right back down the slope to the
lower trackway. The noise of the barrage was deafening.
Wilder wondered how much of his order had been
heard.

Nearby, the six crew members of an Exterminator had
abandoned their machine and were fleeing down the
slope. Wilder was about to leap down after them when
he saw Commissar Hark appear out of the smoke wash.
Hark had drawn his sidearm, a plasma pistol.

'You men!' he yelled, the loudest thing Wilder had
ever heard him utter. 'Get back to your stations!'

The tankers hesitated, then continued to run.

Hark turned away.

Wilder jumped down. 'What the hell was that?' he demanded.

Hark glanced at him. 'If they're scared enough to ignore me, my rank and my weapon, then they're too scared to be of any use. Why? Would you like me to have shot them?'

'Hell, yes!'

'What, to assuage your current anger?'

'You and I are going to have a conversation, Hark.'

Hark nodded. 'As you wish, colonel.'

'Now rally the men!'

Wilder ran down the left wing of the broken line. Some of the Eighty-First First were in place at the crest of the slope, sniping into the mist. He passed Novobazky, who had expertly grouped most of D Company's first troop into firing positions and was delivering a variation on one of his favourite themes, The Shores of Marik.

'On the Shores of Marik, my friends,' Novobazky declaimed, head-high as he walked the line, oblivious to the whizzing shells, 'the fathers of our fathers made a stand under the flag of Belladon. Shells fell like rain. Were they afraid? You bet they were! Were they trepidatious? Absolutely! Did they break and run? Yes! But only in their minds. They ran to friendly places and loved ones, where they could be safe… and then, by the providence of the God-Emperor, they saw what those friendly places and loved ones would become if they did not stand fast, and so stand fast they did! How do you feel?'

There was a throaty murmur.

'I said, how do you feel?'

Louder shouting.

'Belladon blood is like wine on the Emperor's lips! Belladon souls have a special place at his side! If we spill our blood here today, then this is the soil He has chosen to bless and anoint! Oh, lucky land! Rise up and load, my friends, rise up and load! If they're going to have our precious blood, then they'll find the cost is dearer than they can afford! Fury of Belladon! Fury! Fury!'

A piece of art that. Honed over the years. The skilful acknowledgement of fear, the patriotic strand, the unexpected sucker-punch of 'Did they break and run? Yes!'. A piece of art. The thundering cadence and gathering rhythm. Simple words that carried over the tumult. Too many commissars told men they were invulnerable when they patently weren't. Too many commissars harangued and scolded, stripping away pride and confidence.

Or turned their backs on fleeing cowards, Wilder thought.

'Commissar!' Wilder called.

'Colonel, sir,' Novobazky answered, hurrying over.

'Good work. We're in a patch of hell here.'

'I noticed.'

A shell struck twenty metres away and they both winced.

'I want you down the left flank. I need you to pull the sections down there in tight. If the enemy start a ground push, we'll be exposed at the base of the hill.'

Novobazky nodded. 'I'll get to it.'

'Fury of Belladon, Nadey.'

'Fury of Belladon, Lucien.'

Novobazky hurried off down the slope.

Wilder turned and took stock. He hoped to see Baskevyl or Callide, but neither Belladon was in view. Little was in view, in fact, apart from flames, roiling smoke-fog and scattering figures. Wilder comforted himself that at least a half-dozen Hauberkan machines were now firing, including an Exterminator, which shattered the thickened air with the hammer of its heavy autocannons. Wilder doubted any order had been given. He was fairly confident that once he'd got the Chimera firing, others had joined in because they supposed that was what was meant to be happening.

Whatever works, Wilder thought.

He came up on a troop section dug in around the cover provided by a shattered and smoking Chimera. They'd got their field support weapons set up: two thirty calibre cannons and a trio of light mortars.

None of them was firing.

It was G Company. Wilder read that from their shoulder flashes.

He ran across, ignoring the raining dirt and biting wind.

'Where's Daur?' he yelled.

Captain Ban Daur, tall, solemn and good-looking, clambered up from a slit trench to face him.

'Colonel?' he saluted, his head hunched down in that 'shrapnel's flying and I'd rather I wasn't so tall' attitude.

'Nice position, Tanith,' Wilder said.

'Thank you, sir. It's Verghastite, actually.'

Wilder smiled humourlessly. He should have known that. The influx from the First-and-Only had been allowed to retain their patriotic badges, which they wore next to the 81/1 (r) silver emblem of the mongrel unit, just as the Belladon retained their brass carnodon head. A skull and single dagger for the Tanith-born, an axe-rake motif of the Verghast miners. Ban Daur wore the latter.

'My apologies.'

'No need, sir.'

'Much as I'd love to spend the rest of the day in genteel conversation with you, Daur, might I ask, since we're being shelled, why the hell your troop isn't firing?'

'Because we're being shelled, sir,' Daur replied.

'Make this good.'

Daur turned and gestured out at the fog-bank lapping the far edge of the slope. 'We're being shelled, colonel. Whatever's lobbing these munitions is well beyond our small-arms or even light support range. Four or five times that, maybe more. If there are hot-body targets out there too, well, they're likely to be two or three times beyond our range too. Any closer, and they'd stand the risk of taking the back-creep of their own artillery. I've got a limited amount of ammo and mortar loads. I'd rather not waste any of that until I can be sure of a target.'

Wilder frowned, turned away, and then looked back at Daur. He was grinning. It was that grin that had made Daur like him on the first day of the mix.

'You're smart, Ban,' Wilder said. 'You after my job at all?'

'No, sir.'

'Sure?'

'I'll admit to nothing, sir.'

'That's fine. Good job here. I like sense. Sense is good. Hold this just as you are... but you'd better start wailing on them the moment they show.'

'It's my purpose in life, sir,' Daur said. 'Correction, it's G Company's purpose in life.'

There was an enthusiastic roar from the men.

'Keep doing what you're doing, then,' Wilder said, moving away. 'You need a piper or anything to get you going?'

'No, sir. Unless you can produce Brin Milo out of nowhere.'

'Who?'

'Never mind. We're fine.'

'Yes, I think you are, captain. Carry on, G Company.'

COMMISSAR NOVOBAZKY SCRAMBLED down the lank, wet grasses to the base of the slope at the left end of the Hauberkans' disastrous line. Fyceline smoke billowed down from the hammering shell-strikes, and the skyline looked as if it were on fire.

The Eighty-First First troops on the left flank had accumulated in the long ditch watercourse at the foot of the hill. They seemed unformed, un-unified, cowering in the lapping water.

'My friends!' Novobazky cried as he moved in amongst them. They looked at him. 'On the Shores of Marik, my friends,' he continued. The text had worked earlier, and it was fresh enough for another go-get. 'The fathers of our fathers made a stand under the flag of Belladon. Shells fell like rain. Were they afraid?'

'Who?' asked a man nearby.

'The sons of Belladon!' Novobazky smiled.

The man looked the commissar up and down. 'My name is Caober. I'm a scout, born and raised on Tanith. I honestly don't know what you're talking about, but I'm sure it matters somehow. Why don't you talk to the captain?'

A big man approached them, drawn by the voices. He studied the commissar for a moment. Novobazky shook his head at his own mistake. This was C Company.

'Commissar?'

'Major Kolea. Wasting my time with the whole Shores of Marik riff, right?'

Gol Kolea half-smiled. 'Not the best crowd to try that material on. Pretty much Ghosts here, through and through.'

'Can I retain any sense of cool at all?'

'I doubt it. You entered like a pantomime chorus. I'd love to hear the story, mind you. Where's Marik?'

'Damned if I know. I wasn't there.'

Gol Kolea chuckled. 'Gaunt never told stories, you know that?'

'I'm sure he did,' Novobazky said.

'Well, maybe. I don't remember any to tell. Derin? You recall any of Gaunt's stories?'

'Only the ones we lived through, major,' a trooper nearby called out. 'I've still got the scars from Hagia.'

'Yes, yes, all right,' Kolea said. He looked back at the commissar. 'You got a reason for being here, sir? Apart from pantomime, that is?'

Novobazky nodded. 'Instructions from the colonel. Get tight.'

'Any tighter and we'd be spitting pips.'

'Good. You don't seem tight.'

'We're tight. We're tight, aren't we?' Kolea called to the crouching figures along the watercourse.

'Tight as tight can be, Gol!' someone called back.

'That's good,' said Novobazky. 'Wilder's anticipating a ground push.'

'Nice to hear he's on the same page,' Kolea said. 'So are we. The moment the shells stop.'

'Well…' Novobazky began. He paused. An ominous, lingering silence, broken only by the crackle of flames and the cries of the wounded, had fallen across the slope. The shelling had stopped.

'I…' he continued, but Major Kolea waved him to silence.

'Saddle up,' Kolea hissed.

With a clatter of weapons and munitions belts, C Company rose and steadied.

The first las-shots began to pink out of the smoke. Small-arms fire pattered across the position. On the slopes, the dug in sections of the Eighty-First First began firing, supported by the heavy guns of the few Hauberkan machines that had not fled or died.

Enemy infantry was slogging up out of the mist, assaulting the slope. They emerged one by one, but soon became hundreds strong, thousands. They came yelling and baying, bayonets fixed.

'All right, C Company,' Kolea said. 'Like Gaunt himself would have wished, up and at them.'

The enemy troopers came forward out of the mist. Dawn light was now filtering down across the floor of the compartment, enough to glint off black and red armour, steel blades, and iron grotesques.

At brigade strength, the echelons of the Blood Pact assaulted the hill.

NINE

08.17 hrs, 193.776.M41
Frag Flats HQ
Sparshad Combat Zone, Ancreon Sextus

DRESSED IN A clean field uniform and a black leather jacket, a heavy kit-bag across one shoulder, Nahum Ludd stopped in front of the cabin door, paused for a moment, then knocked smartly.

He waited. Officers walked past along the quarters deck hallway. There was a faint smell of breakfast coming up from the mess-deck, mixed with the caustic odour of rat poison that always seemed to build up in the Leviathan's air systems over night.

Ludd was about to knock again when the door opened. He found himself staring up at Eszrah ap Niht. The sheer size of the partisan was intimidating enough, but now Ludd took a step back in surprise. Complying with orders, Eszrah had bathed and shaved. Or had *been* bathed and shaved. The tangled hair and the long, wode-matted moustache had gone, as had the iridescent mosaics around his eyes. His bald skull, regally and firmly domed at the back, his wide shoulders and his long neck gave him a noble aspect. His skin was entirely dark grey, as if that was its natural pigment, or as if the Nihtgane paste was simply too chronically ingrained to come off. The feathered cloak and tribal trappings had gone too. Eszrah was wearing laced boots, fatigue trousers and a woollen sweater, all Guard issue, all black. They served only to emphasise his height and slender build.

'I'm here to see the commissar,' Ludd said.

Eszrah's dark face was impassive. His grey, creaseless skin had a polished sheen to it, like gun-metal. His eyes were invisible behind an old, scuffed pair of sunshades.

'The commissar?' Ludd repeated, a little louder.

Eszrah stepped aside to let Ludd past, then closed the door behind him. Gaunt had been given high-status quarters in the officers' wing. The room Ludd stood in was part of a suite. Through an open door across the room, Ludd could hear a whipping sound, as if a flogging were underway.

Ludd put his kit bag down beside the door, and dropped his cap on top of it. The Nihtgane had returned to a chair in the corner of the room, and was busy cleaning some kind of ancient weapon that looked for all the stars like a crossbow. Around the room, equipment had been laid out, most of it still in the plastek wrap it had come bagged in, fresh from the quartermaster's stores. Ludd saw a fleece bedroll, a field-dressing pouch, a leather stormcoat, a ten-to-sixty field scope, and a brand new commissar's cap, the brim gleaming, still half-wrapped in cushion paper. On a side table, in an open steel carrier, a matched pair of chrome, short-pattern bolt pistols lay in moulded packing. Ten spare clips were fastened into the carrier's lid with elastic webbing.

On the main table lay a pile of dataslates and open dossiers. Walking past, Ludd noticed one slate was a set of current data codes and protocols. Another was loaded with the tactical charts of Sparshad Mons. With particular interest, Ludd noticed a brand new paper copy of the *Instrument Of Order*, the Commissariat's 'rulebook'.

Ludd stepped through the doorway. The room beyond, larger, was the bedchamber, but the cot and all other furniture had been pushed back against the walls, and the twin-ply matting on the floor had been rolled up.

Gaunt was in the cleared centre of the room. He was wearing highly buffed black boots and a pair of dark grey jodhpurs with green piping down the legs. High-waisted, the jodhpurs were held up by a tight pair of black, service-issue braces. Apart from the straps of the braces, Gaunt was unclothed from the waist up. His lean, muscular body was flushed with perspiration. He held a beautiful, polished power sword in a two-handed grip, and was executing masterful turns, sweeps, blocks and reprises, circling and crossing, never putting a foot wrong, each motion exact and severe. As it moved, the blade made a hard, whistling sound like a whip.

Ludd watched for a moment. He had no wish to interrupt. Gaunt was evidently a brilliant swordsman who took practice very seriously. As he swung round, Ludd noticed with a slight intake of breath the huge and old pucker of scar-tissue across Gaunt's wash-board stomach. It looked like he'd taken a hit from a chainsword or–

'Ludd.' Gaunt stopped mid-stroke and lowered the sword. 'Can I help you?'

'Good morning, commissar,' Ludd said. 'I came to tell you we've been routed. Transport will be made available at noon.'

'So soon?' Gaunt said. He picked up a hand towel and scrubbed it across his face and neck.

'They want you in the field as soon as possible.'

'I'm sure she does,' Gaunt said. 'Noon. All right. Do we have a deployment?'

Ludd reached into his jacket and handed Gaunt a message wafer. Gaunt took it, deactivated his sword and passed it to Ludd.

'Hold that, would you?'

Ludd took hold of the weapon. It was old, superb, deliciously heavy. The grip was worn from use, and the hilt patinaed with age, but the perfectly-balanced blade shone like a mirror. Switched off, it was still warm, and gave off a scent of heated oil and ozone.

Flopping the towel over his left shoulder, Gaunt tore open the wafer and read the tissue-thin form inside. 'Third Compartment Logistical Base. Uhm hum. Good as anywhere, I suppose. We're to report to the staff office of Marshal Sautoy. Know him?'

Ludd shook his head.

'I do,' Gaunt said, and left it at that. He balled up the wafer and dropped it into the little incineratum on his nightstand.

Gaunt turned back to Ludd and held out his hand for the sword. 'Like it?'

'It's a very fine weapon, sir,' Ludd replied, handing it over carefully.

'The ceremonial blade of Heironymo Sondar,' Gaunt said, flicking the blade back and forth one last time before returning it to its leather scabbard. 'A trophy, Ludd. It was awarded to me by the ruling families of

Vervunhive as a mark of respect.' Gaunt looked at Ludd. 'It's just about the only thing I took to Gereon with me that came back intact. It's been in holding since I arrived here. They just sent it along to me. I'm glad to have it. I missed it.'

'I requested that all of the effects taken from you during processing at Camp Xeno be forwarded,' Ludd said.

'Processing,' Gaunt smiled. 'How nice you make it sound.'

Ludd blushed.

'Forget it, Ludd,' Gaunt said, pulling down the straps of his braces and towelling his armpits and shoulders. 'If we're going to work side by side, I can't have you going a shade of puce every time I make a dig about the circumstances of our meeting.'

Ludd nodded and tried to look happy. 'I want to say, sir… I want to say that I consider it a real honour to be assigned to you.'

Gaunt stared at Ludd as he finished rubbing down. 'I didn't request you, you know.'

'I know, sir.'

'You were appointed to me.' Gaunt tossed the towel away and reached for the clean vest and tunic shirt hung over a nearby chair back.

'You could have requested an alternative, sir,' Ludd said.

Gaunt pulled the vest over his head and tucked the hem into his jodhpurs. 'I suppose so. But after that bang-up job you did at the tribunal…'

Ludd sighed. 'Do I take it, sir, that I should expect this kind of ribbing to be an everyday aspect of serving as your second?'

'Yes, why not?' Gaunt said, buttoning his shirt. 'It'll keep you on your toes.'

Ludd nodded.

'I appreciate the sentiment, though,' Gaunt added, tucking the shirt in and pulling up his braces. 'The fact you think it's some kind of honour. I was under the impression it was more like a duty. Aren't you supposed to be my watcher?'

'Sir?'

'Come on, Ludd. I can deal with the idea you're watching my every move, reporting back, making sure I'm on the level. But I can't abide dissembling. You're Balshin's appointed spy. I know that. You know that. Let's be open about it, at least. I can't stand deceit, Ludd. Be a man and be frank about it, and I won't have to kill you.'

Ludd cleared his throat. 'Another example of your trademark humour, I take it?'

'Oh, let's hope so,' said Gaunt. He'd carefully pinned two small badges to the breast of his shirt, and now was searching for something on the dresser.

'Lost something, sir?' Ludd asked.

'More than you could possibly imagine, Ludd,' Gaunt replied. He squatted down, peering under the cabinet. 'Feth it, where the hell…'

Looking around, Ludd noticed something small and shiny down beside the night stand. He went over and picked it up. It was a regimental crest, a skull surrounded by a wreath, with a blade transfixing it top to bottom. There was a motto on it, but age had worn it indecipherable. The badge had rough edges, as if parts of it had been broken off.

'Is this what you're looking for, sir?' he asked.

'Yes,' said Gaunt. He took the badge and pinned it beside the other two on his shirt.

'May I ask…?' Ludd began.

Gaunt pointed to the emblems in turn. 'The pin of the Hyrkan 8th. The axe-rake of Vervunhive. The badge of the Tanith First-and-Only. All lost to me now, Ludd, but I'll not wade into war without them about my person.'

'Lucky charms?' Ludd said.

'I suppose. Ludd, have you ever lost anything that really mattered to you?'

Ludd shrugged. 'Not really, I… yes. Yes, sir. I lost my father at Balhaut.'

'Really? Was he a commissar?'

'Yes, sir. Serving with General Curell's staff at Balopolis. As far as I know, he was slain in a gas attack during the first few days of the battle.'

'What was his name?'

'The same as mine, sir. Nahum Ludd. Commissar Nahum Ludd. I'm Junior Commissar Ludd in so many ways.'

Gaunt nodded. 'I didn't know him. I was up at the Oligarchy during Balhaut. I know Balopolis was a bad show. The worst. I knew Curell, though. A little.'

'The Oligarchy,' Ludd said. 'That was the heart of it, wasn't it? You were with Slaydo?'

'Yes, I was.'

'Holy Throne. Is that where you–'

'What, Ludd?'

'The scar on your belly, sir…'

Gaunt shook his head. 'I won that a long time before Balhaut. In honour of my father. We have something in common then, I suppose. Following in our fathers' footsteps.'

'Yes, sir.'

'Careful where they lead, Ludd,' Gaunt said.

He walked back into the outer room where Eszrah was still cleaning his antique weapon. They exchanged a few words Ludd didn't understand. Gaunt pulled his fresh, new stormcoat out of its plastek wrap and put it on. It had been bundled up so long it still had fold creases in it as it hung from his shoulders. The room was filled with the pervasive smell of new leather.

Gaunt crossed to the main table and started to work through the dataslates and dossiers. He called up a plan of the third compartment and studied it for a while.

'The *Instrument of Order*?' Ludd asked, picking the book up.

Gaunt glanced over. 'I thought I should refresh myself. I'm a rogue, Ludd. I've been in the wilderness for a long time. I thought it was as well that I reminded myself of the actual rules.'

'And?'

'They're a nonsense. Starchy, high-minded, tediously prim. I find it hard to remember now how I ever managed to discharge my duties as a commissar without breaking down in tears of frustration.'

'You're a commissar again, now, sir,' Ludd said.

'Yes I am. And not that rare beast a colonel-commissar. I'll miss command, Ludd. Miss it dearly. Tell you what, you'd better slide that volume into your coat. I'll need you to remind me what the feth I'm supposed to be about.'

'Sir?'

Gaunt laughed and shook his head. 'A trooper is afraid for his life, as is quite natural in war. He breaks the line. What am I supposed to do?'

Ludd hesitated.

'Well, here's a clue, Junior Commissar Ludd. It's not speak to him, calm his fears, improve his morale and get him back in line. Oh no, sir. The correct answer, according to that vile text, is to execute him in front of his peers as an example.' Gaunt sighed. 'How did we ever build this Imperium? Death and fear. They're not building blocks.'

'This is another example of your off-beat humour, isn't it, sir?'

Gaunt looked at him. 'If it makes you sleep better at night, I'll say yes.'

Gaunt put down the dataslate. 'I want to see the Ghosts.'

'Sir?'

'The Ghosts. They're about to be reassigned too, right?'

'Yes sir. In a day or so.'

Gaunt nodded. 'They're going to be sent to join this new company?'

'The lord general thought that made the best sense, sir. Provided the company commander agreed.'

'I see. What's his name?'

Ludd thought for a moment. 'Colonel Lucien Wilder, sir.'

'Feth me,' Gaunt said. 'How truth seeps into dreams.'

'Sir?'

'Never mind, Ludd. I want to see the Ghosts. Before I go.'

'Is that wise, sir? Surely a clean break–'

'Too much history, Ludd. Too much blood under the bridge. I have to see them, one last time.'

'Barrack E Nine, sir. Awaiting dispersal.'

Gaunt walked to the door. 'Thanks. I'll be back before noon. Make yourself useful and pack up my kit for me.'

Ludd paused. 'Me?'

'I wasn't talking to Eszrah,' Gaunt said as he opened the cabin door. 'He has many fine qualities, but packing

a Guard field kit as per regulations isn't one of them. I
meant you, Ludd.'

'Yes, sir.'

'There's a place for Eszrah on the transport, right?'

'He's coming with us?'

'Of course.'

'Then I'll make sure of it, sir.'

GAUNT WALKED AWAY down the hallway, under the harsh
bars of the lumin strips. He knew what was coming and
he hated it. He'd never imagined, never at all, that he'd
have to do what he was about to do…

Say goodbye.

He passed various fresh-faced young officers as he
strode along. Most pretended not to look at him, but he
could feel their eyes as he went by.

Scared. Wary. Unsettled.

Damn right. They should be scared.

Right then, Ibram Gaunt felt like the most dangerous
fething bastard in the whole Imperium.

THE GHOSTS ROSE as he came in, but Gaunt waved them
back down. They looked strange in their clean, black
fatigues, like newly-founded draughtees. Only their
faces betrayed their experience. All of them except Criid
had shaved scalps. On various bare forearms, Gaunt
noticed medicae skin-plasts, little adhesive patches that
were releasing drugs into their systems to clean them of
parasites and lice.

Gaunt sat down on one of the bunks, and they
formed a casual huddle around him.

'I've been routed, and I'll be leaving this morning,'
Gaunt began. 'So I probably won't see any of you again
for a while.'

There was little comment. Rawne just nodded his head gently. Beltayn stared at the deck.

'Well, don't go all mushy on me,' Gaunt said. Varl and Brostin laughed. Bonin murmured something.

'Mach?' Gaunt said.

Bonin shrugged. 'Nothing. I just said… it's not how you expect.'

'What are you talking about?' asked Feygor.

'He's talking about the end,' Mkoll said, his voice low.

Bonin nodded. 'You never think about it,' he said.

'Except for the times you do,' Larkin whispered.

'Yes, except then,' Bonin agreed. 'And then all you can imagine is… oh, I don't know. A glorious last stand, maybe. Or a triumphal parade and a Guard pension. One or the other.'

'Dead or done,' Varl said, raising his eyebrows mockingly. 'Some choice.'

'Mach's right,' said Larkin. 'That is all you ever imagine. The two extremes. Not this.'

'Not this,' Bonin echoed.

'It all just seems so…' Beltayn began. 'So… mundane.'

'This is the real world, Bel,' Rawne said. 'The life of the Guard, hey ho. Forget the glory songs. Slog and disappointment, that's our lot.'

'Well,' said Gaunt. 'Now I've raised morale to a fever-pitch…'

More of them laughed, but it was generally hollow.

'You know where you're going?' Gaunt asked Rawne.

'We're waiting for despatch,' Rawne said, getting to his feet. He crossed over to his field pack and started rummaging inside it. 'But we know roughly. And we know what we are.'

He pulled a waxed paper pouch out of his kit and tossed it to Gaunt. It was heavy and it clinked. There was a Munitorum code-stamp on the wrapper. Gaunt shook the contents out into his palm. Shiny silver pin badges marked with the emblem 81/1(r).

'I don't know much about them,' Gaunt said, studying one of the pins. 'But the Munitorum will have tried to make sure that any mix of leftovers like this makes field sense. And Van Voytz gave the mix his personal approval.'

Someone snorted disparagingly.

'All right, I know he's not your favourite person. But I think he's still on our side, even now. I've been given to understand your new commander is a decent sort.' Gaunt looked over at Criid. 'His name's Wilder.'

Half-hidden behind her mane of hair, Tona Criid's eyes widened for a second.

'Yes, I wondered if you'd remember that, Tona.'

'What?' asked Varl.

'Nothing,' she said.

Gaunt slid the badges back into the pouch and handed it back to Rawne. He got up. 'I'm not going to make goodbyes, because that's a sure way to jinx us ever meeting again. And I'm not going to make any grand speech. This isn't the place, and it's not really in me anyway. And I don't want you thinking you've got to go out there and make me proud. You don't owe me anything. Not a thing. Do it for the Throne, and do it for yourselves.'

He walked to the barrack room door. He wasn't even going to look back, but at the threshold, something made him turn one last time. Silently, the Ghosts had risen to their feet. They hadn't formed a rank, or any kind of formal row, but they were all facing him, standing stiffly to attention.

Gaunt saluted them, and then walked away.

TEN

TWICE IN HALF an hour, they had pushed the enemy back from the top of the hill. Support weapons and well-disciplined rifle drill had done most of that work, but in places it had been brutal. Callide reported casualties from a face-to-face scrap where Blood Pact troops had come up along a blind defile and flanked his second section.

Wilder sensed they'd reached the tipping point in this particular scrap. Was the enemy going to break, or was it going to force a third attempt at the slopes?

It was hard to tell. Daylight had come, heavy and white, but the visibility was cut drastically by the waves of smoke running off the hill crest. Reports said his own line was still in position, but where the enemy stood was a matter of guesswork.

Wilder was finding it difficult to see anyway, because of the blood in his eyes. He'd been halfway along the escarpment when a nearby Hauberkan Chimera had taken a rocket. The vehicle had gone up like a demolition mine, and Wilder had been flung forward by the blast, gashing his forehead against the bole of a dead, splintered tree.

Now he had to keep blinking away the drops, dabbing his head. He could taste the salt in his mouth.

He reached the position commanded by one of the Tanith company officers, a Captain Domor, and his own Captain Kolosim. Throne, he had to stop thinking like that. They were *both* his own now.

'Are you all right, sir?' Domor asked as Wilder scrambled up. Domor was a solid, four-square man with a reliable air about him. His eyes had been repaired at some point in his career by heavy augmetic implants. The Tanith had a nickname for him, but Wilder couldn't remember it.

'I'm fine,' he replied. 'What have we got?'

'They've pulled back to the stream down there,' replied Kolosim, a burly redhead. 'Lot of cover sweeping that way. Lot of rocks. We've got a line of sight overlap with Sergeant Buckren's troop, but neither of us can determine what they're doing.'

'I've pushed two units down the flank,' Domor said. 'Raglon's and Theiss's. In case they suddenly stab that way, across the ditch.'

Far away to their left, the meaty chatter of an autocannon throbbed the air.

'Think they're coming back for another go, sir?' Kolosim asked.

'How stupid do they look, Ferdy?' Wilder grinned.

'Stupid enough we could be here all day,' replied Kolosim.

'What about those tankers, sir?' said Sergeant Bannard, Ferd Kolosim's adjutant. 'Coward-bastards!'

'We've all got our own words for the tank-boys, Bannard,' Wilder said, 'and I'll be having most of them with that leper-brain suck-pig Gadovin the moment I find him.' Wilder held up his hand suddenly. 'What was that?'

A low note, a machine noise, had just reached them.

'That's armour,' one of the Belladon troopers said with some confidence. Some of the men crawled forward to try and spot enemy vehicles in the smoke.

'It's behind us,' said Kolosim.

'No, that's just the echo roll. Backwash,' Bannard said.

Captain Domor had turned, and was gazing up into the smoke bank pluming off the hill behind them. 'Kolosim's right,' he said.

'What?' Wilder said.

'Oh feth!' Domor said suddenly, and grabbed the voice-horn from his vox-officer. 'Inbound, inbound, report your position!'

Static.

'Inbound, I say again! Report your position! If you are on approach, be advised we have troops in the grid!'

More static. A pause, then: 'Inbound at two minutes. We are hot for strike on grid target.'

To Wilder's eyes, the smoke was just smoke, but Domor's augmetics, enhanced beyond human vision, had picked up the heat trails chopping in at low level. He glanced at Wilder.

'Order retreat. Right now!' Wilder said. Domor started yelling into the vox. 'Up and back! Now!' Wilder yelled. 'Double time it! Get off this hill!'

Grabbing kit and weapons, the men started to scramble back down the slope, running between the burning shells of Hauberkan machines. All along the saddle of the hill, the troops of the Eighty-First First began a frantic pull-back towards the trackway.

About a minute later, with the men still running, the gunships slammed out of the smoke. The roar of their turbojets preceded them like the bow-wave of a ship. Twenty-five Vulture attack ships, boom-tailed, jut-jawed and painted in cream and tan dapple, burned in through the smoke-bank at tree-top altitude. Their vague shadows slid over Wilder's men in the hazed sunlight. He heard the *hiss-whoosh* as their underwing rocket pods began to fire. Spears of vapour shot out ahead of the thundering Vultures and the top of the hill disappeared in a necklace of fireballs that quivered the ground.

Wilder saw men on the slopes knocked down by the shockwave. 'They're coming in short!' he yelled at the nearest vox-man. 'Tell them they're coming in short!' The man started shouting into his link.

A second wave drummed over, rippling the hanging smoke with their powerful backwash. Another salvo of fragmentation rockets squealed out over the hill. Another riot of fire and hurled soil chewed up the landscape.

'I've got strike control,' the vox-officer reported. 'I think I've persuaded them to redirect beyond the hill.'

A third wave came in, or maybe it was the first on its reprise, Wilder couldn't tell. The third rocket strike went in behind the hill, detonating down the far slope. The thick black smoke from the first strike eddied in wild patterns as the Vultures travelled through it.

Wilder clapped the vox-man on the shoulder. 'Nice piece of fast-talk, my friend. What's your name?'

The man looked at him in surprise. 'Esteven, sir. It's Esteven.'

It was. Esteven, Belladon born and raised, vox-man in Baskevyl's troop. Wilder had become so overcautious about correctly identifying his new mix, he failed to recognise a man he'd known for years. Esteven's face was smeared with soot, but it was no excuse.

'Of course it is,' Wilder said. 'I was just testing,' he added, trying to joke it off. Esteven just laughed, and scooped up his vox-caster to head for the nearest ditch. It was indeed a laughing matter, but Wilder hadn't felt much like laughing all day.

'Hey, Esteven!' Wilder called. 'Did strike control explain the grid error to you?'

Esteven nodded. 'They said it wasn't an error. They were locked on the plot the Hauberkan had given them.'

THEY GOT THE signal to retire about half an hour later, and moved back down the trackway road to post 36, four kilometres back down the compartment. It was mid-morning by the time the Eighty-First First began to reassemble.

Post 36 was one of the field HQs set up at the friendly end of the fifth compartment. It lay close to the west wall and within sight of the gargantuan gateway leading back into the fourth compartment. The post covered about two square kilometres, most of which was taken up with supply dumps and field tents. Some of the post facilities, including the field hospital, had been set up in the crumbling house the Imperials had found as they pushed into the fifth. The house was a single storey stone structure, as old and ragged as the Mons walls themselves. Ruins like it could be found throughout the explored compartments of the step-city, some just wall-plans proud of the dirt, others still upright and flaking. No two were alike, and no purpose for them had yet been decided. There was some talk that they were the remains of primitive domiciles, that the compartments had once been filled with populated cities. Others said the houses were shanty relics built by local tribes who had come to scrape a living and dwell inside the walls long after the Mons itself had become a ruin. A third theory ran that the compartments had always been open areas of contained wilderness, constructed with some mystical purpose, and the houses were the temples and shrines left behind by the original builders of the Mons.

Wilder didn't much care. The place made a decent enough foothold camp from which the exploration and clearance of the compartment could be run.

Several regiments of infantry were gathered at post 36. On the high road up to the great gate, others could be seen moving in. An armour column. Supply vehicles. Valkyrie drop-ships were swinging down onto a wide table-rock of basalt, west of the post, dropping off wounded from the field. Some of those bodies on the stretchers were Wilder's men. Once they'd dropped, the Valkyries either lifted off and headed back out into the compartment for a second run, or flew on south, through the massive arch of the gate, heading to their landing fields at the fourth compartment forward posts.

Wilder walked off the roadway track and up the dusty slope into the post. Sunlight was burning off the grasses and the islands of scrub behind him, and the far wall of the compartment rose like a desert cliff. He looked up as a flight of cream and tan Vultures went over, heading home.

There was a bunch of armoured vehicles parked by the roadside, most of them black-drab numbers from a regiment Wilder didn't recognise. But amongst them were at least five Hauberkan treads, and other Hauberkan units were grumbling up the winding track out of the valley floor.

'Get the men rested and watered,' he told Baskevyl. 'Ration detail, and a weapons check by fourteen hundred. I want every one with a full load, no excuses.'

'Yes, sir.'

Wilder headed up the dirt causeway to the hospital.

MUNITORUM PIONEERS HAD roofed the house with precast armour-ply sheeting, and reinforced the walls with flakboard and sandbags. The north end contained the post command station in an area extended from the building with tent canopies. A pair of vox masts had been set up nearby, trailing cables off to the bank of generators behind the building. The rest of the place was given over to the triage station and infirmary. There was a pervading smell of sawdust and new chip-panel that almost choked out the regular odours of a field hospital.

Neither the severely wounded nor the dead stayed there long. There was no facility for them. Regular transport runs ferried them away to main station compounds at Frag Flats and Tarenal, or to the gradually swelling cemetery out in the desert. Post 36's hospital was a processing point, superficial and efficient, treating minor wounds, illness, infection, and patching the less fortunate up for evac.

The *less fortunate*. Wilder thought about that. Were they? Were they really? He walked in under the low arch, stepping aside to let a procession of stretcher bearers inside. To the right lay a pair of rooms given over to triage, with an adjoining chamber fitted up as a field theatre. There were two more theatres in habi-tents outside on the causeway. To the left were three small wards where men with minor wounds could be given bedrest and treatment for a few days before returning to active duties, and the grossly injured could wait for transport.

The place was busy. It hadn't stopped being busy since the Guard had moved in and occupied the position five days earlier. Wilder saw a few of his men amongst the injured, most of them walking wounded with cuts and burns. He exchanged encouraging words with a few. So far there were about five more seriously hurt. Two were unconscious: one of them Sergeant Piven, who Wilder had always had a lot of time for. Piven looked like he'd been smacked in the face with a flat iron. The other, Trooper Boritz, had been shot eight or nine times. Lumps of his torso and legs were missing. Two corpsmen were busy intubating him.

Further down, Wilder found trooper Raydee on a cot. The Belladon was woozing in and out of consciousness, high on painkillers. His foot and ankle had been crushed by a stalker.

'Big bastard it was, sir,' Raydee said.

'You get it?' Wilder asked.

'Not me, no sir, but it was got.'

Wilder smiled. Raydee's injury would be a long time healing. He would soon be one of the *less fortunate*.

'Did Mkard make it, sir?' Raydee called out.

'Sorry?'

'Mkard, sir. He was with me when it happened. I hope he made it, sir,' Raydee said.

'I'll find out,' Wilder said. Raydee had expressed genuine concern, and for one of the influx. Mkard was a Tanith name. Maybe the alloy was strong already.

Nearby, Wilder spotted the elderly chief medicae who had joined with the Tanith. He was strapping up a Verghastite's arm-wound.

'Doctor?'

Dorden looked around. 'One moment, colonel,' he said, finishing up. Dorden seemed fragile and brittle to

Wilder, too old for battlefield duty, but he had the seniority and the skill, and since the Belladon had lost most of its medicae staff, that counted for a lot.

'This way, colonel,' Dorden said. He led Wilder over to a vacant dressing table. 'Just tilt your head back, please.'

'What? Oh!' Wilder had almost forgotten his own injury. 'I'm not here for that, doctor. I just stopped in to get some idea of numbers. We had to pull out of the line in a hurry, and I've no idea what kind of hit we took.'

Dorden shrugged. 'I'm sorry, colonel, I can't answer that. They're still coming in, as you can see, and I've not been keeping a tally of badges. Just bodies to patch. The Kolstec 50th took a hammering early this morning up along the bluff. They've been airlifting them in for the past hour.'

'A bad hammering?'

'Is there a good kind? What about you?'

'Fairly intense. A mess, actually. I'll go talk to the men.'

'I'd prefer to treat that wound right now, actually,' Dorden said.

'Later. Get to someone who needs you more urgently.'

Dorden looked at him for a moment then turned away.

Wilder was about to cross over into the wards when he saw that the door at the back of the house was open. In the patch of sunlight outside, body bags lay on the dry earth. He went out, removing his cap despite the glare. Nearly forty bodies lay in neat lines, drill ground perfection. Orderlies were carrying more over from nearby trucks. Wilder walked down the line, looking at the tags tied off round the bag-seals. He found two Belladon, and a Tanith. *Mkard*.

An ancient, hunched man was slowly moving down the rows, reading from a hymnal and blessing each body in turn. Last rites, field style.

'Ayatani,' Wilder nodded.

Zweil peered at him. The old priest always struck Wilder as a little mad, but he was just another part of the influx.

'Colonel. Another day in the dust, unto which we will all return, most of us faster than we'd like, at this rate.'

Wilder wasn't quite sure what to say. The old man had a knack of blindsiding him.

'Some days, you know, I pray to the beloved beati for some skill that I can contribute. I don't fight, as you know, and I don't fix... not like Dorden. I often pray to her for the gracious ability to bring them back from the dead.'

'Who, father?'

Zweil gestured at the bodies on the ground. 'Them. Others. Anyone. But so far she's refused to grant me that knack. Can you do it, Wilder?'

'What?'

'Bring them back from the dead?'

'No, father.'

'It's funny, sometimes you look to me exactly like the sort of person who can bring them back from the dead.'

'Sorry, no. I'd like to think my area of skill lay in not getting them killed in the first place, and even that's not infallible.'

Zweil sniffed, and wiped his nose on his sleeve. 'None of us are perfect.' He stared up at Wilder, then, to Wilder's surprise, grabbed hold of Wilder's jaw with his less than clean fingers.

'You should get that looked at,' Zweil said, twisting Wilder's face around so he could scrutinise the head wound.

'Yes, I will. Thanks, father,' Wilder said, prying the priest's hand away. 'Dorden already offered to patch it, but I said it could wait.'

'Why?'

'Triage, father.'

'Exactly.'

'What?'

Zweil took a dried fig from his pocket and sucked it thoughtfully. 'Triage. Degrees of priority. Only a scrape, but you are the company commander. What if you leave it and it gets infected? That's the regiment, at this early, delicate stage, without a chief.'

'I suppose so, father.'

'So get it done. Priorities.'

'Yes, father.'

'Before the whole mob of them starts flailing around for the want of proper leadership with you in bed, feverish with blood poisoning–'

'Yes, father.'

'And gangrene of the eyebrows. And black pus oozing from–'

'Thank you, father. I'll go right away.'

'That's my other skill,' Zweil called out as Wilder turned away. 'I just remembered. It's to give sage advice and good counsel. I bless the beati for granting me that talent.'

'Yes, father.'

'Are you sure?' Zweil called out as Wilder reached the door into the house.

Wilder looked back. 'About what?'

Zweil was staring down at the bagged bodies on the dry earth. He was subdued again now. His sudden mood swings and skipping trains of thought had a bi-polar quality to them.

'You can't bring them back?'

'No, ayatani father, I can't.'

Zweil sighed. 'Carry on, then.'

* * *

'LOSE THE HEADSET and the hat,' Dorden said, and Wilder obliged. 'Head back.'

Dorden washed the wound and pulled it shut with some plastek staples. 'I'd dress it, but it'd be better to get the air to it,' Dorden said. He handed Wilder a small tube of counterseptic gel. 'Put that on it every few hours, keep it clean, come back in a day or two.'

'Thanks,' Wilder said.

Baskevyl appeared in the triage bay doorway, and sighted Wilder. 'DeBray wants a field debrief, sir. I don't think he's too taken with the mess this morning.'

'He can join the queue behind me,' Wilder said. 'When does he want me?'

'At your convenience. I told him you were being patched.'

Wilder nodded. 'We got a tally yet?'

'Eight dead,' Baskevyl said. 'Thirty-eight wounded, twelve of those serious. That's so far.'

'Could have been a whole lot worse,' Wilder said. 'A whole hell of a lot worse. Pass on my compliments to Captain Domor, by the way. He's one of the reasons it wasn't.'

'Sir.'

'And we'll get the company leaders together and–' Wilder was tucking the counterseptic tube into his coat pocket, and his hand had just encountered the forgotten message wafer. He pulled it out and read it.

'Sir? Something the matter?' Baskevyl asked.

'What?'

'There's a look on your face like... like I don't know what.'

Wilder looked up at his first officer and was about to reply when Dorden interrupted. He was holding Wilder's microbead headset and cap.

'Your link's squawking,' he said.

Wilder pulled the headset in place, in time to hear a repeated call.

'Wilder receiving, go ahead.'

'This is Hark, colonel. Please come down to the dispersal area.'

HARK SALUTED AS Wilder and Baskevyl approached. The wide dirt-pan of the dispersal area was filling up with vehicles: treads returning from the front, and the inbound convoy from the gate. Hark was standing beside a trio of dirty Chimeras sporting Hauberkan livery.

'This way,' Hark said. A crowd of Hauberkan troopers had gathered around the rear of one of the AFVs. Wilder felt his fists tighten.

'Stand aside!' Hark snarled, and the tanker crews broke to let them through. Gadovin, the Hauberkans' commander, was cuffed by one wrist to a tie-bar on the Chimera's rear end. He was a sallow-faced man with thin, yellow hair. His tunic had half-moons of perspiration under the arms.

'Release me!' he snapped at Hark. 'This is ridiculous!'

'Ridiculous?' Wilder said.

Gadovin saw him for the first time and stiffened.

'You were supposed to advance, Gadovin,' Wilder said.

'The zone was mined.'

'Not so much you had to stop dead and cut engines. I warned you what would happen.'

'I listened to you!' Gadovin protested. 'When the assault came, I took immediate action–'

'You reversed.'

'To regain the trackway!'

'Through my men, who had moved in to support you. You nearly ran them down, and left them stranded, line broken. Then you called down an air-strike.'

'The situation was extremely dangerous! We might have been overrun. It was essential that–'

'It was dangerous all right. You'd seen to that. My men were still in the target grid, fighting your fight for you, when the Vultures came in. Didn't you think? Didn't you care?'

'I thought you'd pulled back too!'

'Why? Because you did? We're not all gutless worms, Gadovin.'

Gadovin didn't answer. He was staring over Wilder's shoulder. Marshal DeBray was approaching, led by Major Gerrogan, Gadovin's second in command.

The men drew back further, respectfully. DeBray entered the circle of tank troopers. A slightly-built man, with white hair and a permanently listless expression on his lined face, DeBray looked them up and down.

'Stand down, Colonel Wilder,' he said. 'This isn't your place to direct reprimand. Did you cuff this man, commissar?'

Hark nodded.

DeBray stared at Gadovin. 'I've been reading through the preliminaries, Gadovin. Not a pretty picture. In the first place, you should have pushed on. In the second, you should have held tight, like Wilder told you. Third, the air-strike was a fantastically bad call.'

'The situation was critical, sir,' Gadovin said. 'There were mines and–'

'Funny that, mines. It being a war. You're an arsehole, Gadovin. But you and your entire unit is new to this theatre and fresh-founded. You're off to a famously bad start, but I hope you can learn from this and get your bloody act together. Quickly. Be bold, be decisive, stick to the plan, and when an experienced officer like Wilder gives you advice, bloody follow it. Are we clear?'

'Sir.'

'Being cuffed up, humiliated and called an arsehole by me in front of your men is probably punishment enough. Uncuff him, please, commissar.'

Hark paused, then stepped forward and released Gadovin's restraint.

'Are you just going to let him–' Wilder began.

'Ub-bub-bup!' DeBray said, raising a hand. 'I appreciate your rancour, Wilder, but I did tell you this wasn't your place to direct reprimand.'

'Actually, marshal, it's not yours either,' said Hark bluntly. 'This man was found wanting in the service of the God-Emperor today. Sorely wanting.' He turned. A small autopistol had appeared in his hand. The single shot made everyone around start. Gadovin slammed back against the rear of the Chimera, a fern-leaf of blood from the back of his head decorating the plating. He fell on his face.

The Hauberkan men all around gazed in speechless horror. DeBray glared at Hark.

'Discipline and punishment are the provinces of the Commissariat,' Hark said clearly, so all could hear. 'We do not need to hear another word from you on the matter, marshal. The Hauberkan crews will learn from this demonstration that the Imperial Guard, Warmaster Macaroth, and Emperor himself will not tolerate incompetence or cowardice, especially from line officers. Major Gerrogan, I hope this is ample inspiration to you to be a much better regimental leader than your predecessor. Clean this up, and clean up your act.'

He holstered his pistol and walked away. DeBray sniffed, glanced humourlessly at Wilder, then stalked back to his command station. 'That report please, Wilder!' he called over his shoulder.

Wilder caught up with Hark half way to the Eighty-First First billet.

'What now?' Hark said.

'Nothing, I just…' Wilder shrugged. 'Men desert in the field, and you let them run, but you're quite happy to execute a ranking officer.'

'Yes. Let that be a lesson to you,' Hark said. He stopped walking and turned to face Wilder. 'I'm joking, of course. I'd like to think this might have illuminated you a little as to my approach. Men desert in the field. They're afraid. Why are they afraid? Because they're not being led soundly. Should they be executed, for a simple, human failing? No, I don't believe so. I think they should be given a solid leader so it doesn't happen again. An officer fails, then the whole structure falls down. Gadovin was why those men were running. Gadovin was the failure. So I reserved my censure for him.'

Wilder nodded.

'Are we good?' asked Hark.

'Yes.' Hark began walking again.

'Hark?'

'What, colonel?'

Wilder held out the message wafer. 'I received this earlier. I think maybe you should see it.'

Hark read the note. 'Is this confirmed, sir?'

'Yes.'

'Holy Throne. They're alive? After all we… Well, that's unexpected. Have you told anyone?'

'No. You're the first.'

Hark nodded. 'We'd better decide how to handle this. How do we tell the Ghosts that Gaunt's still alive?'

ELEVEN

IN THE STARK NOON heat, the Valkyrie's turbojets whined up to power, shaking the airframe. The flight sergeant checked Ludd's harness with a tug, then Gaunt's, but drew back from doing the same with Eszrah's.

'He's fine,' Gaunt said.

The flight sergeant nodded, then signalled to the pilot. The roar of the engines suddenly intensified, as if they were going to burst, and then the assault carrier lifted off.

The flight sergeant had left the side doors of the cargo bay open, and he stood in the left hand doorway beside the swung-out heavy bolter mount, one hand raised to clutch a grip-bar. Past his silhouette and the shading arch of the port wing, Ludd could see the bright world flashing by. Low level at first, as they raced away from the Leviathans across the tent city and vehicle depots of Frag Flats, the jigging flags, the fence-post vox masts, a

145

blur of passing detail. Then they began to climb, bearing north. The view outside became the unbroken white expanse of the Flats themselves, a glaring vista of reflected light. The Valkyrie banked slightly in a wide, climbing turn, and through the mouth of the right-hand door, Ludd could see their tiny, hard shadow, a black dart, chasing them across the bright desert floor far below, flickering and jumping as it was distorted by dune-caps and ridges.

'Flight time's about fifteen minutes to the Mons,' the flight sergeant shouted.

Gaunt nodded and checked his wrist chronometer. Ludd noticed Gaunt was fiddling with the strap. The timepiece was Guard issue, chunky, well worn, but its bracelet strap had long since gone, replaced by a woven braid of what looked like leather and straw.

'We should have checked you out a fresh one from stores, sir,' Ludd yelled over the engine noise.

'It's fine,' Gaunt called back. 'It kept time on Gereon, it'll keep time here.'

Ludd glanced back at Eszrah. Arms folded, the Niht-gane looked like he was asleep. But with his old, battered sunshades on, it was impossible to tell. Ludd suddenly got a queasy feeling that Eszrah was actually staring right back at him. He looked away quickly.

Below, in the blinding white desert, he saw black dots, dark lines and twists of dust. Massed troop and vehicle columns moving up-country from Frag Flats to lend their muscle to the fight at the Mons. It was an immense undertaking. Ludd wondered quite what sort of obstacle could require such effort. Sparshad Mons was just one of eight step-cities on Ancreon Sextus currently under assault by Van Voytz's armies. Driven from the plains and the modern cities of Ancreon during the first phase of the liberation, the cult armies of the Ruinous Powers had taken refuge in the ancient monoliths, where they were now, reportedly, doing a very fine job of keeping the Imperium at bay.

There was a clack of vox, and the flight sergeant deftly slammed the side doors shut and locked the seals. The engine roar did not abate, but it changed tone and became deeper.

'Coming up on the smoke bank,' the flight sergeant explained. As if on cue, the small window ports in the cargo doors suddenly washed dark with ashen fumes, and the Valkyrie began to buck and tremble. They were flying through the vast smog field that veiled Sparshad Mons from view at Frag Flats.

The vibration eased, and after about three minutes, the flight sergeant reopened the side doors. Vapour still streamed off the sides of the carrier, but the air outside was clear again, and the sunlight dazzling.

The Valkyrie began to bank around again, and Ludd caught sight of new details on the ground below. Jumbles of rocks, slabs of tumbled stone, the occasional flash of sunlight on metal. Gaunt unstrapped, and got to his feet, moving to the door beside the flight sergeant. Ludd couldn't hear their conversation, but the crewman was pointing to various things out of the door.

Ludd snapped off his harness, and went to join them. It was harder to keep balance on the shaking, tilting metal deck than Gaunt had made it look. Ludd made sure he kept hold of the safety rail.

'Sparshad Mons,' Gaunt said to him, with a tip of his head.

From the open door, Ludd got his first sight of the Mons. He was expecting something big, but this dwarfed his expectations. The Mons was vast: wide, towering, cyclopean, not so much a man-made monument as a mountain peak cut into great angular steps from its broad skirts to its cropped summit. The stone it had been hewn from – not local to this desert region, but actually quarried in the lowland plains thousands of kilometres west, and conveyed here by means unknown – glowed pink and grey in the sunlight.

From the briefings, Ludd knew the Mons was a structure of concentric walls, ascending to the peak. The walls, hundreds of metres high and monumentally thick, enclosed the so-called compartments, significant tracts of wild country open to the sky. By some quirk of climate and topography, these compartments – some of them as much as twenty kilometres by ten – supported entire eco-systems of plant and wildlife, nurtured by untraceable underground water courses, defying the deserts outside. The encircling compartments were linked in chains, connected end to end by gigantic inner gateways, and the Imperial invaders had found, perplexingly, that the eco-system and terrain of one could differ wildly from that of its immediate neighbour.

The brief had also emphasised that there was no direct route into the heart of the Mons. A gateway compartment – dubbed, with the military's typical lack of imagination, the first compartment – allowed entry at the base level, and then connected to further compartments like a maze. Each area had been heavily defended, each compartment forming a walled-off 'lost world' that the Guard had to fight its way through to the next gate. So far, only seven of the compartments had been breached.

'What was it for?' Ludd shouted.

Gaunt shook his head, still staring out. 'No one knows. No one even knows if it was built by humans.

But the multicursal plan suggests some ritual or symbolic purpose.'

'The *what*…?'

'Multicursal, Ludd. A pattern of alternate pathways, some leading nowhere, some to a dead centre.'

'Like a labyrinth, sir?'

'Actually, no. A labyrinth is unicursal. It has just one path, with no blind ends or alternates. A maze is multicursal. Designed as a puzzle, a riddle.'

'So the archenemy is right inside the heart of that thing, and we have to find the correct way of getting to them? Since when was warfare so complex?' Ludd yelled.

'Since forever,' Gaunt called back.

'Why don't they just flatten the place from orbit and save all this bloodshed?'

'I was wondering that myself,' said Gaunt.

The Valkyrie dipped lower. The passage of time and the ministries of the desert had collapsed what had once been the outer rings of compartments around the base of the Mons. The white sand was densely littered with fallen stone blocks and the tatters of once-immense walls. Within these eroded ring patterns, Ludd could see the long emplacements of Imperial artillery, dug in and lobbing shells up at the higher steps of the inner Mons.

Lower still, they came in towards the bulwarks of the first compartment. The density of Imperial machines and manpower beneath them increased. There was other air traffic too now: carriers and gunships, passing them in formation.

The mouth of the first compartment was gone, its grand gate shattered into loose stones. Within its broken throat, lines of truncated columns, each ten metres in diameter, marched off into the scrubby wilderness of the compartment interior. Ludd saw field stations, seas of tents, marshaling yards of AFVs, the portable bridge units of the pioneer corps spanning streambeds and ravines. He saw tanks on the move, flashing in the light. The scene was starkly half-shadowed by the hard shade of the sunward wall.

They seemed to be flying straight towards the colossal end wall of the compartment, but Ludd realised that what he had taken to be part of the shadow was in fact a yawning gateway, black as pitch. It was a hundred metres high at least, almost as wide, coming to an arched top. As they closed in, Ludd found he could make out the worn marks of carvings and bas-reliefs around the giant gate, smoothed out by the ages and shrouded in massive drapes of dry creeper and lichen.

There was a sudden pressure hike and change of engine sound as they swept on into the gateway. They were plunged into cool darkness, a long cave of rock lit at lower levels by burner lamps and rows of stablights. The far end of the gateway shone ahead of them, an arch of sunlight in the dark.

With another suck of air, they were out into the second compartment. The immense floor space was a mat of brown undergrowth and islands of pinkish scrub, interlaced with the white lines of roadways and the occasional stone jumble of an old ruin. There were areas where the undergrowth was black, where fires had scorched away great patches of the plant cover. Ludd saw the twisted hulks of war machines and other dead relics of the first fighting phase. To the north of them, far away down the compartment, an area was still on fire. Stray scuds and puffs of black smoke fluttered back past them on the slipstream.

They banked to starboard. About three kilometres along the right hand wall of the compartment, another massive gateway loomed, its facade severely pock-marked and burned by shelling. Ludd glimpsed rocket batteries and artillery positions clustered around its mouth as they flew on through, into darkness, and out the other side.

'Third compartment,' the flight sergeant said.

This section of the Mons, as wide and vast as the previous two, ran north-east, and curved away to the left gently, following the orbit of the step-city. Below, the land was rough and irregular, with outcrops of jutting granite and wide pools or lakes that reflected the tiny image of their carrier back like mirrors. There were more trackways, more areas of damage and scorching. Ludd saw several large blast craters, hundreds of metres across, their shallow pits filled with dark water.

Gaunt nudged him and pointed ahead. On a large outcrop of lowland before them, an Imperial station of considerable size was spread out. Close-packed avenues of tents, net-covered depots, uplink masts, prefab structures, portable silos and hangar-barns, an extensive jumble of local ruins that had been converted for military use. Third Compartment Logistical base, also known as post 10. Even from the air, it was clear the station was heaving with activity.

In a stomach-rolling series of soft swells, the pilot dropped the carrier down, circling wide across the post before nosing in towards a wide patch of flat, baked earth to the south of the main complex where a giant eagle had been crudely stencilled in white paint on the ground. Two Vulture gunships and a Nymph-pattern recon flier were tied down at the edge of the field. A member of the ground crew ran out into the middle of

the scuffed eagle, and cross-waved a pair of luminous
paddles. The Valkyrie eased into its descent, jets wailing,
and landed with a jolt. Immediately, the engine sound
began to peter away.

Gaunt and Ludd jumped down into the sunlight and
the dry, scented heat. Eszrah followed them, stepping
out more cautiously, his head bowed low under the
wing stanchions. The flight sergeant unloaded their kit-
bags and holdalls, and Gaunt tipped him a thank you
nod. The sergeant nodded back with a quick salute, and
then went to unstrap the freight of medical supplies and
perishables that had ridden with them to the station.

Ludd went to gather up their bags, but Eszrah had
already picked them up – all of them except Ludd's own
kit bag.

'That too,' Gaunt said.

Effortlessly, the Nihtgane hefted Ludd's kit as well.

'Do you need a hand there?' Ludd asked him.

Eszrah made no reply. He just stood there, impassive,
laden with bags.

'Maybe not then,' Ludd said. Gaunt was already walking away across the pad, and Ludd ran to catch up.

'I don't think he likes me, sir,' he said.

'Who?'

'Eszrah.'

'Oh. You're probably right. He doesn't take to people
quickly. He probably thinks you're after his job.'

'His job, sir? What job?'

'Looking out for me. He takes it very seriously and
he's very good at it.' Gaunt looked back at the Nihtgane
following them. 'How many times, Eszrah? Preyathee,
hwel many mattr yitt whereall?'

'Histye, sefen mattr, soule,' Eszrah replied, his voice
thick and dense.

'Seven. Seven times he's saved my life,' Gaunt told Ludd.

They'd nearly reached the edge of the pad. Windspeed streamers and garish air-buoys fluttered on their wire-braced poles. An officer in a beige uniform was coming to meet them, escorted by two troopers. They stopped short and the officer, a captain, saluted Gaunt. He was a pale-skinned man with a narrow mouth and watery blue eyes.

'Commissar Gaunt? Captain Ironmeadow. Welcome to post 10. The marshal's waiting for you.'

'Thank you, captain. This is my junior, Ludd.'

'Sir,' Ironmeadow nodded. He paused and squinted at the Nihtgane. 'And that is?'

'Eszrah Night. He's with me, captain. Don't bother him and he won't kill you.'

'Well, that's excellent,' said Ironmeadow, trying not to show that he had no idea what had just been said to him. 'This way, commissar.'

They fell in step and headed up the flakboard walk-way towards the main station post. It was a rambling local ruin, a house, as old as the ages, patched and shored up by the pioneer crews. Hydra batteries lurked in dug-out nests along the north side, their long barrelled autocannons slouched at the sky.

'What's your unit, captain?' Gaunt asked as they walked.

'Second Fortis Binars, sir,' Ironmeadow replied.

'Really? I'd heard Fortis had at last grown strong enough for a founding.'

'Three now, sir, actually. We're very happy to get into the fight. I have to say, I requested the honour of greeting you. Every man of the Binars knows the name Gaunt. From the liberation.'

'I was one of many, captain.'

'One of many without whom Fortis Binary forge world would still be under the yoke of the archenemy.'

'It was a good while ago,' Gaunt said. 'I don't want you treating me like a hero.'

'No, sir.'

'Just with the abject fear and suspicion that is normally afforded an officer of the Commissariat.'

Ironmeadow blinked. He noticed Gaunt was almost smiling, so took that as permission to laugh at what he dearly hoped was a joke.

'Yes, sir.'

They entered the gloom of the house. The place, almost window-less, was lit by glow-globes and lumin strips. The hallway was piled with cargo and munitions cases, and the floor covered with metal grilles to overlay the extensive web of power and data cables. Ludd could hear the chatter of cogitators and the hum of equipment.

'This way, sir,' Ironmeadow said. 'The marshal's just down here.'

MARSHAL RASMUS SAUTOY rose from his chart table as they entered the station command room. Of medium build, he had a thick, grey goatee and soft eyes, and wore a row of citation ribbons across the left breast of his purple coat.

'Ibram Gaunt!' he declared, extending a hand as if welcoming an old friend.

'Marshal,' Gaunt returned, shaking the hand briefly. He had no particular wish to use first names. Sautoy clearly wanted to demonstrate there was some old history between them.

'Long time since Fortis,' Sautoy said.

'Long time indeed.'

'Quite a record you've notched up since then. Inspiring reading. Funny how fate brings us back together.'

'Fate is quite the comedian.'

Sautoy barked out a laugh. 'Have a seat, Ibram. Your junior too. Is this your man?'

'Eszrah, wait for me outside,' Gaunt said. Without even a nod, the Nihtgane stepped out.

'Can I offer you caffeine? Something stronger?'

'Just water, thank you,' Gaunt said. He could already feel the water debt from the heat of the trip in.

'Ironmeadow, some water, please.' The Binar captain scurried away.

'So, Ibram, welcome to this end of the war.' Sautoy resumed his seat, but turned the chair to face his guests. The command room was long and low-ceilinged. Away from the marshal's area, with its chart table, wall maps and stacks of document cases, the bulk of the room was filled with tactical codifiers and cogitators, manned by Guard officers and advisors from the Tacticae Imperialis. There was a general background murmur.

'You've come to us in the capacity of a commissar, I understand,' Sautoy said. 'Throne knows, we need it. This theatre is plentifully supplied with men, Ibram, but for the most part they are new-mustered and green.'

'So I understand,' said Gaunt. 'What's the per capita ratio of Commissariat officers?'

'Roughly one in seven hundred,' Sautoy said. 'Woefully thin. It needs sorting out. Discipline, discipline. There's a lack of backbone and spirit. Desertion is high. Though it's fair to say this place would spook even experienced Guardsmen.'

Ironmeadow returned with flasks of water and handed them to Gaunt and Ludd.

'Would you bring us up to speed on the situation in this compartment, sir?' Gaunt said.

Sautoy nodded, and cleared the surface of the large-scale chart on his table. 'Third compartment, so designated because it was the third section to be penetrated. Heavily defended in the early stages, though the enemy has dropped back. I've nine regiments here, infantry, plus armour support to the tune of three mechanised outfits. I've petitioned for more, but we'll have to wait and see. Main force concentration is here at post 10, here at post 12, and here, post 15. Now, the hot zones are as follows: we breached the gate in the north wall here four days ago so we're fighting up into the compartment designated "seven". Early days, very fierce. Then, about four kilometres further along the same wall, here, you see, is the gate to compartment nine. We're not through that yet. The country around the gate mouth is seriously defended and wooded. There's quite a tussle going on up there. In fact, I'm due to go up tomorrow to see first hand, if you'd like to join me?'

'I may well do that, marshal. I'd like to get orientated as quickly as possible.' Gaunt pointed to the chart. 'There appears to be another gate here at the very north end of this compartment.'

'That's right. It leads through into compartment eight. Our scouts reached that early on. Eight's empty, a dead-end. The gate wasn't defended and the area's abandoned. We've found other dead-end spurs like it. We just crossed it off our list and concentrated on Seven and Nine.'

'What's the enemy disposition extant in Third, sir?'

Sautoy shrugged. 'Very little. Pockets of insurgents, the odd clash. Most have been wiped out or driven back. I'm not saying it's safe – patrols do run into firefights, but Third is pretty much ours. Oh, except for the stalkers.'

'Stalkers?' Gaunt asked.

'Nocturnal threat, Ibram,' Sautoy said. 'We can't work out if they are natural predators in this habitat, or something the archenemy is able to unleash in the cover of darkness. They've been encountered in all the compartments, though more heavily the deeper in we reach. Bastard things. The boys have various names for them: stalkers, spooks, wights, ogres. Wretched, wretched creatures. The most puzzling thing is we've not been able to track them to their source. No lairs, no sign of where they go to ground during the day.'

Sautoy turned from the table and looked at Gaunt. 'So how do you intend to work things, Ibram?'

'I'll spend a few days getting the way of things, meeting with unit commanders and other commissars. Make my own deliberations, and then focus my efforts where they seem to be most useful.'

'And what do you need from me?'

'Accommodation here, just habi-tent space. Transport, and an authorised liaison, an officer, to start me off. Also, full clearance for the compartment, communication day codes, and an up-to-date disposition list.'

'No problem,' said Sautoy. 'I can give you the list right now.' He took a dataslate from the shelf over his desk and handed it to Gaunt. 'As you'll see, most of the units are as green as an ork. Fresh blood. Oh, Ironmeadow, don't look so worried. The Binars are new too, but they're proving themselves quite nicely, thank you very much.'

'Yes, marshal,' Ironmeadow nodded.

'Ironmeadow here can be your liaison, if you've no objections?'

'None,' said Gaunt.

'Well, I won't keep you from your work,' Sautoy said. He held out his hand again, and Gaunt shook it as briefly as he had the first time. 'My senior staff dines at twenty hundred local, if you'd like to join us. I'll make sure there's a seat if you make it.'

'Thank you, marshal.'

'By the way, Ibram?' Sautoy said. 'What happened to that unit of yours? You had command for a while, didn't you?'

'I lost them, sir,' said Gaunt.

BEHIND IRONMEADOW, WITH Eszrah in tow, Gaunt and Ludd headed to the logistics office at the far end of the house.

'Just wait here, sir,' Ironmeadow said. 'I'll get a billet assigned for you.' The captain disappeared into the office.

'You didn't drink all your water,' Gaunt said to Ludd.

'I wasn't that thirsty.'

'Drink it next time. All of it. Every chance you get. Water debt in this heat is going to be high, and I want you sharp, clear-headed and reliable.'

'Yes, commissar.'

They waited. 'You said you know the marshal, sir? He certainly acted like you were friends,' said Ludd.

'You'd be better off reading my body language than his. Yes, I know Sautoy. Back on Fortis Binary. I was serving under Dravere then. Odious bastard, cruel as a whip. Sautoy was a colonel back then, part of Dravere's oversized general staff. Toadies and runts, the lot of them. Sautoy was a desk-soldier, as I knew him, and I doubt he's matured. He's inherited his old commander's habit of wearing medals that mean little. And he's anxious to show himself well in with combat veterans like me. You heard how he kept using my first name, like we were pals? That was all for Ironmeadow's benefit. It'll get back to the rank and file.'

'You don't like him?'

'Sautoy's probably harmless enough, but that's just it. He's harmless. Toothless. He was so keen to impress on us how green the Guard strengths are here. Fresh-founded, draughtees, kids, most of them, getting their first taste of a real combat zone. What Sautoy neglected to mention was that the same can be said of the officer cadre, even the senior staff. Oh, there are exceptions… Van Voytz, naturally, and Humel and Kelso… but for the most part, Macaroth's taken the cream with him to the front line. This Second Front's being fought by children, commanded by inexperienced or unqualified commanders. No wonder the desertion and taint rate is so high.'

Ludd tried to look thoughtful, hoping that the conversation wouldn't come round to his own utter lack of combat experience.

'Damn,' said Gaunt suddenly. 'I completely forgot to ask Sautoy the key question.'

'Which one, sir?' asked Ludd.

'The one you asked.'

Ironmeadow returned. 'I've arranged a billet. It's alongside the Binar section. I'll show you to it.'

They stepped out into the bright sunlight. Ludd reached for his glare-shades.

'I wonder if you can answer a question for me, Ironmeadow?'

'I'll try, sir.'

'Why is the Guard prosecuting the step-cities this way? Why haven't they been neutralised from orbit?'

Ironmeadow frowned. 'I… I never thought to wonder, commissar,' he said. 'I'll find out.'

Ironmeadow led them a short way across the busy post into the neat files of the Fortis Binar billet area. In the row upon row of habi-tents, young troopers in beige fatigues relaxed and chatted, smoked, kicked balls around, or simply lay out of the sun in their cots, the sides of their habi-tents rolled up and secured. Many of the young men made to greet the captain, then backed off warily when they saw who was with him.

'Will this one do?' Ironmeadow asked, indicating an empty habi-tent near the end of one of the rows. It was a four-man model designed for officers.

'That'll be fine, captain,' Gaunt said, nodding Eszrah inside to deposit the kit. The habi-tent was close to the main through-camp truckway, and only five minutes' walk to the Command station.

'All right, captain,' Gaunt said to Ironmeadow. 'Give us an hour to settle in here. Go scare me up some transport. And get some water brought here.'

'Yes, sir,' Ironmeadow nodded, and went off.

Gaunt took off his coat and cap, and sat down on one of the small camp chairs inside the tent. He was flicking his way through the disposition list Sautoy had given him.

'Throne,' he said after a while. 'They weren't lying about the desertion rates. Nineteen troopers sequestered in the last week alone for suspected corruption and taint.' He looked at Ludd. 'Know how that feels. And look–'

Gaunt held the slate up so Ludd could see it. 'There's sickness too. Above the normal rate, I mean. There's an especially bad case at post 15. A serious attrition of manpower.'

He put the dataslate down. 'Let's go for a walk,' he said.

'Where to?'

'Just around,' Gaunt replied. He looked over at Eszrah. 'Restye herein, soule,' he said.

The Nihtgane lay back on one of the cots.

Outside, Gaunt turned to two Fortis Binar troopers playing cards under the awning of their own habi-tent.

'You men.'

They jumped up. 'Yes, sir!'

'No one goes to that tent or disturbs the man inside, got that? I'm counting on you both.'

'Yes, sir!'

THEY STROLLED THEIR way around the limits of post 10. It was a typical large-scale Guard encampment, the kind Gaunt had seen so many times before. The large prefab structures that housed mess halls, the stores and work-shops, the canvas drum-tents of field stations, the ordered aisles of the billets, the rows of parked vehicles. Transports and light armour grumbled down the road-ways, troopers hurried about their duties. On parade areas, companies were being drilled. Ludd saw a mob of newly-arrived infantry disgorging from a line of trucks while power lifters unloaded their equipment crates. There was a smell of cooking, and the chemical tang of well-maintained latrines. In front of one large tent assembly, a platoon of Guardsmen in full battle dress were kneeling to receive the benediction from a robed ecclesiarch.

'Hardly the horrors of war,' Ludd remarked.

'Those await up-country in the hot zones,' Gaunt said. 'And in here.' He tapped his own chest. 'The single most likely reason a man has to desert is fear of the unknown.

In new recruits, that fear means everything. They've not seen combat, they've not seen injury or death. They've probably never left their home worlds before, and certainly not ever been this far away from their families and all things familiar. This post looks decent enough, but to most of them it's probably a lonely, alien place. And their dreams are full of the horrors to come. So they break and they run.'

'My heart bleeds,' Ludd muttered.

Gaunt smiled. 'For such a young man – and, forgive me for saying so, such an inexperienced person – you're quite a hard sort, Ludd. Are you past this, or were you always made of stern stuff?'

Ludd shrugged, delighted by the sort-of-compliment. 'I understand what you've said about these young men, sir, but I've never known those sentiments myself. I never had much attachment to any home. Since I was very young, I've wanted to do nothing except follow in my father's footsteps. And you seem to forget, I am a product of Commissariat training.'

'You know, somehow I do seem to forget that. Which scholam?'

'Thaker Vulgatus, like my father. You, sir?'

'Ignatius Cardinal, more years ago than I care to remember.'

They had paused on the edge of the vehicle pound, at the west end of the post site. Gaunt took off his cap, mopped his brow and gazed out at the granite outcrops and shimmering lakes of the third compartment.

'What a strange place to fight a war,' he said.

'We should be getting back,' Ludd noted, checking his time-piece. 'Ironmeadow will be checking back, and I doubt you'll want him left alone in Eszrah's hands.'

The thought made Gaunt chuckle. He checked his own chronometer, and then started reaching down the sleeve of his coat.

'Sir?'

'Fething thing,' Gaunt grumbled, wrestling with his sleeve. He finally fished out his wrist chronometer. The primitive band had come loose and it had fallen back inside his cuff. He retied the instrument to his wrist.

'We should have–'

'Don't say it, Ludd.'

They started to retrace their steps to the Binar billets. Ludd suddenly realised he was walking alone. He looked round. Gaunt had moved into the shadow of a depot shed and was standing quite still, staring at something.

'What is it?' Ludd asked, joining him.

'Those men there,' Gaunt said. Across the truckway, which was busy with passing traffic, Ludd saw a hardstand where several cargo-8's were parked behind a Munitorum storage prefab. Seven troopers in khaki fatigues, the sleeves of their jackets rolled up, were loading ration boxes onto the back of one of the trucks.

'What about them?'

'They were doing that when we passed by ten minutes ago,' Gaunt said. 'How long does it take seven men to load a pile of boxes?'

Ludd shrugged. 'I don't see–'

'Then try, son. What exactly do you see? As a commissar, I mean?'

Ludd looked again, anxiously trying to identify whatever it was Gaunt's practiced eye had seen.

'Well, Ludd?'

'Seven men…'

'What company?'

'Ah, Kolstec Fortieth, Forty-First, maybe.'

'What are they doing?'

'Loading ration packs onto a transport.'

'Is that all you see?'

'They look… relaxed.'

'Yes. Nonchalant, almost. As if *trying* to look relaxed.'

'I don't think–'

'Where's the Munitorum senior, Ludd? In a depot, you can't move for a grader or a senior checking things off. And since when did combat troops load field supplies? That's servitor work.'

Ludd looked at Gaunt. 'With respect, sir, is that all? I mean, there could be hundreds of reasons to explain the circumstances.'

'And I know one of them. Stay here. Right here, Ludd. Come only if I call you.'

'Commissar…'

'That was an order, junior,' Gaunt snapped. He stepped into the road, paused to let an ammo carrier sweep past, then swung in behind it into the middle of the truckway, skirting round a dusty cargo-12 grinding the other way, and arrived on the hardstand before any of the men had seen him approach.

'Hot work, lads?' he said.

They stopped what they were doing and stared at him. All of them were wearing glare-shades, but Gaunt read their body language quickly enough.

'I said, hot work?'

'Yes, commissar,' said one of them, a thick-set man with the stripes of a gunnery sergeant. 'In this weather.'

'Tell me about it,' Gaunt said, removing his cap and making a show of wiping his brow. 'Does it need seven of you to shift these cartons?'

The sergeant tilted his head slightly, good-humoured. 'They're heavy, sir.'

'I'm sure they are.' Gaunt eyed two of the other men, who were still hefting a box between them. 'Please, lads, put that down. You're making me sweat.'

Uneasily, the men set the box down. The others stood around by the open tailgate of the cargo-8, watching.

'Oh, look, I'm making you jumpy,' Gaunt said apologetically. 'I know, I know, the uniform does that. Relax. I'm new at the post, just settling in. I came over because I recognised the uniform. Kolstec, right?'

'Yes, sir.'

'Which outfit?'

'Forty-First, True and Bold,' the sergeant said. Some of his men grunted.

'I served alongside the Hammers. At Balhaut. Great soldiers, the Kolstec Hammers. Big old boots for you young men to fill.'

'Yes, sir.'

'How are you finding it?' Gaunt asked. He started patting down the pockets of his storm coat. 'Damn it, where did I leave my smokes?'

The sergeant stepped forward and plucked a pack out of the rolled-up cuff of his fatigue jacket. Gaunt took a lho-stick and let the sergeant light it with his tin striker.

'Thanks,' Gaunt said, blowing out a mouthful of smoke. He took a step backwards, and his heel kicked the box the two men had set down. It slid back across the dry earth lightly. Gaunt back-kicked it again without looking. It slithered another good half-metre.

'Here's a tip,' he said. 'When you pretend to load heavy cartons, bend at the knees and make it look like it's an effort. Break a fething sweat. Just so you know, next time.'

He looked at the sergeant. 'Not that there's going to be any next time.'

The sergeant lunged at Gaunt. Gaunt slapped the approaching fist aside and stabbed the man in the cheek with the lit lho-stick. The sergeant staggered back with a yelp. The other men were moving. One swung at Gaunt, missing him entirely as the commissar ducked, and got a fist in the mouth. He stumbled back, spitting blood and fragments of tooth, and Gaunt spun round, his coat-tails flying out, to deliver a side-kick to the man's belly. Doubled up, the trooper slammed over onto the empty carton and crushed it flat.

Three more rushed in. One had a tyre iron in his hands.

On the far side of the truckway, Ludd started forward. 'Oh Throne!' he murmured. 'Oh Holy Throne!'

He ran out into the street, then jumped back, narrowly avoiding a personnel carrier that blared its horn at him. Ludd waited for it to pass, then ran out, dodging between transports and mechanised munitions carts. Halfway across, he was forced to stop dead to let a massive tread transporter grumble by the other way.

'Come on!' he yelled at the crawling load. 'Come on!'

His cap flying off, Gaunt ducked low and punched a trooper hard in the chest, grabbed him by the front of his tunic, and punched him again. As the man fell away, paralysed and winded, Gaunt swung round and kicked the legs out from under the next man running at him, then rose to tackle the trooper with the tyre iron. This man was big, big and young. For a second, he reminded Gaunt of Bragg, big, dumb and eternally innocent.

Gaunt crossed his arms to meet the youth's double-handed swing, and caught him in a tight, scissoring block. The trooper struggled back, trying to use the advantage of his size, but Gaunt had already kicked him in the kneecap and spilled him over. As the trooper slumped sideways, Gaunt wrenched him sharply around with his scissor grip, and the flailing blunt end of the tyre iron smacked into the face of the next attacker so hard his legs went up in front of him like he'd run into a tripwire.

'Come on!' Ludd yelped. The tread transporter was taking forever to move by.

A fist caught Gaunt's jaw, snapping his head hard round. Gaunt tasted blood on his tongue where he'd bitten his own lip. He feinted left, dummied the man, and then felled him squarely with a socking straight-armed jab that Colm Corbec had once taught him. The old Pryze County Number One feth-your-face.

The Kolstec fell over, rolling up in a ball, wailing. Gaunt turned to the last one. The remaining trooper fell down onto his knees, shaking. 'Please, please, sir, please… they said it would work. They said we'd get out of here… please… I only wanted to…'

'What?' Gaunt snapped.

'My home, sir. I wanted to go home.'

Gaunt squatted in front of the blubbering boy and slapped his clumped hands away from his face. 'Look at me. Look at me! *This* is home now, trooper. This is the zone! It doesn't make friends and it doesn't like you, but by the Throne, it's where you are! The Emperor wants you, boy! Did no one ever tell you that? The Emperor wants you to make his glory for him! How can you ever do that if you run for home?'

'I'm scared, sir… they said it would be all right… they said…'

'You're scared? You're scared? What's your name?'

The boy looked up at him. His eyes were red and wet. He was no more than seventeen years old. Like Caffran, Gaunt thought. Like Milo, Meryn, Cader, on the Founding Fields at Tanith Magna.

'Teritch, sir. Trooper third-class Teritch.'

'Teritch, if you're scared, I'm terrified. The archenemy is no playmate. You're going to see things, and be expected to do things your poor mother would have a fit at. But the Emperor expects and the Emperor protects, all of us, even you, Teritch. Even you. I promise you that.'

Teritch nodded.

'Get up,' Gaunt said, rising. The boy obeyed. 'I thought you were going to execute all of us,' he whispered.

'I should,' said Gaunt. 'I really should. But I think–'

'Lie still! Right where you are! No moving! Not a flinch!'

Gaunt looked round. Ludd was hurrying forward across the hardpan, head low, his laspistol aimed in a double-handed grip at the men sprawled and moaning on the ground.

'Not one move, you bastards!'

'Ludd?'

'Yes, sir!' Ludd replied, switching his aim from one supine form to the next, diligently.

'Put that weapon away, for Feth's sake.'

Ludd straightened up and slowly returned his gun to its holster.

'Everything's under control,' Gaunt told him. 'Call up the post watch and get these men put into custody. I'll deal with them later.'

Ludd nodded. He gazed at Gaunt's handiwork. One boy, sobbing fretfully into his hands, and five able-bodied troopers rolling and groaning in the dust. Gaunt had taken on and felled seven men with–

One plus five equalled–

'Sir, where's the other one?'

Gaunt looked round at Ludd. 'What?'

'There were seven of them, sir.'

The gunnery sergeant was missing. Gaunt's crushed and bent lho-stick still sizzled on the ground.

'Ludd–'

The cargo-8's engine roared into life. It pulled out of the rank and started to turn wide across the hardstand towards the street exit.

'Hold these men here, Ludd!' Gaunt yelled, running after the transport. 'Wave your sidearm or something!'

Ludd drew his laspistol again. 'Everyone face down on the dust. You too, boy.'

Gaunt ran across the pan. The truck was kicking up dirt and exhaust plumes as it turned around the end of the next bank of parked transports, and headed towards the road.

Gaunt drew one of his brand new bolt pistols, shiny and clean, virgin and unfired, and ran out into the path of the cargo-8. He could see the gunnery sergeant at the wheel, driving madly.

Legs braced, Gaunt stood his ground and raised the bolt pistol.

'Pull up! Now!' he yelled.

The truck skidded to a halt ten metres short of him. The turbine engine continued to rev hard. Exhaust pumped from the stack like the angry breath of a dragon. Gaunt realised how small and flesh-made and vulnerable he was compared to eighteen tonnes of fat-wheeled transport.

'Engine off. Get out.'

The exhausts belched again, another rev.

'You haven't quite crossed the line yet, gunnery sergeant. But you will soon,' Gaunt yelled, squeezing back the hammers of his aimed weapon. 'Shut down, get out, and come quietly, and we'll deal with this like men. Keep going and I promise you, you'll be dead.'

The engines revved again. The cargo-8 jerked forward a pace or two.

Gaunt sniffed and lowered the bolt pistol to his side. 'Go on, then. You can run me down just like that. But then what? Where are you going to run to? There's nowhere to go except here, and here's where you stop.'

The engine revved one last time, then died with a mutter. Arms raised, the gunnery sergeant clambered down from the cab and lay on his face.

Gaunt walked over to him.

'Wise choice. What's your name?'

'Pekald.'

'We'll be chatting later, Sergeant Pekald.'

Horns were blaring now. Post security personnel were rushing in across the hardpan.

'My arrest,' Gaunt told one of the approaching troopers as he walked away from the spread-eagled Pekald. 'My name is Gaunt. Secure them all in the stockade pending my interview. And mine only. Understood?'

'Yes, sir!' said the trooper.

ESZRAH WAS WAITING for them as they came back to the habi-tent. The Nihtgane tilted his head questioningly

'Nothing for you to worry about,' Gaunt told him, and Eszrah stood aside. Inside the tent, Ironmeadow was waiting for them. He was sitting bolt upright in one of the camp chairs, taut and terrified.

'Hello, Ironmeadow,' Gaunt said as he came in and stripped off his cap and coat. 'Been waiting long?'

'Your man...' Ironmeadow murmured nervously. 'Your man there, Eszrah Night. He...'

'He what?' Gaunt picked up one of the water canteens and took a deep drink.

'He had this crossbow thing, and he waved it at me, and he made me sit down, and-'

'That's common pleasantry where Eszrah comes from, captain. I'm sure you weren't put out.'

'No, sir. Just a little frightened.'

'Frightened? Of Eszrah?' Gaunt said. 'Good. How's the transport coming?'

Ironmeadow cleared his throat. 'I've got a cargo-4 and a driver ready at your convenience, commissar.'

'That's fine work, captain, I appreciate your efforts.'

'I...' Ironmeadow coughed delicately. 'I understand there was an altercation-'

'It's done. Forget it, captain. Just another chore for the Commissariat.'

'I see. So everything's all right for today?'

'It is,' said Gaunt, sitting back on his cot. 'Get yourself off duty, Ironmeadow. We'll start again tomorrow. A tour of the stockade, I think.'

'Yes, sir. Well, goodnight.'

'Sleep tight,' said Ludd, removing his jacket and his webbing belt.

'Oh, commissar,' said Ironmeadow, swinging back in through the flaps of the habi-tent. 'I got an answer for that question you posed.'

Gaunt sat up. 'Indeed.'

Ironmeadow fished a dataslate out of his coat pocket and handed it to Gaunt. 'The tacticae prepped this for you. It's all there. We're not annihilating the step-cities from orbit because the Ecclesiarchy says there is a possibility they are sacred places.'

'They're what?' Ludd asked.

Ironmeadow shrugged. 'There's a lot of argument about what these structures mean and who built them. You'll see it all there in the text, sir. Some say they are relics of the Ruinous Powers, some say they are the vestiges of a prehuman culture. But there are signs, apparently, tell-tale clues that archaeologists have identified, that this Mons and the others like it are edifices raised in the name of the God-Emperor, circa M.30.'

'In which case…' Gaunt began.

'In which case they are preserved holy sites,' Ludd said.

'In which case they must be cleansed and not obliterated,' Ironmeadow finished. 'Does that answer your query, sir?'

TWELVE

11.23 hrs, 195.776.M41
Post 36, Fifth Compartment
Sparshad Mons, Ancreon Sextus

WILDER HAD BEEN at the observation point on the southern edge of the post for the best part of an hour. Officers from all the regiments housed at post 36 had gathered there, training the tripod-mounted scopes out across the grasslands and the broken, rocky terrain of the compartment. Five kilometres north, a battle was raging.

Just before dawn that day, scouts had reported a concentration of enemy war machines moving south. Best guess was that they'd used the cover of darkness to move forward through the gate from the sixth compartment. DeBray had sent out the newly-arrived 8th Rothberg Mechanised to meet them, with the Hauberkan squadrons, very much on probation, to establish a picket line at their heels. The engagement had begun rapidly, and escalated quickly, with the Rothbergers' Vanquishers assaulting the enemy treads across a series of water meadows east of the main trackway.

The din of tank-fire had been rolling back ever since, and the wan daylight across the wide compartment had become tissue-soft with smoke. Numerous clots of solid, black vapour trickled up into the sky, marking the demise of armoured vehicles, friendly and hostile. The Rothberg commander had reported the fighting as 'intense, though the line is holding'. He had identified stalk-tanks, AT70 Reaver-pattern tanks, AT83 Brigands and at least two super-heavies. Many displayed the colours and emblems of the despised Blood Pact.

At the observation point, the infantry commanders waited nervously. If things went well, or if the enemy suddenly produced ground troops to support their push, units like the 81/1(r) and the Kolstec Fortieth would be rapidly moved forward to reinforce the armour. If things went badly, really badly, everything up to and including a withdrawal from post 36, and the other fifth compartment field HQs, was on the cards.

The one eventuality DeBray would not allow was withdrawal from the compartment itself. It had taken too much time and blood to force a way in through that ancient gate in the name of the Golden Throne.

Wilder was accompanied by Baskevyl and Kolea, respectively the senior Belladon and Tanith officers under his new command. Wilder liked Major Kolea immensely, and had admired his solidity and command-sense from the outset. He wondered if it was significant that the most senior ranking officer in the influx was not a Tanith at all, but a Verghastite. The Tanith, on whose bones the regiment had originally been composed, didn't seem to resent Kolea's position. Since the siege of Vervunhive that had brought the Tanith and Verghast together, the two breeds had bonded well. Wilder knew of other 'forced mixes' where the regiments had ended up at war with themselves, stricken with factions, feuds and in-fighting. Apart from a few rough edges and teething problems, the Tanith First – the so-called Gaunt's Ghosts – had meshed admirably, according to the records. Now the game of 'leftovers' was happening all over again, and so far it seemed to be going reasonably well.

That was until the news had arrived. After consulting Hark, Baskevyl, Kolea and a few others, Wilder had made the announcement to the Eighty-First First. It had been greeted with stunned silence. Wilder had looked out across the shocked faces of the Tanith and Verghastites, and sympathised completely. The news had done away with most of the key reasons for the mix.

As a consequence of the action on Herodor, and the classified Gereon mission, the Tanith First had found itself deprived of its key leaders. Colonel Corbec had died heroically on Herodor, and the beloved Verghastite Soric had been removed from active duty under difficult circumstances. Then the Gereon mission had apparently robbed the Ghosts of Gaunt, Major Rawne, and the scout commander Mkoll. Despite the valiant efforts of Gol Kolea and Viktor Hark, neither one of them Tanith founders, the Ghosts had been considered, by High Command, as woefully lacking in the charismatic and essential leadership that had made them strong in the first place. Gaunt, Corbec, Rawne, Mkoll: without those men, the Ghosts were a headless entity.

For its own part, the Belladon Eighty-First had also suffered. Founded two years before the start of the Sabbat Crusade, the regiment had once been eight thousand strong, and had enjoyed a series of notable victories during Operation Newfound and the push into the Cabal Salient. Then had come the hellstorm of Khan III, the war against Magister Shebol Red-Hand. As a victory, it would remain pre-eminent in the regimental honours of Belladon, but the cost had been great. Nearly three-quarters of the Eighty-First had been killed, almost a thousand of them in one stroke during the desperate stand-off at the Field of the Last Imagining. The Belladon Eighty-First had defeated the notorious 'Red Phalanx' elite there, destroyed the Rugose Altar, slain Pater Savant and Pater Pain, and put the Magister himself to flight, an act that led to Shebol's eventual destruction at the hands of the Silver Guard at Partopol. But it had been a pricey trophy. Reduced to around two thousand men, the Belladon had been in danger of being redesignated as a 'support or auxiliary company'. However, their command structure was remarkably intact.

Thus, as Wilder understood it, the lord general himself had approved the mix. The two partial regiments – both light, both recon oriented – complemented one another. The Ghosts would swell the Belladon's depleted ranks, the Belladon officer corps – most especially Wilder himself – would provide the Ghosts with much needed command muscle. That was how the dry, distant decisions of staff office were made, that was how men were added to men to make the Munitorum ledgers add up.

That was how the Eighty-First Belladon and the Tanith First had become the Eighty-First First Recon, for better or for worse.

And now all of that was up in the air again. Gaunt was alive. The Ghosts had accepted the change, believing their singular leader dead. Now he wasn't any more. Whichever way you sliced it, Wilder thought, the Ghosts were going to resent the mix now. Resent the Belladon. Resent Wilder himself. It had all been for the best. Now there was another best that the Ghosts had never dared hoped for.

'You're over-thinking it,' Gol Kolea said.

'What?' Wilder looked around.

Kolea smiled. He was a big fellow, a slab of muscle and sinew, and his mouth seemed small and lost in the weight of his face. But the smile was bright and sharp.

'You're worrying, sir. I suggest you don't.'

Wilder shrugged gently. His body language was slow and amiable, one of the key things that had made him such a fine leader of men. 'I'm just worried about that, Gol,' he said, nodding his head at the distant thump of tank-war echoing up the compartment.

'No you're not,' said Kolea.

'No, he's not,' agreed Baskevyl, bending over to stare through a scope.

'What is this?' Wilder asked. 'You ganging up on me?'

'You're worried about the message, sir,' Kolea said. 'The one you read to us yesterday.'

'You're no fool, Gol Kolea,' Wilder said.

'Guess that's why I'm still alive,' Kolea replied.

'No, that would be luck,' Baskevyl commented, still staring through the scope.

'Actually, Bask's right,' Kolea said. 'Doesn't matter. I know you're sweating because Gaunt's turned up alive. You're worried about the effect that's going to have on the mix.'

'Wouldn't you be?' Wilder asked him.

'I would,' Baskevyl murmured.

'I'm not asking you, Bask. Wouldn't you be, Gol? I mean, in my place?'

'In your place? Sir, in your place, I'd have kept the name Tanith First and let the Belladon suck it up.'

'Of course you would.'

'That was a joke,' Kolea said.

'I know,' Wilder replied casually.

'I was just joking.'

'I know.'

Several officers from other outfits nearby were beginning to listen in. Kolea beckoned Wilder away to the
back of the redoubt. Baskevyl joined them.

'Here's what I think,' Kolea said frankly. 'This mix
made sense. It made absolute sense to you and it made
absolute sense to us. Have you heard any complaints?'

Wilder shook his head.

'Feth no, you haven't. I'm not pretending it's been
easy, but the Ghosts have gone along with everything.
Losing their name, mixing in. They're experienced
Guardsmen, they understand how it works. We all have
to stay viable, combat-ready. In the Guard, you keep
moving, or you die.'

'Or you go home,' Baskevyl said.

'Shut up,' Kolea and Wilder chorused.

Baskevyl shrugged. 'Just saying...'

'This mix made sense,' Kolea said. 'We got into it, we
didn't complain. It's the way things work. And you know
what made it easy? You. You, and the likes of Bask here.'

'Now you're just blowing smoke up my skirt, Kolea.'

Kolea smiled. 'Do I look like the sort of man who
likes to make nice, Lucien?'

Wilder paused. Kolea didn't. Big as he was, he really,
really didn't.

'No.'

'We were lost and we were hurting. You came along
and we liked you. Liked Bask, liked Kolosim and
Varaine. Liked Novobazky. Callide's an arse, but there's
always one, right?'

'He's not wrong,' Baskevyl said, 'Callide is an utter arse. I'd shoot him myself if he wasn't my brother-in-law.'

Kolea looked mortified. 'Throne, I didn't know that. Sorry, sir.'

Baskevyl looked at Wilder and they both chuckled.

'I'm lying,' Baskevyl said.

'He's not your brother-in-law?' Kolea asked.

Baskevyl shook his head. 'He is an arse, though.'

Kolea ran his big hands across his shaved head. 'Throne, I had a point just then, and you with your jokes...'

'Sorry,' Baskevyl smiled.

'I think what I was going for,' Kolea rallied, 'was that the Ghosts have taken to you, *because* of you. This is starting to work.'

'But Gaunt–' Wilder said.

Kolea showed his palms in a 'forget it' gesture. 'When you told us the news, you know what I thought? I thought... well, I thought how happy I was. Ibram had made it. Come through. Done the gig. Like he swore to us he would. I was happy. I still am. The Ghosts are too. Ibram's a great man, sir, and the fact that he's done this and come back to tell the tale, well that's one more notch for us.'

'But he's alive,' Wilder said.

'Yes he is. But he's not a threat to you. You told us, the despatch was clear... Gaunt's been returned to Commissariat duties. Reassigned. He's not going to rock the boat.'

Wilder looked away. 'The very fact that he's alive is going to rock the boat,' he said. 'The Ghosts are going to want him back. Accept no substitutes.'

'I think they've moved on, sir,' Kolea said. 'And even if they do want him back, High Command has been emphatic. We can't have him back. End of story.'

Wilder nodded. 'I guess. What about the others? They're coming back. What about this Rawne guy? I hear he's a truck-load of trouble.'

'We'll make room,' Baskevyl said. 'I'd slide Meryn out to make a place for Rawne. What do you think, Gol?'

'Not Meryn,' Kolea replied. 'Meryn had become one of Rawne's inner circle and he won't like the idea of stepping out. I'd slide out Arcuda and give Rawne H Company. Better still, have a Belladon give up a company command. That'd send the right signals.'

Wilder thought about that and did some quick maths. 'If I did that, more of the companies would have Ghost leaders than Belladon.'

'Would that be so bad?' Kolea asked. 'I mean, as a gesture. A compromise?'

'It rankles,' Wilder said. 'I know my boys. Is this Rawne fellow that good?'

'He's a gakking son of a bitch,' Kolea said frankly, 'but Gaunt never did anything without Rawne in the front of it.'

Wilder looked at Baskevyl. 'What do you think? Kolosim? Or Raydrel?'

'Throne, neither!' Baskevyl said. 'Demote Ferdy Kolosim and he'll hunt you down like a dog. Raydrel's also an excellent officer. We're talking about pride, here.'

'I agree,' Kolea said. 'Not Kolosim or Raydrel. Look, if it helps, I'll step aside for Rawne.'

'No!' they both said.

Kolea grinned. 'I got a warm tingling feeling right then. So… Arcuda. He'll understand. Or maybe Obel. Or Domor, he's very loyal.'

Wilder sighed. 'This, gentlemen, is exactly what I was worried about. Not Gaunt himself. The others. Mkoll–'

'Oh, that's easy.' Kolea said. 'Form up a dedicated scout unit and give him power. You'll love what he does.

He's like… I don't know. He's a wizard. Give him the Ghost scouts and the best of your recon men and he'll blow your shorts off.'

'My friend here meant that in a good way,' Baskevyl said.

'I know he did,' said Wilder. 'All right, all right… Rawne's still the problem. Leave that with me.'

The microbead link pipped. The three officers looked at each other.

'This is it,' Wilder said. 'Come with me, please, both of you.'

'You think I'd miss this?' Kolea said.

THE NORTH END of post 36 was strangely quiet. As the puff of dust on the highway track from the gateway slowly approached, the Ghosts got up from their sunbathing, their card games and their habi-tent cots and gathered around the roadway.

The trucks approached. Four cargo-10s carrying medical supplies and munitions, and a fifth one stripped out for troop transfer. Changing down into low gear, they grumbled up the escarpment into post 36, kicking walls of dust out behind them.

Wilder, Baskevyl and Kolea arrived a few moments before the trucks rolled to a halt. They joined Hark and Dorden, and stood waiting. Ayatani Zweil appeared, and scurried to join them, holding up the skirts of his robes.

'You lied to me, colonel,' the old priest said.

'What, father?'

'You swore blind to me the other day that you didn't have the power to bring people back from the dead. You were lying.'

Wilder chuckled and shook his head to himself.

The dust slowly billowed away and settled. Wilder looked around, felt the electric expectation in the air. He saw the Ghosts: Domor, Caffran, Obel, Leyr, Meryn, Dremmond, Lubba, Vadim, Rerval, Daur, Haller, DaFelbe, Chiria… all the rest.

Eyes wide. Waiting. *Waiting*.

The tailgate on the fifth truck slammed down. Dark figures jumped clear onto the track. There was a moment's pause, and then they began to stroll down into the post, in a loose formation, black-clad figures slowly looming out of the winnowing dust. Walking in step, slow and steady, weapons slung casually over their shoulders.

Rawne. Feygor. Varl. Beltayn. Mkoll. Criid. Brostin. Larkin. Bonin.

Their faces were set and hard. Their new uniforms, displaying the pins of the Eighty-First First, were bright and fresh. A slow smile dug its way across Lucien Wilder's face. He'd seen some bastards in his time, and many of the best were in the Belladon's ranks.

But he'd never seen such a casual display of utter cool. He liked these troopers already. Coming home when they were believed lost. Coming home, asking for trouble. The slow pace, the lazy stride. Throne damn it, they were heroes before they had even started.

Wilder heard a sound, a sound that started slowly then grew. Clapping. The Ghosts around the post were clapping and it became frenzied. Without really knowing why, the Belladon joined in, applauding the heroes home. Shouts, whoops, whistles, cheers.

Rawne and his mission team didn't react. They came striding in out of the dust towards Wilder, faces set hard and stern.

They came to a halt right in front of Wilder. The clapping rang on. The newcomers made no attempt at an ordered file, they just came to a stop in a ragged group. Then they came to attention in perfect unison.

'Major Elim Rawne, and squad, reporting for duty, sir,' Rawne said.

Wilder took a step forward and saluted. 'Colonel Lucien Wilder. Glad to meet you. Welcome to the fifth compartment.'

THIRTEEN

THE CONTRAST BETWEEN posts 10 and 15 could not have been more striking.

They'd spent a couple of days in the relatively civilised and ordered environs of post 10, orientating themselves, but it had felt much longer to Ludd. Gaunt had insisted on conducting extensive interviews with company leaders, tacticae advisors, Munitorum seniors and Commissariat officers, and Ludd had become a little bored with either sitting in as a silent observer or waiting around. Ludd had been looking forward to beginning actual fieldwork as Gaunt's junior, but there seemed to be no particular direction to what they were doing. Gaunt moved with a purpose, but he didn't share it with Ludd. Ludd wasn't really sure what Gaunt was looking for, and when he pressed the commissar, Gaunt had a habit of replying in oblique riddles.

'We're looking, Nahum, for men carrying empty boxes and not bending their legs.'

Gaunt had also spent a long time in the stockade, talking with the prisoners. Ludd had expected some hard interrogations, but Gaunt had been very low-key and relaxed. He'd interviewed the Kolstec they'd rounded up on the first afternoon. Several of them had almost broken down as they confessed their fears to Gaunt.

'Just frightened boys,' Gaunt told Ludd. 'Totally without strong leadership, lost. They saw a chance to sneak out under cover of a faked freight run. It was all a little desperate and sad. I've arranged for them to receive eight days lock-up here, and then be transferred back to Frag Flats for basic support duties.'

'Shouldn't they just be… shot?' Ludd asked.

Gaunt pretended to search his coat pockets. 'I don't know. Should they? I can't find my *Instrument of Order*.'

'You know what I mean, sir.'

'If we start executing,' Gaunt said, 'Van Voytz will be fighting this war on his own. From what I've seen and what I've been told, the Imperial forces of the Second Front are plagued with fear and lack of resolve. Punishment has its place, Ludd, but what's needed here is a way to give the Guard some focus. Some resolve.'

'Because they've lost it?'

'Because they've never had it. These boys have no experience of war, nothing to insulate themselves with. Under other circumstances, the officer class and the commissars would whip some spirit into them and get them through the first weeks of doubt and fear until they found their feet. But the officers are no more experienced, and there aren't enough commissars. Summary execution is a commissar's most potent tool, Ludd.

Used to effect in a situation involving a veteran unit, it reminds the men of their commitment. Used on units of fresh-faced boys, it destroys what little spirit they have. Worse, it confirms their fears.'

When, on the second morning after their arrival in the Mons, Gaunt announced it was time to visit post 15, Ludd had perked up. Fifteen was right inside the hot zone, close to the fight for the gate into the ninth compartment. They might even see some action.

As they drove down to post 15, Ludd realised the prospect of action was making him twitchy and nervous. Suddenly, he understood how the young Guardsmen had felt.

Ironmeadow had kept a transport and driver on standby for Gaunt's use, and came with them to act as liaison. The transport was a battered, open-top cargo-4 that had seen better days. Its engine made the most desperate clattering sound, as if there were stones in the manifold. The driver was a short, tanned Munitorum drone called Banx who had a slovenly attitude and bad hygiene.

'Only the best for us, eh?' Gaunt muttered to Ludd as they climbed aboard. Ironmeadow rode up front beside the driver, with Ludd and Gaunt in the rear seats. Eszrah, whom Gaunt insisted was to come along, sat sideways in the truck-back, leaning against the column of the roll-bars.

Post 15 lay some nine kilometres north-east of 10, in the sickly woodland around the mouth of the ninth compartment gateway. Ironmeadow insisted they could only make the journey in daylight, and had to get travel papers signed off by Marshal Sautoy.

The trip seemed to drag. The up-country trackway wound around the wide pools and lakes that characterised the third compartment, and passed through wide plains of ill-looking sedge and broken rock, and sudden gloomy forests of black larch, lime and coster.

There were signs of war everywhere: burned-out wrecks, cratered earth, and pieces of tarnished and forgotten kit beside the road. Three or four times, they had to pull over to allow a transit column to go by: big dark trucks and small freight tanks trundling south towards post 10. Once, about halfway to 15, the cargo-4 overheated, and they had to linger on the roadside while Banx nursed some life back into the tired engine. They had a good view of the towering compartment wall, and the massive gateway into the seventh compartment. Somewhere over there was post 12. Beyond the gate, an entirely new phase of warfare was going on.

Post 15 announced itself robustly before they even arrived. Above the grim, undernourished trees, they caught sight of thick smoke and fuel vapour, half-cloaking the massive cliff of the compartment wall and the contested gate. On the wind, Ludd heard the heavy report of energy artillery, and the dull thump of shell-launchers. His guts tightened. He realised he was afraid.

Then they noticed the smell. A rank, sick, organic odour that clung to the gloomy woodland like bad luck.

Banx slowed as perimeter guards appeared and demanded to see paperwork. The guards, hard-edged men with jumpy, nervous dispositions, became a little more obliging when they saw Gaunt.

'Go right on through, sir,' one said. 'We'll vox the post commander to let him know you're inbound.'

'Do me a favour, trooper,' Gaunt said, taking a couple of fresh cartons of lho-sticks out of his kit-bag and passing them to the men without any fuss. 'Let it be a surprise, all right?'

The men nodded. Banx drove on.

Post 10 had been a smart, regimented place, swept and formal, wound like a well-maintained watch. Fifteen was a hellhole. Sitting low in a spongy hollow under the gate, it was waterlogged and damp. The truckways were rutted mires, and the latrines had evidently become swamped. The place stank, and clouds of biting flies swirled in the wet air. They drove past rows of habitents that had become sodden with groundwater, huge scabs of mould and fungus caking the limp surfaces of the canvas. Dirty cooking smoke was thick in the air, and carried the gorge-raising hint of rancid meat and fat. All the men they passed were pale and hollow-eyed, tired and strung out. They stared at the passing transport with fretful, sullen expressions. Ludd began to feel still more anxious.

The north end of the post was a ring of artillery positions, actively hammering fire at the vast gate facade and washing fyceline fumes back over the post. The constant, earth-shaking thump of the guns was enough to put a man on edge. And it was like this every hour of every day.

Ludd jumped as a flight of Vultures went over them, turbojets screaming. The gunships banked wide and shot into the dark mouth of the gateway, disgorging their rockets in a blitz of sparks and smoke.

'Calm down,' Gaunt said.

'I'm calm,' Ludd said. 'Very, very calm.'

Gaunt had particular concerns at 15: the drastic desertion rates and the virulent sickness. The feel of the place reminded him unpleasantly of Gereon and the taint there. He felt his skin itch. It made him think for a moment of Cirk. He wondered what eventual fate had befallen her, and was surprised to realise he didn't care. He doubted he would ever see her again.

He spent a brief twenty minutes with the post commander, a harried colonel who was standing in for the marshal and had far too much on his mind. Ludd saw the medicae tents – five times the size of the infirmary complex at post 10; extra sections had been added on in the last few days to accommodate the Guardsmen stricken by illness. The chief medicae had wanted to ship the sick back to facilities away from the frontline, but the request had been denied for fear of spreading the infection to 'clean' posts.

'They say it's a Chaos taint,' Ironmeadow said to Ludd as they waited for Gaunt outside the command station. 'Something in the water, something in the air.' Ironmeadow had tied a neck scarf around his nose and mouth. Ludd thought the captain looked like a bandit.

He was not at all surprised that sickness had blighted the post. The conditions were dreadful: the damp, festering conditions alone could have incubated the infection, and Ludd was grimly sure that the leaking latrines had a lot to answer for.

Chaos taint? The answer didn't need to be anything like that fanciful. Even so, Ludd had the crawling sensation that infectious microbes were burrowing all over him. He wished he could stop jumping every time the massive cannons at the north end of the camp banged off.

Gaunt reappeared. 'What a hole,' he muttered. 'I'd run away from it myself.'

'I know what you mean,' Ludd said.

'I'll go and arrange some billets for us,' Ironmeadow said.

'Why?' asked Gaunt.

Ironmeadow shrugged. 'Well, sir. It's mid-afternoon already. if we leave in the next hour or so, fine. But if we leave it much later, we'll have to wait until tomorrow.'

'Because?'

'Marshal Sautoy's orders, sir. Under no circumstances are we to travel after dark.'

Gaunt glanced at Ludd. 'We won't be here long, Ironmeadow,' he said. 'Don't worry about it.'

'What do you know, sir?' Ludd asked.

'I have a hunch. I hope I'm badly wrong,' Gaunt replied.

Before he could explain in more detail, an especially violent explosion ripped into the air away at the gate mouth. The detonation shook the ground and threw curls of flame up at the sky.

'Holy Throne!' Ludd grunted. 'Shouldn't we be–'

'What, Ludd?'

'Running, sir?'

Gaunt shook his head. 'That was just a tank. A tank's munitions load cooking off.'

'How do you know?' Ludd asked.

'I've heard it before. Poor bastards. May the Emperor protect their souls. Right, let's head for the mess.'

Ludd stared quizzically at Gaunt. 'You want to eat?'

'No.'

'Sir, I've arranged for you to speak with the chief medicae.'

'That can wait, Ludd.' Gaunt had a dataslate in his hand. 'The post commander gave me this and I've made a quick scan. Hence my hunch. I want to check it out first. Ironmeadow?'

'Yes, commissar?'

'I want to apologise, captain.'

Ironmeadow looked baffled. 'What for, sir?'

'I think in the next half-hour I might wound your pride considerably.'

'I don't follow you, sir.'

'Doesn't matter. Just accept my apology now. Remember it was nothing personal.'

Ironmeadow looked at Ludd, who simply shrugged.

'This way, gentlemen,' Gaunt said, and headed towards the mess tent.

THE LONG ROW of open-sided mess-tents was busy with troopers chowing down, spooning stew out of dented tins. Smoke welled under the canvas awnings, and the smell of meat was ripe and heavy.

At the back of the main tent, a mix of Munitorum workers and Guard service workers ladled out the day's offerings onto the trays of waiting men, stirred the heavy vats sitting on the burners, mashed vegetables that were past their prime.

'Ludd?' Gaunt said. 'Go ask some questions. Engage the staff. Get some basic answers.'

'To what, sir?'

'To anything you can think of. Ironmeadow? Cap and coat, please.'

'What?'

Gaunt took off his commissar's cap and heavy leather stormcoat and swapped them for Ironmeadow's canvas jacket and bill-cap. 'You're pretending to be a commissar now. Say nothing, look aloof, and let Ludd do the talking.'

'Sir, this is highly irregular…'

'*I'm* highly irregular,' Gaunt replied, pulling on the bill-cap. 'And lose that fething bandana. You look like a bandit.'

Ironmeadow put on the coat and hat, and followed Ludd into the mess. They lost sight of Gaunt.

'Hello, there,' Ludd called across the vats of food.

'Meal for you, sir?' returned one of the line workers.

'No, thank you. I just wanted to ask a question or two. Actually, my senior here did, but he doesn't like to talk much.'

Ludd indicated Ironmeadow, who made an effort to appear remote and intimidating. Gaunt's coat was a little too large on him, and it made Ironmeadow look like he was a ghoul or vampire, lurking, about to strike.

'Doesn't he like the food?' asked the menial.

'Do you?' asked Ludd, having to raise his voice above the drone and clatter of the busy kitchen.

'Me? No, sir. I eat dry rations, me.'

'Who's staffing this canteen?'

The menial, a heavy, lumpy man in stained aprons and vest, thought about this. 'Munitorum, mostly. The charge cooks are from the local regiments. First Fortis Binars.'

Ludd looked at Ironmeadow, but the captain was so busy getting into character and frowning that he hadn't picked up on the mention of his kindred unit.

'Point me to one of them,' Ludd said.

The menial looked around. 'Hey, Korgy! Over here!' he yelled.

Another server approached. He was very solidly made, beetle-browed. He wiped his hands on his greasy apron and looked Ludd up and down. Ludd saw the Fortis pin dangling from the man's undershirt.

'Commissar? What can I help you to?'

'Just reviewing. You're Korgy? Something like that?'

The man nodded, wary and, to Ludd, far too defensive. 'Regiment Service officer, first class, Ludnik Korgyakin. Korgy for short. Is there a problem?'

'You run these kitchens?'

Korgy nodded. 'Me and Bolsamoy,' he said, indicating a tall, portly, bald-headed man hurrying past with a full kettle of stew.

'Any problems?' Ludd asked.

Korgy shrugged. 'Like what, sir?'

'I don't know. Camp's down with the fever, but you guys seem all right.'

'We eat well and we live clean, what can I tell you? The Commissariat's never been down here before, nosing. You got an issue?'

'No,' said Ludd.

'You got a warrant for this?' Korgy added.

'No,' said Ludd. 'I don't need one.'

'Well, you're backing up the queue,' Korgy said.

'Yes, we are rather backing up the queue,' Ironmeadow put in.

'Shut up and stay in character,' Ludd hissed.

'Only saying…' said Ironmeadow.

'He speaks,' noted Korgy.

'Ignore him. He's battle-damaged,' said Ludd. 'The queue can wait for a second. Why are you defensive, Service Officer Korgyakin?'

Korgy let his ladle flop loose against the side of his stew kettle. 'I have no idea. Maybe being quizzed by the Commissariat? That might do it.'

'It might,' said Ludd. 'You're real jumpy for a cook. Why is that?'

Korgy looked away at someone. A passing hint, a tip-off. Ludd saw it plainly. Korgy looked back. 'Look, do you want a meal or what? If you don't, move on. There are plenty of hungry guys behind you.'

Some instinct, some part of him that he had never known, brought Ludd up to reflex. Without thinking, he drew his laspistol and aimed it at Korgy.

'Back away and raise your hands!' he said.

'What are you doing?' Ironmeadow was bleating behind him. 'Put that away!'

Korgy took a step back, lifting his meaty hands away into the air and dropping his wipe-cloth. 'You shit-head,' he said.

'Ludd!' Ironmeadow yelled.

Ludd glanced sideways. The other head cook, Bol-samoy, had dropped his steaming kettle and pulled a heavy auto pistol, a Hostec 5.

Bolsamoy started to fire.

GAUNT SLIPPED BACK to the rear of the cook-tents, and waited until the foot traffic nearby had cleared. There was no door, so he pulled out his Tanith straight silver, and slit a line down the canvas back-vent.

Stepping through, he found himself in the meat chiller, a larder kept fresh by powerful freezer pods. Lank pieces of meat hung from hooks, or lay, turgid and slimy, in cooler-crates.

He took a step or two forward. Every ounce of him wanted his hunch to be wrong. He reached the back wall. Flakboards, tight-set, formed a heavy barrier around the rear of the mess area. He looked them over, and saw the scrape marks on the floor, the worn edges on one board that had been pulled out and replaced a number of times.

He pulled it open. It came away after a little effort. On the other side was a loading dock, and a prefab lean-to. It was quiet, a private little space in the heart of the busy camp. Gaunt caught the smell on the air.

'Oh, Throne, no...' he muttered.

He edged across the prefab hatch and opened it.

Cold vapour welled out through the door into the damp heat. Counterseptic stink. He took a glance, and all his fears were confirmed.

He almost threw up.

'You stupid bastards,' he said.

Behind him, in the mess tents, shots rang out, followed by screams and yelling.

Gaunt reached inside Ironmeadow's jacket and drew his twin bolt pistols. He started to run back towards the mess hall.

BOLSAMOY'S FIRST BURST had splintered the nearest tent support pole and killed a junior trooper who had been waiting in line, holding his mess tin. The boy simply tumbled down, his skull burst. Further shots wounded three more men in the canteen queue and caused everyone to flee in riotous panic.

Ironmeadow fell down and covered his head with his arms.

Ludd had thrown himself sideways, colliding with the canteen tables and spilling over several cauldrons.

Korgy was running, along with several other members of the cook-tent staff. Bolsamoy was firing into the tent, screaming.

Ludd rolled up, ducked under another flurry of rounds, and then trained his weapon.

'Commissariat! Drop it or drop!'

Bolsamoy fired again.

Ludd had a perfect angle. He prided himself on his marksman scores. He fired.

Bolsamoy staggered slightly. To Ludd, the world went into some kind of slow motion. The cook shuddered, so hard and so violently, Ludd was able to watch the fat of his belly and jowls quaking like jelly. A tiny black hole, venting smoke, appeared abruptly in Bolsamoy's right cheek. His face deformed around it. His right eye bugled and popped. His head hammered back like whiplash had cracked down his frame. Nerveless, his hand spasmed around the trigger of the auto, which tilted up as he went over backwards, punching holes in the canvas roof.

Ludd rolled up onto his knees, aiming his weapon. He heard a deep, throaty whine that went past his left ear and realised that someone had just shot at him and almost hit him in the face. Korgy was close to the tent flaps, amidst the frantic mass of fleeing service crew. He had a blunt 9 in his hand and was firing backwards on full auto.

For a split-second, Ludd believed he could see one of the bullets in the air, spinning towards him. He tried to turn. The round hit him in the head with a crack like thunder and he went down, slamming his right cheek against the leg of the service trolley beside him.

Ironmeadow was screaming like a girl. The troopers in the tent were fleeing en masse, yelling and shoving.

Gaunt appeared from somewhere out in the back, bursting through the tent flaps that screened the inner kitchens. He had a gleaming chrome bolt pistol in each hand.

Korgy saw him, and blasted away with his auto-blunt, backing away now, yelling out some obscene oath.

Gaunt skidded to a halt, raised his monstrous weapons and unloaded. There was a fury of muzzle flash and Korgy came apart, shredded in an astonishing shower of blood and meat.

'Halt where you stand!' Gaunt yelled 'No mercy! No choices! Run and I'll kill you all!'

The fleeing cooks and servers stalled in their flight and fell on their knees, their hands behind their heads.

One of them turned, reaching for a hide-away pistol.

'Idiot!' Gaunt snapped and shot the man through the back of the skull. He fell over on his folded knees, bent double.

'Ludd?' Gaunt called. 'Ludd?'

'I think he's dead, sir,' Ironmeadow called back.

HE WASN'T DEAD. The bullet had exploded his cap and put a crease of bruise along the top of his scalp.

'Are you all right?' Gaunt asked.

Ludd nodded. 'Did I... Did I just shoot a man?' he asked.

'Yes,' Gaunt nodded.

Ludd threw up.

'The station commander's in a rage,' Ironmeadow said. 'What the hell was this all about?'

'Remember my apology, Ironmeadow?' Gaunt said.

'Yes?' Gaunt led the captain into the back tent and beyond. He left Ironmeadow vomiting on the verge outside.

'I'm sorry the Binars brought this curse with them,' Gaunt said. 'Really, I am.'

'Shut up!' Ironmeadow growled between his retches. 'Shut the hell up!'

BANX, TRUE TO form, said nothing as they drove back towards post 10. The light was fading, but they still had time. Gaunt now rode up front beside the driver, Ludd and Ironmeadow sullen and sickly in the back seats. Eszrah, as always, was silent.

'I'm sorry,' Gaunt said over his shoulder.

'You were wrong,' Ironmeadow replied. 'The Fortis Binars never have–'

'I'm sorry, Ironmeadow, but they have. I was there. On Fortis Binary, food shortages got so serious that the

Munitorum started to take corpses from the morgues and process the flesh for food. It was endemic in the hives at one point. A shameful secret your people put behind them.'

Ironmeadow threw up again, spattering yellow bile over the side of the cargo-4.

'I knew the smell as soon as I arrived. And once the base commander had shown me the spread on the dataslate, it was clear. The Fortis Binars are new blood, but their service staff isn't. The cooks and canteen workers are veterans from the old war on your homeworld, Ironmeadow. They know how to make a meal go round. More particularly, they can make a killing selling fresh food-stocks on the black market, filling in the shortfall with forbidden supplies.'

'You bastard!' Ironmeadow yelled.

'Sickness and plague, Ironmeadow, you do the maths. I'm sorry this tragic piece of Fortis Binary's history has followed you here.'

'Bastard!' Ironmeadow returned, and threw up in his mouth again. Ludd grabbed the captain as he leaned out to spit the sick away.

'All right, Ludd?' Gaunt asked.

'Peachy,' Ludd called back over the engine roar.

'You did fine, son. How's the head?'

'Sore.'

'You did all right.'

'Not good,' Banx said suddenly. The cargo-4's engine cackled and then died completely. They rolled to a halt in the shade of some black-trunked lime trees.

'Get it started,' Gaunt told the drone, climbing out of the transport. Banx hurried round to the front of the truck and lifted the hood.

'Dammit, we don't need this,' said Ironmeadow as he wandered up to Gaunt on the roadside. 'It'll be dark soon.'

'Just relax,' said Gaunt.

Ludd joined them. The sky above was still clear and pale, but the heavy shadow of the compartment wall was approaching fast as the sun sank.

'We'll be fine,' Gaunt said. He looked back at Banx.

A thready, fretful clatter was issuing from the cargo-4 as the drone tried to restart it. Five minutes passed. Ten. Thirty. The cargo-4 coughed and sputtered and refused to live. Banx cursed it colourfully.

The close woodland around them became heavy and mauve. The shadow was close now.

'Sir?' Ludd said, touching Gaunt on the sleeve to alert him.

Eszrah had suddenly got down from the transport, his reynbow in his hands. He was alert, listening, coiled. He took one look at Gaunt, then disappeared up into the undergrowth.

'Shit,' said Gaunt. 'Now we're in trouble.'

A deep roar cut the air, a predatory howl that echoed through the damp glades.

Twilight enclosed them. In the dark thickets nearby, something massive was moving closer.

FOURTEEN

18.47 hrs, 196.776.M41
Open Country, Third Compartment
Sparshad Mons, Ancreon Sextus

THE TEMPERATURE BEGAN to drop sharply as night set in. In the distance, the compartment began to echo with odd, inhuman calls, throaty and rough. Something closer by answered the calls with a whooping roar.

'Stalkers,' said Ironmeadow. 'Holy Throne, stalkers! They come out after dark and--'

Gaunt took him firmly by one shoulder. 'You've had a really bad day, captain. Keep your voice down and don't make it any worse. Get your weapon.'

Ironmeadow nodded, and went to the transport to fetch his lascarbine.

'You too, Ludd,' said Gaunt. 'Neither of you fire unless you hear me tell you to. Understood?'

'Yes, sir,' said Ludd, unholstering his pistol. 'Where… where did Eszrah go, sir?'

'Hunting, Ludd. My guess is before long we'll know who to feel sorry for: us, or whatever's lurking out there.'

Gaunt went over to the truck, and took another look at Banx's efforts. The drone's hands were shaking so hard he could barely work.

'Calm down,' Gaunt told him. 'You've got four armed men covering you. We need to get this heap of junk rolling, so concentrate, work hard, and get it done.'

Banx nodded and wiped sweat off his brow with his cuff.

Something moved in the undergrowth beyond the track. Ludd turned smartly, aiming his weapon. Gaunt hurried to him. He had a bolt pistol drawn now.

'See anything?'

'Something's definitely circling us, sir.'

Somewhere a twig broke and leaves rustled. The distant calls echoed again. Like the forest wolves on Tanith, Gaunt thought, howling as they slowly circled in to pick off the stranded, the unlucky, the lost. He'd never heard them himself, of course, but Colm Corbec had liked to tell such tales by the campfire. 'I like the look on the lads' faces,' Colm had once said of those stories. 'I can see how the tales are reminding them of home.' *Scaring the crap out of them, more like*, Gaunt had reckoned.

He realised, suddenly, that he wasn't frightened. He was quite aware that they were in all kinds of danger, but fear refused to come. If anything, his pulse rate had dropped, and a terrible clarity had settled upon him. He tried to remember the last time he'd actually felt any fear, and realised he couldn't. Gereon had stolen that from him, and from all the members of the mission team. Terror had been such a permanent fixture, around them at every moment, that the fear response had simply burned out. So had everything else: desire, appetite, common feeling. All they had been left with was the simple, pure will to survive. Gereon had hardened them so drastically, Gaunt wondered if any of them would ever get back those basic human traits.

Another rustle in the dark foliage. Ironmeadow's carbine was jumping back and forth at every sound, or imagined sound at least. The cargo-4's engine rattled into life, revved, and then died again.

In the silence that followed, Gaunt heard an odd, rapid whispering. He traced it back to Ironmeadow. The Binar captain was muttering the Litany of Faithful Providence over and over to himself.

'I appreciate the sentiment,' Gaunt said, 'but under your breath, if you don't mind.'

There was a rather louder movement in the undergrowth. Boughs shook, shivering leaves. Pebbles skittered. All three men raised their weapons.

Something big suddenly moved in the treeline, crashing through bracken, splintering saplings. It sounded as if a Leman Russ were ploughing in from the outer woods. A dreadful, blubbering roar whooped out of the dark.

'Wait until you can see it!' Gaunt cried.

There was more thrashing, another roar, then a series of odd, muted barks. Something, possibly a tree, fell over with a crash in the outer darkness, and the thrashing stopped abruptly. Silence settled again.

'Oh my Emperor, there it is!' Ironmeadow shrieked.

'Idiot!' said Gaunt, and knocked the man's aim aside.

Eszrah Night emerged from the darkness and walked calmly towards them.

'Preyathee, soule?' Gaunt said.

Eszrah raised one hand to his mouth and made a plucking motion away from the lips with his long fingers. It was a Nihtgane gesture, the equivalent of a Guardsman running a finger across his throat. *The spirit of the foe has been plucked out.*

'It's dead,' Gaunt said.

'What?' said Ironmeadow.

'It's dead. Eszrah killed it.'

'Well, that's bloody wonderful!' Ironmeadow exclaimed. He was so relieved, he was almost in tears. 'Bloody wonderful! That's amazing! Well done, sir!' He held out his hand to the Nihtgane. Eszrah looked at it as if he was being offered a dead rat.

'Anyway, bloody good work!' Ironmeadow said, as Eszrah walked past him.

The cargo-4 made a nasty grinding sound, then roared into life. The engine sounded decidedly unhealthy, but it was running. As the engine turned, the headlamps came on, bathing Banx in bright yellow light. He slammed down the hood, and turned to them in the spotlights of the twin beams, arms spread, like a showman taking an encore.

'Slow but sure,' he called out to them, 'the Munitorum gets the job done. You can all thank me later!'

For Banx, later lasted about a second. A gigantic shadow rose up behind his lamp-lit form, leaned over into the glare, and bit his head off.

Arms still wide, what remained of the driver took two shuffling steps forward, shaking and jerking, and fell over onto the track. Violently pressurised jets of blood sprayed into the air from the ghastly wound, and now blood fell like rain.

Ironmeadow lost control of his bladder and dropped onto his knees.

'Holy Throne...' gasped Ludd.

The wrought one came forward into the light, hunched low, its throat tubes baggy and loose. Its huge arms, locked at the elbow, supported the titanic bulk of its head and upper body. Its flesh was florid and pink, and a mane of tangled brown hair draped forward over the segmented metal armour of its massive skull. Tiny, fierce eyes glowed in the deep recesses of the visor slits. They could smell it, smell the rancid sweat-stink of its mass, smell the sour blood and meat rotting in its vast maw.

The stalker's vast lower jaw thrust forward, underbiting the plated snout, and long steel teeth, as spatulate and sharp as chisels, rose up out of the gum slots and locked back into position.

'Hwerat? Hweran thys?' Eszrah murmured, evidently surprised. 'Ayet dartes yt took haff, withen venom soor, so down dyed yt!'

'Well, somehow,' said Gaunt, 'it got better.'

The creature gazed at them for a moment. Then its slack, heavy throat tubes began to swell and distend. It opened its mouth and let out a deafening, trumpeting roar, exhaling bad air and blood vapour in a mighty gust.

'Kill it. Right now,' Gaunt said. He had both of his bolt pistols out. They began to boom, lighting the gloom with vivid muzzle flashes. At his side, Ludd started firing too, his laspistol slamming off at maximum rate. Eszrah raised his reynbow and thumped another iron dart deep into the meat of the thing's shoulder.

The combined firepower would have felled most of mankind's known humanoid enemies. Even a dread Traitor Marine might have reeled from the force of two bolt pistols at such tight range. Certainly, the monster's flesh tore, burst, exploded. Grave wounds ripped across its upper torso and arms, and two deep dents appeared in its armoured snout.

But it didn't seem to care. It charged them.

'Move! Move!' Gaunt yelled.

Ludd threw himself to the left. Eszrah disappeared to the right. Gaunt went after Eszrah, and then remembered Ironmeadow.

The captain was still on his knees in the thing's path, weeping and helpless.

'Oh feth,' Gaunt snarled.

He turned back, skidded on the muddy track, almost fell, and then righted himself. Wrapping his arms around Ironmeadow, his pistols still in his fists, he yelled 'Move it! Now!'

Just about all of Captain Ironmeadow's higher functions had by then become devoted to emptying his body as quickly as possible. The frantic weeping was the most wholesome aspect of this evacuation. Gaunt felt the ground shake as the monster thundered in at them. He put all his strength into a desperate body throw.

Gaunt went over backwards, and Ironmeadow flew over him, landing on his back in the trackway mud. He slid on his shoulders for quite some distance and ended up beside the cargo-4. The massive beast thundered past, its quarry suddenly missing.

The wrought one turned heavily, grunting and snuffling. Its throat sacs puffed out and went limp, puffed out and went limp. Its vicious teeth retracted and then snapped back, bright and murderous.

It saw Gaunt, spread-eagled on his back.

Gaunt tried to rise. He saw the iron quarrels, eight of them, stuck in the beast's pink flesh. Eszrah hadn't lied. He'd put eight reynbow darts into the thing, loaded with Untill toxin, and still it was moving.

With another roar, the stalker came at Gaunt.

Gaunt had lost his grip on one of his bolt pistols, but, still on his back, he fired the other one at the hideous thing as it bore down.

Gaunt rolled hard, to his left. One of the stalker's huge paws, claws extruded, dug up a bucketful of mud as it struck at the place where Gaunt had been lying.

Gaunt leapt onto his feet. Just three rounds left in the clip. He put them all into the side of the beast's skull as he backed away.

Shaking its long, armoured head, the stalker turned to look at him with its glinting, piggy eyes.

Clip out. Another in his coat pocket. Two seconds to load, maybe? Three? Nothing like enough time for that.

Holy Throne, Gaunt thought. *I'm afraid. Great God-Emperor, I'm actually afraid!*

'Well done, you son of a bitch!' he cried into the monster's face.

It lunged forward at him, raising an arm so thick, so corded with reinforced muscle, Gaunt knew his bones would be pulped.

Before the blow could land, the stalker winced away, blinking. Las-rounds were striking it in the ribs. Heavy, hard, a sustained and serious assault.

'That's right, you bastard!' Ludd shouted. 'This way! This way!' He fired again.

With a raging, phlegmy rattle, the wrought one turned aside and went for the new target instead.

'Oh! Bugger…' Ludd said.

The empty bolt pistol flew up into the air, discarded. Gaunt ran forward, drawing the power sword of Heironymo Sondar. He lit it up and felt the crackle of ignition.

He sliced at the wrought one.

The amplified blade cut clean through the monster's body. If he'd hit the backbone, Gaunt was sure he'd have severed it and crippled or killed the beast. But he didn't quite manage that.

The wrought one let out a huge howl of pain that shook its flapping throat tubes. It turned back to find out what had hurt it so. A copious amount of black, stinking blood gushed out of the deep slice Gaunt's sword had put through its torso.

It swung at him. Gaunt guarded and sliced back, his blow deflecting off the monster's reaching claws. Several talons flew off into the air, sizzling from their cut ends.

The beast opened its mouth. The stink of it hit Gaunt like a body slam. It was going to lunge forward, a biting strike. Gaunt braced his blade in both hands. He was certain he could impale it, kill it, maybe. Of course, he would be dead in the same exchange, as the huge killing jaws snapped forward and closed.

There would be a symmetry to that, at least. To die, killing your killer. That might be enough. After all this time, all these battles, after the unremitting horrors of Gereon, it might be enough. Enough to die with. He almost welcomed it.

'Finally…' he sighed.

The wrought one fell on its face at his feet.

It gurgled once, then the breathing stopped. It was dead. Really dead, this time.

'Holy…' Gaunt said. He sank to his knees, leaning on his sword.

The potent toxins of Eszrah's bolts, quite enough to kill a regular human with the slightest scratch, had finally worked through the stalker's system.

'Sir? Are you all right? Sir?' Ludd called, coming closer.

'I'm fine. I'm alive,' Gaunt replied. He rose upright again. 'I'm alive. Still, I'm alive!' he shouted the words at the dark woods around them. Ludd took a step back. 'You hear me? I'm alive, you bastards! You can't kill me! You just can't kill me, can you?'

Gaunt held his arms up, holding the sword aloft, and slowly turned in a circle. 'I'm alive, even now! You bastards! What have you got left?'

He began to laugh, violently, full throatedly, his head back, almost manic.

Nahum Ludd had seen plenty during that day that had scared him, and the stalker had almost topped the list. But Gaunt's defiant laughter was the scariest thing of all.

ESZRAH NIGHT LOOMED out of the dark and placed a hand on Gaunt's shoulder.

'Restye, soule,' he whispered.

Gaunt nodded. 'It's all right, my friend. I'm all right. Ludd?'

'Yes, sir?'

'Good work there. I won't forget it. Get Ironmeadow cleaned up.'

'How exactly, sir?'

'Find a stream or a pool. Make him stand in it.'

'Yes, sir.'

Gaunt looked back at the partisan. 'Howe camyt be, soule? Sow suddan, sow vyle?'

Eszrah shrugged. 'Stynk offyt I hadd. Thissen steppe.'

The Nihtgane led Gaunt into the undergrowth. Away from the track, and the lights of the truck, huge slabs of granite loomed in the dark between the trees. They were slumped and fallen askew, like a monolith that had been sunk and toppled by the measures of eternity.

'Histye,' Eszrah said, touching parts of the stone and the foliage as he led the way. 'Herein, herein y twane. Thissen spoor, here alswer, yt maketh spoor, alswer, alswer over.'

He came to a stop before a massive slab of quartz, as big as a superheavy tank. The lump of rock reclined among the draping, sickly trees. Gaunt had to feel for its shape in the dark.

'And here's where the track stopped?' he asked.

'Namore stynk, namore spoor yt leaf. Comen fram Urth yt dyd.'

'Are you sure?' Gaunt asked, feeling the rock. Eszrah did not reply. Gaunt could feel the Nihtgane's reproach. Of course Eszrah was sure. He was partisan, a Nihtgane of the Untill. What he couldn't track was beyond the limit of measure.

Gaunt looked up at the night sky. In the cold, hard frieze of the air, stars twinkled beyond the trees. Somewhere out there, across the dim, distances of space, the proper face of this war was being fought, by experienced, determined men.

But it would be lost here. If he was right, and Gaunt was pretty sure he was, the Sabbat Worlds Crusade would be lost right here, in the step-cities of Ancreon Sextus. The Warmaster was going to get stabbed in the back.

He would get stabbed in the back and die.

And there was nothing Gaunt could do about it. After all, he was a loose cannon, a suspect officer, regarded as so dubious in his loyalties, he'd been issued with an observer to keep an eye on him. Regarded as so untrustworthy, he hadn't even been given back a command of men.

Just because they thought he was tainted. Well, it was that very poison essence in his blood that made him know this now. Know it for sure.

Somehow, despite all the odds against him, he had to find a way of getting the senior staff to take him seriously.

And there was one way he could think of…

'Let's get back to the transport,' Gaunt said to Eszrah. On the trackway below them, the cargo-4's engine was still running, and its lights were burning. The distant cries of hunting stalkers flooded the night.

'Ludd? Ironmeadow?' Gaunt yelled as he scrambled back down to the transport, Eszrah behind him. 'We're leaving. Now.'

FIFTEEN

04.02 hrs, 197.776.M41
Fifth Compartment
Sparshad Mons, Ancreon Sextus

RAWNE'S TEAM HAD been back amongst them for nearly two days, and Wilder was now convinced they should never have returned. It wasn't that he didn't know them – and by the Throne, he didn't – but he had been counting on the Tanith men to absorb them back into the company, to smooth over the transition, to welcome the squad's return. And that just wasn't happening.

There'd been an attempt at greeting on the first afternoon. Once they'd cheered and applauded their arrival, the Ghosts had mobbed forward around their long-lost comrades, shaking their hands, embracing them, asking the first of a thousand questions. Rawne's team had, for the most part, simply suffered this attention. They'd smiled back thinly, accepted the handshakes and embraces stiffly, quietly said hello to old faces.

Gol Kolea had marched straight up to his old friend Varl and squeezed the smaller man in a big hug. Varl

213

had grinned an empty grin and patted Kolea on the back until he stopped.

'All that, and they still didn't get you?' Kolea said.

'So it seems,' said Varl. 'I suggested they tried harder, but their heart wasn't in it.'

'Holy Throne, it's good to see you,' Kolea admitted.

'Yeah,' Varl seemed to agree. He was simply looking around at the camp, anywhere but at Kolea's face.

'So… when do we hear all about it?' Kolea asked.

'Not much to tell,' Varl replied.

The Tanith scouts had surrounded Mkoll and Bonin. From what Wilder could overhear, those greetings were oddly muted too.

'What did you see, sir?'

'What happened?'

'Gaunt's alive, right?'

'What happened to Ven?'

'Good to see you all still breathing,' Mkoll had replied. This Mkoll, the famous Mkoll the scouts had boasted proudly about, didn't look like much to Wilder. Small, unprepossessing, tightly wound.

'But what did you see out there?' Leyr asked.

'Not much worth speaking of,' Bonin replied.

'Somebody give me a sit rep,' Mkoll had said, as if he'd just wandered in from a routine, half-hour sortie.

Trooper Caffran had pushed his way through the huddle towards Tona Criid, and stopped short in front of her. He started to move to embrace her, but there was something in her manner that seemed to persuade him not to.

'Tona,' he said.

'Caff.'

'I knew… I knew you'd make it back.'

'Glad someone did.' Then she'd moved on past him, heading towards the billets, leaving him alone, a puzzled expression on his face, the muscle in the corner of his jawline working tightly.

Only Brostin, Rawne's flame-trooper, had seemed in a remotely expansive mood. Greeted by company flame-troopers like Lubba, Dremmond, Neskon and Lyse, Brostin had accepted a lho-stick from a proffered pack.

'What was it like, Bros?' Dremmond asked.

'Well,' Brostin had replied, looking down at his smoke, 'there weren't enough of these for a start.'

A despondency had settled in. The returning 'heroes' appeared to want nothing more than to be left on their own. The day's celebratory mood ended up fizzling away as pathetically as a badly connected det-tape.

THE FOLLOWING MORNING, Wilder had called them all to a briefing at his field tent. He summoned other officers too, including Baskevyl, Kolosim, Meryn and Kolea. The down country squabble with the Blood Pact was still grumbling away inconclusively, the spat holding over from the previous day. Daylight in the compartment was a patchy grey that seemed as shiftless as the mood. According to the post advisors, DeBray was likely to order an infantry advance in the next thirty-six hours. This made sense to Wilder. The enemy armour wouldn't have been gripping on so tightly if they weren't trying to hold a door open for a ground troop push.

'Chances are we'll be moving into the compartment again tomorrow,' Wilder had said. 'Maybe even as soon as later today. Details to follow, but I'll be looking at a firm foot advance from the main companies, with scout units combing ahead. A secondary issue is getting you fixed into place neatly.' By 'you' he had meant Rawne's team. The major nodded.

'I've got various ideas about where to slot you,' Wilder said, 'but I think a little familiarisation is needed first. This is odd fighting country–'

'We're used to odd,' Rawne said.

Wilder paused. He wasn't accustomed to being interrupted, certainly not by a man he didn't know.

'Noted, Rawne. Thank you. I'm going to divide you up and post you with three forces. Sergeant Mkoll and Trooper Bonin, given your speciality, I want you moving in with the recon force, to get a good feel of the way we like to run scouting operations. Captain Kolosim is one of our recon leaders, so you'll be with him.'

Kolosim nodded a greeting to Mkoll and Bonin that was only just acknowledged.

'Varl, Criid, Brostin and Larkin. I'm sorry I don't yet know any of you better. I'm going to put you with C Company, that's Kolea's bunch, so you'll be in with the main infantry advance. Try and find your feet. I don't think you'll have much trouble doing that.'

'I'll keep them in line if they don't,' Kolea remarked, shooting for a good-natured quip. It fell flat.

'Major Rawne, I'd like to attach you to E Company, along with Feygor and Beltayn. E Company is Captain's Meryn's unit. If I can be frank for a moment, I know that might be a little strange, as Meryn was very much your junior when you left. Rub along, please. This is simply about acclimatisation. Meryn, you know Major Rawne is a seasoned and experienced officer. I think we all know we're lucky to have him back with us. I won't lie – there's every chance I'll be moving E Company to him before long. I know that'll feel like a demotion to you, but suck it up. If it happens, it'll be no reflection on you, Meryn. There will be other opportunities.'

'I understand perfectly, sir,' Meryn said. There was not even a hint that he was put out by the suggestion. He must have seen that coming, Wilder thought. Wilder saw how Kolea looked briefly unhappy that Wilder didn't seem to be following his recommendation about Meryn and Rawne.

'All right, that's it,' Wilder said, rising to his feet. 'Major Rawne, I'm sure you'll remind your team that this is all about getting to know your old comrades again, and getting to know your new ones as fast as possible.'

'Of course,' said Rawne.

'And may I take this opportunity to say that the Eighty-First First has nothing but admiration for what you've accomplished in the last eighteen months. We haven't been told everything, naturally. Parts of your mission details remain classified. But you don't have to prove anything to us... except that you can fit back into company level operations.'

Now ANOTHER DAWN was on the way. Wilder woke and immediately felt uneasy again. It wasn't just the cold. The cool, aloof attitude of Rawne's team still bothered him deeply. There were only nine of them, but that was enough to unsettle the entire balance of the regiment. The Belladon didn't know what to make of these surly newcomers and their hard-as-nails reputation. For the Tanith and the Verghastites, it was just a huge disappointment. These people were heroes, back from the dead. They'd built them up so much in their minds, the reality was like a cold shower.

The Eighty-First First and the Kolstec Fortieth had mobilised in the pitch dark. The eerie hoots of stalkers echoed up from the blackness of the compartment.

Baskevyl brought the signals up from the command station. A pre-dawn advance, just as Wilder had suspected, the Eighty-First First leading off the Kolstec into the eastern side of the compartment. By oh-nine hundred, DeBray wanted Wilder's regiment secure along Hill 56, preferably having made contact with the Rothberg armour.

Down on the trackway, and on the assembly areas, the companies were forming up: men, numb and cold from their billets, canteens full, adjusting webbing and the fit of battledress, checking weapons. The sky overhead was as clear as glass, and only the bright pattern of the stars showed where the black sky ended and the black shape of the high compartment walls began.

Twenty minutes to the go. Wilder buttoned up his fleece-lined coat, did a quick intercom test, and went to check a carbine out of the stores. He normally only carried the powerful laspistol strapped to his thigh, but today he had a feeling, and it wasn't pleasant.

On his way back out of the post, he saw Hark and Novobazky talking to Dorden.

'Morning,' he said, joining them.

'Just off to join the ranks, sir,' Novobazky said.

'Problem?' Wilder asked.

'We were just discussing Rawne and the others,' Hark said.

'Anything you'd like to share?'

Hark shrugged and looked at the old medicae. 'I can't imagine what they've been through,' Dorden said. 'I can't imagine, and therefore I have no real idea, because none of them are at all willing to talk about it. I checked each of them over yesterday, just the expected routine exam. I'd been so looking forward to seeing each one again, and they were like strangers. Not actually unfriendly, but… distant.'

Hark nodded. 'That'd be my reading too, sir.'

'Any conclusions?' Wilder asked.

Dorden frowned. 'They've been on their own for so long, it may take them a while to settle back into company. I mean, they're just not used to being around people they can trust. I think they've had to ditch a lot in order to survive as long as they have. In fact, that's all they have left. Survival. I don't know if they'll ever be the people we knew again.'

Wilder knew the old doctor was bitterly disappointed his beloved colleague, Curth, hadn't returned with the team. 'Are they fit?' Wilder asked.

'Physically, they're supremely fit. Even Larkin, who's the oldest one of them. And Larks is the one who gave me most pause, I suppose. He was never–'

'Go on,' said Wilder.

'Dorden is diplomatically trying to say that Larkin was a little poorly wired in the head department,' Hark said. 'He had personal issues, edgy and nervous. The only reason he made the cut for the Gereon mission was that there's no better marksman in the Tanith First.'

'Larks has got a hard edge to him now,' Dorden said. 'A lot of the old shakes and tics have gone. I'd have expected a horror show like Gereon to push him right over the edge. Maybe it did, and he got pushed so far, he came back the other way. Point is, if that's what it's done to the most psychologically weak member of the team…' his voice trailed off.

Wilder sighed. He checked his watch. 'All right, gentlemen, let's get this circus moving.'

THE SIGNAL TO advance came over their microbead links, quiet and simple. Standing with C Company, Larkin felt the pip in his ear and picked up his weapon. It was new, an Urdesh-pattern mark IV long-las, finished in satin black with dark plastek furniture. Quite a nice weapon, all things considered, but he was still getting to know it. He'd left his own weapon – the old nalwood-fitted long-las that had seen him through every firefight from Tanith to Herodor – back on Gereon. In fact, it was still hard for him not to think they'd left three friends behind on that arse-end world: Ven, Doc Curth and his sniper rifle. It had been a simple thing, in the end. About six months into the Gereon tour, he'd run out of hot-shot rounds, run out of even the means to manufacture or recook hot-shot rounds. Dead, mute, his old long-las had become about as useful as a club. He'd switched to a simple, solid-slug autorifle that Landerson had found for him, an old hunter's bolt-action.

As they moved forward down the trackway into the darkness, Larkin found himself walking beside a young Belladon soldier who was also carrying a long-las.

'Kaydey,' the youth said, offering his hand.

'Larkin.'

'Major Kolea's asked me to travel with you. Wants us up the front with the point men.'

'Lead on,' Larkin said. They double-timed for a couple of minutes, moving up the file of troopers.

'So, you take some shots on this Gereon place?'

'One or two.'

'What was it like?'

Larkin looked at the boy. 'Aim and squeeze, just like here.'

'No, I meant–' Kaydey began.

'I know what you meant.'

After that, Kaydey didn't say much.

* * *

KOLEA GOT HIS company moving north into the scrublands off the track. Dawn was still a while off, and most of them were using goggles, painting the world as a green image, as if they were underwater.

Kolea gave point to Derin and moved back, checking the company line, troop by troop. He saw Criid, and fell in step with her.

'You been avoiding me, Tona?' he asked.

'Yes, Gol. That's why I went to Gereon, to avoid you.'

'I don't suppose you got a chance to see the kids on your way in here?' he said.

Criid and her partner Caffran had rescued two young children from the Vervunhive warzone, and had been raising them as their own as part of the regimental baggage train of camp followers, support staff and non-combatants. It had turned out that the kids, in one of the more quirky examples of the God-Emperor's sense of humour, were Kolea's. The children he thought he'd lost back there. Kolea had let things be, left Criid and Caff in charge, not wishing to screw up the kids' minds any more than they already had been.

Since the regiment had arrived on Ancreon Sextus, the kids, Yoncy and Dalin, had been in the care of the regimental entourage back at Imperial Command.

'No,' said Criid.

'You going to?'

'Eighteen months since I've been gone, Gol. You seen them yet? You been to them and told them the truth that daddy's not actually dead?'

'No,' he said.

'You talk to Caff at least?'

'No,' Kolea said.

'Throne's sake, Kolea! He knows! I told him all about it. Feth it all, eighteen months and the two of you haven't even had a conversation? You're as bad as each other!'

'Tona–'

'Don't talk to me,' Criid said. 'Maybe later, but now you don't talk to me. We're in the fething field here, you dumb gak. Shut up and choose your moments better.'

She walked on. Some of the men nearby looked at Kolea. They hadn't caught much of the exchange, but they knew something spiky had just gone down.

'That's *major* dumb gak...' Kolea called after her.

E COMPANY, ALONG with Callide's H Company, were the last to move out from post 36. In the bitter darkness, lit by lumen paddles and lamp-packs, the Kolstec units that would follow them were already forming up and filling the assembly areas vacated by the Eighty-First First.

As he waited for the off, Feygor kept looking back at the Kolstec assembling on the hardpan thirty metres behind them. He tutted silently and shook his head. The Kolstec were making a fair bit of noise.

Rawne stood beside him, huddled deep in his new leather coat. He'd spent some time in the last few days working at the coat with oil and wool to soften it, but the new leather still creaked slightly as he moved.

'Murt?'

'Fething craphounds,' Feygor whispered. 'Zero noise discipline.'

Rawne nodded. He'd actually been fairly impressed with the manner in which the Eighty-First First had drawn together and moved out. Some noise, and some chat, but nothing too disgraceful. He had assumed the good practice of the Tanith had rubbed off on these Belladon people.

The Kolstec though, they just wouldn't shut up. He could hear whining and complaining and occasional bursts of laughter. And even though they clearly had low-light goggles as standard, they were flashing lamps and torch paddles like it was Glory of the Throne Day.

Rawne saw the Belladon commissar – what was his name again, Novobazky? – talking with Captain Callide and several junior officers Rawne couldn't name. He went over.

'Major Rawne? Good morning.'

'Commissar. I assume you'll be doing something about that?' He inclined his head towards the Kolstec forces.

'I'm sorry?'

'The noise and light. It's not acceptable.'

'They'll settle once we're underway.'

Rawne smiled. 'Will they? Oh, that's all right, then.'

'Besides, it's a matter for their own commissars to–'

Rawne stared into Novobazky's eyes. 'It will be our matter when those fething idiots bring down the hurt on our heads by yabbering at our heels. If you just assume something will get done, it never will. And somebody else's problem never stays somebody else's.'

'Are you telling me how to do my job, major?' Novobazky said.

'Yes, I fething well am. Someone has to.' He turned and walked away.

'Major! Get back here!'

'I don't think I will, fethwipe,' Rawne said, still walking.

'Major Rawne!

Rawne ignored Novobazky and rejoined Feygor. 'We just got the signal to move,' Feygor said.

E Company began to stir. Ayatani Zweil was moving down the column, issuing a few last blessings to troopers. He reached Beltayn and smiled, about to speak the simple prayer of protection.

'Save it, father,' Beltayn said.

'Son, I'm only–'

'Just save it. I'm blessed or I'm cursed. Either way, a few words from you won't help.'

Zweil closed his mouth and watched the young trooper move away with the rest of the company. Dughan Beltayn had once been one of the most devout troopers in the regiment, always amongst the first to arrive for the daily service. But the look in his eyes just then…

Meryn was near the head of the formation, leading the men off into the darkness. For all he'd nodded along with Wilder's placement orders the previous day, he was twitchy and uncomfortable. He felt as if Rawne's eyes were boring into him wherever he went. Before Gereon, Meryn had styled himself on the Tanith's second officer, admired him, sided with him, and had benefited from being one of 'Rawne's men'. Now he was a captain and a company leader, and Rawne had come back from the dead, threatening to take that away. Meryn didn't blame Rawne; ironically, the situation made him focus ever more intently on the skills and philosophies Rawne had drummed into him: self-reliance, cunning, the desire to protect what was his with brutal and exclusive efficiency.

He'd make nice, he'd nod along with Wilder. But there was no fething way Flyn Meryn was going to let Rawne come in and steal this command from him.

Jessi Banda was up ahead of him, moving forward with the marksmen taking point. There was another little sticky point. It hadn't been common knowledge, but Rawne and the caustic, sharp-tongued sniper had been an item before the mission. Once Rawne had gone, Banda had chosen Meryn as a replacement partner. Meryn was no fool. He knew that Banda was an ambitious woman, who liked to keep the company of promising officers, or men on the rise. Like Rawne before him, Meryn was one of the sniper's trophies. He knew she didn't love him, and he didn't much care. They were good together, and had a hard-nosed, volatile relationship that seemed to cater for their basic needs.

The trouble was, Meryn had become terribly possessive. He didn't love Banda either, if he was honest, but he was intoxicated by her; intoxicated by her cruel wit, her laugh, her flirtatious manner, by the very heat and smell of her. She just had to look at another man – or another man look at her – and Meryn would brew up. Two days earlier, a Belladon sergeant called Berenbeck had wound up in the infirmary, badly beaten. Berenbeck was a loud-mouth, and it was presumed – even by Berenbeck himself – that he'd been jumped by Hauberkan tankers who had overhead him opining that a bullet had been too good for Gadovin. The truth was it had been Meryn, waiting for Berenbeck behind the latrine tents after dark with a sock full of stones. Meryn had heard the man telling his buddies how 'hot the Ghosty sniper girl' was.

Banda hadn't said anything about Rawne's return, nothing to get Meryn thinking, at any rate. But Meryn could barely fight down the furnace in the pit of his gut. His command and his girl. Fething Rawne wasn't going to take either one from him.

E Company, with H Company on their right flank, moved out across the scrublands, closing up on the

Eighty-First First units already slogging up north through the compartment. Rawne thought they moved well. The Belladon were evidently a decent enough regiment. In all probability, the Ghosts were lucky to have been mixed with them. But Rawne felt empty and cold, and it wasn't just the biting chill of the pre-dawn air. There was nothing about this he engaged with any more, no point, no purpose, no sense of loyalty. The Tanith First was gone, even though so many familiar faces were around him. There was no longer any intensity, no passion. The world had become empty, its lustre gone, and Elim Rawne was simply going through the motions.

NORTH-EAST OF post 36, the landscape of the compartment was downland scrub for three kilometres, a stubbled expanse of tumbling rough ground speckled with stands of lime and thorn-bush. At its lowest point, the scrubland gave way to marshes and oxbows of brackish water, thickly clogged with black rushes and reeds. East of the depression, past a vestigial trackway overgrown with moss, the land rose again, becoming bare and flinty, the scrub broken by ridges of quartz and ouslite that looked like the gigantic exposed roots of the compartment's massive eastern wall.

Ridge 18, so marked on the charts, was a particularly high example, a hard-sided buckle of sharp rock that ran east-west for about half a kilometre, its upper surfaces thick with dogwood, bramble and flowering janiture. Kolosim's recon unit was about halfway up the southern side.

Four recon units had set out ahead of the main advance, one to the west, two across the central basin of the scrub, and the fourth, Kolosim's, around to the east.

It had taken them about forty-five minutes to move down country from the post. Dawn was still not yet a glimmer above the western wall.

Ferdy Kolosim, red-headed and bluff, was Mkoll's equivalent amongst the Belladon. A recon specialist, he had risen to company command by dint of his experience and his leadership skills. He was well liked. Even the Tanith had warmed to him.

There were eight men in his unit. The Tanith Scouts Caober and Hwlan, the Belladon Recon Troopers Maggs, Darromay, Burnstine and Sergeant Buckren, and the newcomers Mkoll and Bonin. Already, Kolosim had made a mental note of the scary way the last two performed. He'd always believed the Belladon to be pretty good stealth artists, and it had been a wake-up call to witness the extraordinary abilities of the Ghosts when the regiments first amalgamated.

But Mkoll and Bonin were something else. Kolosim had to keep checking they were still there, and every time he did, neither Mkoll nor Bonin was where he'd last seen them.

It was to the Belladon's credit, as a recon division proud of its skills, that there had been no ill will when the Ghosts first came along. Rather than resenting the way the Ghosts showed them up, the Belladon had got busy learning all the woodcraft and battle-skills the Tanith could teach them. They'd got rid of the netting shrouds they'd been using since their founding, and adopted Ghost-style camo-cloaks. They'd stopped using their clumsy sword-form rifle bayonets for close work, and got hold of smaller, double-edged fighting knives. The knives were nothing like as handsome as the Ghosts' trademark straight silver, but they were far handier than the long bayonets. They'd even started dulling down their regiment pins and badges with boot black. Caober, pretty much the senior Ghost scout since Mkoll, Bonin and Mkvenner had gone, had taught Kolosim that himself. He'd pointed out the faintly ludicrous fact that the Belladon drabbed up buttons, blades, fasteners, bootlace eyelets, skin and uniform patches for stealth work, but still wore a shiny, scrupulously gleaming regimental badge on their tunics.

'It's a matter of pride,' Kolosim had said. 'Pride in our unit identity.'

'Pride's great,' Caober had replied. 'Great for a lot of things, except when it gets you seen and killed.'

Kolosim liked Caober's frank and fair attitude, and the two were forming a decent working relationship. He wasn't sure how things would sit now the famous Mkoll was back. Every tip and piece of advice Caober, or any of the other scouts, had ever imparted, came with a phrase like 'as Mkoll taught us' or 'like Mkoll always said'.

So far, Mkoll had said a dozen words to Kolosim, and six of those had been, 'You Kolosim? Right. Let's go.'

The unit reached the crown of Ridge 18 and slid through the bramble cover. From the top of the ridge, they got a decent view, via night-scopes, across the deep basin beyond, a steep-sided, scrub-choked vale that widened as it ran west. On the far side of the basin, parallel to them, ran Ridge 19, a lower and more jagged escarpment. At its western end rose Hill 55, and behind it, the broader, loaf-like bulk of Hill 56, where the Eighty-First First was meant to form up later in the day. Hill 56 was back-lit by a jumping, trembling light, brief flashes and bursts that lingered as after-images on their goggles. Even from half a dozen kilometres away, they could hear the crump and report of tankfire. The

Rothberg armour had pushed the archenemy back up the compartment, but the fight was still in them, even at this early hour.

Kolosim studied the area and made a few jotted notes with his wax pencil.

'At least they're where we thought they'd be,' he muttered. Buckren nodded. There had been a danger that the Rothberg would have been shoved backwards overnight, or worse, which would have made Hill 56 unviable as an infantry objective. One of the key objectives of the recon units was to make sure DeBray's orders still made sense. Thanks to the high ground and the efficiency of their advance, Kolosim's unit was the first to get a visual confirmation.

'Signal it in?' Buckren asked.

'Do that,' said Kolosim. Buckren crawled over to Darromay, who was carrying the vox-caster, and began to send in the details.

The other duty of the recon units was to assess the approaches. The tacticae advisors at the post reckoned there was a high probability that the archenemy might use the distraction of a drawn-out armour fight to sneak infantry down the eastern side of the compartment.

Mkoll stared northwards. He studied the charts in detail, but there was nothing like seeing the land first hand. Feeling the lie of it. And there were so many lies here. For all it seemed like a natural landscape, the compartment was artificial. It was a giant box full of dirt and rock. He didn't trust any part of it. He turned his scope towards the far north end, and was just able to pick out the suggestion of the end wall, the great bastion enclosing the next massive gateway. That would be the real objective in the days to come: burning a path to that monumental gate and breaking through. What lay beyond that, none could say. Even orbital obs and spy-tracking had come up with nothing. The only thing anyone knew for certain was that the next compartment was another step towards the centre of this ancient puzzle, and that it was capable of launching forth armoured columns and companies of warriors to face them.

Hooting roars echoed up the ridge from the basin. Mkoll swung his scope to look down that way.

'You'll never spot 'em,' said Maggs.

Bonin looked across at him. 'The stalkers?'

'Yeah, you never see 'em. Not until it's too late.'

'That so?'

Maggs nodded, and patted the butt of his mark III. 'And one of these babies won't stop one, not even on full auto. Even if you do see it first. Which you won't. You never see 'em till they find you.'

'You maybe, not the chief,' Bonin replied.

Wes Maggs frowned. He was a short, well-built man with a broad, swimmer's back and heavy shoulders. His hair was cropped and brown, and he had a little vertical scar running down from the outside corner of his left eye. Maggs was one of Kolosim's best scouts, known amongst the Belladon as a likeable rogue and joker, who sometimes had too many words in his mouth for his own good. Bonin hadn't made up his mind about Maggs yet. Too much personality for his liking.

'I'd like to see your old man try taking a stalker...' Maggs began.

'Stick around,' said Bonin.

Kolosim was ignoring the quiet exchange. He was studying the ridgeways ahead of them.

'No way they'd bring a force this way on foot,' Buckren said.

'Too much like heavy going,' Burnstine agreed. 'The lateral ridges would slow them down. And if they got into trouble, they'd have no easy retreat.'

'The Blood Pact don't often think of things in terms of retreat,' Mkoll said.

'You think they'd come this way?' Maggs asked.

'I think it's possible. I think it should be checked,' Mkoll said.

'You're crazy–' Maggs remarked.

'Pin that lip,' Kolosim snapped. He rose to his feet and stood beside Mkoll. 'I was going to have us follow the line of this ridge west until we hit the open table-land, then hike up the escarpment to Hill 56. Something tells me that's not what you want to do.'

Mkoll shrugged slightly. 'Your unit. You call it.'

'We're meant to be getting to know one another, Mkoll. I'd like to hear what you have to say.'

'All right,' said Mkoll. 'The ridges break the terrain along this east wall. It wouldn't be the approach of choice. The enemy would be better off trying to cinch an infantry column around Hill 55, and come in on the trackway. But I think we should stop thinking about this like normal open country. We're boxed in by walls. We're enclosed. If I wanted to outflank us, I'd send in troops this way.'

'Over the ridges?'

'Over the ridges. They're steep, but we made the top of this one in, what? Under an hour from the post? It's well covered too. The densest undergrowth in the compartment. It would be hard going, but it would pay off. Besides, we don't know what's down there or behind the next ridge…' he gestured down into the basin. 'And we don't know how much better our enemy knows this place.'

'Meaning what?' asked Caober.

'Meaning tunnels. Meaning trenches. Meaning sally-ports we can't see. It's artificial.'

'There's been no sign of any tunnels or anything so far,' said Hwlan.

'Doesn't mean there aren't any there,' said Mkoll.

Kolosim pursed his lips. 'Let's take a look.'

'You're kidding me!' Maggs grunted.

'Darromay,' Kolosim said, ignoring Maggs. 'Signal post command we're moving onto Ridge 19. Maybe another hour. We'll vox them again when we're on site, and take it from there.'

'Yes, sir.'

DOWN IN THE dark, overgrown basin between Ridge 18 and Ridge 19, in a dank glade between lichen-heavy lime trees, Crookshank Thrice-wrought paused. Something was coming, something moving down the steepness to the south of him.

Other, lesser wrought ones, once-wrought or twice-wrought, were hunting in the damp groves nearby, but they all knew to give Thrice Crookshank a wide berth. The sun, and the time of going back, was a long way off.

Crookshank puffed breath through his floppy throat tubes and made a dull, idle rasp. He clambered forward, rolling his gait through all four, powerful limbs, head low.

He sniffed the air. He could smell it now for sure.

Something was coming, and it was called meat.

SIXTEEN

05.26 hrs, 197.776.M41
Fifth Compartment
Sparshad Mons, Ancreon Sextus

EVEN IN DAYLIGHT, the basin would have been dark. An off-set bowl between the two long ridges, it was choked with undergrowth that blocked out the sky. Back on Tanith, it was what the woodsmen would have called a combe.

The southern slope was steep, almost sheer in places. The ground was a mix of loose, flinty loam and exposed quartz. Thick gorse and bramble spilled down the slopes, hanging like frozen waterfalls. Resilient lime, and some form of tuberous, gnarled tree species, sprouted from the thicker deposits of soil, and provided handholds for the recon unit to brace against as they descended.

A musty smell of damp and mud and leaf decay welled up from the basin below. It was several degrees warmer out of the open.

The men moved with their weapons strapped over their right shoulders, right hands on the grips, left hands free to grip and grasp. Distant noises came up out of the darkness below. Scrabbling, snorting, the occasional half-heard grunt. Mkoll had no doubt there was at least one stalker loose down there.

Mach Bonin was listening carefully. The other members of the recon unit were making precious little noise, but it still sounded loud and clumsy compared to the total silence he and Mkoll were managing. It wasn't just the Belladon. Even Caober and Hwlan seemed to him to be heavy footed, and they were two of the Ghosts' best scouts. Had their technique really slackened off in Mkoll's absence?

No, he realised, watching them for a moment. They were as good as ever. The difference was with him. Heading to Gereon, Bonin hadn't thought he could get any sharper. The place had proved him wrong about that, like it had proved them wrong about so many things.

About halfway down the slope, Mkoll perched on a jutting crop of quartz and held up his hand for a silent halt. The others arrested their descents quickly, and waited, watching him.

Mkoll paused for a moment, listening, breathing in the air, working out what was there and what wasn't. No birds, no insects to speak of. Possibly burrowing worms and beetles, but nothing flying. Nothing chirruping and stirring. No small rodents, no lizards. Just the still, damp, stringy undergrowth.

He smelled wet stone, bark, musky leaves, humus. He smelled free flowing water, and he could hear that too: rills and rivulets gurgling down the slope below.

The noise of the stalker or stalkers had receded for a while, and the few louder sounds he heard were actually the echoing thumps from the distant tank battle beyond the hills, which were hard to screen out.

But he could smell blood. The rank sweat, body odour scent of blood, as from a poorly healing wound. The smell of rotting meat between the teeth that a carnivore carries with it.

He signalled them to move again. As they got up and carried on, Maggs shook his head, as if amused by Mkoll's painstaking manner.

Kolosim reached the bottom of the slope, where the depth of the basin began to round out, and was glad to have both hands back on his weapon. He began panning round, then jumped in surprise to find Mkoll right beside him.

'Shit!'

'Let's spread that way,' Mkoll whispered.

In a lateral line, they moved out across the basin floor, their boots sinking into the thick black mud, dense bramble and branches pushing in around them. Bonin could smell the blood scent too, and glanced at Mkoll.

The smell had changed a little, as far as Mkoll was concerned. It had become more like sweat, dirty human sweat.

Something moved up ahead. A tree shivered and there was a snort.

Weapons came up.

Mkoll took a step forward.

CROOKSHANK THRICE-WROUGHT salivated at the air's taste. He was close now, moving with astonishing grace and care for something so big and heavy, delicately parting gorse stems and saplings as he slid forward.

Nearby, off to his left, a lesser wrought one, a twice-wrought, was active, snuffling. Much longer, and the lesser thing would spoil it.

Crookshank opened his jaws and unslid his steel teeth. His dark-sight stained red. He could see the meat at last, twiggy shapes of pink heat in the red darkness.

His teeth locked into place.

RIFLE UP TO his cheek, Mkoll waved Maggs and Bonin to his left. Caober and Burnstine were just away on his right-hand side, and the others were coming in behind.

Maggs moved through the undergrowth as instructed, sliding his body this way and that, so it barely touched a twig. He'd had enough of the newcomers' showboating. They weren't the only ones who knew how things should be done.

Maggs came in under a twisted lime and looked back for Bonin. There was no sign of the man. Where the h–

A hand clamped over his mouth. Maggs stiffened in terror and then realised it was the Tanith.

Bonin took his hand away. Somehow, he'd come up around Maggs without Maggs noticing. How the hell did a man do that, unless he was a–

Ghost.

Maggs glared at Bonin. Bonin ignored the acid look, and pointed ahead. There was something there all right. Something stalking them as surely as they were stalking it.

Maggs swallowed. This was insane. The truth was, and Maggs wasn't about to admit this to Mr Know-it-all Bonin, he'd never actually seen a stalker. But he'd heard plenty of stories since the Eighty-First First had moved into the Mons. Horror stories of the bogeymen that stalked the compartments after dark. Bestial ogres that refused to drop, even when you were hosing them with full auto fire and saying please nicely. Everyone knew you didn't go looking for stalkers, even when you were part of a fire team. Kolosim should have turned back from the ridge, not come down here, not down here where–

Bonin was slowly lifting his weapon. From the dense, black undergrowth ahead, there came a wheezing snort. The crack of a root breaking under a great weight.

Maggs raised his rifle too. He toggled it to *full auto* anyway.

CROOKSHANK THRICE-WROUGHT tensed, muscles pulsing, his breathing short and sharp. He began to puff up his throat tubes. His fighting spines rose erect. Saliva oozed from the long, dagger-toothed line of his jaw.

WITH A LUNG-BURSTING howl, the wrought one tore out of the undergrowth and ploughed towards Maggs and Bonin. Maggs began firing at once, loosing a bright cone of energy flash as his weapon discharged at maximum sustain.

Twenty metres back, Mkoll started running forward, and the rest of the unit came after him. Mkoll couldn't see anything of the situation ahead, apart from the bright, flickering wash from the lasfire backlighting the undergrowth. He could hear the shooting, and the roaring.

Maggs kept firing as long as he dared. He had made a real mess of the stalker's armoured face and throat. His furious shots had chewed at it, ripped and stippled the flesh. But still it came on, bawling aloud, trailing flecks of blood and saliva into the air. *You never see 'em*, he heard himself saying, *not until it's too late*. It was too late now. The thing was a freaking *nightmare…*

Then Maggs realised something else. He was alone. Bonin had vanished. Somewhere between the thing bursting out at them and Maggs opening up, the Throne-damned runt-head spineless Ghost had just *disappeared*, without even firing a blessed shot. He'd run, and left Maggs to face the music.

'You lousy shithead bastard!' Maggs yelled, his voice all but drowned out by the whooping roar of the monster's throat tubes. He turned and ran. Maggs got about five metres, tripped on a root in his terror, and fell.

The wrought one came after him.

Maggs looked up, screamed, tried to untangle himself from the brambles. The thing was right on him, right on him, mouth agape, those teeth, those teeth, those f–

The wrought one abruptly flailed, and fell hard on its face, as if it had tripped too. It landed so suddenly that its lower jaw smashed into the loam and slammed its gaping mouth shut. It had come down less than a metre from Maggs's outstretched feet.

It wasn't even slightly dead. It thrashed and roared, reaching with its huge arms, its maw snapping and slicing the air. Maggs screamed again, and scrabbled backwards, out of reach. He fumbled for his lasrifle. Why had it fallen down? Why the hell had it fallen down?

And why in the name of the God-Emperor had its roaring, bellowing sound become so shrill and wretched?

Like it was… in pain.

The wrought one heaved itself forward again in a mighty surge, rising up on its massive arms, muscles bulging, veins prominent like cables. Curds of foam glistened around its drawn lips. It lunged at Maggs.

He found his weapon and fired into its gullet, glimpsing the scorched punctures his shots made in the ribbed, pink roof of its mouth. Then he rolled aside hard, lacerating his face and arms on spine-gorse and thorny bramble.

Bonin suddenly appeared in mid-air behind the wrought one, propelled by a leap that must have needed a run up. He was no longer holding his lasrifle. In one outflung hand, he clutched the Tanith trademark weapon, the straight silver fighting dagger. The blade of Bonin's dagger was black-wet with blood.

Bonin landed astride the wrought one's hunched back with a grunt of effort, and grabbed hold of the raised fighting spines for purchase with his free hand. Maggs realised that the stalker was half-prone on its belly, dragging its rear limbs.

The monster shook and bucked, trying to shake the man off its broad back. Bonin clung on, and thumped his dagger down into the base of the stalker's skull.

Thirty centimetres of straight Tanith silver punched into its brain case. Thick, dark blood squirted out, hitting Bonin like a pressure hose. He wrenched the knife out and stabbed again.

The wrought one quivered, spasmed, convulsed, and then fell over on its side with a jolt that seemed to rock the ground. Bonin was thrown off.

An almost silence fell. The only noise was the last, tremulous breathes rattling phegmatically in and out of the dead stalker's throat tubes, the gurgle of the blood weeping out around the hilt of the embedded knife.

'Holy Throne…' Maggs said.

'You all right, Maggs?' Bonin asked, getting to his feet and slicking the thing's blood off his face with the palm of his hand.

'Yeah, I'm dandy…' Maggs said.

'Bonin?' Mkoll said. He had suddenly appeared beside them, weapon raised. Kolosim and the others arrived a moment later.

'Golden Terra…' Kolosim murmured, gazing in astonishment at the stalker's huge corpse. 'I mean… Golden bloody Terra…'

'Was that you, Mach?' asked Hwlan.

'Oh, none other,' Caober chuckled. 'See the silver?'

'Yes. Good work, Bonin,' Mkoll said. He was still stiff, as if uneasy.

'Good work? Good work?' Maggs stormed. 'He left me to face it! He left me to deal!'

Bonin walked over to the stalker and plucked out his dagger. When he turned, Maggs was in his face. 'You ditched me, you bastard!'

'I killed it, didn't I?' Bonin asked.

'Yes, but–'

'Before it chomped on you.'

'Yes, you bastard, but–'

'You told me even full auto wouldn't stop a stalker,' Bonin said quietly. 'And so I took your word on that, Maggs. It's a hell of a beast, but it's still an animal. It has anatomy. Anatomy that obeys the simple laws of hunting.'

'What?'

'It has hamstrings. So I cut them. It fell down. It has a brain. That's where I stabbed it. See the skull there? The grafted armour plating at the front? That's why they can't be stopped, even by full auto. Whoever made them armoured their braincases at the front. You have to hit them from behind.'

Maggs stared at Bonin for a long moment.

'Wait a minute,' said Sergeant Buckren. 'Whoever *made* them…?'

Caober was about to speak when he saw that Mkoll had slowly raised his hand.

The Tanith chief scout pulled his weapon up to his chin and aimed back into the undergrowth behind them.

'Get ready,' he hissed. 'We're not out of this yet. Not at all.'

CROOKSHANK THRICE-WROUGHT was panting. The twice-wrought had rushed in early, and ruined his kill. It had almost spoiled the hunt with its inexperience and haste. Later, back under the Quiet Stones, once they had gone back in, Crookshank would have most definitely slain it for its insolence in depriving a thrice-wrought of its meat.

But such punishment was no longer necessary. The lesser thing was dead. The meat twigs had killed it.

Crookshank drew a breath. His throat sacs filled and swelled pink. The sun, and the time of going back, was close now, but he would still feed. The meat had no idea how close he was. They had no notion just how near his claws were to their–

No. One had. The smallest one. The one with no meat on his bones. That one had turned, and was looking directly at Crookshank Thrice-wrought.

Crookshank's blood-hunger was too enflamed by then for him to be troubled by such a curiosity. He extended his claws and pounced.

THE SECOND STALKER came out of the bramble screen like an avalanche. Lime stems cracked and splintered as its bulk pulverised them. It was massive, at least twice as large as the monster Bonin had brought down.

Kolosim, Hwlan, Buckren and Caober began to fire. Mkoll was already unloading at full rate. Bonin ran towards his fallen weapon. Maggs turned and gasped at the stupendous bulk of the new monster. Burnstine simply ran.

Darromay died.

The middle claw of Crookshank's splayed left paw cracked down into the top of Darromay's skull like an augur, right through the hardened steel helmet he was wearing. Then the weight of Crookshank continued to press down, crumpling Darromay into the ground, snapping him like a grass-stalk, breaking all his bones, and rupturing the splintered ends of them out through his deforming skin.

Darromay became a crushed, trampled mess in the loam, his burst blood steaming in the cool air. Crookshank hadn't even meant to kill him. Darromay had simply been underfoot.

The broken vox set on Darromay's twisted back sparked and crackled.

Backing away, the unit fired together, hammering bright lasfire at the charging monster. Full auto from five Guard weapons wasn't even slowing it down. Maggs retrieved his gun and joined the fusillade. So did Bonin.

It wasn't anything like enough.

Oan Mkoll threw aside his spent weapon and drew his warblade.

'Let's go then, you ugly bastard,' he growled.

There was a sudden, piercing buzz that made all the Guardsmen wince and reach for their microbeads.

Crookshank faltered, lifting his massive paws to the sides of his head.

He roared in frustration.

The call. The call to the quiet stones.

Mkoll yanked the microbead plug out of his ear. He could still hear the buzzing. It was in the air, all around them, so low and intense all the leaves were shivering. The rest of the recon unit were stumbling around, clawing at their intercoms to pull the plugs out.

Crookshank backed away a pace or two, fighting the command, twisting his massive head from side to side, and gouging at his ears. Shuddering with the queasy, infrasonic buzz, Mkoll took a step towards the monster.

It looked at him. Blinked. Grunted.

'Next time we meet, I'll kill you.' Mkoll said.

Crookshank Thrice-wrought roared, turned, and then vanished into the heavy sedge and bramble.

The buzzing stopped.

Slowly, the men of the recon unit straightened up.

'What the hell was that?' Caober asked.

'Some kind of call,' Kolosim said. 'Right, Mkoll? Some kind of call?'

Mkoll nodded. 'It reminded me of something,' Bonin said to him quietly.

'Yes, you too?' Mkoll asked, picking up his lasrifle and reloading it.

'It reminded me of the sound the glyfs made, back on Gereon.'

'That's what I thought,' Mkoll said. He turned back to the others.

'We have to find Burnstine,' Kolosim was saying.

'Burnstine? Burnstine?' Buckren began yelling.

'Shut up!' Mkoll spat. He looked at Bonin. 'Why would they call their monsters off, I wonder?'

Mkoll paused. He could smell it again. The smell of dry, soured blood that he had detected from higher up the slope. He had supposed the reek belonged to the stalkers, but now he knew different. The stalkers stank of sour-sweat, human meat.

This dry, blood smell was different.

Familiar.

'We need to move,' he said.

'What about Burnstine?' Kolosim asked. 'Dammit, Mkoll, what about Burnstine? And Darromay? We can't just leave the poor bastard's body there.'

'We can and we will. Forget him, captain, forget Burnstine. I'm not joking around here. I think the enemy's close. Very close. Just like we suspected.'

'What?'

'Let's go take a look, then get the word out if I'm right.'

'Without a vox?' Buckren said. The unit's caster had died with Darromay.

'We'll find a way,' Kolosim said. 'Do as Mkoll says.'

They clambered through the dense vegetation, heading north-east, cutting away fronds of strangling gorse that blocked them. Behind them, in the west, the first light of dawn was hazing in over the far wall, slowly turning the sky red.

'What's that?' Kolosim asked, coming to a halt, whispering.

'Machine noise,' Hwlan responded.

Clack-clack-clack the noise went, drifting through the vegetation. There were footsteps too. A lot of them, crunching and squishing on mud and grit. Kolosim waved the unit into cover. They dropped down, fast and obedient, skulking in behind tree boles and dense thorn, their weapons gripped ready.

Into view, into the realm of their lambent night vision, figures appeared, advancing through the tangled undergrowth of the basin, a column of men moving down from the northern ridge.

Men wearing dark grotesque masks. Men sporting the signs of the abominable and the forbidden.

Mkoll knew he had smelled that dry-blood aroma before. Too often before, in fact.

It was the stink of the Blood Pact.

From his vantage point, Mkoll estimated at least a hundred Blood Pact infantry, probably more. With them – *clack-clack-clack!* – came stalk-tanks, rattling along on their calliper legs, light and nimble enough to manage the steep terrain of the ridges.

Kolosim signalled the unit to stay low and silent. They didn't even dare dropping back.

Nice and quiet, let them go by, then slip away and–

'Captain? Captain? Respond, please…' Burnstine's anxious voice suddenly crackled over the intercom. Kolosim quickly muted his mic, but the damage was done.

One of the stalk-tanks shuddered to a halt, its body raised. The head turret tracked round until it was pointing towards the undergrowth where the scouts lay concealed. They could see the tank's operator, a surgically augmented human, prone in the fluid-filled blister cockpit under the tank's tail, making adjustments to his controls. The cannon mounts on the tank's head clattered as they autoloaded.

'Voi shet tahr grejj!' The command echoed out of the stalk-tank's external speakers. Immediately, two squads of Blood Pact troopers broke formation and began moving towards the scouts' hiding place, weapons ready. Almost at once, one of them spotted Buckren.

The warrior called out. As he raised his weapon to fire, a las-shot took him off his feet.

'Concealment's no longer an option,' said Mkoll, firing again and taking down two more troopers. 'Hit and run.' The rest of the recon unit joined in his gunfire.

In reply, the Blood Pact began shooting, blasting into the undergrowth with their rifles as las-bolts began to rip into their ranks.

And then the stalk-tank's cannons opened fire too.

SEVENTEEN

06.10 hrs, 197.776.M41
Fifth Compartment
Sparshad Mons, Ancreon Sextus

AT FIRST LIGHT. Wilder allowed himself a little, satisfied glow of contentment. The bulk of the Eighty-First First was still advancing across the tableland scrub, but Hill 56 was less than a kilometre away, and Baskevyl's company had already reached it. They were well ahead of schedule.

It was going to be a cold, grey start to the day. Mist still lingered in the lowlands. Beyond the soft curve of Hill 56, the thumping drone of the tank fight echoed like distant thunder. Occasional flashes lit the sky.

Wilder called up his vox-officer and got himself patched through to Baskevyl. He walked along beside the vox man, talking into the speaker horn.

'Tell me what you've got, Bask.'

'…see some business…' Baskevyl's voice came back, chopped and sliced by atmospherics. Sunrise did that sometimes, though this seemed worse than usual.

'Say again, Bask. You're phasing on me.'

'I said I think we'll see some business this morning, sir. The Hill's secure. I can see the Rothberg line, and I've had a brief connect to their commander. It's a hell of a tussle down there. The–'

'Repeat that last, over.'

'I said it's a hell of a tussle. The armour's holding, but from what I can see, the enemy's throwing a lot this way. The Rothberg mob have brought the Hauberkan in to support them now.'

'Are they behaving, over?'

A wash of static.

'Baskevyl? Baskevyl? Come back, B Company lead.'

'…me now? I repeat, are you hearing me now, Eighty leader?'

'Check on that, Bask. The air's bad today. I asked how the Hauberkan were doing.'

'According to the Rothberg commander, the Hauberkan have raised their game. I can see a line of their treads over to my north-west, guarding the track-way. Lot of smoke, lot of dense smoke. The trouble seems to be that the Rothberg have been at this for the best part of three days. The crews are dog-tired. A signal's gone to post command for more armour to relieve them. I understand some Sarpoy treads are due to join us around noon. That will be the critical time. The enemy may try to push for the advantage if they see the Rothbergers breaking off.'

'Understood,' Wilder replied. That would be when a picket line of well dug-in infantry would come into its own. Anticipating armour, both the Eighty-First First, and the Kolstec Fortieth behind them, had come loaded for a spot of tank-hunting. Every fireteam unit had been issued with at least one anti-tank launcher, devices which Wilder had learned the Tanith referred to as 'tread-fethers'. He consulted his chart again. They'd have to hold the hill and the adjacent trackways, and also the watercourse along the west side. Tread-fethers, crew-served weapons. They had about six hours to dig in effectively. That was doable.

'You still there, Eighty leader?'

'Reading you, Bask. I want you to start scoping the land there for good, defensible positions. I want a breaker line, you understand me? A breaker line to stop anything we don't like the look of.'

'Understood. I'm on it,' Baskevyl's voice crackled back. A 'breaker line' was Belladon shorthand for a defensive position constructed to maximise crossfire support, so that every element was backed up by the enfilading cover-fire of its neighbour.

'Bask, any sign of foot advance?'

'Not at this time, sir, but like I said, dense smoke. Likelihood is they've got infantry massing in the wings to storm up once the tank fight's done.'

'You got the recon units there with you?'

'Two of them. Raydrel's unit's still over in the west, circling through the marshes. He checked in about ten minutes back and says there's zero chance of the enemy trying anything that way.'

'Like we supposed. What about Kolosim?'

'Negative on Ferdy, Eighty leader. Nothing from him since the routine check over an hour ago.'

'Understood. Get to work. I'll be with you in about twenty minutes. Eighty leader out.'

Wilder handed the speaker horn back to the vox officer, who shrugged the harness of the heavy caster set on his back to make it sit more comfortably.

'Get Kolosim for me.'

'Yes, sir.'

Still walking, the vox officer adjusted his earpiece and began to tune through the channels using the caster's secondary control panel, which was strapped around his left forearm. Wilder heard the man test-calling for Kolosim on the channels reserved for recon forces.

Wilder turned and looked east across the tableland towards the distant compartment wall. Beyond the dotted lines of his men trudging north, long-shadowed, through the broken scrub, the land fell away and became jagged and jutting along the steep rock ridges. The woodland was deep there, dark pockets still smoking with mist. Somewhere over in that direction, Ferdy Kolosim's recon unit was supposed to be cutting around west towards Hill 56.

Wilder tried to shake off the nagging feeling that had entered his head. It wasn't like Kolosim to miss a check, and he should have been on or near the hill by now.

'Nothing, sir,' the vox-officer reported. 'Zero return from the captain's designated channel.'

'Try the other bands. He may be having reception trouble.'

'I have, sir. Nothing. Post command says he voxed in just before five and reported his position as Ridge 18. He told them he was going to scout the next ridgeline before turning west.'

Wilder nodded. He scratched the corner of his cheekbone where two hours of wearing low light goggles had started to chafe.

'I want you to keep trying him, every five minutes.'

'Yes, sir.'

'Before that, get me the Kolstec commander. Then I'll want a general patch to our company leaders.'

'Yes, sir.'

The field commander of the Kolstec Fortieth was a man named Forwegg Fofobris. The Fortieth was a fine bunch of experienced heavy infantry, packing some serious crew-served support pieces, which would be useful come noon. However, Fofobris had come across as a bit of a blowhard to Wilder in the brief encounters they'd had. Baskevyl and Wilder had taken to referring to Fofobris as 'Foofoo Frigwig', which was a bad habit, because it was all to easy to slip and call a man by his nickname to his face. The pair of them had once developed the name 'Jonny Frigging Glareglasses' in reference to a archly posing Volpone officer they'd had to deal with on Khan III. When Wilder had called the man that by accident during a briefing, he'd been challenged to an honour duel.

He'd got out of it, thanks to Van Voytz. A formal apology and a case of amasec. Funny thing was, Baskevyl, who usually coined these derogatory terms, never slipped. It was always Wilder. Wilder wondered if Baskevyl had a nickname for him too.

Most probably.

Foofoo Frigwig came on the line. 'Wilder, is that you, sir?'

Wilder suddenly got a fit of the giggles. He remembered a moment in the post 36 billets, several nights earlier, when Gol Kolea and Ban Daur had introduced the Belladon officer cadre to the mysteries of home-brewed sacra. A Tanith tipple, evidently. One sip made you smile like a lovely bastard. It was during that little session that Baskevyl had come up with the name 'Foofoo Frigwig', adding that the 'foofirst class arsehole' was in command of the 'Kolstuck Foofortieth' fighting 'foofor the Golden fooFrigging Throne.'

Ah well, it had been foofrigging funny at the time, and such childish humour had a habit of sticking in places where it was no longer funny or appropriate. Unless you'd been there.

'Fofobris? This is Eighty leader.'

'What's the matter with this link, man? It sounds like you're giggling.'

Wilder covered the vox horn and looked at the comms officer. 'Slap me real hard, Keshlan.'

'Sir?'

'Across the cheek. If you don't mind.'

'Sir… uh, what?'

Wilder shook his head. 'Never mind.' He looked out east towards the ridges and the thought of Kolosim straightened his face pretty quick.

'Sorry, Kolstec lead, the atmospherics here are bad. You're at our tail, I understand?'

'Affirmative, Eighty leader. Forty minutes from the hill at this time.'

Fooforty minutes. Really, still funny.

'The Rothberg are going to be pulling out around noon, Fofobris. By then, we're going to need to be providing serious ground cover. Are you good for that?'

'As soon as we're on site, Eighty leader.'

'That's good to hear, Kolstec lead. We're going to need tread-fethers and–'

'Say again?'

Throne, how easy to fall into slang. *I'm my own worst enemy*, Wilder thought. 'Anti-tank, Fofobris. A lot of it. Expect heavy shit. Patch to my number two, Baskevyl, on 751. He's scouting the terrain now. I want you placed as per his recommendations.'

'Not a problem. Understood, Eighty leader.'

Wilder handed back the horn to vox-officer Keshlan. 'Now the company leaders, please.'

Keshlan hooked him up, and Wilder briefed the officers of the Eighty-First First on the bare bones of the gig ahead.

All the while, he stared east.

Where are you, Ferdy, and what's the problem?

C COMPANY HAD reached the foot of Hill 56. 'Double time it, you slugs!' Kolea shouted. 'Up the slope now. You can rest when you're dead.'

The troopers began jogging up the scrubby incline.

Kolea turned, and saw Varl. Varl had stopped moving. He was standing on the slope, looking west, his hand to his left ear.

'Varl?'

It took a moment for Varl to look round. When he did, there was no hint of the man Gol Kolea had once known.

Varl adjusted his microbead plug. 'You hear that?'

'What?'

'It's clipping in and out. Through the static.'

Kolea shook his head. 'Atmospherics, Ceg. Just atmospherics. The weather's bad for that today. Solar radiation, or something.'

'No,' said Varl. 'It's the chief. He's in trouble.'

'Mkoll?'

Varl looked at him.

'You know, you're going to have to tell me some stories, sometime, Ceg,' Kolea began gently. 'I mean, you and me. We were friends once. And the Ceglan Varl I knew was the biggest blabbermouth story-teller I ever met. I'm beginning to think the archenemy sent us back a copy that looks all right, but is actually–'

'That some kind of joke?' Varl growled. His eyes were suddenly hard.

'Gak, yes!' Kolea said, taking a step back, mortified. 'A joke, Varl. A fething joke. You remember them, right?'

Varl breathed deeply. A tiny smile crossed his face. 'Sorry, Gol. Sorry, man. It just seems like everyone I meet suspects me. Thinks I'm tainted, because I was there so long. I had the fething Inquisition on me, you know.'

'I know.'

'We all did. How fething right is that, after what we did? A tribunal? I served, for Throne's sake! I fething served!'

Kolea blanched. He held out his hand. 'Gak it, Ceg. What happened to you? What did they do to you on Gereon?'

Varl laughed. 'Nothing, Gol. *They* did nothing. I did it all to myself. Just to survive…'

Varl's voice trailed off. He looked at his old friend. 'Sometimes, you know…'

'What, Ceg?'

Varl shook his head. 'Nothing. It's just that sometimes I wish my old Ghost buddies had the first fething clue about what we had to deal with on Gereon.'

'So tell me. Then I will.'

Varl laughed again. It pained Kolea to see his old friend so conflicted. 'Tell you? There's nothing I can tell you. Gereon didn't make for anecdotes and war stories. Gereon was fething hell on a stick. Sometimes I want to scream. Sometimes I just want to cry my heart out.'

Kolea smiled. 'Either. Both. It'd just be between you and me.'

'You're a good man, Gol. How are the kids?'

'The what?'

'Tona told us all about it. You have to see your kids, Gol.'

Kolea turned away, bruised with anger. 'You better watch your lip, Varl.'

'All right. Whatever you say, poppa. Stings, does it? Close to home? I tell you what, Gol, Gereon's closer than that to me. To all of us that were lost. It fething hurts, it's so close.'

Varl looked east again. 'The chief. He's in trouble. I know it.'

CAPTAIN MERYN RAN back down the scrubline and summoned his troop leaders out of the advancing mass of E Company.

'Coming up on 56 now,' he told them as they huddled around him. 'Wilder wants us into a line, with close support to the front. Fargher, Kalen, Guheen, Harjeon, that means your teams. Into position, quick smart, and listen for Baskevyl's instructions.'

'Yes, sir,' they chorused.

Meryn paused and looked around. 'Where's Major Rawne?'

Guheen pointed back to a gaggle of figures down the slope.

'All right,' said Meryn, 'move it up. I'll be there in a minute or two.' He hurried back down the slope towards Rawne.

Rawne was standing with Feygor, Caffran and Beltayn. The vox-officer was fiddling with his set's dials.

'Is there a problem here?' Meryn demanded.

Rawne looked at Meryn as he approached them. 'I think so, captain.'

Throne, how Meryn hated the way Rawne said '*Captain*'.

'And it is?'

Beltayn looked up at Meryn, fiddling still with his caster dials. 'Something's awry.'

Meryn managed a smile. It had been a Throne-awful long time since he'd heard that refrain.

'Like what?' he asked.

'Mkoll's in trouble,' Feygor rasped, his voice issuing flat and bald out of his metal throat-box.

'How the feth can you know that?' Meryn asked. 'Come on, Tanith. We're meant to be setting in at the top of this fething hill and–'

'Mkoll's in trouble,' Rawne repeated. He stared at Meryn. 'Beltayn tells me so. How much more do you need?'

Meryn squared up to the major. 'I need to know,' he said, 'why you think that. I need to know the details. Don't push me around, sir, I still have command here.'

Rawne gestured towards Beltayn. 'I'm getting static shunts, pulse, three after one,' Beltayn said, adjusting his set.

'It's just the atmospherics,' Meryn said. 'Wilder just warned us about that. Solar radiation. It's just futzing the link.'

'No, sir,' Beltayn said. 'It's a signal.'

'Oh, come on now, please, we've–'

Meryn shut up quickly as Rawne grabbed him by the lapels. 'Listen to him, you little jumped-up fethwipe,' Rawne snarled. 'It's a signal we learned on Gereon.'

'What?'

'Pulse three after one. That was our signal for trouble. Back on Gereon, my young friend, we often didn't have full gain vox. We had to improvise. Pulsing static, shunting vox burps. Three after one was the signal for trouble.'

Meryn pulled himself away from Rawne. 'Is that true, Beltayn?' he asked.

'Yes, it's true,' the vox officer replied.

'All right, all right,' Meryn said. 'Maybe I can spare a couple of troops to head east. Maybe.'

'Do it quick, or I'll tell Banda you let the chief hang out to dry,' Rawne said.

'You bastard.'

'Yeah, yeah, whatever.'

'It's coming again,' Beltayn called, working his set.

THREE PULSES, THEN ONE. It was hard to manage on the run. Mkoll had torn off his microbead and split the plastek casing open so that he could trigger the vox-send key manually. Finger and thumb.

Three, then one. Just the way they had done back on Gereon. Improvisation. It created a hell of a lot of inter-ference, binding out the main vox channels, but Mkoll knew it was worth it.

Three, then one.

The recon team scattered through the undergrowth of the basin. Buckren was already dead, and Hwlan had been hit so badly he was limping and falling behind.

Into the dense vegetation, the Blood Pact chasing them, weapons firing. Clinking and clanking, the stalk-tanks scurried in pursuit, their gun-mounts blasting into the thickets, spraying out leaves and charred bark.

Three, then one.

Three, then one.

'COLONEL WILDER?' vox officer Keshlan said.

'Yes?'

'I'm getting reports, sir.'

'Of what?'

'I'm not sure, sir… Uh, it seems that C and E compa-nies have turned east.'

'They've *what*?'

Keshlan shrugged. 'Like I said, I'm not sure, sir. They seem to have turned east, both of them.'

'They realise that they're supposed to be on that hill right now?' Wilder asked.

'Yes, sir. I've spoken to both Kolea and Meryn. They apologise. But they're heading east.'

Wilder held out his right hand and slapped the fingers against the palm repeatedly. 'Give me that vox horn, mister. Give it to me right now.'

EIGHTEEN

06.59 hrs, 197.776.M41
Fifth Compartment
Sparshad Mons, Ancreon Sextus

THE RECON TEAM ran clear of the gloomy basin into the pale, misty daylight. The ground ahead was barren, a flinty slope of sedge and thin gorse. Blazing las-bolts followed them out of the thickets, whining in the cold air.

'Cover would be good,' Kolosim said, almost casually.

Mkoll pointed. Five hundred metres up the open slope, the land levelled slightly, and there were what appeared to be boulders or part of a wall.

'That'll do!' Kolosim agreed. They started running. Hwlan fell behind again, limping and stumbling. Mkoll tossed his rigged microbead to Bonin. 'Keep sending!' he ordered, and ran back to the wounded scout. Hwlan was a good deal taller and heavier than Mkoll, but the Tanith chief scout didn't hesitate. He stooped, grabbed Hwlan around one thigh with his left hand, and hoisted him up over his shoulders. Then he started running towards the promised cover.

'Ditch me…' Hwlan gasped.

'Shut up,' Mkoll grunted, taking quick, short steps, trying not to fall. Several powerful las-bolts hit the dirt nearby, coughing up powder ash and dust. A couple more hissed past.

Kolosim and Bonin had reached the litter of rocks. It proved to be the ruin of one of the Mons's curious house structures. This particular relic was beyond the hope of reconstruction: little more than a plan of the walls that had once stood there, sketched out in rubble amid the patchy grass. In places, enough of the walls remained for them to kneel behind. Kolosim and Bonin leapt the ragged stones and took position, firing back down the slope to cover the others. Maggs joined them, then Caober. Mkoll and his burden were still a little way back.

'Come on!' Kolosim yelled. 'Come on!'

The first of the pursuers had broken from the dense undergrowth behind them. At least a dozen Blood Pact troopers, their heavy kit and battle plating rattling as they ran up the slope, began firing their weapons from the hip.

'Pick 'em off!' Kolosim roared.

The four scouts in cover started blasting single shots. Las-bolts whickered up and down the slope, crosshatching the air. Caober hit one of the Blood Pact in the chest and walloped him heavily down on his back, then immediately hit a second of the enemy number in the head. The shot exploded the trooper's leering black iron mask and sent pieces of it spinning away as the man toppled onto his front. Kolosim got another, who fell down in a sitting position, clutching his throat, before he slumped over backwards. Maggs and Bonin managed to kill the same target.

'There's a waste,' said Maggs grimly, resighting and blasting again.

Bonin made no reply. He tapped another pulse on the microbead, then took up his weapon again and dropped two more of the enemy troopers.

Mkoll reached the ruin. Kolosim and Maggs threw down their rifles and grabbed him and Hwlan, hauling them in over the wall. Shots smacked into the stones.

Hwlan cried out in pain as he landed. He'd been shot in the right hip, and in the side of the torso just above it.

'I've got him!' Maggs yelled, his head low as he went to work. Kolosim and Mkoll joined Bonin and Caober at the wall, and started firing. A great deal more Blood Pact infantry had begun to spill out of the undergrowth behind the front runners. Three, four dozen, perhaps more. Some ran forward, others dropped to their knees, or onto their bellies, and started loosing aimed shots. Las-bolts filled the air like sleet.

Maggs yanked open one of his webbing pouches and pulled out his field kit, spilling paper-wrapped dressing wads onto the ground.

'Hold on, you hear me?' he murmured at Hwlan. Hwlan, on his back and going into hypovolaemic shock, nodded weakly, his face drawn and pale with pain.

Maggs ripped open the leg of Hwlan's fatigue trousers and loosened the scout's webbing belts. The wounds were messy. The flesh had burned and cauterised, the usual consequence of super-hot energy hits, but the concussive impact had ruptured the flesh and caused severe secondary bleeding. Hwlan's skin was sickly white and beginning to bruise. Maggs's hands became slick with blood.

'Hold on,' Maggs said again. 'Hwlan? Hwlan! Don't you grey out on me! Hwlan!'

'I'm here, I'm here!' Hwlan insisted, snapping back awake. 'Feth, Wes, it hurts.'

'No, really?' Maggs was washing the wounds with counterseptic gel. 'Come on, stay with me. Talk to me.'

'What about?'

'Tell me something. Anything. Tell me about your first time.'

'What, getting shot?'

'No, you dipstick. Your first time with a girl.' Maggs had packed adhesive dressing across both injuries, and was now using Hwlan's belt to tourniquet his leg around the groin.

'Hwlan?'

'What?'

'Your first girl.'

'Oh. Her name was Seba.'

'Sabre? Like a sword?'

'No. No. Seba. Feth, she was sweet. Oww!'

'Sorry. It's got to be tight.' Maggs wiped his hands on his jacket and pulled the cap off a single-use plastek syringe.

'Seba, eh? Was she any good?'

'I don't know. Yes. I was only sixteen. I didn't know what I was doing.'

Maggs stabbed the needle into the meat of Hwlan's thigh. 'Story of my life,' he said. 'Hwlan?'

'Uhn. Yeah.'

'The shot should take the edge off the pain, but you might get a little woozy. I've got another shot if you need it.' Each of them carried a field kit with two doses of painkiller, but the medicaes never advised using more than one at a time.

'I feel better already.'

'Good. I got to get to it now. You lie here and don't move.'

'Prop me up by the wall. I can fire my weapon.'

'Oh, be quiet. You a hero now, too? Shut up and lie there.'

Maggs crawled back to the wall. 'What did I miss?' he asked.

'Just another highlight of life in the poor fething Guard,' Caober said, snapping off shots.

Maggs looked down the slope at the distressingly large number of enemy troopers massing there. Between them, the scouts had killed more than twenty, littering the patchy soil with the jumbled bodies. But more than a hundred were now shooting their way up the slope towards the ruin. The density of las and hard rounds flying up at the scouts was frightening.

'How's Hwlan?' Mkoll asked, between shots.

'Stable,' Maggs replied. 'At this rate, he'll outlive us.'

An explosion just beyond the wall line tossed grit and soil into the air. The Blood Pact warriors were starting to hurl stick grenades, though they were falling short. Kolosim saw one Blood Pact trooper rise, arm back to throw, and put a las-round into his chest. The warrior fell, and a second later the four or five troopers around him were knocked flat by the blast of his grenade. Two more grenades dropped in front of the wall and flung dirt and flame up.

Bonin grunted as a las-round sawed across his right shoulder.

'Mach?' Caober called.

'I'm all right. Just scratched me,' Bonin replied, though in truth his shoulder throbbed like it had been struck by a red-hot sledgehammer.

Another shot, a hard slug, exploded part of the wall top and ricocheted off into Kolosim's face. He staggered backwards, blood pouring from his mouth. The deformed bullet had torn his upper lip and philtrum. Spitting out blood, he continued shooting.

'I don't like the sound of that,' Bonin said suddenly. Maggs cocked his head. 'No, me neither,' he agreed.

The first stalk-tank lumbered out of the undergrowth, trailing vines and brambles from its spidery legs. Behind it came a second one. The Blood Pact sent up a fierce cheer.

The sound of the cheer roused Hwlan from his stupor. 'Are we winning?' he asked.

Maggs and Caober laughed. Even Bonin cracked a grin.

'No,' said Mkoll sadly. 'I don't think we are, this time.'

Striding forward, the stalk-tanks began to fire.

'BASKEVYL!' WILDER SHOUTED into the vox. 'You've got command, you hear me?'

'Reading you, Eighty leader.'

'Form up the defence here and get this hill secure. Don't take any shit from anyone.'

'Understood. What's going on? Where are you?'

'No time to explain. Get on with it.'

Wilder tossed the speaker horn back to his vox-man. 'Follow me,' he ordered, and set off down the slope, heading east. 'And patch me to Meryn, Kolea or Rawne. Any of them. Immediately.'

'Yes, sir.'

The pair of them were running cross-country, against the tide of advancing men. 'Keep moving up the hill! Keep moving!' Wilder yelled at the troops as he pushed through. 'Novobazky!'

The commissar, marshalling squads near the foot of the hill, turned at the sound of his name.

'Yes, colonel.'

'Come with me.'

Novobazky hurried over and ran along with Wilder and Keshlan. 'What's going on?'

'In a nutshell, Rawne. We've got two companies breaking formation and heading east.'

'What? Why?'

'Like I said, I think this is Rawne's doing. Why the hell did he have to come back?'

'I wasn't going to mention it, sir, but he gave me some crap first thing this morning.'

'Then you've got my permission to shoot the bastard.'

The three of them were out in the empty scrub land now, pressing away from the Guardsmen deployed on the hillside. Wilder had to slow down to let the heavily-laden vox-man keep up.

'Major Rawne, sir,' Keshlan reported, panting. The three men stopped and Wilder took the horn.

'Rawne? This is Wilder. What the hell is going on?'

'We've got a situation, sir,' Rawne's voice came back. 'Contact from the missing recon unit. They've run into trouble.'

'What kind of trouble?'

'Can't say. The contact was non-verbal.'

'It was what?'

'Emergency pulse code, improvised. I know it's Mkoll. I know the code.'

'Rawne, I'm fit to choke you with your own genitals. What the hell happened to chain of command? Why in the name of the Golden Throne did you not run this by me?'

'No time, sir. This was priority.'

Wilder lowered the horn from his mouth for a second. 'That bastard's going to be the death of me,' he told Novobazky. 'I can just about imagine him pushing Meryn into this, but what the frig is up with Kolea? I thought that man was sound.'

'Old loyalties,' Novobazky said. 'This Mkoll, he's a pretty big deal to the Ghosts. Almost as big a deal as Gaunt, as I understand it.'

'And what am I? Dried rations? This is no way to run an army. I'll have them all up on charges. *You'll* have them all up on charges. Things are hard enough without these idiots…' He trailed off, shut his eyes, and cursed.

'Rawne?' he said, trying to inject a little calm and control into his voice as he raised the speaker horn again. 'Where are you?'

'Moving south-east of Hill 55, towards Ridge 19.'

'Find it,' Wilder told Novobazky, who pulled out his chart and began examining it.

'And where do you think the recon unit is?'

'Somewhere near the ridge. There's a lowland ahead. We can hear shooting. Heavy gunfire.'

'Rawne, I'm heading to join you. When you know anything for certain, tell me. And do not, repeat *do not* engage without my express permission. Wilder out.'

'Come on,' he said to Novobazky and the vox-officer. They had to run to keep pace with him.

RAWNE PASSED THE vox horn back to Beltayn.

'What did he say?' Feygor asked.

'He's coming to join us,' Rawne said.

'What else did he say?' Meryn asked.

Rawne shrugged. 'I really don't remember. Atmospherics kept cutting him off.'

'You're lying,' Meryn said.

'Yes, but I outrank you, so live with it.'

They were moving as they talked. E Company was slogging double-time across the rough scrub. The body of C Company was about fifteen minutes behind them, to the north.

'Lot of shooting ahead,' Caffran called out. 'Down under the ridge, about half a kilometre. Serious exchanges.'

Rawne came to a halt. 'Give me a scope, someone.' One of the Belladon sergeants, Razele, handed Rawne a set of magnoculars. Rawne played them left and right.

'Feth,' he said. The swell of the land was obscuring much of the view, but Rawne could see a shroud of gun smoke leaking up into the sky, and serious back-flashes of lasfire. 'Caff wasn't kidding. Someone's started a little war down there in private.'

He handed the scope back. 'Line advance!' he shouted. 'Straight silver! Weapons live!'

There was an answering clatter as the company fixed their bayonets.

'I thought Wilder said we weren't to engage?' Meryn said.

'Meryn, if you know what he said, why the feth do you keep asking me?'

'Company ready, sir,' Feygor said.

'Let's get busy,' Rawne yelled. 'Company advance! For the Emperor and for Tanith!'

'What about Belladon?' Razele demanded.

'Screw Belladon,' Rawne told him. 'This is a family thing.'

THE DEVASTATING FIRE of the advancing stalk-tanks disintegrated another section of the ruined wall. Flame and stone debris showered into the sky. Crouching down, Mkoll, Kolosim and Bonin crawled back from what remained of the wall cover, still firing. Caober and Maggs dragged Hwlan between them.

A third stalk-tank had now emerged from the undergrowth. This one had an oversized head turret, like a deformity, and appeared to be armed with a plasma weapon or a multi-laser. With that in play, the game really would be done. Cheering and howling, the Blood Pact, now two hundred-strong, was on its feet, advancing at the pace of the rattling tanks. Two minutes, and they'd be at the wall.

'You're a piece of work,' Maggs said to Mkoll. 'I've known you about twenty-four hours and you get me into this shit.'

'Just think what I could do if I was really trying,' said Mkoll.

Another salvo hit the feeble barrier of stones, blowing a stretch of it onto them in a spray of stones and chipped fragments. Then the lead stalk-tank rose into view over the ruined wall, its gun-pod head lifted high on greasy hydraulics, smoke gusting from the exhaust vents of the heavy cannon.

There was a loud, sucking woosh of air and something screamed in low over the heads of the cowering scouts. It struck the stalk-tank squarely between the gimbal-joints of its front pair of legs and exploded. The entire forward section of the stalk-tank vapourised in a blinding orange blur. Concussive overpressure flattened the scouts into the soil.

Shrouded in smoke, coughing, they struggled back up.

'All right,' said Kolosim. 'Which of you jokers had a rocket launcher in his pocket all along?'

'Eighty-First First!' Maggs yelled out. 'Eighty-First First!' He was pointing back into the open country behind them.

'Holy feth,' said Caober.

The soldiers of E Company were yelling as they came charging in around either side of the house. The cry they made was incoherent, but the intent, the passion, unmistakable. Warriors of the Imperium, blood up, with the enemy in sight. The scouts saw the flash of fixed blades against the dark battledress of the running figures.

'Now that's a sight,' said Bonin.

THERE WOULD BE no time for finesse, Rawne realised. This was going to be a pitched battle in the antique sense of the word, infantry line against infantry line. There was no cover, no terrain for ranged fighting, and no room for flanking moves. Face to face, hand to hand, the way wars used to be fought.

E Company had the slope on their side. They poured over the rim of it, running towards the enemy, firing shots from weapons that they were brandishing like spears. The Blood Pact seemed to balk en masse, as if they could not quite understand what was happening. Those at the top of the slope froze in dismay, those further back hesitated because they couldn't see what was coming.

The lines struck with a visceral, crunching impact of bodies, helmets and battle-plating. The sounds of shooting, shouting and striking became frenetic.

Caffran and Guheen ran into the ruin with the scouts. Both were lugging launcher tubes. Dunik followed, carrying a drum of rockets.

'Welcome to my world,' Caober said to Guheen.

'That your handiwork?' Bonin asked Caffran, who was loading up another rocket.

Caffran glanced at the headless stalk-tank smouldering beyond the wall. 'Yes. Bit of a risk at the range I had, but I thought you'd appreciate the effort.'

Guheen had already shouldered his tread-fether and taken aim at the second tank. 'Ease!' he yelled. The men around him opened their mouths to help with the discomfort of the pressure punch. Guheen's tread-fether barked out a hot backwash of flame and spat a rocket into the shoulder of the second tank. It shook with the impact, badly damaged but still active.

'Load me!' Guheen shouted to Dunik.

Caffran was crouching by the wall with his own tube. 'Ease!' he warned, and fired. His streaking rocket hit the second tank and finished the work Guheen had begun. The main body section blew apart with huge force, probably helped by the detonation of the tank's own munitions, and dozens of the Blood Pact around it were roasted in the firewash.

'Aim for the third tank,' Mkoll told Caffran. The formidable plasma mount had opened up, slicing beam-energy mercilessly into the ranks of E Company. The air was suddenly ripe with the smell of cooked blood and bone.

Rockets squealed out from several points in the E Company spread. A Belladon trooper called Harwen scored the winning shot. The third tank went up, its oversized head spinning away, decapitated, still firing plasma beams wildly like a firecracker as it bounced amongst the Blood Pact lines.

Rawne and Feygor were right in the thick of it, lost in the punching, whirling, deafening violence of the fight. Rawne shot those he could shoot, and smashed his bayonet into those who were too close. The last proper action he'd seen had been back during the last days on Gereon, and he'd briefly forgotten the way killing had come to feel. This slaughter quickly reminded him.

Once, combat had been about pride and fury for Elim Rawne, the honest, hot-blooded endeavour of a fighting infantry man. Such a romantic notion, that seemed to him now. He recalled Gaunt and Colm Corbec debating the styles and types of combat, as if it came in different flavours or intensities, like love or sleep.

Today, his blood was cold, his pulse barely elevated. His blood was always cold. Gereon had done that to him. On Gereon, every single fight, from the full-blown open battles to the savage blade-brawls of infiltration missions, had been about survival, merciless survival, totally undressed of sentiment, honour or quarter. He'd learned to use everything, every opening, every advantage. He kicked, stabbed, crushed, stamped, bit and gouged; he ripped his straight silver into backs and sides and buttocks, he'd butchered men who had already fallen wounded, or who had turned to run.

Rawne had never been a particularly honourable man, but now his soul was cold and hollow, utterly devoid of honour or courage. Fighting had simply become a mechanical absolute; it no longer had degrees. Rawne either fought or did not fight, killed or did not kill. Combat's purpose had been reduced to a point where it was simply a way to ensure he was still alive when everything around him was dead. He had no use for caution, no use for fear.

Feygor, fighting at his commander's back, was much the same. Death was no longer something he feared. It was something he used, a gift he dished out to those that opposed him. Death was just a tool, an instrument. The only thing Murt Feygor was afraid of any more was being afraid.

Near to them, struggling in the melee, Meryn became aware of the sheer fury he was witnessing. It took his breath away to see the two men, so completely unchecked by fear. When Mkoll and Bonin broke through the scrum of bodies to lay in beside Rawne and his adjutant, Meryn faltered completely and backed away. He hated the archenemy with a passion, but his own courage and intent seemed to leak away when he saw the Blood Pact broken apart by these daemons.

Daemons. *Daemons*! Not Ghosts at all. Not even human.

THE BLOOD PACT broke. Engulfed and overwhelmed, surprised by a foe it had not expected to meet, it scattered back towards the deep cover of the basin. E Company, enflamed by Rawne's brittle fury and example, gave chase.

Meryn limped back up towards the smoking stones of the house. He'd taken a gash in the knee somewhere along the line, he couldn't remember how. The ground was carpeted with bodies, the vast majority of them crimson-clad Blood Pact. Steam rose like mist. The air was clammy and smelled like a butcher's hall.

In the house ruin, and along the ridge beside it, E Company teams were setting up crew-served weapons. Leclan, the corpsman, was treating Hwlan. Maggs and Caober had vanished into the fight. Kolosim was sitting against a pile of stones, a dressing pressed to his torn mouth.

'What's the matter with you?'

Meryn glanced round. Banda had been using part of the stone wall as a sniper nest, but the enemy was out of range now.

'Nothing,' he said.

'Are you just going to let him do that?' she asked, stripping out her long-las to take a fresh barrel.

'Do what?'

'Just come in and take over. Last I heard, you were E Company's commander.'

Meryn sat down on part of a stalk-tank's buckled undercarriage. He tore off his helmet and threw it on the ground.

'It's Rawne,' he said.

'So what?' she asked.

'You think I could have done this?'

'You give the order, captain, E Company jumps,' Banda said.

He really wasn't enjoying her tone. 'Jessi,' he said, 'if it had been up to me, I wouldn't have even broken us east. Rawne recognised the signal, I didn't.'

'Wilder's going to be pissed.'

'I know.'

'You want Rawne to get E Company?' Banda asked.

'He'll be up on charges for this.'

'You think, Flyn?' she asked. 'You really think so?' Jessi Banda's face was unusually beautiful and expressive, but when she got angry, it became ugly and repellent to Meryn. 'Take a look, Flyn. Take a long look,' she said, gesturing down the body-littered slope towards the dark basin. E Company was near the line of undergrowth now, picking off the enemy troopers as they tried to escape.

'Rawne just picked up on a counter-offensive and squashed it flat. Wilder may have words with him, but that's a commendation in the eyes of high command. Maybe a pretty medal.'

'So what?'

'So you just stood there and let him do it,' she said, getting to her feet and slamming a fresh hot-shot pack home.

'Something's happening,' Kolosim said abruptly, rising to his feet.

'You're right. They're coming back,' Leclan agreed, getting up from beside Hwlan.

Meryn turned. Down the long slope, E Company was suddenly pulling back. Heavy fire was driving them into reverse out of the undergrowth. Plasma fire, lancing beams of blistering force.

Meryn realised he was smiling, despite the situation. Rawne had taken a big bite, and it had proved too big. The Blood Pact force Mkoll's scouts had alerted them too was a great deal bigger than they'd first imagined.

'Shit,' said Kolosim again, coming to stand beside Meryn. 'We thought it was a small strike brigade. They must have been pushing a whole frigging army along the east side.'

Meryn took a deep breath and reached for his dangling microbead. Now he could take charge and settle in a proper defence. Now he could make Rawne look like an impulsive idiot for–

'We heard there was a party. Are we too late?'

Meryn looked around. Gol Kolea calmly strolled up beside him. Behind him, C Company had fanned out in a wide line, covering the top of the slope. Support-weapon teams were assembling their pieces.

'Fix your silver,' Kolea called out, casually.

His words were answered by a clatter.

'Looking good, digger,' Banda called out to Kolea with a cheeky grin.

'I always look good, girl,' he called back. 'C Company! Get your act together. Let Rawne's people come back to us and then we'll get busy.'

Rawne's people. Meryn glared at Kolea.

'Come on, C Company!' Kolea was shouting. 'Let's get some torches up to the front.'

Brostin, Lyse, Mkella and a Belladon called Frontelle hurried forward out of the C Company line, their heavy flamer tanks clanking.

'I spy undergrowth,' Kolea said. 'It looks flammable to me. What do you say, Bros?'

Brostin smiled. The last stub of a lho-stick dangled from the corner of his mouth. He reeked of promethium, as if he'd been bathing in it.

'I say good morning flammable undergrowth, sir. Just say the word.'

'Heat 'em up,' Kolea said.

Brostin moved forward, trudging down the long slope. 'Line up on me, torches, wide spacing,' he called out. 'Fat-blue, wide-wash, keep it near the ground. And keep your pressure up.'

Lyse, Mkella and Frontelle came forward with him, adjusting their regulators. The stink of promethium jelly was now sharp and acute.

'Hey, Larks!' Brostin called out as he went forward. Larkin emerged from the C Company line, toting his long-las. The Belladon, Kaydey, came with him.

'Yeah?'

'Little airburst special?' Brostin said.

Larkin nodded. 'Whatever makes you happy.' He toggled off his long-las and shook out his shoulders, following the flame-troopers down the slope.

'What are we doing?' Kaydey asked him.

'I'm taking a shot,' Larkin said. 'You're watching and learning.'

'Hey, sniper,' Banda said as Larkin walked past her.

'Hey yourself, doll,' Larkin replied, smacking hands with her.

'Go do some hurt,' she called.

'I intend to,' Larkin replied, snuggling his long-las up into his shoulder as he walked forward, like a game-keeper seating his shotgun.

E Company was coming back up the slope. It wasn't so much a retreat as a survival measure. Whatever was massing in the undergrowth behind them was angry and well-armed.

The C Company flamers, tooling down the slope in a wide spread formation, as if they were on a country walk, met the men of E coming back up. Rawne, spat-tered with blood, came up to Brostin.

'Good to see you,' he said.

'Trouble, major?' Brostin asked.

'The hostiles we just minced were only the forward section of something a lot bigger. They're right behind us and about to come calling.'

Brostin nodded. 'Fine. Mister Yellow is at home for visitors,' he replied. 'Got a smoke on you, boss?'

'Feygor?' Rawne called.

Feygor hurried over and pulled out a pack of lho-sticks. With the troops of E Company flooding past back towards the top of the slope, Feygor drew a stick out and posted it into Brostin's mouth.

Brostin lifted his flamer gun up and lit the stick off the blue pilot flame sizzling beside his weapon's regu-lator. Bubbles of promethium were dripping from his torch's hoses.

'Ah, yes,' Brostin said. 'That draws nice. A fine brand, Mister Feygor.'

'Only the best,' Feygor smiled.

Brostin exhaled. 'Flamers? Let's get this done.'

As the last tail-enders of E Company ran back past them, the flame-troopers plodded down the slope, spreading wider. The tanks on their backs were gurgling and sputtering, and their pilot flames hissing. Larkin, his gun half-raised, tailed them, Kaydey behind him.

Twenty metres from the edge of the undergrowth, Brostin brought his team to a halt. He took a flamboyant drag on his smoke and then flicked it away.

'Wait for a heartbeat,' he called out. 'Let's see their faces.'

Blood Pact troopers began to emerge from the edges of the undergrowth cover. They raised a cry, a howl. Weapons cracked and barked. Behind them, machine noise betrayed the approach of more stalk-tanks.

'All right,' said Brostin. 'That's enough faces. Cook 'em. Fat-blue, wide-wash, keep it near the ground. Let's do it.'

The four flame-troopers triggered their weapons and sent searing plumes of fire down the slope. Caught in the sudden inferno, the front line of the Blood Pact shrieked and staggered, enveloped. A moment later, the edges of the dried undergrowth caught too. A mess of flames boiled up the basin, storming and furious.

Brostin squeezed his flamer's paddle gently, nursing out gouts of liquid flame. 'Easy does it,' he urged.

The hem of the undergrowth was a blitz of fire now. Screams and shrieks rang out of the furnace. Several Blood Pact troopers emerged, stumbling, encased in fire.

'Now, that's real nice,' Brostin said.

Something big exploded in the undergrowth – a stalk-tank's munitions cooking off – and the fire spread.

Brostin shrugged off his flamer tanks and glanced at Larkin. 'Larks?' he said.

'I'm ready,' Larkin replied, raising his weapon. Brostin uncoupled his feeder tubes and dropped his gun.

'Wind it up,' Larkin said. He and Brostin had pulled the 'airburst special' more than once back on Gereon.

Brostin was a big, hulking man with a heavy upper body. He began to turn slowly, picking up speed as he rotated, like a hammer thrower. His flamer tanks were in his right hand, spinning out as a counter weight.

With a grunt of effort, he released them, and the heavy prom tanks flew up into the air over the basin undergrowth. Larkin tracked them, and, as they began to dip, he fired.

The hot-shot round smacked into the pressurised tanks and ignited them. A torrential rain of liquid fire fell across the basin and brought it up in searing flames.

'Holy crap,' Kaydey said.

Brostin turned away from the crackling heat of the firestorm in the basin. The screams and popping explosions drifted back with the smoke.

'Say hello to Mister Yellow,' he said.

A THICK BELT of black smoke was climbing into the sky when Wilder reached the scene of the battle. Keshlan sat down to catch his breath. Novobazky wandered in beside Wilder, gazing at the litter of the fight.

C and E Companies had taken up a heavy defensive position facing Ridge 19. A large portion of the lowland countryside was on fire.

'The God-Emperor protect us...' Wilder said, surveying the devastation. Kolea approached and threw a salute.

'I want full details, including casualties, later, Kolea. Right now, the short version.'

'Kolosim's recon party picked up hostiles in the woods thataway. E Company moved in and pretty much crushed them before we got here.'

'This would be the E Company that I ordered specifically not to engage without my permission?'

'I'm guessing yes, sir.'

'Go on, Kolea.'

'But the hostiles were just part of a much larger force.'

'How large?'

'Eight, nine hundred troops, maybe more, with stalk-tank support. The enemy was definitely out to mount a major offensive through the difficult terrain in the east compartment while our attention was on the tank fight.'

Wilder nodded. 'And you've held them?'

'Flamers did a lot of damage. Drove them back. We assume they're either in retreat, or they're waiting to come at us along the ridge there.'

Wilder looked around. 'Understand me, Kolea. You, Meryn, Rawne and I will be having a serious talk about this later. I know it's going to be hard for me to tear you off a strip when the results are this good, but believe me, this will be settled.'

'Yes, sir.'

'You stay in my command, you follow my orders, or I throw you to the commissars.'

'Yes, sir.'

Wilder walked over to Keshlan. 'Get me post command,' he said to the vox-man. 'We'd better tell DeBray that the enemy's just gone proactive on us.'

'Not just here, sir,' Keshlan said. 'From the reports coming in, the whole Mons has gone crazy.'

NINETEEN

THE SOUND OF gunship engines woke Gaunt from a curious dream. Dawn had come, grey and damp, and a cold wind flapped the seams of the habi-tent. Ludd was still sound asleep, but Eszrah was crouching in the flapway of the tent, looking out into the camp. There was a lot of activity out there. Trucks and transporters were revving, and men were shouting. Another squadron of Vulture gunships droned low overhead, snouts down, heading into the north-east and the bleak morning.

Gaunt stepped past Eszrah, who rose to follow him. Gaunt shook his head, and motioned that the Nihtgane should stay where he was.

He went outside into the billet area. Most of the habi-tents around had already been vacated. There really was a hell of a lot of activity going on. Gaunt pulled his shirt and vest off over his head and walked to the standpipe of the nearest service bowser. He cranked the pump handle, and sluiced out cold water to wash his armpits, his neck, and his face.

More attack ships went over, Valkyries this time. Gaunt stood upright and shook the water off his face like a dog as he watched the gunships slide past. Twenty of them, then another fan of at least thirty. Their combined engine noise was deafening.

Something about them, or about the cold, grey sky behind them, reminded Gaunt of his dream. He'd been in a room, a small, oblong room, with a door in each of the shorter walls. The room had been open to the sky, lacking a roof. Every time he'd looked up, he'd been able to see a vast stretch of wild heavens, deep and florid with banks of cloud that were ominously edged with a fiery russet.

In the dream, Gaunt had been aware of a deep compulsion to get out of the room. Some odd part of the dream's internal logic told him that if he didn't leave the roofless room, he wouldn't be able to do any good. Any good at what, the dream wasn't particularly bothered to identify.

But every time he walked towards one of the doors, it was no longer there. The doors wouldn't stay put. He'd move towards a door, and suddenly it would be in another wall.

For a few weeks on Gereon, early on, he'd been plagued by a recurring dream where he'd been stuck in a stone chamber that had no doors or windows. It had bothered him deeply, scared him, back at a time when he still could be scared. The claustrophobia, the sense of imprisonment, had lingered on him each morning, long after he'd woken. Ana Curth had told him it was simply an anxiety dream, a nightmare about being trapped on Gereon. After a few weeks, it had passed.

This new dream didn't scare him, but it left him with an unsettled sensation that fed uncomfortably into his current troubles.

Gaunt was pulling his vest and shirt back on when Ludd appeared, bleary-eyed.

'What's going on, sir?' he asked.

'I don't know. Something big. I'll go and see Sautoy. I have to report to him, after all.'

They'd arrived back late the previous night after their bloody encounter on the road. Ironmeadow had wanted to file a full report at once, but Gaunt had told him to get some sleep. He'd assured the captain he'd make his damning report about post 15 in the morning.

'I'll come with you,' Ludd said.

'No. Stay here and get some caffeine brewed. We both need some. I'll be back soon.'

GAUNT PUT ON his coat and cap, and headed down the truckway to post command. There was activity all around. Young troopers, their faces pale and anxious, were boarding transporters or loading munitions onto cargoes and armoured cars. A line of Chimeras grumbled past. The sky was overcast and grim, and there was a real wind picking up. It was hard to tell, but Gaunt was sure he could hear heavy, booming blasts echoing from far away.

Post command was busy. The place was heaving with officers and tacticae advisors, message runners and technicians. Briefings were underway in some of the side chambers, and a constant flow of shouted updates rang from the bustling vox station.

Gaunt pushed inside. There was a smell of fear. Stale sweat, morning breath, the ugly odour of men who had been living in the field and now had been roused early, unwillingly, to face a cold, unfriendly day. Faces were pinched, troubled, unfriendly. The younger men in particular looked like a slow horror was dawning on them.

Sautoy was in the station command room. He looked harried and bothered. The start of his day had evidently been so brusque that he hadn't even had time to pin his handsome collection of medals to his purple coat. Officers had gathered around his chart table, and Sautoy was throwing orders and directives left and right as he sorted through an increasing pile of status forms and message papers that the runners were bringing in from the vox-station.

'Gaunt!' he called as he saw the commissar in the doorway. No false bonhomie this morning. 'Come in. I just sent Ironmeadow to find you.'

'I must have crossed him on the way,' Gaunt said. 'It's busy out there.'

Gaunt stepped inside and took off his cap. Half a dozen of the junior officers around the marshal's chart table hurried out to get on with their orders. The others remained, bent over the table in a serious huddle, conferring and pointing out various details on the underlit map image.

'I wanted to file a report, sir,' Gaunt began. 'My visit to post 15 yesterday. Serious code violations led me to–'

Sautoy held up his hand. 'I know all about it, Gaunt. Ironmeadow came to see me last night.'

'I see.'

'He was shaken, Gaunt. Understandably. What you found there was vile.'

'Symptomatic of an underlying–'

'It's academic now, anyway, Gaunt.'

'Why, sir?'

'Because a total crap-storm broke about two hours ago, Gaunt. Post 15's gone. Twelve's maybe about to fall too. The archenemy has decided, this morning, to mount a full scale counter-offensive.'

He led Gaunt over to the chart table. It took Gaunt very little time to make sense of the markers and deployments on display.

'Significant enemy forces struck through compartments seven and nine just before first light,' Sautoy said anyway. 'They stormed out of the ninth compartment and overran post 15. Our forces there abandoned the site rather hastily. They've also pushed us entirely out of the seventh compartment. We're currently throwing everything we've got into this compartment to try and establish some resistance in the lowland sector here, behind post 12. Trouble is, as it stands, post 12 is pretty much cut off and taking the brunt of both advances. We've had no contact with them for thirty-eight minutes.'

Sautoy beckoned Gaunt away from the junior officers and lowered his voice. 'We've not seen anything on this scale since we first chased the bastards into this step-city. It's barely credible that they've got such resources built up in here. Our boys are rattled. Seriously rattled, and on the back foot. There's a real danger we could get pushed right back out of the third compartment unless we rally soon.'

A vox-officer came in, saluted Sautoy and gave him a message wafer. Sautoy's face darkened as he read it. 'Throne above,' he whispered, and handed the slip to Gaunt. Post 36 in the fifth compartment was reporting a major enemy offensive too.

Gaunt sighed. He'd had a plan that morning. He'd intended, one way or another, to find a way of persuading Sautoy to allow him to transfer to fifth compartment operations. It was a long shot, and Sautoy was certainly no ally. Gaunt had already debated with himself at least a dozen possible excuses or reasons for the transfer, none of them satisfactory. He'd even considered contacting Van Voytz and going over Sautoy's head. But now this had happened, and everything, as Sautoy had remarked, was academic. There was no point even asking.

Gaunt did, anyway.

'I'd like to request permission to transfer to the fifth compartment, sir,' he said.

Sautoy blinked. 'Out of the question, man. Why would you even ask that?'

Gaunt paused. In the light of the current situation, he quickly decided which of his excuses sounded the most plausible. 'My old outfit, the Tanith First, is up in the Fifth, sir. If this is as bad as it sounds, I'd like to be with them and try–'

Sautoy shook his head. 'Admirable, Gaunt. Very admirable. Loyal. I like that. It's why I've always liked you. But the answer's still no. I need you here, for Throne's sake. I need you right here, you and every experienced cadre officer I've got. I want you forward in the line as soon as possible. Intelligence says the greener regiments, especially those falling back from 15, are in total disarray. We have to rally these young men, and that'll take veterans like yourself.'

'I understand, sir.'

'Get into the field and start whipping those boys back into shape. Get them forming up a proper line of resistance. I'll be sending all the officers I can forward to help get the situation under control.'

'Will… you be joining us, sir?' Gaunt asked.

Sautoy stared at him. 'Damn you, Gaunt. Of course I will. Now get about it.'

Gaunt saluted. 'My apologies, marshal. I intended no slight.' He turned for the door, then looked back at Sautoy. 'Why today, sir?'

'What?'

'Why is this happening today, I wonder?'

'I have no idea, Gaunt!' Sautoy snapped.

'Then you might want to relay that question back to Frag Flats Command and get the tacticae advisors thinking about it. Historically, ritually, there may be a reason the archenemy is stirring in such force this morning.'

GAUNT LEFT THE command room. Instead of heading outside, he pushed through the men hurrying to and fro along the internal corridor and entered the vox room. Twenty-five vox-officers worked at independent high-gain sets, all of them speaking at the same time as reports came in and went out.

Gaunt wandered to the nearest one. The operator, a small man with a pencil moustache, looked up and took off his heavy earphones.

'Commissar, can I help you?'

'I need you to patch me a link, operator,' Gaunt said.

'On what authority?' the officer asked.

'On the authority I'm wearing, soldier,' Gaunt said. The operator swallowed. 'Yes, sir. Sorry, sir.' Gaunt told him the comm-code he required. The operator tuned it in. He didn't look entirely comfortable.

'This is… non-standard, commissar,' he said as he adjusted the dials. 'It will have to be recorded in my day-book.'

'You do what you have to do,' Gaunt said. 'By all means note it was a direct order from the Commissariat.'

'I have contact, sir,' the operator reported. He indicated a spare set of headphones on the desk, and keyed the channel through as Gaunt put them on.

'Unit receiving,' said a voice on the line, cut by static. 'Identify sender, over.'

'This is One. That you, Beltayn, over?'

A pause. 'Yes. Yes, it is, sir. Didn't expect to hear your voice, over.'

'Sorry I don't have time to catch up, Bel,' Gaunt said. 'I need to talk to Rawne or Mkoll. That possible, over?'

'Stand by, over.' Gaunt waited, listening. Burbles and fluting wails of distortion echoed over the channel.

'This is Rawne. That you, Ibram, over?'

'Affirmative. What's the situation, over?'

'A fair mess, Bram. Hell in a handcart. Where are you, over?'

'Not as close as I'd like to be, Eli. Listen up. I've got very little time to explain this to you, but I need you and Mkoll working on something, over.'

'Copy that. We're a little busy right now, but go ahead, over.'

'All right. Listen to this, and tell me what you think…'

ONCE HE'D FINISHED the brief conversation, Gaunt handed the phones back to the vox-man, thanked him, and left the command post. The operator, a little bemused, wrote up the track in his day-book, and was about to resume his work when another voice said, 'May I see that, operator?'

The operator looked up and saw a second commissar standing by his caster set. What *was* this?

'Your day-book, please,' the second commissar said. The operator handed it to him. 'This was a confirmed patch?'

'Yes, sir.'

'Authority?'

'The commissar's own, sir. He said it was Commissariat business.'

'And this is authenticated? The code?'

'Yes, sir. A field vox-caster. Ident 11012K. That's with the Eighty-First First.'

'Patch me to Commissariat command, Frag Flats. Immediately, please. Use this code.' The commissar wrote a numeric serial down on the vox-man's message pad.

'Channel open,' the vox-officer announced a moment later.

The commissar picked up the speaker set. 'Command, this is Ludd. Put me through to Commissar-General Balshin.'

GAUNT RETURNED TO his billet.

'Where's Ludd?' he asked Eszrah. The Nihtgane shrugged.

'Get your stuff together,' Gaunt told him. 'We'll be leaving shortly.'

The wind was quite strong now. There seemed to be spots of rain in it. Gaunt touched his cheek where he'd felt the droplets land. Rain? The sky was a mass of crinkled grey cloud above the towering walls.

Ludd appeared, hurrying down the track between the habi-tents. Empty, they stood on either side of him like an honour guard, their door flaps rippling like cloaks in the rising air.

'Where did you go?' Gaunt asked him.

'I went looking for you, sir,' Ludd said.

'I told you to stay here, Ludd.'

'Yes, sir. I know. But Ironmeadow came by just after you'd left. He had transport placings for us. We're to move up because–'

'I know, Ludd. Where is he?'

'Waiting with our transportation, sir. So I came looking for you. I thought you'd want to know.'

Gaunt looked at him. Ludd seemed a little more tense than usual, but then this day was doing that to everyone. 'Where did you look, Ludd?'

'Oh, in the command station. Around there. One of the Binar officers said they'd seen you heading back this way.'

Gaunt held Ludd's gaze a little longer. 'All right, Ludd. Grab your things.'

They took only their weapons and basic field kit. Eszrah zipped the rest of their kit up in the habi-tent, and then hurried after Gaunt and Ludd.

The main assembly yards were packed with transports filing out along the east trackway. Most of the transports were carrying men dressed in the beige battledress of the Fortis Binars.

Ironmeadow waved them over to a pair of Salamander command vehicles, both of which had been newly painted in Binar livery.

'Sir!' Ironmeadow said, saluting and handing over a message wafer. 'The marshal asked me to find you and–'

'Old news, Ironmeadow, I've spoken with him.' Gaunt read the paper slip. It was a brief, curt order-tag requiring Gaunt to advance with the Second Binars into the hotzone, and 'accomplish the maintenance of decent battlefield morale and discipline.'

Gaunt handed the wafer to Ludd. 'Keep that for me, Ludd. If I get a chance later I may want to choke Sautoy with it.'

'You and your sense of humour, sir,' Ironmeadow laughed.

'Did you think I was joking, Ironmeadow?' Gaunt asked. Ironmeadow half-laughed again, then blinked.

Gaunt could tell how desperately scared the young officer was. He remembered how little combat experience Ironmeadow had – how little anyone of his regiment had. Sautoy was sending novice, frightened boys up country to assist novice, frightened boys. On top of that, Ironmeadow was most likely still very rattled by the events of the previous day.

Just for a moment, Gaunt reminded himself who and what they all thought he was. 'Things will be fine, Ironmeadow,' he said. 'Our spirits may be tested today, but if we keep our faith in the Throne and remember our training, we will prevail.'

'Yes, sir,' Ironmeadow nodded.

'Make it known that I regard it as a privilege to be advancing alongside the men of the Second Fortis Binars.'

That actually got a flush of pride into Ironmeadow's face. 'Thank you, sir. I will.'

One of the open-topped Salamanders had been reserved for Gaunt, with a driver, gunner and vox-operator assigned. The other belonged to Major Jernon Whitesmith, Ironmeadow's direct superior. He was a slender, craggy man in his fifties, with receding hair, and the look of a veteran about him.

'PDF?' Gaunt asked him as he was introduced. Whitesmith smiled, as if impressed that Gaunt should notice. 'Yes, sir. It was my honour to serve in the liberation war.'

In founding their regiments to assist the Crusade, the people of Fortis Binary had selected some of their planetary defence force veterans to serve as line officers. That was something at least, Gaunt mused. It would be the experience and steadiness of the few older men like Whitesmith that would keep the rookie companies together.

There was no time for further conversation.
Whitesmith climbed into his Salamander and set off
down the truckway, the vehicle's heavy track sections
clattering. Gaunt, Ludd and Eszrah followed
Ironmeadow aboard the second machine, and rattled
off after him, the light tanks skirting swiftly around the
column of slow-moving troop trucks on the road.
Heavier tanks and armour pieces formed the bulk of the
column's front portion, including Trojan tractor units
tugging heavy field artillery.

The inky grey storm clouds were firmly settled above
the compartment, leaching most of the daylight away.
Again, Gaunt felt the cold spits of rain in the air. It was
so overcast that many vehicles had activated their headlamps and running lights.

'Damned weather!' Ironmeadow said, raising his
voice over the roar of the Salamander's engines. 'It's getting as black as night out here!'

He's right, Gaunt thought. As black as night. Then he
wondered if anyone in high command or the senior
staff had considered just how *literally* nocturnal the
stalkers were.

LESS THAN AN hour later, powering north-east into the
middle lowlands of the third compartment, they met
hell coming the other way.

It was an astonishing sight. The scrubby, shelving
landscape that Gaunt and Ludd had driven up through
the previous day was masked with wind-driven smoke-
banks, great tidal waves of choking black soot and ash
that billowed off firestorms raging across the central
compartment. From wall to wall, it seemed that the
whole landscape was ablaze, except where it was broken
by the lakes and deep ponds, stretches of water that now

flashed back the reflected flame-light like mirrors. There were men and machines moving everywhere, not just on the trackways. Thousands of Guardsmen and a ramshackle multitude of vehicles were crawling back across country, chased by the firestorms.

As the Salamander slowed, Ludd got to his feet and stared out over the cabin top. He'd never seen anything like it.

The column was bunching up ahead. The relief forces from post 10 were coming up against the exodus from the north. There was panic and confusion. Over the Salamander's vox-caster, Gaunt could hear frantic chatter. Calls for help, calls for clarification, calls for orders. He knew the sound only too well. It was the sound of defeat. It was the terrible sound the Imperial Guard made when it fell apart.

'Post 12?' he asked the Salamander's vox operator. The man shook his head.

'Sir!' Ludd called out sharply. Gaunt joined him at the front of the Salamander's compartment and took up a scope. The ragged edge of the firestorms lay about three kilometres in front of them, and through it, the first enemy units had just emerged. Tanks, some churning fire, scrub and earth ahead of them with massive dozer blades; self-propelled guns, lurching out of the smoke; platoons of troops in rebreathers. Gaunt could see the flash of shells landing amongst the fleeing Imperial forces. He saw the bright surge-fires of the flamer weapons the Blood Pact was using to drive all before it. A quick estimate put the number of enemy vehicles at three hundred plus, and that was just what he could see. There was no telling the infantry strength.

'Throne, this is awful,' Ludd said.

'Nothing gets by you, eh, Nahum?' Gaunt replied. He jumped down from the Salamander and hurried on up the track on foot to the brow of the hill. There, Whitesmith stood in conference with some of his senior unit officers.

'Situation?' Gaunt asked.

'We've just had an unconfirmed report that Colonel Stonewright has been killed.' Stonewright was the Second Binar's commanding officer, who had led the support forces in an hour in front of them. Whitesmith's orders had been to move in to support him.

'That puts you in charge, Whitesmith,' Gaunt said. 'These men are waiting for your orders.'

Whitesmith straightened himself up, as if he'd only just realised that. 'Yes, commissar, of course.' He paused. 'I've called in for more air cover.'

'That's good. That's about the only advantage we have right now.'

Whitesmith gestured to his left. 'The bulk of our armour is down that way, though Throne knows it's hardly deployed properly. Beyond it, towards that lake, I think we've got auxiliary light armour, the Dev Hetra 301, but I've no idea what shape they're in.'

'Other side?' Gaunt asked, glancing south.

'The bulk of our infantry, and two columns of Sarpoy armour. See for yourself, though. It's a shambles.'

Whitesmith looked at Gaunt. 'I can't raise Marshal Sautoy. I can't even get a clean patch through to the Sarpoy or Dev Hetra commanders. And I'm afraid I can tell for a fact that my boys are close to breaking. They've had no experience of this. Line discipline has gone and–'

'Line discipline is my job, Major Whitesmith. Stop worrying whether the men will do as you tell them, and start worrying about what it is you're actually going to order them to do.'

Whitesmith shook his head. 'I believe I have two options on that score, sir. The first is to hand command to you.'

'Whitesmith, I'm a commissar, not a command officer. It's my place to advise, muster control and make sure orders are followed. It's not in my remit to decide strategy.'

Deep, rolling booms echoed in across the lowland floodplain. The enemy tanks were shelling with more fervour. 'With respect, Gaunt,' Whitesmith said soberly, 'you were a line officer and a commander for a long time. A successful, decorated commander. You've had a damn sight more experience of front-line engagement than me or any of my staff, and you've lived to carry that wisdom forward. For pity's sake, sir, I hardly think this is a moment to stick to some feeble rule of authority. Are you honestly going to stand by and watch while I struggle and lead these young men into a shambolic disaster?'

'No, major. In my capacity as an agent of the Imperial Commissariat, I am going to support you in the implementation of your command decisions. You were given your rank for a reason. You are an officer and a leader of men, and your training should tell you what to do under these circumstances.'

Whitesmith smiled sadly. 'Then there's the second option, commissar. My forces are in disarray. The enemy's right upon us. I must order an immediate retreat in order to salvage what lives and materiel I can.'

'What about a third option, major?' Gaunt said.

'Dammit, there is no–'

'There's always another option, Whitesmith!' Gaunt snapped. 'Think of one! You were kind enough to remember I was once a successful commander in war.

Do you think for a moment those successes came easily? That I never had to wrack my brains and think beyond the obvious? Tell me, quickly, what would you do if this was more to your liking?'

'What?'

'Ignore the immediate problems. Imagine you've got the Jantine Patricians here under your command, or a phalanx of Cadian Kasrkin. Battle-hardened veterans, ready and eager for your orders. What would those orders be, Whitesmith?'

'I'd...' Whitesmith began. 'I'd order them to hold this ridge line, and the open fen down to the lake there. That would give us the best defensive file.'

'Good. Go on.'

'I'd spread the infantry out, right along the line, and swing two squadrons of armour up over the ridge onto the right flank. I'd deploy artillery in the low land behind us and start shelling the enemy before they got any closer. And I'd make damn sure the Dev Hetra and Sarpoy understood that I needed their firm support.'

Gaunt smiled and smacked the Binar on the shoulder. 'That sounds like a plan to me, sir.'

'But–'

'Call up your officers. Finesse that plan for five minutes, get it solid and workable, make sure everyone knows what they're supposed to be doing.'

'Where will you be?' Whitesmith asked.

'Holding up my side of the bargain,' Gaunt replied, 'by making sure your orders are followed when they come.'

Gaunt hurried back down the dirt track to Ludd and Ironmeadow. Eszrah lurked behind them, gazing dubiously at the creeping curtain of fire and smoke approaching like doomsday across the scrubby landscape.

'Ironmeadow,' Gaunt said. 'Your services as a liaison are no longer required.'

'Sir?'

'Look about you, man. Whitesmith needs every officer he can get. Go to him, listen to him, obey him. You've got rank there, Ironmeadow. Use it. Give an example to your men and they will follow you. Whitesmith's counting on you.'

'Yes, sir!' Ironmeadow said.

'I know you're young and this is new to you, Ironmeadow, but I have faith. You faced down a stalker last night and lived to tell the tale.'

'Only because you saved my bloody life, sir,' Ironmeadow groaned.

'It doesn't matter. You've looked death in the eyes, and survived. That's more than any of these young men can say. That makes you special, tempered, like any good officer or fine piece of steel. It almost makes you a veteran. Strength of character, Captain Ironmeadow.'

Ironmeadow smiled.

'Tell every Binar you meet that Ibram Gaunt is with them, and Ibram Gaunt expects to be honoured by the company he keeps. And Ironmeadow?'

'Yes, sir?'

'I expect to read your name in despatches tomorrow, you hear me?'

'Yes, sir!' Ironmeadow replied, and ran up the slope to where Whitesmith was convening his officers.

'Ludd?' Gaunt said, turning to his junior. 'I want you to go find every commissar on this hillside and get them assembled here in the next ten minutes.'

'Sir?'

'The Binars have at least three, Ludd. Find them for me.'

Ludd hesitated. The sound of shelling was rolling ever closer. There were dark strands of smoke in the wind.

'What are you waiting for?'

'Nothing, sir. I'm on it.' Ludd hurried away.

With Eszrah at his heels, tall and ominous, Gaunt crossed the trackway to the left and hurried down a slope of patchy grass onto a muddy strand beside a long pool. Almost a hundred Binar troopers were gathered there, gazing at the oncoming horror. Behind them, several Binar treads had come to a halt, bottled up.

'You men!' Gaunt yelled. Some of them turned and straightened up at the sight of an approaching commissar.

'What the hell are you doing?' Gaunt demanded, splashing closer. There were a few, miserable answering grunts. Gaunt leapt up onto a limestone boulder at the edge of the pool so that they could all see him.

'You see the emblem on my cap?' he cried out. 'Commissariat, that's right! You know what that means, don't you? It means bully! It means discipline master! It means the lash of the God-Emperor, driving you cowards to a miserable end! Let me show you something else…'

He drew a bolt pistol in one fist, his power sword in the other, and held them both up so that the crowd of men could see. 'Tools of my trade! They kill the enemy, they kill cowards! Either one, they're not fussy! Now listen to this…'

Gaunt dropped his voice, made it softer, but still injected the well-practiced projection qualities he had honed over the years, so that they could all still hear him. 'You want to run, don't you? You want to run right now. You want to get out of here. Get to safety. Throne, I know you all do.' He sheathed his sword and reholstered his gun. 'I could wave those about some more. I could tell you, and Throne knows I wouldn't be lying, that whatever it is coming this way in that wall of smoke is nothing compared to my wrath. I could tell you *I'm* the thing to be frightened of.'

He jumped down off the boulder and walked in amongst them. Some of the men backed away. 'If you want to run, men of Fortis Binary, then go ahead. Run. You might outrun the archenemy, bearing down on us now. Feth, you might even outrun me. But you will never, ever outrun your conscience. Your world suffered under the yoke of the Ruinous Powers for a long time. You're only here today, as free men of the Imperium, because others did not run. Your fathers and uncles and brothers, and young men, just like you, Imperial Guardsmen from a hundred scattered worlds, who had the courage to stand and fight. For your world. For Fortis Binary. I know this because I was there. So, run, if you dare. If you can live with it. If you can face the dreams, and the pangs of conscience. If you can even bear to think of the fathers and uncles and brothers you lost.'

He paused. There was a strained silence, broken only by the booming sound of the shelling behind him.

'Alternatively, you can stay here, and follow Major Whitesmith's orders, and fight like men. You can stay, and honour the memory of your fathers, and your uncles and your brothers. You can stay and stand with me, for the Imperium, for the God-Emperor. And for Fortis Binary.'

Gaunt walked back to the boulder he had vacated and climbed back onto it. 'What do you say?' he asked.

The men cheered approval. It was hearty, and just what Gaunt had been looking for. He smiled and raised a fist. 'Squad leaders form up! Get this trackway cleared so the treads can roll through! Unit commanders! Where are you? Come on! Get yourselves up onto the trackway so Whitesmith can brief you! Support weapons, through to the front and get set up! Let's move!'

The men started moving. Gaunt jumped down. He turned to Eszrah. 'Come on,' he urged.

They splashed across the edges of the pool, onto the far slope and ran towards the next gaggle of Binars, milling purposelessly on the adjacent ridge top. The men there had seen the activity below, heard the sudden cheer, and stood bewildered.

'Histye, soule!' Eszrah called.

'What?' Gaunt looked back over his shoulder, still running.

'Preyathee, wherein wastye maden so?'

'Blood,' said Gaunt simply. 'My blood. My father.'

Eszrah nodded, and followed Gaunt up the slope. The Binars crowded there spread back from the commissar. Gaunt hurried to a parked Chimera and clambered up the access rungs onto its roof. He stood there for a moment, looking down at the huddled men. So young, all of them. So scared.

'Sons of Fortis Binary,' he began, 'I'll keep this simple. I'll tell you what I just told your comrades down in the vale…'

IT WAS ALMOST fifteen minutes before Gaunt and Eszrah returned to the trackway. The enemy line, indeed the firestorm itself, was much closer. The forward edge of the Binar formation was now less than a kilometre from the advance, and the rain of shells from the Blood Pact armour had begun to find range. Binar and Sarpoy tanks started to open up in reply. From behind the Binars' forward position, the artillery commenced barrage firing, lofting shells over into the Blood Pact lines.

Gaunt checked in with Whitesmith. The man was pale with tension, but also enervated. 'I've lined them all out,' he told Gaunt. 'And the armour's all but deployed. Some slackness from the infantry. Most of them are still scared. It's the ones in flight, you see.'

By then, the exodus of troops and machines fleeing before the invasion had begun to trickle through the reinforcement line. The sight of them, and the stories they were bringing with them, were steadily eroding resolve.

'Tell your officers to let them come through,' Gaunt said. 'Don't oppose them. They're running anyway, nothing's going to change that. Let them through and ignore them.'

'That an order, sir?' Whitesmith smiled.

'No,' Gaunt smiled back. 'Just an informed suggestion. It's going to get bad in the next half-hour or so, major. I won't lie. Keep the line, and trust your men. The Emperor protects.'

Whitesmith saluted Gaunt and ran back to his Salamander. Shells were now whistling down and impacting on the lower slope of the rise where the track fell away. Gaunt hurried back down the roadway to Ludd.

Ludd had assembled five commissars. An elderly senior attached to the Sarpoy called Blunshen, two of the primary Binar commissars – Fenwik and Saffonol – and two young juniors.

'Gentlemen,' Gaunt said as he came up to them.

'The state is parlous,' Blunshen said at once. 'With such woeful measure of resolve, and such feeble unit connection, we must supervise an immediate fall-back and–'

'Blunshen, is it?' Gaunt asked.

'Yes, commissar.'

'Chain of command places Major Whitesmith in charge of this action. I am Major Whitesmith's commissar, and so that gives me authority here. Do you agree?'

'I suppose so,' said the old commissar.

'Good. No more talk of retreat. From anyone, especially someone wearing that badge. Marshal Sautoy's last orders to me were to accomplish the maintenance of decent battlefield morale and discipline along this line. That's right, isn't it, Ludd?'

'To the letter, sir.'

'Good,' said Gaunt. 'There will be no falling back. Not on my watch. Whitesmith has devised a scheme of resistance. Are you all familiar with it?'

'I made sure the major's orders were circulated,' Ludd said.

'The archenemy has us on the ropes here,' Gaunt said. 'They must not be allowed to prevail. If we break now – or fall back, Commissar Blunshen – then the third compartment will be forfeit. Do you know what that means?'

'A severe set-back to our advance into the Mons structure–' Blunshen began.

'No, Blunshen, It means Lord General Van Voytz will be angry. I happen to know him, and I do not want to be on the receiving end of that anger. The seven of us will make the difference between success and failure today. The Guardsmen here are well-armed, well-trained, and capable. The only thing they lack is discipline. They're scared. It's up to us to enforce the control they need. It's up to us to make sure Whitesmith's entirely workable strategy pays off. The Guard needs inspiration and motivation, gentlemen. Few though we are, we have to accomplish that. Blunshen, I'd like you to return to your Sarpoy units and make sure they hold the right flank. A great deal depends on their crossfire and support. Explain to them if you have to, that the Fortis Binars in the middle width of the line will be slaughtered if they don't maintain fire-rate.'

Blunshen nodded. 'I'll see to it at once.'

Gaunt turned to the others. 'What's your name? Fenwik? And you? Saffonol ? Good to meet you. Whitesmith has drawn his armour line out across this ridge, and laced the infantry in between it. We have to hold that echelon stable. Fenwik, go south. Maintain firing discipline there, keep the tanks shooting. Range is all we have. Saffonol, head forward, take charge of the units at the head of the rise. Do not, and I emphasise, do not, allow the troop units to charge and lose the advantage of gradient. Use your crew-served support weapons.'

Both men nodded.

'You juniors, step up. What are your names?'

'Kanfreid, sir.'

'Junior Loboskin.'

'Move to the rear, sirs. We won't survive this without the artillery support, and artillery units have a habit of getting edgy and pulling out because they're too far away from the visible line to understand what's happening. Assure them everything's fine. Dissuade them from leaving. How you do that I leave up to you. Just keep your cool, and keep the rate up. Even if we break, we'll need the field guns to cover us. They must keep firing. In the event of a rout, they can ditch their cannon and run at the last minute.'

'Yes, sir,' the young men echoed.

'Get on with it!' Gaunt cried with a clap of his hands. The commissars hurried away. Gaunt turned to Ludd.

'I'm intending to cover the northern flank of the Binars,' Gaunt said. 'I need you to press on further north and link up with the Dev Hetra units. I need you to keep them solid.'

Ludd paused. 'Sir,' he began.

'What is it, Ludd?'

'Sir... I'm not supposed to leave you. I mean, my orders are that I should stay with you at all times.'

Gaunt glared at him. 'Throne's sake, Ludd! Feth, I'd forgotten you didn't actually take orders from me.'

Ludd pulled back, stung. 'That's not fair, sir. Not at all.'

'Really? You're Balshin's spy. You never denied that. You're my... what is it? Minder? That was all fine when this was just a game, but it's not a game any more, Ludd. You see what's going on out there? You see what's coming?'

'Yes, sir. Yes, I do.'

'Then show some wit, Ludd,' Gaunt snarled. 'Us commissars have got to spread thin, to maximise our effect. Are you really telling me that Mamzel Balshin's orders are so intractable you're going to stick with me like a bad smell instead of getting the job done?'

'No, sir.'

'Louder so it means something, Ludd.'

'No, sir!'

'Find the Dev Hetra, Ludd. Get them into formation. This is war now, lad. Not politics. Not games.'

'Yes, sir.'

'Get on with you. You're an Imperial commissar, Ludd. Act like one. And if Balshin chews your ear, send her to me.'

'Yes, sir,' Ludd shouted, scrambling down the wet, grassy bank.

'Ludd?' Gaunt called after him.

'Sir?'

'Don't die, all right?'

'No, sir.'

IT WOULD TAKE a two kilometre dash, cross-country, to reach the Dev Hetra 301. Ludd ran as fast as he could, stumbling through the loose, plashy mires of the lowland belt. He crossed behind the drawn-up retinues of the Binar infantry, behind the hasty dug-outs where they had secured their infantry support weapons. He dodged through lines of battle tanks, squirming through the mud to their deployment positions.

By some miracle, he realised, Gaunt and Whitesmith were bringing the Binar line together. It was strong and it was firm. Men were singing battle-songs that had last rung out over the field of war between the ruined refineries of Fortis Binary. Behind the Guard front line, a kilometre south-west, artillery positions were thumping shells into the air with maintained vigour.

Shells sang back. The enemy was dreadfully close. That roiling belt of smoke and flame. Huge explosions ripped into the Guard line, hurling bodies into the air, rupturing tanks. The Blood Pact was at the door and their assault was slicing mercilessly into the ranged forces of the Emperor.

Ludd ran on, slipped, and righted himself. A shell dropped just behind the next rise and lifted a huge column of water, fire and mud into the air. Drenched by it, Ludd sprinted forward. There was a buzzing sound, which got louder, and then much louder still. A wave of Vultures flocked overhead, fifty or more machines, wrenching off rocket fire into the closing enemy line. A long, snickering wildfire of overlapping explosions crackled along the target spread. The Vultures peeled away. A second wave went in, another fifty or so. Ludd could hear their rocket pods banging like snare drums, and their autocannons grinding like whetstones. Less than half a kilometre away, he saw Blood Pact AT70s disintegrate in twitchy puffs of smoke and fragmenting metal.

Lasfire from the advancing enemy infantry started to kiss into the Imperial lines.

Ludd reached the upland above the Dev Hetra position. Something hit the ground behind him, and turned the whole world into fire.

GAUNT DREW HIS powersword and ignited it. In his right hand, he clutched one of his paired bolt pistols. The sky was as black as a coal-star now, and thick smoke billowed in from the ends of creation. All along the line beside him, Fortis Binar officers blew whistles and demanded order. Gaunt could hear mumbled prayers and frightened moans addressed to mothers and loved ones. Shells wailed down. Gritty blasts tore the air and quaked the earth.

'Men of Fortis Binar, stand firm!' he yelled.

It was no use now. They couldn't really hear him.

The first of the Blood pact AT70's were in view. Gaunt could hear the distinctive whistle-whoop of their main weapons discharging. He saw figures in crimson battle-dress massing forward alongside the tanks, running in through the smoke towards the raised ground where the Imperials had chosen to meet them. He saw the black masks, grotesques, like faces frozen in agony, the glint of bayonets.

'Rise and address!' he yelled. Whistles blew in answer. The young, virgin troopers of the Second Fortis Binars stepped up to meet the onrushing tide of the Blood Pact.

Gaunt leapt over the ledge of the hastily dug slit-trench and greeted the enemy head on. Binar troops either side of him buckled and died under sudden, hailing gunfire.

Gaunt's blade cleanly decapitated the first Blood Pact trooper to reach him. The second and third fell victim to his booming bolt pistol.

Mayhem descended. Bodies clashing in the smoke, blood flecking the air. Gaunt fired his bolt pistol at point-blank range, right into the chest of a charging Blood Pact soldier. He leapt over the fallen body and fired again, knocking another of the archenemy host onto his back. Figures rushed in around him: the Binar boys, yelling, firing, stabbing with their bayonets.

'For the Throne!' Gaunt bellowed. Two rifle rounds punched through his coat. Gaunt twisted round and shot a Pact trooper to his left, hurling the man into the air in a tangle of limbs. The sloping ground was treacherous. He found himself sliding into a scrum of enemy troopers that was trying to scale the muddy bank. Gaunt stroked left and right with his power blade, sliced off a trooper's arm at the shoulder, took out the throat of another. A third fell over in the mire in his frantic effort to dodge the slashing blade.

A Blood Pact officer, barking orders and curses, ploughed up the low bank and assaulted Gaunt with a keening chainsword. Gaunt deflected the first stroke with his power blade, and then was driven backwards, knocking aside the demented, hacking cuts that swung at him.

'Bastard!' he yelled, throwing the force of his arm into a ripping cross-cut that caught the chainsword halfway down its length and buckled it. As the enemy officer attempted to defend with the broken weapon, Gaunt sliced back in a reprise, and the tip of his blade found the side of the warrior's face. The officer recoiled and fell, blood pouring from his head, his silver grotesque hanging off to one side.

Guardsmen in the charging line dropped and sprawled as las-shots streaked across the mud and hit them. Shells detonated with huge, sucking roars. Explosions plumed like geysers across the miasmal fen.

Gaunt strode on. He buried his blade into the helmet of a Blood Pact trooper, wrenched it free, and shot another, who was wading in with his bayonet. A hard round skimmed his right shoulder and knocked him down for a second.

Strong hands grabbed him. Gaunt looked up and found Eszrah Night dragging him back to his feet. The partisan had streaked his face with wode, a ritual symbol of his intention to make war.

'I told you to stay back!' Gaunt yelled over the din. Eszrah put a hand to his ear as if to sign he couldn't hear. The Nihtgane turned and aimed his reynbow. The electromag weapon spat out a quarrel that dropped a nearby enemy trooper. Eszrah reached into his satchel and loaded another barb, sliding it down the reynbow's tube. The partisan weapon fired the iron darts with such force that they would easily kill a man if they hit squarely, but the fact they were tipped with powerful Untill venom meant that even a scratch was lethal.

Eszrah fired again. What little sound the reynbow made was lost entirely in the roar of battle. Another

Blood Pact trooper collapsed, an iron quarrel jutting from an eye slit.

Gaunt picked up his fallen sword and resumed his advance. Almost immediately, he lost contact with Eszrah as the smoke swirled in. There were stalk-tanks ahead, trotting through the filthy air, hosing laser fire from their gun-pods. Gaunt saw one of them blow out as a rocket struck it. The flash was so bright, it left an afterimage on his retina.

Another wave of vile figures emerged from the hellish smoke. Blood running from his shoulder wound, Gaunt urged the Binar infantrymen into them. Bodies slammed together along the course of the ditch, clubbing and stabbing.

Gaunt broke free, breathing hard. His clip out, he holstered the pistol and dragged out its twin. He looked around for the next enemy to kill. Nearby, three Vanquisher tanks lurched and splattered forward, their hulls bouncing. The support weapons on the tanks chattered, licking out brilliant tongues of ignited gas. Several dozen enemy troopers fell back before the approaching tanks.

Beams of light lanced through the smoke wall ahead of them. Gaunt saw one of the tanks simply disintegrate in front of him.

Churning out of the vapour, clearing a path for the archenemy advance, the stumble-guns had arrived.

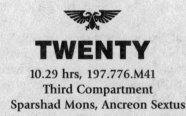

TWENTY

WHEN HE WAS a boy, Nahum Ludd had been particularly taken with the frescoes on the ceiling of the scholam chapel. He'd loved all pictures of war, and pored over old books and military texts, but the frescoes had been special. The domed ceiling had been a wide, cloudy blue, an imitation sky through which Imperial angels of war had flown on golden wings, swords aloft. With them, depicted in that quaint, slightly primitive style of old murals, there had been gunships and strike fighters, the hosts of the air, radiant and mighty.

He opened his eyes, and thought for a moment that he was still a boy, still in the old chapel. The roof above him, swollen with white cloud, full of gunships and angels.

His hearing returned like a hammer blow. Ludd sat up quickly. He'd been lying on his back in the muddy grass. A blast had knocked him down, he remembered that now. He was numb and cold, but there seemed to be no obvious signs of injury.

Ludd looked around. Overhead, Vulture gunships were making approach passes, chasing low and hunting for surface targets. To the east, the vast horror of the battle spread out against the encroaching black cloud. It was turmoil. Ludd took a moment to accept the scale of it, the blinding flash and blast of the shelling, the stink of mud and fyceline, the juddering buffet of overpressure.

Individual figures were almost too small for him to make out, but he saw dark, sparking lumps that were evidently tanks engaging as they thundered into the lowland belt. He saw the fiery breath of flamers, the strafing blizzards of autolaser fire in the sky, detonations of extraordinary violence. In the thick of the fighting, he could make out obscene banners and battle standards, waving aloft, mocking the sanctity of the Emperor and the purity of man. He saw rockets fly like sparks from a bonfire.

A bonfire. That's what it looked like: a gigantic, blazing bonfire, filling the entire compartment, crackling with sparks and embers, lashing with tongues of yellow flame, choking out the sky to the east with a mountainous block of charcoal smoke.

He realised that this was finally it. This was war. He'd yearned for it, trained for it, prepared for it, and worked hard to earn a place for himself in the ranks of the Imperium so he could pursue it. This, ridiculously, was what he had been searching for all his life. This madness, this chaos, this calamity.

It had no sense or shape, no structure or meaning. It was simply a maelstrom of hurt and damage, a sundering whirlpool laced with fire and blood and splintering metal. It was as if Ludd had been let in on some giant, private joke. Men trained for war, rehearsed, honed skills, solemnly studied military teachings, as if warfare was something that could be learned and controlled and conducted, like a formal banquet or a great country dance. But here was the raw truth of it. All theories of combat perished immediately in the furnace heat of real war.

How foolish lord generals seemed, plotting in their back rooms and command cells, dreaming up principles and schemes of battle. They might as well be trying to govern and contain a supernova.

Ludd had almost forgotten why he had been running north, or what it was Gaunt had demanded of him. Surely he could serve no purpose now? The frenzy of war was feeding itself, fire into fire. It just *was*, and no man could alter that.

Ludd wondered where Gaunt was. He tried his microbead, but there was nothing except sizzling distortion. Gaunt had to be somewhere down there, in the jaws of the beast.

And probably dead by now. Could anything human survive in that horror?

He wondered where to go, what to do. Binar tanks and infantry groups were advancing past him on the flanks of the ridge. He could see where the foremost sections were entering the battle, riding forward into the fierce gunfire. Shells were slamming into the fenland, and showering water up from the long, wide lakes.

On the far side of the ridge lay the Dev Hetra positions. Over two hundred units, most of them Hydra and multi-laser mobiles, along with some bulky Thunderer siege tanks and heavy Basilisk platforms. There was very little fire coming from them.

Ludd began to head down the slope towards the light support line. There was an abrupt bang overhead, as if the vault of heaven had finally split. Ludd looked up, and watched in helpless awe as a Vulture gunship fell out of the air, trailing ochre smoke. Sub-assemblies disintegrated off it as it dropped. It hit the fenland short of the main line and tumbled over and over, ripping apart, leaking fire.

Ludd turned and ran on into the Dev Hetra position. Motors were running, and gun-crews were stacking munitions and power-chargers. The Dev Hetra machines were of the finest quality, and polished like they'd just rolled out of the forge silos. The uniforms the men wore were almost regal in their decoration: dress white with gold braiding, with gleaming silver crest-helmets for the officers, and black fur shakoes for the rank and file. They looked like the ceremonial escort detail of a sector governor. Ludd had never seen such resplendent troops.

'Who's in charge here?' Ludd shouted. His voice was hoarse from the smoke. The men, magnificent in their regalia, looked at him archly, as if he was some filthy low-life blundering uninvited into their midst. 'I said who's in charge here, dammit?'

The men around still didn't answer. They continued to regard him with what appeared to be utter disdain. No, he thought, they're just dazed, frightened. That was it. Despite their finery, the soldiers here, all of them young, all of them no doubt first-timers and fresh recruits, were simply too shocked by the spectacle of the battle to form any coherent reply. Ludd knew how that felt. He swallowed hard, tried to clear his throat a little and put some authority into his words.

'Who's in charge?'

A sergeant came forward. He wore a blue sash and carried a silver power-sabre. He bowed curtly.

'Who may I say is asking?'

'Ludd. Commissar Ludd.'

'Do you not have a hat, sir?' the man enquired.

Ludd realised his cap had come off somewhere, probably when he'd been knocked down. He tried to stroke back his hair, and felt it was caked with mud. His coat was torn and smeared with drying dirt. He realised his first instinct had been correct. The haughty Dev Hetra had chosen to ignore him because of his dishevelled appearance.

'No, I don't have a hat! I've also not got much patience! Get me a ranking officer! Now, if you please!'

The sergeant bowed again, and led Ludd over to a gun platform where a very young officer, a captain, was working a vox-caster set. The sergeant had a few quiet words with the captain. The captain put down the vox-horn, and turned to face Ludd. His white uniform was frogged up the tunic front with gold braid, and his high peaked cap was a sumptuous affair of silverwork and yet more braiding. He wore a mantle of black fur around one shoulder, secured by a golden clasp.

'Are you really a commissar?' he asked. He was handsome, in a fey, high-born way, his slightly-slanted eyes disapproving.

'I fell down,' said Ludd.

The captain looked Ludd up and down. 'Did you? How unfortunate.'

'Who am I addressing?' Ludd asked.

'Captain Sire Balthus Vuyder Kronn.' The young man was very softly spoken, and his accent betrayed fine breeding. Ludd remembered his briefing. The Hetrahan came from a highly structured world ruled by an aristocratic elite. They appointed officers by merit of birth and breeding.

'Why aren't you engaged, Kronn?' Ludd asked.

'I would prefer it if you used my full nomenclature when addressing me,' the captain said, and began to turn away.

'I would prefer you answered my frigging question, Kronn,' Ludd said. 'Why isn't this unit engaged?'

Ludd might as well have slapped him by the look on Kronn's face. 'At this time,' Kronn said, 'it has been deemed inappropriate for us to engage.'

'Really? By whom?'

'My commander, Colonel Sire Sazman Vuyder Urfanus.'

'Well, I'd better have a word with him, then.'

'He has gone. He has already quit the field. I have been given charge of the withdrawal of the war machines.'

'He's gone? Your commanding officer has left you here?'

Kronn raised his eyebrows. 'Of course. There is some jeopardy here. Sire Vuyder Urfanus is a high-born man, first cousin to the Hzeppar of Korida himself. His security takes precedence.'

Ludd began to laugh. He couldn't help it. The sheer insanity of it all had got to him. Behind him, the amoral, elemental fury of war was loose, defying comprehension and logic. In front of him, stood men hidebound by tradition and breeding, who were packing away for the day like their garden party had been rained off.

'I do not like the way you laugh,' Kronn said. 'It is uncivil.'

'I don't much like anything about anything at the moment,' Ludd replied. 'Look, you were given orders.'

'The communication systems are inoperative,' Kronn said, gesturing to the vox.

'You were sent orders. By runner. Orders from the Fortis Binar commander.'

'The orders were garbled, and the runner refused to address Sire Vuyder Urfanus with a correct measure of formality. Sire Vuyder Urfanus will only respect orders given to him by the marshal.'

'Listen to me carefully, *captain sire*,' Ludd said. 'If he survives today, Sire Vuyder Urfanus will find himself in deep trouble with the Commissariat. This will be because he has disobeyed orders. Most likely, he will be shot without trial.'

Kronn began to speak, outrage in his face.

'Continue with your intent to retreat now, and you… and all your fellow officers… will suffer the same, ignoble fate. If that doesn't appeal, get your arses in gear, and start doing what you're supposed to be doing.'

'You are uncouth,' Kronn announced. He unbuttoned his leather glove and smacked Ludd round the face with it. Then he threw the glove on the grass.

'You have grossly offended my honour, the honour of my sire, and the honour of Hetrahan. I will be pleased to settle this matter in a bout of merit at your convenience.'

'Did you…' Ludd paused as he fought to get his head around it. 'Did you just challenge me to a duel?' he asked, rubbing his smarting face.

'Are you such a base thing you do not know common manners? Of course I did. By the Code Duello, we will–'

Ludd punched Kronn in the face and broke his nose. The young captain staggered back a few steps and fell down against the tracks of the weapon platform.

'Duel's over.' said Ludd. 'You did say it would be at my convenience. That was a good time for me. Now, get the hell on!'

Kronn looked up at Ludd. There were tears in his eyes, but that was probably just pain.

'Throne's sake!' Ludd cried. 'How far have you and your men come to be here, Kronn? How many frigging light years have you travelled? Your war machines are shiny and new, your uniforms pressed and clean. What are these, gold buttons? You come all this way, dress up in your finest, get to the front line… and then just decide to go home again without firing a shot?'

'It was deemed inappropriate–' Kronn gasped. He paused, and swallowed. Ludd realised the tears were real. For all his bluster, the captain was embarrassingly young, just a precocious child. Kronn looked up at Ludd, and his voice became thin and piteous. 'Look at it out there! Look at it! It's simply madness! Just blind madness! Tell me you do not think so!'

'No,' Ludd lied. He dragged Kronn to his feet, and jerked him round to face the calamitous battle. 'Break now, and you simply postpone your deaths. Break now, the line breaks, the line breaks, the city falls, the city falls…'

He looked at Kronn. '…the city falls, the world falls. Death and glory, Kronn. Or cut down running away. What does your breeding tell you a man should choose?'

Kronn wiped the blood from his face. His hand was shaking. 'I am afraid,' he said, simply.

'So am I,' said Ludd. 'And there'd be something wrong with us if we weren't. But it's worth remembering that the Imperium of Man, which has endured these thousands of years, was forged by men who were afraid, yet who faced down the daemons anyway.'

He let go of Kronn, bent down, and picked up the captain's fallen cap. It was heavy with gold thread and finely-worked bands of silver. He dusted it off and handed it to Kronn. 'Let's begin again, Captain Sire Vuyder Kronn.'

Kronn turned to the men who had gathered nearby. 'We will engage, Sergeant Janvier. Make ready.'

'Yes, captain sire!'

'Crews to your platforms! Load munitions! Connect power cells!'

Ludd followed Kronn back to his command vehicle, a gleaming super-Hydra with twin quad turrets. Standing before the machine, Kronn paused and looked back at Ludd. 'What do we do, commissar?'

'The line's left us behind a little. I suggest you move forward in formation about five hundred metres, maybe a touch more. We have to seal up this side of the line. More importantly, we have to start hitting the enemy sections. You may not have a large complement of treads, sir, but your Hydras and multi-laser carriages pack a serious fire rate. We need to lay down a blanket of sustained firepower across that stretch there.' Ludd pointed. 'Carve into them, and maybe even split up their spearhead phalanx.'

Kronn nodded and clambered up onto the footplate. 'I would appreciate your advice as we progress,' Kronn said. 'As you so easily detected, this unit is new to war. We are... novices. We have never seen anything like this. We would benefit from your experience in these things.'

Ludd was startled for a second. 'My experience?'

'Whatever it is that allows you to remain so calm, so centred. Assist me, please, commissar. I'm sure you can sympathise with our situation. You must remember your own first taste of battle.'

Ludd climbed up onto the riding board. 'As a matter of fact, I do,' he said. 'You never forget your first time.'

STUMBLE-GUNS WERE virtually spherical frames of plated steel, three metres in diameter. The muzzles of plasma-beam cannons jutted out from their carcasses like the spines of a sea-urchin. They rolled and bounced across the field of war, heavy and relentless, propelled by some kind of inertial drive, spilling out random beams of destructive energy.

Gaunt had never seen one in the flesh, but he'd heard far too many reports of their devastating effect in other conflicts. They were like murderous playthings, gew-gaws rolled out of the archenemy's toy-box, blitzing out slaughter wherever they bounced.

Phalanxes of cult troopers followed the tumbling advance of the stumble-guns. The cultists were heavily armoured in black plate, and brandished flamers to scour the ground wracked by the ball-weapons. The cultists also carried heavy censers, bearing them along like litters. The censers were vomiting out the dark, black cloud that marked the archenemy advance, sheeting up swirling cover that amplified the smoke of the firestorms.

'Hold fast! Form a line here!' Gaunt yelled

Some of the Binars obeyed. Others broke. The lead stumble-gun rolled in across a line position, massacring men with its lancing blasts, crushing others under its metal frame. Gaunt saw men die. Too many men.

The stumble-guns weren't solid. Well armoured and heavily plated, as well as being wrapped in rusty razor wire, they were still frameworks. Gaunt glimpsed the operators inside the balls, supported in stabilized, gyro-mounted cockpits that remained upright against the turn of the ball-cages around them.

They made a terrible sound as they advanced: a clanking, rattling noise overlaid by the screech and whine of the sputtering weapons.

Gaunt turned to shout another rallying cry, and a plasma beam destroyed the ground beneath him. He fell, squirming, into the mud, into a jagged furrow where the ground water steamed, super-heated.

Explosions burst overhead. Gaunt clambered up from the furrow, drenched in muck. He saw a stumble-gun buffet past, and ducked as more plasma beams speared his way. The Binar line had broken back. Men were running. Some caught fire and fell as the randomly lancing beams touched them. Others were cut in half, or decapitated, by direct hits. A direct plasma beam, especially the crude, stream-blasts of a stumble-gun, severed a human body quite thoroughly. A bright beam ripped along an entire platoon of fleeing men, and their torsos left their legs behind. Gaunt saw a Fortis colour sergeant trying to struggle out of a ditch. A beam touched him, bright as the sun, and the man fell in two directions, bisected vertically down the length of his spine.

Gaunt got up, and began to run back towards the broken Binar formation. Men were milling around him, running. A Binar Vanquisher stormed forward over the ditches, and hit one of the stumble-guns squarely with a shot from its turret weapon. The stumble-gun rocked back, over and over, like a kicked ball, and then began to rotate towards the tank again. It squealed and fired.

The tank's armour caved in like wet paper and it began to burn.

'Hold fast!' Gaunt yelled.

'They're killing us!' a man protested.

'So kill them back!' Gaunt shouted.

But how? The line had crumpled. All the precious gains they had made in the first few minutes of the battle were slipping away. How did you even begin to kill machines like that?

Gaunt found himself wishing he had Larkin with him. The grizzled marksman would have had the wit and ability to put a round in through the stumble-gun cages and kill the operators, at least.

But the Ghosts weren't with him any more, nor would they ever be again. He was surrounded by frightened youths, who were fleeing and soiling themselves in the face of death.

And he couldn't blame them.

'Someone give me a grenade!' he yelled.

The nearest stumble-gun suddenly stopped firing, and rolled to a halt. Gaunt ran towards it, expecting at every step to be incinerated. He approached the smoking ball. Even from a few metres away, through the frame and plating, he could see that the operator was dead, bent over in his cradle.

An iron dart transfixed the operator's throat.

'Eszrah! Eszrah!' Gaunt yelled.

The tall, slender figure of the Nihtgane appeared, bounding towards Gaunt across the mud. He reloaded his reynbow.

'Hwat seythee, soule?'

'You did that?'

Eszrah plucked his fingers from his mouth again. The Nihtgane's kiss of soul-taking.

'Do it again, if you please.'

He might not have Hlaine Larkin, but he had the hunter skills of an Untill's partisan.

Gaunt and Eszrah ran towards the next stumble-gun. It had rolled past them into the soft footing of the fen.

Men were running before it. A few of the Binar troops had taken cover behind some scorched boulders.

'You! What's your name?' Gaunt yelled.

'Sergeant Tintile, sir. Georg Tintile.'

'Good to know you,' Gaunt said as he ran up to the man. 'My name is Gaunt.'

'We all know who you are, sir,' Tintile said.

'I'm flattered. Listen to me, sergeant. Our line's broken, but the day's not lost. I want you to send a runner to Whitesmith and tell him you're advancing.'

'Why, sir?'

'Because you are advancing. The stumble-guns are terror weapons. See for yourself, they've already burst through our ranks. The enemy believes that when that happens, we'll break like fools. Prove them wrong. Advance. Hit those bastards coming in.'

'But the stumble-guns, sir…' Tintile began.

'Leave them to me. Do this for me, please, Tintile. The Emperor protects.'

'Yes, sir.'

'Do you have grenades, Tintile?'

The sergeant handed his last two hand-bombs to Gaunt.

'Good luck, sir,' he said.

Tintile rallied his men and continued to advance. Piecemeal at first, then more urgently. The rattled and broken structure of the Binar line re-formed and pushed ahead again.

Gaunt and Eszrah approached the next stumble-gun. It had trampled into a break of larch and coster, and was slicing out plasma beams at the Binar armour as it revved its inertials to clatter free.

Eszrah killed its operator with his second shot. As the stumble-gun died and rolled back into the mud-wash,

Gaunt ran up close and tossed one of Tintile's grenades into the cage.

The stumble-gun blew out with such force that Gaunt was thrown flat. Eszrah helped him up and away from the burning sphere.

'That's two,' Gaunt said, looking around for the other terror-weapons.

'Histye,' Eszrah said, and pointed.

Away to the north, a monumental rain of shells and lasfire had begun to sweep across the archenemy advance. The phalanxes of cult warriors shrieked and fell as multi-laser fire, at a fabulous rate, rippled across them. Censer-bearers collapsed. A deluge of shots, like torrential flame, was engulfing the enemy's right flank.

The Dev Hetra had moved forward and, at last, brought their gun-platforms into the fight.

TWENTY-ONE

15.50 hrs, 198.776.M41
Fifth Compartment
Sparshad Mons, Ancreon Sextus

FOR A WHOLE day, they held them off.

About three hours after Rawne's unilateral repulse of
the Blood Pact, the enemy struck again from the east,
using the quartz bastion of Ridge 19 to shield its
approach onto the compartment floor. By then, following consultation with DeBray, Wilder had brought the
entire bulk of the Eighty-First First into position on the
eastern flank in anticipation of just such an event, leaving the Kolstec Fortieth to assume responsibility for Hill
56.

At that point, the day seemed to turn spectacularly
bad. Massed in much more considerable numbers than
before, the Blood Pact poured out into the scrub, res-
olutely determined not to be denied a second time. The
Eighty-First First became locked in place, rigidly defend-
ing a two-kilometre line of rough ground from hasty
dug-outs, relying heavily on its crew-served weapons.

In apparent coordination with the Blood Pact's attempt at an eastern breakthrough, the archenemy armour brigades beyond Hill 56 renewed their assault. All possibility of the fatigued Rothberg tankers withdrawing evaporated. With the Hauberkan reserves, they became tangled in an increasingly feral struggle, which was only relieved by the arrival of the promised Sarpoy armour, the force that had been supposed to replace them on the field. More Kolstec infantry was rapidly sent down from post 36 to reinforce both Hill 56 and Wilder's line, and strings of Valkyries began flying urgent munition runs back and forth across the southern compartment to keep both fighting zones supplied.

By nightfall, it became evident that the archenemy was not going to back down from either fight.

Through the course of that long, wearisome day, Wilder had kept himself updated with news from the Mons as a whole. From the sound of things, the third compartment was in an even worse state. Both Wilder and Fofobris had sent requests to high command, via DeBray, for reinforcement, but got little satisfaction. Significant reserves had been sent through to the third compartment, where the situation was described as 'grave'. After a while, even that choked off. Wilder listened to frantic and disheartening vox traffic describing mayhem in the first and second compartments, where relief columns were becoming boxed in by personnel fleeing the third compartment fighting. There were also ominous reports that some of the relief forces themselves had broken back, too scared of what they had heard was happening ahead of them. Some of these units were actually reported to be 'in flight'. Others, more cautious perhaps, were declaring 'mechanical problems' and other set-backs that were preventing them from moving.

It was an ugly picture. The two key 'hot' compartments, three and five, were enduring massive offensives, and the rest of the Imperial strength was milling around in headless confusion, unable or unwilling to come to the aid of either.

It had been Wilder's professional experience that warfare ebbed and flowed. Quiet days, quiet months, could be suddenly disrupted by angry flares of enemy activity. He did not see anything especially sinister in the fact that the enemy had chosen that particular day to coordinate and unify its defence of Sparshad Mons. In many ways, he'd been waiting for it to happen.

But there was no denying how successful the archenemy had been. No one knew for sure how centralised the enemy command was in the mysterious heart of the Mons, but by whatever means, it had orchestrated a shatteringly well-timed attack on all sides. And the systems and discipline of the vaunted Imperial Guard had seized up, paralysed, as a result.

In the fifth compartment, fighting continued after nightfall. As the temperature dropped, the ferocious tank battle behind Hill 56 raged on, lighting up the low horizon and painting the looming black walls of the compartment with a shadowplay of coloured flashes. At Wilder's line, the intensity dropped a little, but all through the night the support weapons of the Eighty-First First continued to hammer away at invasive attempts by Blood Pact strike teams to edge their way forward in the darkness. Just after midnight, one force almost broke through, but it was denied by Callide's Company after a brutal, forty-minute gun battle across the frosty scrub.

Other dangers lurked in the darkness. Stalkers appeared again, some inexplicably, haunting the darkness behind the Imperial front, as if they had somehow lurked hidden during daylight in dens or lairs in the southern part of the compartment. Two munitions convoys were attacked, and men lost, and Fofobris's Kolstec troops on the hill suffered a series of predatory raids from the rear.

The next day dawned, but the sun was only a little bruise of light against the black undercast. The unnaturally dark smoke rising off the third compartment war zone was blanketing the entirety of Sparshad Mons. The surreal twilight it created seemed like the product of some foul sorcery.

Along the Eighty-First First's position, things were quiet for the first few, chilly hours of the day. Vox distortion levels rose, and the inexplicable daylight winds groaned across the scrub and clumpy thorn-rush. Then the Blood Pact renewed its assault on the eastern flank.

This time they sent stumble-guns to shatter the infantry line that had repelled them time and again the previous day. Wilder had been forewarned about these things via the garbled reports flowing out of the third compartment. They were supposed to strike down everything before them like skittles, random and wild, and make a path for the ground forces.

There were three of them. They came down across the escarpment of Ridge 19, rattling like pebbles in a mess can. At a distance, they seemed so odd, so unthreatening, Wilder's troops just stared at them. Steel balls, trundling in across the damp, gritty soil. Then their spines started to glow and they began to flash out searing plasma beams in all directions, like jumping firecrackers.

The men and women of the Eighty-First First, veterans all, did not break in panic as the inexperienced Binars had done the day before in the third compartment. They held their line. That resolve cost them nearly thirty lives in the time it took to kill the stumble-guns.

The worst of the losses were amongst L Company, Varaine's troop. Oblivious to the stupendous rally of gunfire they sent at it, the stumble-gun rolled into them and crushed those that it did not dismember and char with its beams. Corporal Choires, one of Varaine's toughest, finally halted its progress. Luck, more than anything else, had left Choires unscathed as the ball-weapon rolled past, and he bowled a grenade in through its armoured structure, annihilating the operator. Choires did not live to celebrate. As it expired, one of the stumble-gun's final, spasmodic plas-beams vapourised his head.

Commissar Hark led an attack on the second weapon, determined to stop it before it reached the Eighty-First First's position. Despite the loss of four of the troopers bold enough to go with him into the reach of the lethal device, Hark blasted shot after shot into it with his plasma pistol, and managed to kill the operator. Directionless, the stumble-gun rocked to a halt, smoking.

Caffran, Guheen and the Belladon Gespelder, each of them armed with a tread fether and supported by anxious teams of loaders, used up fourteen rockets between them stopping the third. One of the last two rockets managed to penetrate the heavily armoured sphere deeply enough to touch off its plasma vats or cause some kind of critical weapon failure. The stumble-gun exploded like a miniature star. Guheen and Gespelder argued amiably over which of them should claim the kill.

The Eighty-First First line rippled with mingled cheers at the sight of the last stumble-gun's demise, but the relief was short-lived. With stalk-tanks and modified cannon platforms to the fore, the Blood Pact main assault came in.

Three hours of intense fighting followed. More than once, Wilder was afraid they would be overrun and slaughtered, but Hark and Novobazky, along with the company leaders, kept the position firm. Even Rawne, Wilder noted, with a mix of satisfaction and annoyance, led from the front, spurring the Guardsmen on.

Just before noon, a phalanx of Hauberkan treads, part of the reserve element from post 36, arrived in support. The formidable range and effect of their main weapons crippled the coherence of the Blood Pact front, and forced it into retreat.

Wilder was amazed. He'd never thought he'd be glad to see a Hauberkan tank.

AFTER THE BATTLE, an uneasy lull settled. Keeping a careful eye on the ridge, the Eighty-First First took advantage of the quiet spell to eat rations, service weapons, and even catch a few, quick minutes sleep. Though it was long past the middle of the afternoon, conditions had not improved. The day was still lightless and dismal, the air bitter cold, and the ground hard as lead. Wrapped in camo-cloaks and bedrolls, troopers huddled down beside boulders or nested in patches of stiff grass. Some just sat, looking out across the scrubland, where hundreds of corpses, and the wrecks of fighting machines, lay scattered all the way back to the jagged quartz of Ridge 19.

The Hauberkan treads had taken up position on the left flank of the Eighty-First First position, and Wilder went to liaise with the crews, leaving Baskevyl to supervise munition distribution from a pair of Valkyries that had just arrived from post 36.

'I think we should go now, while it's still quiet,' Mkoll said. 'If we leave it much later, it'll be dark.'

Rawne nodded. They'd found a place to talk away from the others, behind some broken lime trees about thirty metres away from the E Company slit trenches. Criid, Varl, Feygor and Larkin were with them.

'All right. Everyone gather what you need and meet up out beyond those rocks in fifteen minutes,' Rawne said. 'We–'

Varl suddenly made a brusque, throat-cutting gesture with his finger and Rawne shut up. Gol Kolea and Ban Daur were approaching.

'Everything all right?' Kolea asked.

'Fine,' said Rawne.

'Just taking a breather,' Varl said.

Kolea glanced at Daur. 'See? They're just taking a breather. I told you there was nothing dodgy going on.'

'You're right,' said Daur, leaning against the trunk of a lime and folding his arms.

'And you said they looked conspiratorial,' Kolea said to Daur.

'I did. I did say that.'

Kolea looked at Rawne. 'There's nothing conspiratorial going on here, is there?'

Rawne said nothing. Kolea looked at Mkoll instead. 'Is there, chief? Just a bunch of comrades, taking a breather, hanging out. I shouldn't read anything into the fact that all of you are lost souls who went to Gereon?'

Mkoll held Kolea's gaze without any sign of discomfort. 'There's nothing going on, Kolea,' he said.

Kolea pursed his lips and looked up at the sky for a moment, as if watching the black clouds chase. 'I got roasted a little bit,' he said at length. 'For siding with you yesterday, Rawne. Wilder was pretty gakking pissed off we pulled C and E out of the line without his say so, even though it turned out we had a good reason. I don't blame him, either. If I was Wilder, I'd be mad as hell. This is a good unit, and most of that is down to his hard work pulling it together.'

'Noted,' said Rawne. 'Why are you telling me this?'

'Because I'd hate to see that happen again,' Kolea replied. 'It's a great thing all of you made it back to us, but if you refuse to settle, it's going to cause problems. If you're chasing secret agendas, for instance. It'll be divisive. How will Wilder maintain authority if you constantly refuse to work with him? The Eighty-First First will suffer. And everything and everyone that used to be the Tanith First will suffer too.'

'I understand that,' Rawne said. 'But there are just some things…'

'Like what?' asked Daur.

Rawne inhaled deeply before replying. 'Some things that won't fit into your nice, ordered boxes. Gut instincts. Feelings. I don't dislike this man Wilder. And I honestly have no intent to damage this unit. But there are just some things.'

'Are they important?' Daur asked.

'Feth, I think they are,' Rawne replied.

'So bring Wilder in. Get him on your side, instead of sneaking about behind his back, pissing him off, and undermining his command.'

'Wilder won't–'

'How do you know what Wilder will or won't do, Elim?' Kolea asked. 'Have you asked him? Have you given him a chance? Ban's right, Wilder's a good man, and when us Ghosts thought you and Mkoll and Gaunt were all dead and gone, we counted ourselves lucky to get him as a commander. I say you go talk to him.'

Rawne looked at the others. None of them made any comment.

'Gereon really messed you lot up, didn't it?' Kolea said softly. 'I think you all got so self-reliant, you've forgotten how to trust anyone.'

'You don't know what it was like,' Feygor growled.

'No, I don't. You bastards still won't tell me. But I think I just hit a nerve, didn't I? You've forgotten how to trust.'

'We trust each other,' Rawne said. 'And we trust Gaunt.'

'Is this about Gaunt?' Daur asked.

'Perhaps,' Rawne said.

'So where do your loyalties lie?' Kolea demanded. 'To this regiment or to Gaunt? Because if the answer's Gaunt, this isn't ever going to work.'

'Do you remember his last command?' Criid asked. They all looked at her. The wind gusted and lifted her long hair away from her face, and they all saw the ugly scar across her left cheek, the blade wound she'd grown her hair to hide.

'His last command to the Tanith First,' she repeated. 'Before we left for Gereon, Gaunt told the Ghosts that if he didn't come back, they were to serve whoever came in his place as loyally as they had served him. We should tell Wilder, Rawne. As soldiers of the Imperium, we're obliged to, because that's what Gaunt ordered us to do.'

'GOOD NEWS,' BASKEVYL said to Wilder and Novobazky. 'We just got a signal from 36. We should expect some serious reinforcement by dawn tomorrow. Van Voytz has committed the entire Frag Flats reserve to the front line.'

'Everything?' Wilder said.

'The full works,' Baskevyl confirmed. 'I guess he's getting as tired of this place as we are.'

'Don't look now,' Novobazky said. Rawne, Mkoll and Kolea were walking across the scrub towards them.

'Great,' said Wilder. 'Don't go far, either of you. I've seen friendlier looking mutinies.'

He took a few steps forward, and Kolea and Mkoll fell back a little so that Rawne came up face to face with Wilder.

'Major?'

'Colonel. I think there's a good case to be made for us starting over.'

'Really?' Wilder raised his eyebrows.

'The situation is difficult, and the return to this regiment of the Gereon mission team, particularly myself and Sergeant Mkoll, must have unsettled loyalties.'

'You could say that.'

'My actions yesterday can't have helped much.'

That brought a smile to Wilder's face. 'All right, Rawne. And don't think I'm not appreciating you making this effort, but I get the feeling there's something more to it.'

'You'd be right. There's something that has to be done. I was just going to go ahead and do it, but Major Kolea took the trouble to remind me that I am an officer of the Imperial Guard and have a responsibility to clear things with my commander.'

'Bonus points for Major Kolea,' Wilder said. 'All right, shoot. What's this thing?'

'It'll be dark soon,' Rawne said. 'After last night's experience, we should form a secure rearward perimeter to prevent any stalker trouble.'

'Agreed. Absolutely. See, that wasn't too hard, was it Rawne?' Wilder said. He paused and saw the look on Kolea's face. 'There's more, isn't there?' Kolea nodded.

'Sir,' Rawne said. 'I'd like to take advantage of the current lull not only to set up a perimeter, but also to try tracking these stalkers.'

'Tracking them?'

'Mkoll's pretty sure he can do it.'

'Tracking them?' Wilder repeated.

'To find out where they're coming from,' Mkoll said.

'You mean dens or lairs or whatever?'

'Or whatever,' Mkoll agreed.

'Why?' Wilder asked.

'That's the part you're not going to like,' Kolea said.

'We've not had that already, then?' asked Wilder.

'I received a message from Gaunt,' Rawne said.

Wilder took a casual step backwards and looked sidelong at Novobazky and Baskevyl. 'You know that feeling?' he asked them. 'When you find out your girl's still writing letters to an ex-lover?'

Baskevyl sniggered.

Wilder looked back at Rawne. 'Rawne. Rawne, I couldn't feel much more undermined if you… if you got hold of a frigging land mine and… and put me under it.'

'That probably sounded better in your head, didn't it?' Rawne said.

'Yes,' said Wilder. 'Really, much, much better.'

'Listen to me, Wilder,' Rawne said. 'As everyone – including high command, the Commissariat, the Inquisition, and our old comrades in the Tanith First – has been quick to point out, the team that went to Gereon came back different. You don't spend that long on a Chaos-held world and not have it affect you. It changed the way we fight. It changed the way we live and think, the way we trust. All of those changes were alterations forced on us by the simple need to survive. Gereon left its mark on us.'

'Like a taint?' Novobazky asked. He was only half joking.

'Yes,' said Rawne. 'But not the kind you mean. Just to stay alive, we developed a… a hunch. An instinct. What would you call it, Mkoll?'

'A sensitivity,' Mkoll said.

'Yes, a sensitivity. A little inkling that rang alarm bells when things weren't right. When the ruinous powers were playing tricks or about to strike. I've got that inkling now. So's Gaunt. We've had it since we first set foot in this place.'

'And what does it mean?' Wilder asked.

'We don't think Sparshad Mons is what it seems to be. It's not just an old ruin with the archenemy hiding inside it. Something else is going on. Think about the stalkers. Where in the name of feth do they keep coming from at night?'

'I don't know,' said Wilder.

'No one does. Gaunt suggested it was high time someone did. He contacted me because he thought it was a job ideally suited to the Tanith scouts, to Mkoll and Bonin especially. If they can't track these things to their source, no one can.'

'And what does he expect you'll find?' asked Baskevyl.

'Let's hope lairs and dens,' Mkoll said. 'Burrows, maybe. Natural hiding places that no one has yet detected.'

'But your inkling tells you…' Wilder began.

'That they're getting in a different way. That this place isn't what it seems.'

'If that's true,' said Novobazky, 'it could change everything.'

'All right, you've convinced me,' Wilder said. 'I'm not happy, but you've convinced me. Assemble a team, Rawne. Not just Gereon survivors, though. Include Novobazky and at least a couple of Belladon scouts.'

'Yes, sir.'

'And keep checking in with me.'

'Yes, sir.' Rawne saluted and walked away. Wilder turned to Baskevyl and Novobazky.

'That was right, wasn't it?' he asked.

Baskevyl nodded. 'If there's even a shred of truth,' Novobazky said, 'this is important.'

'And if there's not, at least it gets Rawne out of my face for a few hours.' Wilder grinned. 'Who knows, we might get lucky. Something might eat Rawne.'

THE HUNTING PARTY left the Eighty-First First position half an hour later, and headed south into the broad scrub of the compartment's centre. Rawne had brought Mkoll and Bonin, Varl, Criid and Beltayn, and left the choice of Belladons to Commissar Novobazky. Novobazky selected Ferdy Kolosim, Wes Maggs and two recon troopers Rawne hadn't met called Kortenhus and Villyard.

They moved south in a wide circle, through thickets of gorse and thorn-rush, and across fields of loose flint and ashy soil. Three times in the first hour, Mkoll announced he'd detected a trail, but each one was at least two or three days cold, in his opinion, and too vague to bother with.

'I don't see anything,' Maggs complained each time.

'Why am I not surprised?' muttered Bonin.

Mkoll led them on through a belt of dead trees: leafless, desiccated costers, bleached by the elements, clawing at the sky with gnarled branches. Massive boulders slumped between the trees every few dozen metres, mossy blocks of misshapen granite that looked as if they might have tumbled down from the compartment walls generations before. Mkoll and Bonin studied each one.

'What's the interest in the rocks?' Novobazky asked Rawne.

'Gaunt told me he'd tracked a stalker in the third compartment, and its trail seemed to go dead at the foot of a large rock.'

'He tracked one?' the commissar queried.

'Actually, the tracking was done by Eszrah Night, a Gereon partisan who kind of attached himself to Gaunt. Excellent tracker, mind you. Quite brilliant.'

'If this Night fellow is so good,' said Novobazky, 'why has Gaunt got us doing this?'

'Gaunt wants to support his theory with clean evidence,' Rawne said. 'If you were high command, Novobazky, who would you trust? The heathen claims of a primitive hunter, or the authenticated findings of an Imperial Guard recon expedition?'

'Point,' said Novobazky.

'Here's something!' Mkoll called.

They hurried over. Criid, Varl and the Belladons formed a perimeter.

'It's getting dark!' Varl called out, weapon raised.

'I know,' replied Rawne. Mkoll was crouching beside the foot of a large rock.

'Trail here,' Mkoll said. 'Pretty fresh too. It seems to go right in under this rock.'

'How can that be?' Kolosim asked.

Maggs bent down beside Mkoll. 'I see it this time. Throne, Mkoll, your eyes are good. No doubt about it, it runs right in under this rock.'

'Here's another!' Bonin called.

The main group moved across to where he was kneeling in an open patch of rush-grass. The troopers on watch moved with them, rifles steady.

'Really, getting dark now!' Varl called.

'I know,' said Rawne.

'Just saying,' said Varl.

'Fresh. Moving that way,' Bonin said, examining the trail. 'Maybe last night or this morning, early.'

Mkoll nodded. 'This way.'

'Hang on,' said Kolosim. His voice had an amusing lisp to it because of the swelling around his split lip. 'I thought Bonin said it was moving that way?'

'I did,' said Bonin.

'So… why are we going in the opposite direction?'

'Because we don't want to know where it went, Ferdy,' Maggs said. 'We want to know where it came from.'

'Say what you like about Maggs,' Bonin said to Mkoll, 'he's a quick learner.'

'He is,' Mkoll agreed. 'He really is.'

Criid suddenly held up her hand. The party froze. From not too far away, a whooping roar rang through the dead forest.

'Oh, tremendously not good at all,' said Varl.

'Full auto,' Rawne said. 'Safeties off.'

'Never mind that,' Novobazky said. He drew a pistol from under his coat. Heavy, matt-black and ugly, it was unmistakably a plasma weapon. 'Hark lent me this. Thought we could do with the extra oomph.'

'I've always loved Commissar Hark,' Varl said. Beltayn grinned.

Criid signed. *Something moving, thirty metres.*

Mkoll nodded, and signed the party to move on anyway. Criid and Varl brought up the rear, walking backwards, rifles aimed into the gathering dark.

The trail led into another clearing. At the centre lay yet another big rock, a three tonne ovoid, gleaming with a varnish of glossy green lichen.

'Stay back,' said Mkoll. The party halted at the edge of the clearing.

'What is it?' asked Novobazky.

'You feel that?' Mkoll asked.

Bonin and Beltayn nodded. 'I sure as feth do,' Rawne said. 'It's faint, but it's there. A tiny buzzing.'

'Like a glyf,' said Beltayn.

'Exactly,' said Rawne. 'Exactly like the sound a glyf makes.'

'What's a gliff?' asked Kortenhus.

'You don't want to know,' said Bonin.

'Damn, it's making my skin crawl,' said Rawne.

'It's making my tongue itch,' said Varl.

'I can't feel anything,' said Novobazky. 'Except… except a sense of unease. Is that just me?'

Rawne shook his head.

'Not the first time I've heard this on Ancreon Sextus,' Mkoll said. 'You heard it last time, Maggs. You too, Major Kolosim.'

'That buzzing?' Kolosim replied. 'That was deafening.'

'This is much more low level, but it's the same thing,' Bonin said.

'Oh shit,' said Villyard. 'Look!'

The Belladon scout was pointing towards the boulder in the clearing. Something *wrong* was happening to it. It was distorting: bending and twisting, as if they were seeing it through a ripple of heat haze. The buzzing increased in intensity until all of them could hear it.

There was a noise like cloth tearing, the sudden pop of a pressure change, like an airgate opening, and the lifeless trees around them shivered in an exhalation of cold wind.

The boulder was no longer there. Occupying its precise space and shape was a doorway. A gate. A simple, impossible hole in the fabric of the world.

The hole shimmered. Mist, frost white, slowly drifted out of its dark, yawning gulf. Reality had somehow folded up on itself to allow this hole to be.

'There's Gaunt's answer,' Bonin said.

'I don't understand what I'm seeing,' Novobazky murmured.

'What you're seeing is a very bad thing, commissar,' whispered Mkoll.

'Hate to correct you, chief,' Varl began.

The stalker, thrice-wrought, eight hundred kilos, emerged from the hole as if it was sliding out of the surface of a mirror. It prowled forward on its knuckles, shoulders hunched and rolling loose. It sniffed the air.

'Yeah,' said Varl. 'See, *now* it's a very bad thing.'

TWENTY-TWO

18.01 hrs, 198.776.M41
Fifth Compartment
Sparshad Mons, Ancreon Sextus

'Novobazky!' Rawne yelled

'What?' the commissar stammered.

'Novobazky! The weapon!'

Genadey Novobazky, quite unmanned by his first glimpse of a mature stalker, slowly remembered who and what and where he was, and started fumbling with the plasma pistol Hark had given him.

'Hit it!' Kolosim bellowed. The stalker was coming forward, increasing speed. Its throat sacs puffed out like bellows, and its vast jaws opened to allow the steel teeth to engage.

The hunting party opened fire. Ten lasrifles on full auto lit up the clearing with a blitz of laser fire.

Shrugging it off, the monster came on, turning its bounding progress into a pounce.

The Guardsmen scattered in desperation. Maggs managed to smash Novobazky over in a side-tackle that saved both of their lives. The stalker went over them, and caught Villyard in its mouth.

The Belladon screamed the most appalling scream any of them had ever heard as the stalker's massive bite sheared him apart. Varl turned and began firing at the huge brute. Varl was no fool. He knew full well he couldn't kill the creature with his mark III. He was trying to hit Villyard. He was trying to spare the poor bastard any more agony.

Busy with its kill, the stalker lashed out with its left paw and smacked Varl into the air. He hit a tree, snapped it, and tumbled onto the cold ground.

Maggs rolled off Novobazky. 'The plasma gun! The plasma gun!' he yelled.

'I can't work the safety!' the commissar babbled, fighting with Hark's favourite weapon. 'I can't get it to–'

Maggs snatched the pistol out of Novobazky's hands. He slid the toggle and aimed it at the stalker.

The huge beast turned, its muzzle slick with Villyard's blood. It hooted and roared, and began to charge the Belladon scout like a fighting bull.

'Eat this,' said Maggs, and fired. The searing beam from the pistol vapourised the stalker's enormous skull in an astonishing burst of blood and bone chips.

But the sheer momentum of the thrice-wrought's attack carried its mammoth, headless carcass on. It slammed into Maggs, and knocked him backwards through the air.

Limbs flailing, a look of despair on his face, Maggs fell backwards into the hole and vanished. The headless stalker collapsed onto the soil in front of the shimmering gate.

'Maggs!' Bonin shouted, and ran towards the hole. Mkoll was behind him.

'Feth!' Bonin said, coming to a halt in front of the hole. He reached out his hand and the light rippled like water around his finger tips. 'Maggs! Maggs!'

Bonin looked at Mkoll.

'Never leave a man behind,' Mkoll said, and leapt through the portal.

'Mkoll! No!' Bonin roared.

There was a shout from behind him. Criid had opened up. A second stalker, the one that had been trailing them, exploded out of the treeline and came lumbering across the clearing towards Bonin.

The Tanith scout dived away, coming up to spatter lasshots into the thing's flank as it turned. It wasn't as big or mature as the beast that had come out of the hole, but it was still big enough. Three hundred kilos plus, thick with muscle, its plated skull half a metre long, its teeth the size of fingers.

It made for Bonin, roaring. Rifle fire smacked into it from the left and forced it to turn away. Kolosim and Criid were coming forward, firing at it, trying to distract it from Bonin.

Their efforts worked. It went for them instead.

Dughan Beltayn landed on its back. He stabbed his straight silver down into the rear of the monster's skull. Black blood burst up across his hands and forearms. The stalker convulsed and bucked, throwing Beltayn off its back like an unbroken horse.

Hurt, panting, its throat sacs swelling in and out like a respirator pump, the stalker took a few, unsteady steps. Beltayn's dagger was still buried in the back of its head.

Rawne stepped towards it. There was something in his hand.

'Hello, you,' he said. The beast turned, blood dripping from its gigantic mouth. It gurgled and opened its jaws, slotting its teeth in and out of position as it tasted a new target to bite.

Rawne threw the tube-charge into its wide open smile.

The stalker's jaws closed. There was a brief rumble, and then it blew apart, showering the whole clearing with greasy blood and lumps of meat.

Rawne wiped the hot, rank gore off his face. 'All right, Mach?'

Bonin got to his feet and nodded.

'Criid? Kolosim? Bel?'

'I'm fine,' said Beltayn. He looked at Bonin. 'Back of the skull, that's what you told me. Back of the skull, you said.'

'You did fine,' Bonin replied. He wasn't really interested. He was gazing at the boulder.

The gate had closed. It was just a boulder again.

'Mkoll? Come back. Maggs? Respond.' Beltayn delicately adjusted the dials of his vox-caster. 'Mkoll. This is hunting party. Do you receive?'

'Maybe you broke the caster jumping on that thing's back?' Bonin suggested.

'Well, I wouldn't have done an idiot thing like that if you hadn't told me the back of the skull was the weak spot,' Beltayn snapped.

'It worked for me,' Bonin said.

'Children, hush,' said Rawne. 'Bel? Any joy yet?'

Beltayn shook his head. 'Something's awry. I'm not picking up Maggs or the chief, but they're close. I mean, I've got their signals. I'm picking up their microbeads.'

'Why can't we talk to them?' Kolosim asked.

Beltayn shrugged. 'Microbead links have a range of about ten kilometres, tops, major. This baby–' he patted his vox-caster set, 'well, she's good for global work. The point is, look here.'

Beltayn indicated a particular gauge on the vox-set. 'That's the range finder. We call it the booster. See, see how it's hunting?'

'What does that mean?' Criid asked.

'It means… it means something's awry,' Beltayn replied. 'I've got signals from their microbeads, which suggests they're somewhere within a ten-kilometre spread from here. But the set is hunting madly for a fix. Like they're also out of range.'

'Out of range?' said Rawne. 'Out of *global* range?'

Beltayn shook his head. 'I can't explain it. They're close by… but they're also not actually on…' his voice trailed away.

'Not actually on Ancreon Sextus any more?' Rawne finished.

'Um, yes, sir. I said it was awry.'

Rawne turned away. 'How's Varl?' he asked Kortenhus.

'Sore,' said the Belladon. 'He'll live.'

'All right, Novobazky?' Rawne said.

'I froze,' Novobazky said. 'I'm sorry. I've never seen anything like that before. I still can't–'

'No blame,' Rawne said. 'That was a shock to us all.'

'Sir!' Beltayn cried. 'I have something. Throne, it's coming through like it's on a delay. Why would it be on a delay?'

'Speaker!' Rawne demanded.

Beltayn threw a switch on the vox-caster. They all stood silently as the crackling, distorted voices breathed out of the vox-set.

'–shit hole now!'

Crackle. 'It's not good, is it?'

'Is this what you meant? The shit you could get me in if you really tried?'

'Shut up, Maggs.'

Indistinct garbage followed for a while.

'–the sky? What the hell's wrong with the sky?' That was Maggs. '–the frigging stars are wrong. They're just wrong. It's so frigging cold.'

'Shut up.'

'So cold. Look at the roof.'

Crackle.

'Why?'

'It's like a roof. I mean, a ceiling. Stones. Huge stones. What's holding it up?'

'Shut up.'

Crackle.

'Mkoll, Mkoll, we're picking you up,' Beltayn said. 'Respond!'

Crackle.

'–are we? I mean where the f–'

'–swear Maggs, if you don't shut u–'

Crackle.

'Beltayn? Beltayn? Is that you? This is Mkoll. I can read you, but you're not clear. Say again.'

Beltayn keyed the send button. 'Mkoll, this is Bel. We're reading you, over.'

Crackle.

'–can no longer hear you. If you can hear me, get Rawne to the set.'

'I'm here,' Rawne said.

'–getting nothing over the microbeads. I hope you can hear me. Tell Rawne we're not on Ancreon Sextus any more. Tell Rawne–'

Crackle.

'–place is like a vast chapel. There's no supports for the roof. Stones hanging in the air. It makes me want to cry. It's all so impossible. Maggs has lost it. There are stalkers here. All around us. Hundreds of them, climbing the rocks towards us. I think they have our scent.'

Crackle. A long whine of distortion.

'–me the pistol! Give me the fething plasma pistol, Maggs! They're coming for us! Give me–'

Crackle. Distort. Whine.

'–come on! Move! Don't–'

'–this way! Keep–'

'–right behind us! Keep moving now for feth's sake or we–'

A hideous roar burst out of the vox-caster speakers. Then the channel went dead.

Flat noise droned out of it.

'Oh, Throne,' Criid said.

All of them winced as a bomb went off three hundred metres west. With Rawne in the lead, they started running towards the blast, weapons raised.

Varl, Bonin and Criid fanned out ahead, scouring the woodland, rifles at their shoulders.

'Clear!'

'Clear this way!'

'Over here!' Bonin cried out. The hunting party ran to him.

He was hunched over in another clearing, beside another huge stone. Mkoll and Maggs were sprawled at his feet, lifeless, caked in frost. The corpse of a stalker lay nearby, its skull destroyed by a tube-charge.

Rawne knelt down beside Mkoll and cradled his head.

'Chief?'

Mkoll's eyes opened, slowly blinking. 'Gaunt was right,' he gasped. 'Gaunt was right.'

TWENTY-THREE

GAUNT WOKE TO find Eszrah shaking him by the shoulder. For a moment, he thought he was still on Gereon, in the gloom of the Untill. But this was a different kind of darkness. He remembered where he really was.

He peered at his chronometer. Its glass had been shattered some time during the previous two days. It was still the dead of night. He'd been asleep in the back of the Salamander for less than three hours. He remembered climbing in to rest for a minute, and then nothing. Exhaustion had overwhelmed him.

'What is it?' he asked.

Eszrah pointed. A young Binar corporal was waiting beside the command tread. His uniform was torn and blotched with mud.

Gaunt slid down from the tread's bay. Every atom of him ached, and some pieces of him hurt a great deal more than that. He was slightly dizzy and disorientated.

'Yes?' he said.

The corporal saluted. 'Commissar Gaunt?'

'Yes.'

'A message for you, sir. It came through to my vox station. It says it's urgent.'

Gaunt nodded and rummaged for his cap. He followed the young soldier back down the rutted trackway.

A kilometre behind them, the battle still raged. It was just entering its third day. Somehow, they had endured thus far, somehow they had held that narrow, precious line and kept the enemy at bay. The previous afternoon, reinforcements had begun to arrive. By the evening, the Fortis Binars and their allied units had finally been able to retire from the front and rest.

Gaunt glanced back as he walked down the track. The blackness of the night had been thickened into an almost solid mass by the smoke, and this darkness was underlit by a throbbing orange glow from the vast firezones along the front line. The crackle and shriek of munitions continued to echo up from the fenland positions. Gunships swirled through the murk overhead.

All down the long trackway, men slept or rested in the jumbled troop trucks and fighting vehicles. Most of them were Binars, many of them were wounded. The worst of the injured had been evacuated out in slow-moving processions to post 10.

Gaunt and the corporal reached the vox station, set up in one of a cluster of habi-tents beside the trackway. Figures, mainly junior officers, milled about, dead on their feet from fatigue.

The corporal showed Gaunt over to one of the casters, where the operator made some deft connections, and handed a headset to Gaunt. He removed his cap and slid the set on.

'This is Gaunt.'

'Rawne. We've got what you need, over.'

'Confirm that, Rawne. You have proof, over?'

'Corroboration, Bram. It's solid, over.'

'Where are you, over?'

'Post 36, fifth compartment. That's 36 in the fifth, over.'

'Stay there. I'm coming to you. Gaunt out.'

Gaunt handed the set back and left the tent.

ESZRAH WAS WAITING for him outside. Despite the fact that he'd been in the thick of battle for as long as Gaunt, the Nihtgane seemed untroubled by any sign of fatigue.

'Come on,' Gaunt said to him, and began to walk south down the track, away from the boom of war.

'Restye!' Eszrah called out. Gaunt turned. The partisan was hanging back, glancing behind him up the track.

'What?' Gaunt asked.

'Ludd?' Eszrah said. The last time Gaunt had seen Ludd, the young man had been unconscious from exhaustion in the seat of a cargo-10 parked off the road.

Gaunt shook his head. 'Not this time. Come on.'

THEY FOLLOWED THE track for about a kilometre, stepping out of the road from time to time as heavy transports and armoured cars went by, moving up towards the line. The landscape on either side of them was clogged with troop trucks and munition freighters, along with tanks and Chimeras preparing to advance. A broad patch of bare earth was being used as a forward landing strip for gunships and Valkyries. Six of the machines were on the ground, surrounded by prep crews and fuel bowsers.

Gaunt led Eszrah past a team of bombardiers off-loading tank shells from the payload bay of one battered Valkyrie, and approached the next in line. The pilot, who had been resting on the ground beside his machine, jumped up when he saw the commissar approaching.

'You fuelled and prepped?' Gaunt asked.

'Yes, sir, but–'

'But what?'

The pilot explained that his Valkyrie and the three next to it were on standby for Marshal Sautoy and his senior officers. Sautoy had finally graced the front line with his presence four hours before, to 'oversee the reinforcement phase'.

'The marshal, who's a personal friend of mine,' Gaunt said, 'will have to spare you. I need transit right now. Urgent Commissariat business.'

'It's… irregular, sir,' the pilot said.

'Look around, my friend,' said Gaunt. 'Everything's irregular right now. I can't exaggerate the importance of this. If I hang around and try to go through proper channels to get a bird assigned, I'll be here the rest of the night. If it helps, I'll sign off on a k46-B requisition slip to say that I've commandeered you. You can always show that to your flight controller.'

The pilot studied Gaunt for a moment. There was no doubting his rank, but the commissar was a mess. His clothes were ragged and filthy, and he had fresh scratches and contusions on his dirty face and an agony of fatigue in his pale eyes. He also appeared to have a shoulder wound. The pilot concluded this was probably not a man to cross.

'I'll clear off the fitters and get us up, sir,' the pilot said, buttoning up his flight suit. 'Destination?'

'Fifth compartment,' Gaunt told him. 'Post 36.'

FROM THE AIR, Sparshad Mons was a sprawling, monstrous shadow twitching with ten thousand spots of fire. They flew through reeking banks of smoke that blotted everything out, forcing the pilot to fly by instruments. In clearer patches, once they were over the second compartment, Gaunt could see the columns of troop and armour advance threading up into the step-city: long, winding rivers of lamps and headlights flowing through the dark. Everything was coming. Van Voytz had committed everything he had.

Beyond, to the north, the towering heart of the Mons rose, full of secrets and malice. Implacable, immense, as solid as a mountain peak, it lowered above the outer compartments, half-visible in the night, as ugly as a death threat.

The Valkyrie flew on, down the long fourth compartment, where yet more mighty rivers of military traffic flowed onward. A significant portion of Van Voytz's commitment was heading for the bitter fifth compartment hot zone. Gaunt understood that the Imperial forces were at least making some headway in the fifth. Given the weight of the reinforcement coming through, he was hardly surprised.

They came in under the cyclopean arch and entered the fifth. Far ahead, down country, the baleful glow of a battle lit up the night, amber and red. Gaunt sighted the post, brightly-lit by radiant ground lights and stab-beams, over to the left of them. Another long column of armour and transportation was moving north below.

The Valkyrie circled in, and began its descent towards the wide table of basalt west of the post that served as a landing pad. They touched down with a gently controlled thud and the engines cycled down.

Gaunt slid open the side hatch and jumped out, Eszrah behind him.

'Do you want me to stay on site, sir?' the pilot called out.

Gaunt nodded. 'Yes, thank you. As long as you can.'

'Turn-around checks, please!' the pilot shouted to the approaching ground crew. 'Ten minutes!'

Gaunt and Eszrah hurried up the path towards the house that served as the focus of the post. The low, hillside area around it was encrusted with thousands of habi-tents, like barnacles on the skin of some sea-monster. There was a din of engines from the nearby trackway as the relief column rolled past, without beginning or end. The post itself was bustling with personnel.

'Who's the post commander?' Gaunt asked a passing Kolstec NCO.

'That would be Marshal DeBray, sir.'

'Where can I find him?'

'He's already gone forward to the front line, sir.'

'So who's in charge here?'

'Colonel Beider, sir. Sarpoy 88th.'

'And where would he be?'

The NCO shrugged. 'Maybe in the main dug-out? Or you could try–'

'Never mind,' said Gaunt. He walked past the NCO towards a figure he'd just spotted in the crowd. An old man, all on his own, watching, waiting.

Gaunt began to walk faster, pushing through the crowds. The old man turned, and saw him coming.

Gaunt took a few, last steps, and dropped to his knees in front of him.

'Ayatani father,' he whispered. Zweil bent down and laid his hands on Gaunt's shoulders, gently urging him back onto his feet. The priest gazed up into Gaunt's face. There were tears welling in Zweil's ancient eyes.

'I've seen plenty, life I've had,' Zweil said. 'But the sight of you here gives me the most joy.'

'It's good to see you too,' said Gaunt. He swallowed hard. 'I've been a long time without blessing, father, too long. My sins are heavy on me. Sometimes, I think they're too heavy now to be lifted away, even by the beati.'

'She's a strong lass,' Zweil said. 'I'm sure she'll be up to the job.'

Zweil continued to stare into Gaunt's face. 'By all that's holy, Ibram, you have been to hell, haven't you?'

'It wore a different name, but yes.'

'I like the beard, though,' said Zweil.

ZWEIL LED GAUNT up towards post command, his arm linked around Gaunt's for both comfort and support. Ayatani Zweil, permanently ancient, had become much more old and frail since the last time Gaunt had seen him.

'Rawne's here?'

'Yes, yes. You've lost weight too. Have you not been eating?'

'Father…'

'And you're hurt. These scratches on your face.'

'Yes, father. There was a battle.'

'And your shoulder. What's wrong with your shoulder?'

'A wound. A flesh wound.'

Zweil tutted. 'Flesh wound? Flesh wound? They're all flesh wounds! No one ever says "Ooh, look! I've just been shot in the bones, but it missed my flesh completely!" It's a load of old nonsense, is what it is. It's a phrase you heroic warrior types trot out so you can sound manly and stoic. "Bah, it's just a flesh wound! Only a flesh wound! I can carry on!" Nonsense!'

'Father–'

'I've heard men say that when a leg's come off!'

'Father Zweil…'

Zweil suddenly leaned close and whispered up into Gaunt's ear. 'I don't want to worry you, Ibram my dear boy, but there's a very large man following us. Very large. Great tall fellow. He looks pretty sinister to me, but I'm sure you're aware of him, ever-vigilant coiled spring that you are.'

Gaunt halted and turned.

'Eszrah? Come here.' The Nihtgane approached.

'Eszrah ap Niht, of the Gereon Untill. This is my old friend Father Zweil of the Imhava Ayatani.'

The towering partisan nodded slightly in Zweil's direction.

'Biddye hallow, elderen,' he said.

'What did he say?' Zweil asked, sidelong to Gaunt.

'He greeted you.'

'He's very tall. Alarmingly tall. I say, you're very tall, sir.'

'Hwat seythee?'

'I said, you're very tall. Tall!' Zweil gestured with his hand above his own head. 'Tall? You know? Not short?'

'Hwat, elderen?'

'Is he simple in the head, Ibram? He doesn't seem to understand.'

Eszrah looked questioningly at Gaunt, nodded towards Zweil and plucked his fingers away from his lips.

'No, that's all right,' Gaunt said. 'I've suffered him this long.'

'That was a rude gesture, wasn't it?' Zweil whispered to Gaunt. 'He just made a rude gesture towards me.'

'No, father. He was just concerned for my welfare.'

'Hnh! Tall is one thing, rude is quite another. Strange acquaintances you pick up in your travels, Gaunt.'

'I've often thought so,' Gaunt smiled. 'Now, where's Rawne?'

'In here, in here,' Zweil muttered, pushing open the doors into the wards of the infirmary. A smell of counter-septic and body waste suddenly filled the air. Medicae personnel were treating the latest batch of wounded shipped back from the fifth compartment front line.

'This way!' Zweil called breezily, apparently oblivious to the suffering around him. He strode on into the field theatre.

Gaunt followed him and came to a halt. The massive, badly damaged corpse of a semi-mature stalker lay on the theatre bed. A masked surgeon was in the middle of a rigorous autopsy.

The surgeon looked up at the interruption and slowly set down his bloodied instruments. He struggled for a moment to take off his gloves and mask, and then came quickly across the room to Gaunt and embraced him.

'Throne of Terra, Ibram!'

'Hello, Tolin.'

Dorden took a step back. 'Let me look at you,' he said. 'Feth, is it really you?'

'In the flesh.'

'That's why I brought him to you first, doctor,' Zweil said. 'So you could look at him. He has a flesh wound, he says. In the flesh, precisely, *in corpus mortalis*. He blusters he's fine, but you know these warrior types. Off comes a leg and they blither on regardless.'

'You're hurt?' Dorden said. 'Leg, is it?'

'Just ignore Zweil for a moment. I've scraped a shoulder. You can look at it later. Rawne's here, isn't he?'

Dorden nodded.

'Was this his idea?' Gaunt asked, gesturing to the autopsy.

'One of your lot suggested it, actually. A commissar, Novobazky. He's with Rawne. They dragged this carcass out of the scrubland with them.'

'Find anything?'

Dorden shrugged. 'Yes. Things I'd rather not have found. But I'm still collating data.'

'I need to see Rawne. Do you know where he is?'

THE HUNTING PARTY was waiting in one of the larger habi-tents outside the infirmary. Dorden led Gaunt across, with Zweil and Eszrah behind them. Gaunt went inside the tent, and embraced Criid, Varl and Beltayn. Bonin shook him firmly by the hand. The Ghosts greeted Eszrah warmly too, though the partisan made no response. Rawne waited, facing Gaunt.

'Bram.'

'Elim. Same old, same old. eh?'

'There's only war, sir.'

'Show me what you have.'

'Introductions, first,' Rawne said. 'This is Kolosim, Eighty-First First.'

'I've heard a lot about you, sir,' Kolosim said.

'And this is Commissar Novobazky.'

'Gaunt,' Novobazky nodded.

'Commissar,' Gaunt nodded back.

'Over there,' said Rawne, 'that's Recon Trooper Kortenhus. On the cots there, Recon Trooper Maggs and, well, Mkoll.'

'Poor devils,' said Zweil.

Mkoll and Maggs were supine on simple bed frames. Both of them were hooked up to intravenous drips and bio-feeds. Both looked unconscious, cold, pinched.

'What's wrong with them?' Gaunt asked.

'They went through,' Rawne said. 'They left this planet entirely for a few minutes. Dorden says they're hypothermic and run-down, but they'll live.'

'They left this planet entirely for a few minutes?' Gaunt repeated.

'The proof you were asking for,' Rawne said.

'Start at the top,' Gaunt said.

RAWNE RECOUNTED THE hunting mission for a few minutes. What detail he left out was readily reinforced by Varl, Novobazky and Beltayn.

'Bonin said the back of the skull was the weak point, so that's what I did,' Beltayn complained. 'He'd already killed a stalker that way.'

'You killed a stalker by stabbing it in the back of the head?' Gaunt asked Bonin.

'Yeah. Sure,' said the scout. 'They're not armoured in the back.'

'That's not the point I was trying to make, sir,' Beltayn continued. 'I tried it, on good faith, and–'

'Let's move along,' said Gaunt. 'Commissar Novobazky? Maybe you'd like to report?'

Novobazky nodded. 'I can only confirm what these people have told you, Gaunt. The stalkers clearly enter the compartments via portals. Warp gates. I don't know what you'd call them. They're like trap doors, letting the bastards out after dark, right in amongst us.'

'This is a character of the Mons, you think?'

Novobazky shrugged. 'The various standing stones in the inner terrain seem to be the focal points of the gates. Throne, I don't know. I'm no expert in these things. In my opinion, the Mons is wired to let them through. It's built into the architecture. Established warp gates, networked to I don't know where. This isn't a level playing field.'

'And the stalkers themselves?' Gaunt asked, looking at Dorden, who was standing in the doorway of the habi-tent.

'Tissue samples say they're ogryns,' Dorden said, 'with some human genetic material. The creations of some vicious eugenic program. Their brains are modified for absolute aggression. We're talking about human and ogryn specimens who have been stripped down, rebuilt and programmed just to kill.'

'You've proof?'

Dorden shook his head. 'I'm still collating. I don't have the right instrument back-up here to be conclusive. This is just a field hospital. Maybe if I had access to the body scanners and biopsy vaults at Frag Flats or Tarenal. Right now, it's just a hunch.'

'We do hunches,' Rawne said. 'Inklings too.'

Gaunt looked at Dorden. 'But from what you've seen, doctor, you'd say these were modified human or human-allied troops?'

Dorden nodded. 'The corpse I was autopsying, it had dog tags buried in the flesh of its throat. I mean overlapped by skin graft and regrowth. The tags identified a Trooper Ollos Ollogred, Fifth Storm Faction (Ogryn), 21st Hurgren Regiment. I checked it out. The 21st is currently in action on Morlond.'

'They're sending our own people back to fight us,' Novobazky said.

'It seems so,' Gaunt replied. 'And they're sending them back through punctures in the warp. Anyone here remember the *jehgenesh*?' he asked.

Rawne, Varl, Criid and Bonin nodded. Beltayn moaned at the memory.

'The what?' asked Novobazky, but Gaunt had already moved on. 'Mkoll and...what was his name? Maggs? They went through?' he asked.

'And came back alive,' Rawne replied.

'I want to talk to them,' Gaunt said.

DORDEN INJECTED SOMETHING powerful into Mkoll's drip, and nursed him back into consciousness.

'Five minutes,' he told Gaunt. 'That's all I'll allow.'

Gaunt nodded. He crouched down at Mkoll's bedside. 'Oan? Hey, Oan? It's Gaunt.'

'...never come back...'

'Mkoll?'

'Thought you'd never come back,' Mkoll slurred, opening his eyes.

'You're going to be fine, Oan. Dorden says so. I just want to talk to you.'

'So talk. I'm not going anywhere.'

'What did you see, Oan? What the feth did you see?'

Mkoll rolled over and stared at the roof of the habitent. 'Maggs went through, so I followed him. Never leave a man behind, that's what you always taught me.'

'I did. I did.'

'So I went after him. It was cold, that place. Really cold. I knew at once that I'd stepped off Ancreon Sextus completely. I was… somewhere…'

'Oan?'

'Sorry sorry, drifting off. I was somewhere else. The stars weren't right, that was the first thing I noticed. The constellations were entirely different. I navigate by the stars. I notice these things.'

'Go on, Oan.'

'It was cold. Did I mention that? I mean really cold. Rocks, slabs. Everywhere you looked. Maggs was shouting about the sky, and I noticed that too. I could see star patterns, but directly overhead, it was a roof. A ceiling. Massive blocks of stone hanging in the night sky. It made no sense. How could stones be just hanging there? And they were so quiet.'

'Quiet?' Gaunt asked.

'Really quiet,' Mkoll whispered. 'They should have been making a huge noise, a sky filled with stone slabs. But they were quiet.'

His voice faded away. Dorden reluctantly pushed another vial into the drip.

'No more,' he told Gaunt.

Gaunt nodded. 'Oan? Tell me about the place. Was it empty?'

'No! No, no, no. Hordes of stalkers, massing to attack. Inhuman things too. Machines. War machines. Blood Pact. We ran, and we tried to hide. The stalkers came after us. The wrought ones. I saw legions of the damned, assembled, en masse, waiting for the gates to open.'

'The gates?' Gaunt asked.

'You have to understand,' Mkoll murmured. 'There's nothing inside the Mons. It's empty. It's just a gateway.

A massive gateway, sucking us in so it can open and destroy us. The gates in each compartment don't lead into the next compartment along. I saw them. Laid out in a row. They open into somewhere else….'

'Mkoll?'

'That's enough!' snapped Dorden. 'He's passed out again.'

Eszrah suddenly unharnessed his reynbow and moved to the entrance.

'What is it?' Varl asked. He and Criid switched round, training their weapons on the mouth of the tent. Bright lights were flickering outside. Gaunt rose, hearing the whine of a gunship.

'Put your guns away,' he said. 'You too, Eszrah. I've been waiting for this.'

The tent flaps pulled aside and Commissariat troopers came in, firearms raised.

'Nobody move!' the squad leader said, playing his hellgun around the tent.

Nobody did, not even Rawne.

His pistol aimed squarely at Gaunt, Faragut entered the tent. Behind him came Commissar-General Balshin, Inquisitor Welt and Nahum Ludd.

'You will surrender yourselves to the authority of the Commissariat!' Faragut barked.

'End of the road, Gaunt,' Balshin smiled.

'I'm really very sorry, sir,' Ludd said.

TWENTY-FOUR

'WE GAVE YOU a chance, Gaunt,' Balshin said smoothly. 'I was against it, but the lord general insisted. We gave you the chance to prove yourself. And as is usually the case when someone is given enough rope…'

'All the things you could be focusing your attention on, commissar-general,' Gaunt said, 'and you fixate on me. I really bother you, don't I?'

'My foremost task is the removal of the heresy of taint in the Imperial Guard, Gaunt,' she replied. 'It is endemic on this front of the Crusade. I have never seen its effects so pernicious, so deep-rooted. Of course I am bothered when a senior commissar, a man of influence and authority, walks free amongst us, riddled with the touch of ruin.'

Gaunt almost laughed out loud. 'Based on what?'

Balshin stared at him levelly, as if scolding a recalcitrant child. 'I was never satisfied with your testimony at the tribunal. It was hollow. To be exposed for such a length of

time to an afflicted world? The notion you remained
untainted is laughable. Since returning to duty, your
behaviour has been wayward to say the least. You have
meandered from duty, pursued your own private agendas.
There have been unauthorised communiqués, conspiratorial exchanges conducted under the guise of official
Commissariat business…'

Gaunt shook his head. 'Is that all you've got?'

She smiled blandly. 'Let's consider the fact that just a
few hours ago you deserted your post, broke your
orders, misappropriated an Imperial transport, moved
from one location to another within a martial cordon
without clearance or validation… and here I find you,
plotting again, in a little huddle with some of the very
people who stood accused of taint beside you.'

'I suggest you modify your language, madam general,' Novobazky said sharply. Ignoring the
Commissariat troopers all around them, he took a
step towards her.

'That's close enough!' Faragut warned.

'I take issue with your characterisation of us as tainted or
heretics,' Novobazky said. 'There are matters here that–'

'Novobazky,' Balshin said. 'I always thought of you as
a dependable man. Thank you for demonstrating how
odiously and malignantly Gaunt's contamination can
be spread.'

Novobazky's face hardened and his cheeks flushed
with fury, but he kept his mouth shut. Gaunt looked
directly at Inquisitor Welt, who had not spoken a word.
'Inquisitor? Do you go along with this? I took you to be
far less blinkered than Balshin.'

'Say something to convince me,' said Welt.

Gaunt gestured around the theatre tent. 'I can tell you
plenty. Everyone in this room can tell you plenty. There

is taint here, inquisitor. It's the city itself. The place we're fighting for is sick.'

'That's ridiculous,' said Balshin. 'And borderline heresy. The step-cites of Ancreon Sextus are revered monuments that date back to–'

'Tell me about the stalkers,' Gaunt said.

'What?' Balshin snapped.

'The Ordo Xenos has established, through analysis of recovered specimens, that the so-called "stalkers" are augmetically enhanced humans and, more often ogryns,' said Welt. 'This information has been suppressed for reasons of morale. The unauthorised autopsy you have been conducting here, and all evidence bearing from it, will be sequestered by the Inquisition.'

'And tell me about the warp doors,' Gaunt said.

'What are you talking about?' Balshin asked.

'Tell me about the warp doors that riddle the compartments. Explain to me how the stalkers get in and out during the night.'

'I don't know what you mean. We have assumed burrows, perhaps…'

'There aren't any fething burrows,' Rawne said. 'My team and I witnessed a warp door in use last night, less than five kilometres from where we're standing. We saw a stalker come through. Those two men there passed through the gate themselves and re-emerged through a second one.' Rawne pointed at the unconscious forms of Maggs and Mkoll on the cots.

'They must be examined and interviewed,' said Welt.

'That will have to wait,' Dorden told him. 'They are in no condition.' Welt half-smiled at Dorden, as if amused at the medicae's defiance of an Inquisitorial order.

'The structure of the Mons is unsound, Balshin,' said Gaunt.

'The structure of the Mons has been extensively studied and surveyed,' Balshin exclaimed. 'It is under constant scrutiny from the Fleet and the Tacticae. Do you really expect me to believe that you and a few of your fellow deviants can come here and, in just a few days, uncover secrets that everyone else has missed? If there was a system of warp doors here as you claim, they would have been detected months ago.'

'They are pretty much invisible to standard sensory systems,' Gaunt replied, 'and to regular human senses too.'

'But not to you?' sneered Balshin.

'No, not to me,' Gaunt said. 'Nor to any of the Gereon mission team.'

'He's practically confessing to taint!' Faragut blurted.

'I'm repeating what I've told you all along,' Gaunt said. 'I'm admitting to a sensitivity, an awareness of the vibrations of Chaos. We could not have survived our time on Gereon without developing an affinity. The very instincts that kept us alive there are showing us the truth now.' He stated directly at Balshin. 'The fact that we have worked to expose this danger, the fact that we are telling it to your face... Does that alone not prove whose side we're fighting for?'

Balshin was about to answer back, but Welt raised a hand. 'Commissar-general, perhaps you and your team would be so good as to record full statements from the individuals here. Doctor? Please prepare those two men for transportation back to Frag Flats. Gaunt, walk with me.'

Gaunt glanced at Rawne, and then followed Welt out of the theatre tent. There was a moment's silence.

'That went well, I thought,' said Varl.

***

GAUNT AND THE inquisitor walked together through the habi-tent rows of the post, and came to a halt on a patch of higher ground, looking north. The air was still black, but the compartment was lit by the moving lights and the distant radiance of fire.

'Balshin is under pressure to produce results,' Welt said. 'The Crusade Second Front is truly ailing. If your claims are validated, it will make a big difference to the way the war goes here on Ancreon Sextus.'

'They'd better be validated soon,' said Gaunt. 'Mkoll said he witnessed vast hosts massing beyond the gate. Did no one ever stop and wonder how the enemy was able to keep producing so many troops and fighting vehicles from out of the heart of this Mons?'

Welt paused, as if wondering whether to let Gaunt in on classified information. 'It's not just here, Gaunt. The situation here at Sparshad Mons is being replicated, right now, at every other step-city on the planet.'

'A unified offensive? In cities thousands of kilometres from each other?'

Welt nodded.

'It's because the enemy isn't in the cities,' Gaunt said. 'The cities are just delivery systems to bring them through. The Blood Pact armies are not waiting for us in the next compartment or the one after that. They're simply coming out of the gates. Mkoll suggested that the main compartment gates are large scale versions of the doors the stalkers use.'

'So the enemy gets our attention, draws us into laying siege to these haunted rocks, gets us to commit all our forces deep inside the walls…' Welt let the words hang.

'And then fully opens the gateways.' said Gaunt. 'I sometimes think we're guilty of underestimating our old foe, inquisitor. The Ruinous Powers operate with levels of guile and sophistication that we scarcely credit. On Gereon, we witnessed them using *jehgenesh*. Gigantic warp creatures that were bred to consume a planet's natural resources, such as fresh water or mineral ore, and excrete them via the warp to supply planets light years away. They are not destroyers, they are users. If they work on that kind of scale, why should it surprise us if they deploy entire armies that way, in places like this, where the ancient mechanisms for such transmission still exist?'

'I subscribe to the theory that the Imperium's worst enemy,' said Welt, 'is its own ignorance.'

Welt looked at Gaunt, and studied him curiously for a moment. 'Inquisitor?'

'It's an unhappy position you're in, Gaunt. Despite all the great service you've done for the Imperium, you're regarded as a difficult, dangerous man now.'

'I don't know about difficult,' said Gaunt. 'Dangerous is right, though.'

'You're this close to summary execution,' Welt said baldly. 'And there's only one thing keeping you alive.'

'What's that?'

'Me,' Welt said. 'If you and your team could survive as long as you did on that hell-hole world without succumbing to taint, then for the sake of the Imperium and the protection of our species, I have to find out why.'

WELT RETURNED TO the theatre tent to assist with the interrogations. Two Commissariat troopers were detailed to Gaunt, and kept him secluded in one of the rooms in the post. He sat alone for a few minutes, and then fell into a deep sleep. Ludd woke him four hours later. Outside, a thin light was announcing the day.

'What's going on?' Gaunt asked.

'Commissar-General Balshin's finished here. Rawne's team has been debriefed. They're to return to their unit at the front. Maggs and Mkoll will be shipped back to Frag Flats.'

'How are they?'

'Still unconscious, but showing signs of recovery. I've been sent to collect you, sir. You're to come back with us.'

Gaunt got to his feet.

'Sir, I want to say… I'm sorry,' Ludd said.

'For what?'

'For reporting your actions. Balshin made it quite clear I was to report to her any… unorthodox behaviour on your part. It was my duty. But I didn't like doing it.'

'I was counting on you, Ludd,' Gaunt said.

'What, sir?'

'When I realised something was wrong here, I knew there was no point me trying to convince Balshin. She has no time for me. I needed her to believe I was up to something, that I had something to hide. That way she'd come looking and wouldn't be able to dismiss what I had to show her.'

'So… you expected me to–'

'I expected you to do your duty, Ludd. And luckily, you did.'

TWENTY-FIVE

14.10 hrs, 199.776.M41
Frag Flats HQ
Sparshad Combat Zone, Ancreon Sextus

HE'D BEEN WAITING for hours, almost but not quite a prisoner in a spartan chamber aboard one of the command Leviathans. He kept looking at his pathetic, broken chronometer, watching time creep on slowly.

The chamber doors folded inwards on electric motors. Commissar Faragut stood in the doorway. Faragut stared at Gaunt contemptuously.

'Did you draw the lucky straw, Faragut?' Gaunt asked. 'You must be very happy. Back of the head, please. I don't want your face to be the last thing I ever see.'

Faragut tensed, but didn't take the bait. 'The lord general is waiting for you,' he said.

VAN VOYTZ WAS in the Leviathan's main tactical command centre. Intense activity was taking place all around him. Hundreds of voices speaking all at once, hundreds of logic engines chattering and whirring. The hololithic displays above the main strategium pit were changing fast: coloured patterns and contours symbolising the effects of enormous coordination work.

Van Voytz saw Gaunt approaching.

'Ibram,' he said, and gestured around himself. 'All this, Ibram.'

'Sir?'

'That's all, Faragut,' Van Voytz said, and the commissar left them.

Van Voytz led Gaunt through to a quieter side vault where eight tacticians, including Antonid Biota, were softly discussing their art around an active display table.

'Can I have the room, gentlemen?' Van Voytz asked. 'You stay, Biota.' The other tacticians filed out.

'There's been some preliminary investigation, Gaunt,' Van Voytz said. 'Ordo Xenos, various astropaths. No solid proof can be found of any warp network within the Mons.'

'I see,' said Gaunt.

'But it's all rather hasty, preliminary, as I said. Time is not on our side.'

'No, sir.'

Van Voytz sighed. 'And that's when a lord general earns his pay. Proof or no proof, a decisive tactical decision has to be made, based on the best information. You should have heard the arguments amongst the senior staff this morning. I nearly shot a couple of them. Whatever else, there are two Guardsmen in the infirmary – one a "tainted" Ghost from your Gereon team, the other most definitely not – who are well enough to testify about what they saw last night. I spoke to them both myself...'

Van Voytz looked at Gaunt. 'I know when men lie, and these men are not lying. Their words chilled me.

And when I read substantive evidence, written statements from men like Novobazky, I know I'd be a fool to dismiss what you've stumbled upon.'

The lord general glanced across at Biota.

'Thirty-eight minutes ago,' the tactician said, 'formal order was given for the immediate staged withdrawal of Imperial Guard forces from Sparshad Mons and all other step-cities on this planet. Orbital manoeuvres are now underway to deploy the Fleet in geo-synchronous positions for surface bombardment. It is estimated they will have firing solutions in eight hours.'

'I expect to give the order at around midnight tonight,' Van Voytz said.

'You're going to destroy the cities...' said Gaunt.

'I'm going to wipe them from the face of creation,' Van Voytz said. 'As I wanted to, incidentally, all along. Damn this siege work.'

'It is the prudent thing to do,' Biota said.

'A swift and total victory here could be just what the Second Front needs,' Van Voytz said. 'A robust statement of Imperial domination. An end to a long, slow, drawn-out wrestling match that has sapped and shredded morale.'

'In my opinion, sir,' said Gaunt, 'the problems the Guard has had here on Ancreon Sextus – the desertions, the sickness, the psychoses – much of that can be attributed to the taint in the cities. Exposure to these places has twisted men's minds and souls, even if they haven't been aware of it. The taint Balshin is so desperate to root out is real here, just very, very subversive. But on the Second Front in general, the problem is simply that Macaroth has given you a young, inexperienced army. They're scared, they're improperly supported, they're learning to make war as they go along. In the field here at Sparshad, it's been my honour to serve alongside young men who have never seen battle before. They have brave hearts, general, I can vouch for that. They simply lack the confidence to use that courage.'

'The Imperial Victory of Ancreon Sextus,' said Van Voytz, banging his fist on the edge of the display table. 'That'll put some fire into their bellies. They'll see that the Second Front is capable of accomplishing something.'

Gaunt looked at the display's schematic images of the outer compartments. 'You intend to order the start of bombardment around midnight, sir?' he asked.

'Thereabouts, as soon as it practicable.'

'It will be quite a logistical exercise getting such a huge commitment of troops and machines clear of the cities by then. Especially in situations where they are engaging the enemy.'

Van Voytz glanced uncomfortably at Biota. 'We will orchestrate as full a withdrawal as is feasible,' said the tactician. 'It is regrettable that there may be some losses.'

'Black cross losses, you mean?' said Gaunt.

'Yes.'

'So any Guard unit too slow getting clear of the cities by the deadline… or any that can't break free of enemy engagement…'

'Will be sacrificed,' said Biota calmly. 'Such losses are unfortunate, but, up to a certain proportion, considered acceptable when stacked against the over all strategic advantage.'

'What Antonid means,' grumbled Van Voytz, 'is that if we stick with the siege, we'll most likely lose a hell of lot more men than the ones who'll give their lives in a good cause tonight.'

'I understand what he means,' said Gaunt. 'The poor rearguard will suffer the worst.'

'Don't they always?'

Gaunt turned away from the display and faced Van Voytz. 'Sir, I request permission to return to the field. Discipline will be the deciding factor in how quickly and cleanly the withdrawal can be managed. There will be fear and panic, and also carelessness. You need every commissar you can find to supervise.'

'I expected you to say as much,' Van Voytz said. 'If you must, then–'

'I want to go to the fifth compartment, sir.'

Van Voytz let a slight smile turn his lips. 'Yes, I thought you might. That's where they are, isn't it?'

'Yes, sir.'

'Carry on, Commissar Gaunt.'

GAUNT REMOVED ESZRAH Night from the holding cell where the Commissariat had put him, and together they recovered their confiscated weapons and possessions from a duty officer.

The hull-top flight platforms were seething with activity in the glaring sunlight. Lifters, gunships and fliers were already relaying personnel back from the Mons. Servitors unloaded equipment, and fitter teams in sunshrouds worked on quick turn-arounds. Gaunt found a deck supervisor, who consulted his checklists and told Gaunt there'd be spaces on one of the Destrier-pattern heavy carriers in fifteen minutes.

Gaunt and Eszrah waited by the guard rail. Other passengers, mostly officers and medicae staff, gathered. From the high vantage, Gaunt could see the Frag Flats camp below, spread out under the white sun, baking in the heat. After days in the Mons's drab, dank micro-climate, obscured by smoke, it felt like another world.

The camp was striking. Even the Frag Flats HQ was going to withdraw to a greater distance from the Mons before the midnight deadline. Gaunt watched the temporary city slowly deconstructing itself.

A pair of Valkyries lifted off the pad behind him, and he turned to watch them go. They arced away in the bright blue air towards the great, dark cloud on the horizon.

The deck supervisor called them, and they walked with the other waiting men towards one of the bulky Destriers. It was an ugly, obese flier, its hull flaking grey. The side hatch was open, and they clambered into the battered, bare metal hold and made themselves comfortable in the small, wall-mounted strap-downs.

Another of the Destriers lifted away in a huge din of thrust and flying grit. Their own transport's engines began to turn over.

'Two minutes!' the deck supervisor called.

A figure appeared in the sunlight outside, and climbed into the hold, a last-minute addition to the passengers. He walked across to Gaunt and Eszrah.

'Hello, Ludd,' Gaunt said.

'I heard you were… I mean, I thought I should…'

'Strap yourself in,' Gaunt said.

'This is going to be hard work, isn't it?' Ludd said. 'It's going to be tough getting the men out of there in time.'

'Especially if they're rearguard,' Gaunt said. 'First in, last out.'

Ludd looked over at Eszrah Night.

Slowly, carefully, as a matter of ritual, the partisan was smearing wode across his face, ready for war.

TWENTY-SIX

15.05 hrs, 199.776.M41
Fifth Compartment
Sparshad Mons, Ancreon Sextus

SOMEWHERE, SOME GOD or similar higher being, possibly one seated upon a golden throne, was having a good laugh at Lucien Wilder's expense. Ordinarily, Baskevyl believed, his friend and superior officer had a refined appreciation of good irony, but the special irony of this particular situation was simply making Wilder curse and swear.

They had come so very close.

Wilder darted across the dry gulch and ducked in behind the broken chunks of quartz where Baskevyl and a fireteam were in cover.

'Can you believe that arse?' Wilder spluttered.

'Which particular one now?' Baskevyl asked. 'Are we still on Van Voytz?'

'No!' Wilder growled. 'DeBray! Bloody shithead DeBray!'

'Because?'

'He's only ordered B and C munition trains to pull out! Both of them! That leaves us–'

Wilder broke off as a stream of tracer rounds ripped across their position. Some hit the tops of the quartz boulders, pummelling powdered rock into the stale air.

Wilder looked up and yelled 'Will somebody please kill that stubber for me?'

Two crew-served weapons nearby immediately kicked off, blasting away.

'DeBray's ordered B and C trains out of the zone already,' Wilder continued. 'Which leaves us with what's left of A. And according to the chief armourer with A, that's mostly tank shells and mines, anyway.'

'Not good news,' Baskevyl agreed.

'How does DeBray expect to maintain a successful breakaway?'

Three heavy detonations, in rapid succession, went off close by, and shook them violently. Dirt rained down.

'Dammit,' Wilder said, 'I need to be able to see better. Come with me.'

Wilder and Baskevyl left cover, heads down, and ran around the back of a low ridge where a good portion of Callide's company was dug in. They kept going into slopes of larch and coster on the north side of the ridge. There were Eighty-First First troopers down amongst the trees, N Company. Wilder could hear Captain Arcuda shouting orders.

Baskevyl and Wilder ducked down, and Wilder got out his scope. Stray shots were hitting the tops of the dead trees around them, clattering and rattling like scurrying woodland animals.

'Where's Kolea?' Wilder asked.

Baskevyl pointed. 'To the west there, in support of Obel's mob. Varaine's Company is trying to cover the open stretch there, but it keeps getting pounded by the gun platforms they've got over by the… over on the approach there.'

Wilder swung his scope round, and caught sight of the ugly, multi-barrelled cannon platforms thumping away in the middle-distance, wreathed in white smoke. He knew full well that Baskevyl had said 'on the approach' because he didn't want to use the phrase 'over by the gate'. Baskevyl didn't want to remind Wilder of the irony.

The gun platforms were indeed 'over by the gate'. Throne, they had come so very close.

The battle on and around Hill 56 and Ridge 19 had been curtailed in the small hours by the arrival of the promised reinforcements: huge levels of field reinforcement, with more on the way. DeBray himself had come forward with the advance. Word was that Van Voytz had finally committed the entire reserve into the Mons. Through the end of the night, and into the morning, the reinvigorated Imperial wave had surged forward, making large gains in the fifth compartment. In places, enemy resistance seemed to melt away completely. By midmorning, the towering gate into the sixth compartment had been clearly in view. By midday, the Imperial forces had arrived within a half kilometre of it.

DeBray had offered the Eighty-First First, along with the Kolstecs and the armour groups, the opportunity to stand relieved and retire. They had, after all, been holding the line since the start of the offensive. What remained of the Rothbergers left the field, exhausted and ground down. But for the rest of them, their blood was up. The arrival of the mass reinforcement had bolstered their spirits, and Wilder had certainly not been about to walk his men away from a fight and let somebody else get the glory of finishing it. Fofobris of the Kolstec had been of the same opinion, as had Major Garrogan of the Hauberkan armour. DeBray had graciously allowed them to continue, and together, the three units had made the best of the forward push. There had even developed a sense of friendly rivalry as to which of them would get the honour of taking the gate as a prize.

Then that special god had started laughing. The general order had been relayed forward. Van Voytz had commanded a complete and immediate staged retreat, to be accomplished no later than midnight. He had ordered the Imperial Guard to abandon Sparshad Mons. DeBray had immediately begun the systematic withdrawal of the fifth compartment strengths, starting with the backline reinforcement columns that hadn't even seen action yet.

Wilder wasn't entirely sure what was going through the lord general's mind. Very little, was his best guess. He simply was at a loss to fathom why, after all this time and effort and sacrifice, the Crusade was going to give up on Sparshad Mons.

On top of everything else, one did not simply fall back from a fighting line. A proper breakaway was called for. Certain units had to stay in position until the bitter end, covering the main retreat and holding back the enemy, or they would be inviting a massacre. Standard Guard tactics dictated that any such rearguard action should fall to the units in the most advanced position. For the Eighty-First First, the Kolstec and the Hauberkan, the glory of victory was no longer a prospect. What faced them now was a gruelling, backwards fight, as they covered the main retreat until such a time as they could themselves break off and run.

Simply run. The end of this ludicrous expedition would see them running for their lives. If he got out alive, Wilder swore he would find Van Voytz and–

'Stalk-tanks!' Baskevyl said. Five of them had just emerged from the gate itself, advancing down the rough incline in support of the Blood Pact units along the lower ridge. Fierce gunfire licked up and down the incline. Wilder heard rockets banging.

'Who's down in the rockline there?' he asked.

Baskevyl peered. 'E Company,' he said.

Meryn's lot, thought Wilder. 'I hope they have some live tread fethers left, because those stalks are going to be on them in about ten minutes.'

More loose shots snickered through the dead trees. Pieces of dry branch fluttered down. Away to the east, AT70's were booming away as they tried to prise Garrogan's treads off a shelving escarpment.

'Colonel!' Wilder turned, and saw his vox-man, Keshlan, running towards him down the wooded slope.

Small-arms fire pattered through the trees, and Keshlan fell with a sharp cry.

'Dammit! Keshlan!' Wilder was up and running. More shots pinged down, shattering bark and twigs. Some bastard somewhere had a damn good angle.

'Cover fire!' Baskevyl yelled down to Arcuda, and N Company began to lay las across the enemy positions.

Wilder reached the vox-officer.

'I'm all right, sir,' Keshlan said. His face was white with shock.

'Where'd they get you?'

'Just caught my body armour, sir. Shoulder plate's pretty smacked up, but I'm all right.'

Wilder examined him. A hard round had torn clean through Keshlan's shoulder plating and broken the skin. A few centimetres to the right and Keshlan would have taken it in the throat.

'Teach you to go running about,' he said. 'They *are* armed, you know.'

'Yes, sir.'

'You needed me?'

Keshlan picked himself up. 'Yes, sir. Signal from the marshal, sir. The Hedrogan Light is just pulling out behind us now, and we are to expect the last of the Sarpoy to follow them in the next forty minutes.'

'There'll be no one left to talk to at this rate,' Wilder said. He could see the young man was frightened, and he wanted to keep him steady. But no, it wasn't fear. Something else.

'What is it, Keshlan?'

'Signal from I Company. Captain Raydrel was shot dead about fifteen minutes ago, and both his adjutant and Sergeant Favre were killed trying to rescue him.'

'Holy Throne…' Wilder breathed hard. Favre, and the adjutant, Vullery, were fine men and old comrades. Raydrel had been a friend, one of the best officers in Wilder's command. 'Who's… who's heading up I Company now?'

'Uh, Sergeant Haston, sir.'

'Patch me to him.'

Keshlan started setting his vox. Baskevyl scurried up.

'Raydrel's dead,' Wilder said simply.

Baskevyl looked away, then at the ground. 'We all will be at this rate,' he said. 'The hand Van Voytz has dealt us. Breakaway's going to be nigh on impossible. Throne, if I could plug that gate, just for an hour.'

'Right. Or magically transport us all to a safe world full of wine and flowers. I need practical bloody solutions right now, Bask, not–' Wilder paused. 'All right, that wasn't me talking just then. And it wasn't you listening.'

'Don't apologise, Luc. I know how you feel. I want to kill something just at the moment.'

'Well, as luck would have it,' Wilder grinned, 'we happen to be in the middle of a frigging battle. Take it out on the damn Blood Pact.'

'No response from Sergeant Haston, sir,' Keshlan reported.

Wilder looked at Baskevyl. 'Bask, head down to Meryn and make sure his company is ready for those stalks. If you see Hark anywhere, tell him I need him at I Company immediately. We have to get them rallied.'

'On it.'

'Try Hark on your microbead too,' Wilder called after him. As he moved off, Baskevyl pointed back up the slope. 'More bad news,' he joked.

Wilder looked round. A group of figures was approaching, heads down.

'It's Major Rawne,' said Keshlan.

'That's all I need,' sighed Wilder.

It was Rawne, all right. Novobazky, too, and Ferdy Kolosim, along with most of the infamous 'hunting party'. Wilder scrambled up the bank to meet them.

Throughout the previous night, Kolosim had kept Wilder appraised of the hunting party's movements, though it had all been rather vague and brief. The last Wilder had heard, Rawne's team had been heading for post 36 with 'urgent information'.

'What are you doing here?' Wilder asked.

'We were sent back up the line to rejoin you this morning,' Novobazky said. 'By the time we heard about the general order, we were as good as here, so we kept going.'

'You should have turned back,' Wilder said.

'I'd prefer to withdraw alongside my regiment,' Rawne said. Wilder studied Rawne's face, and realised the man was completely serious. He nodded.

'Are you going to tell me what happened?' he asked. 'I see Kortenhus, Criid, Varl, Beltayn and Bonin. Where are the others?'

'Abe Villyard didn't make it,' said Kolosim. 'Maggs and Mkoll were shipped out, injured.'

'What the hell did you get into?' Wilder asked.

'Gaunt was right,' said Rawne simply.

'He was right?' Wilder said. 'You mean this place isn't… isn't what it seems?'

'No, it's not,' said Ferdy Kolosim.

Wilder felt a sudden rush of understanding, so swooping and immense, it made him feel giddy. 'Is this why… Throne! Is this why Van Voytz has ordered a general withdrawal?' he asked.

'I honestly don't know,' said Rawne. 'We weren't told. We were questioned by the Commissariat, and then sent back to the line.'

'Gaunt,' said Wilder. 'Frigging Gaunt! Ever since he came back from the dead, he's made my life a crap storm of problems and disappointments!'

There was a smack, flesh on flesh. Wilder realised Rawne had swung a fist at him. The scout, Bonin, had stopped Rawne's blow, blocking it tightly in his own hand.

'Don't, Eli,' Bonin hissed, squeezing.

Rawne let his hand drop.

'Oh, please. Go ahead,' Wilder said. 'Give it your best shot. I know you've been itching to, from the moment we met.'

Rawne shook his head. 'That's not true, Wilder. I have great respect for you, believe it or not. But no one badmouths Bram Gaunt in my hearing.'

Wilder thought for a moment. Close by, a series of shells exploded in a rippling line, and the air shivered with overpressure. Renewed gunfire began to crackle below them.

'Enough of this,' Wilder said. 'If you're back, you're back. Start doing some good. Ferdy, take Kortenhus and get back to your company. We'll need the left flank trim and tight in the next two hours, so that the FooFoo Frigwig and his beloved Kolstec can fall back.'

'Sir!'

'Nadey? Head along to I Company and perform your miracles. We lost Raydrel.'

'No!'

'Just do what you can.'

Novobazky nodded and hurried away.

'The rest of you come with me. E Company's in a fix. That's *Meryn's* company, Major Rawne, just so you remember, all right?'

'I understand,' said Rawne.

They hurried down the slope into the rocks. Ahead, the stalk-tanks had begun to spatter lasfire into the Eighty-First First's position.

CAFFRAN RISKED A run between boulders that brought him up behind a particularly large lump of granite. Tank fire crackled past, and Caffran could smell burning stone. The clattering strides of advancing stalk-tanks echoed around the shallow incline.

Nearby, troopers were huddled low, clipping off shots at the enemy ground troops advancing behind the tanks. Caffran could see Larkin, Osket, Kalen and Mkillian close by, obscured by their camo-capes. Several Belladons too. He wished he could remember their names.

Tank fire sizzled in again in great, slamming blasts, and Caffran ducked. He glanced up again in time to see that three of the Belladons had been cut down. Their mutilated bodies lay smouldering on the burned soil. Now he *really* wished he could remember their names.

He took a look out. One of the tanks was very close, waddling along on its slender, insectoid legs, pistons hissing and wheezing. Caffran hefted up his rocket tube, checked the load, and armed the rocket by removing the priming pin. He muttered a little blessing as he did so. Just to make it fly right.

It was his last load. He looked back the way he had come and yelled, 'Guheen! Where the feth are you?' Guheen had his back. And the heavy canvas holder with the last three rockets in it.

'Little hairy!' Guheen shouted back, ducking as small-arms fire licked past.

'Move your Tanith arse!' Caffran shouted. The tank was firing again. It sounded like masses of shingle slithering across a wet beach. It reminded Caffran of the storm landing at Oskray Island. Feth, how many years ago was that now?

'Any time soon, Caff?' Kalen shouted. Caffran shouldered the launcher tube, snuggled it close, and placed his fingers around the trigger spoon.

He swung out of cover and raised the snout of the tube. The tank was right there. Right on them, gun-pods traversing as it hunted for live targets. He clenched his fingers and depressed the metal spoon. The tube jumped violently against his shoulder as the rocket left it. There was a sucking rush, a fart of flame.

The rocket rushed out, trailing white smoke across the air behind it, and smacked into the stalk-tank head on. The blast tore off the stalk's head and thorax, burst the operator's cocoon, and smashed the whole machine over onto its back. It lay there, burning, its long metal legs twitching at the sky.

A cheer went up. *Premature*, Caffran thought. There were still four more stalk-tanks plodding towards E Company's line, and plenty of Blood Pact with them.

He knew he needed a better angle on the next tank. He tensed, then ran out across the open stretch towards the rocks where Larkin was huddled. A squall of gunfire chased him. He threw himself flat and crawled in beside the sniper.

'Very dainty,' Larkin said.

'They were shooting at me.'

'I don't blame them. Look at the mess you made of their nice tank.' Larkin smacked in a fresh hot-shot clip and settled his long-las. 'Speaking of tanks,' he began.

They were getting close. Caffran didn't need the old marksman to tell him that. What he needed was a rocket load. His launcher was smoking and empty.

'Guheen! Any time soon!'

Guheen shouted back something incomprehensible. Lugging the rocket bag, he started to run, and made it to the boulder that had previously given Caffran shelter.

'You know,' Larkin began, conversationally, as if they weren't actually in the middle of a horrendous firefight. 'Those kids. Nice kids. Kolea really ought to wake up and do something. They deserve to know.'

Caffran blinked at him. 'Feth, does everybody know?'

Larkin shrugged. 'Tona told me. On Gereon, there wasn't any place for secrets.'

'Gereon, Gereon, Gereon... I'd give real money if you lot would shut up about that place. It was just a place. Just a fething place.'

'You weren't there,' said Larkin. 'You don't know.'

'I know I'm sick of hearing about it,' Caffran turned. 'Guheen! I need those rockets!'

'One moment you're alive, the next you're dead. In this game, I mean,' Larkin rambled on.

'Shut up, you old bastard!'

'And what are secrets worth then? Even secrets made with the best intentions. Your son and your daughter deserve to know about their other father, Caff. And Gol deserves to–'

'Shut up, Larkin! Shut the feth up! We're in trouble here!'

Heavy-duty lasfire screeched over their heads from the lead tank.

'Guheen! Load me!'

Guheen looked left and right, halted as shots whipped past, and then started his run to Caffran's side, the heavy rocket bag over his shoulder.

He got three metres, and a hard round from the Blood Pact infantry went into the side of his head. Everything inside his skull came out in a shower on the other side. Before he'd even started to fall, two more shots had ripped into him, screwing his flailing body around, forcing it to lose all structure and semblance of humanity.

He hit the dry ground and rolled, one hand clawing impulsively at the sky.

'Oh feth!' Caffran whispered. He started to move forward, but Larkin grabbed him and yanked him back. Gunfire raked the open space, jerking and twitching Guheen's pathetic corpse. The rocket sack was well out of reach.

The Blood Pact troopers were running in close. E Company met them with a flurry of las. Larkin dropped an officer with a perfect kill shot. But still the small-arms fire rattled in relentlessly.

'I can't load,' Caffran said. 'I can't stop those tanks.'

'That's not good,' Larkin agreed casually, thumping home another hot-shot.

'Larks!' Caffran said, keeping his head down. 'Aim for the operator. There, man! In the bubble! Kill him!'

Larkin cosied his new rifle up to his cheek, and drew aim on the nearest stalk-tank. Through his scope, he could see the mutated, augmented operator in his liquid cocoon under the arched, mantis tail.

'Larkin!'

'You don't rush these things,' Larkin said. He exhaled and pulled the trigger. The cocoon burst. The stalk-tank took another few, stuttering steps, and rocked to a halt, dead on its caliper feet.

The Blood Pact wave was almost on them. Caffran dropped his tube launcher and drew his laspistol. He started to fire at the enemy troopers running in. Nearby, Mkillian cried out as a las-round killed him and knocked him back off the rocks.

A torrent of lasfire cut a swathe across the advancing archenemy. They buckled and fell.

'Get up! Up and into them!' someone shouted.

It was Tona Criid, running forward, her weapon on full auto. Beside her came Varl and Bonin. They seemed oblivious to the danger, just running into the zipping fire.

Varl reached the rockline beside Caffran, put one boot up on it to brace himself, and let rip from the hip.

'Having a little trouble?' he asked.

Criid ran forward, shot a Blood Pact trooper in the neck, and scooped up the fallen rocket bag from beside Guheen's body.

'Catch!' she cried, throwing it to Caffran.

'First-and-Only!' Varl shouted as he unloaded. 'First-and-fething-Only!'

Caffran grabbed the bag and began packing a rocket into his tube. 'Tona!' he yelled. 'We need to–'

'Shut up, I'm working here!' she shouted, ripping rounds through a trio of Blood Pact troops.

One moment you're alive, the next you're dead. And what are secrets worth then? Caffran briefly looked at Guheen's body. All the way from Tanith, then just gone. Just gone, like that.

He latched a fresh rocket into the launcher, primed it with a quick blessing, and raised the weapon onto his shoulder.

SEVENTY METRES BEHIND him, Wilder was confronting Baskevyl, Feygor and Meryn.

'This isn't the time,' he was saying.

'I think it is,' Baskevyl said. 'Luc, I came down here and I happened to repeat my flippant comment about how I wished I could plug that gate. And Feygor said we could.'

'It's possible,' Feygor said.

'This is crazy talk,' Wilder said.

'No, sir,' said Baskevyl. 'Hear the man out.'

'We could blow it,' Feygor said. 'If we got sufficient charge in there.'

'And how do you hope to–'

'Mark IX land mines,' Feygor smiled. 'There were plenty of them on the munition train last time I looked. Packed with compressive diotride D-6. Explosive putty, very nasty. Give me half an hour and a decent trigger mechanism, and I could rig up a device that would bring that whole fething gate down.'

'No,' said Wilder. 'This is not an option.'

'It really is,' said Rawne, from behind Wilder.

Wilder looked round. 'Your adjutant is a demolitions expert now, is he? You don't mess around with land mines, and you certainly don't mess around with D-6. If I had an authorised bombardier here, or a tech priest, maybe I'd–'

'Feygor knows this stuff. Always has. And since Gereon–'

Wilder groaned. 'Oh, Rawne! Don't *since Gereon* me. Not now.'

'I think I will. How do you suppose we conducted our sabotage operations there, Wilder? Did we give up the idea because we didn't have an authorised bombardier with us? Feygor knows this stuff.'

'I do. I can handle it,' Feygor said.

Wilder hesitated. Up ahead, rockets were slamming into the advancing stalk-tanks.

'So, Feygor builds us a device. Then what?'

'We get it into the gateway,' Meryn said. 'Sneak it in.'

'What else?' Wilder asked.

'Someone has to carry the device,' Feygor said. 'It'll be heavy. Really heavy. I'd need someone strong.'

There was a clatter of metal tanks hitting the ground. 'I'm up for that,' Brostin said, coming forward. He had let his flamer set slide off his broad shoulders.

'Bask?'

'I think this could work, Luc,' Baskevyl said.

'Get to it, Feygor,' Wilder said.

'I'll assemble a strike team to–' Rawne said.

Meryn cut Rawne off. 'I'll assemble a strike team to get the device in place. This is an E Company initiative. Last I heard, I was still in charge of that.'

Rawne nodded.

'Then it'll be me leading that team,' Meryn said.

'No question, captain,' Wilder replied. Meryn hurried away.

Wilder realised that Rawne was looking at him. 'What?'

'You have to understand about the gateways, Wilder. The enemy isn't coming through from the next compartment. It's simply coming out of the gate. It's warping out of that archway.'

Wilder shrugged. 'Whatever, Rawne. But if we plug that gate, the result's the same, right?'

Rawne nodded. 'I think so.'

As Meryn strode off, Banda caught his sleeve.

'What are you doing?' she asked.

'Getting it done, Jessi,' he said.

'I heard you overrule Rawne just then. Are you trying to prove something?'

He looked at her. 'What if I am?'

'If you are, try not to make me miss you when you're gone,' Banda said.

HALF AN HOUR turned into an hour and a half. The enemy continued to emerge from the gate. Each time it did, sighing winds from another world gusted out across the compartment.

'Feygor?' Wilder called over the microbeads.

'It's ready. A real job. Coming in now.'

'Bask!' Wilder yelled. 'Full spread across the gate mouth! Obel? Domor? Varaine? Company fire for support!'

Near the mid-point of the Eighty-First First line, Novobazky had managed to rally I Company. They had taken up position in and around a long island of thorny scrub, which gave them a good angle on the gate. 'Fire for support!' Novobazky shouted. He could see an alarming number of crimson figures in amongst the broken granite seventy metres ahead. Stray tracer shells sailed by, high overhead, like lost birds.

'Commissar!'

Novobazky turned to see Hark running up.

'We're going to need to rise and push,' Hark told him. 'Sitting here and firing isn't going to cut it. You can't see it from this angle, but there's a mass of hostiles around behind that outcrop. This company needs to come forward to that line and lay down a field of fire, or the bastards are going to cut right down our centreline.'

Novobazky nodded, and relayed instructions to the section leaders. Then he remembered the plasma pistol, and offered it to Hark.

'Yours.'

'Keep it,' said Hark.

'Thank you. It served us well,' Novobazky said.

'It's about to again,' Hark said sourly. 'I understand you met Gaunt.'

Novobazky nodded. 'Briefly. He seemed to me to be an admirable man.'

'I'm glad you think so,' Hark nodded. 'I always believed that was the case.'

The combined companies of the Eighty-First First were now hosing the gate mouth with fire.

'Company up to address!' Novobazky yelled. 'Advance and fire at will!'

MERYN'S STRIKE TEAM, twenty-strong, ran forward, cutting through the Blood Pact resistance on the east side of the gate. Meryn had chosen the east side because it was particularly cluttered with loose rock and fat slabs of stone that had fallen from the walls over the centuries. There was plenty of cover, and for the most part they would be shielded from the main Blood Pact retinues.

It was still murderous. Wildfire sizzled between the rocks, and every few metres, hostile troops would suddenly appear from behind boulders. In the first fifteen minutes, two of the Tanith fell, then three of the Belladon Meryn had selected from E Company.

'Come on! Come on!' Meryn yelled out. They had a brief window of opportunity, all the while the heavy fire from the Eighty-First First line was driving the archenemy backwards towards the end wall of the compartment.

Meryn ran ahead, firing short bursts around the rocks. Behind him came Brostin, struggling under the weight of Feygor's jury-rigged device.

'Keep up!' Feygor shouted, lugging the detonator pack.

'Feth it, Murt, you try carrying this!' Brostin growled back.

Shells slammed in around them. The air stank of scorching lasfire.

Meryn reached the crest of rock in front of the gate. A las-round smacked into his head, and he fell.

Vision blurred and in pain, he reached up and found a wet gash across his scalp. *Almost* a kill shot.

'Advance!' he yelled.

The archenemy had spread wide, out of the gate. Growling armour was now advancing towards Callide's position, and sweeping east towards the Hauberkan line. The gate itself was empty, vacant like the cavity of a skull.

Brostin staggered into the vast, black mouth of the gate.

'How deep?' he yelled back, his voice echoing.

'Into the throat of it!' Meryn shouted. Shots were winging up from the Blood Pact in the lower basin. They had suddenly realised that a recon force had sneaked around behind them. Cager fell, dead. Mkeln toppled over, his chest torn apart.

'Quickly now!' Meryn yelled. His head hurt.

A las-round hit Meryn in the arm, and exploded his bicep in a shower of bloody meat.

Feygor grabbed him and kept him upright. 'Run!' Feygor said.

'But–'

'Just fething run, Meryn!' Feygor screamed. 'Brostin's set the charge.'

Brostin came running back out of the gateway. Lasfire hit him. He fell, and then got up again, blood streaming from multiple wounds

'Set and down!' he shouted. Two more members of Meryn's strike team were hit and killed.

'Go! Go on!' Feygor yelled, setting down the makeshift detonator pack. Meryn began to sprint, lasrounds whistling after him.

'Open wide,' Feygor said, slamming down the plunger.

For a second, nothing seemed to happen. The force of the blast was so severe, its noise and violence were off the scale of human senses. There was a solid, heavy slam, like an immense weight had hit the earth, then a gigantic, volcanic shower of mud and rock and smoke sprayed out of the gate mouth.

Feygor began to laugh. He threw aside the detonator pack and rose to his feet.

A las-round smacked into his chest. He fell down onto his knees, gurgling and coughing blood.

'Murt! Murt!' Brostin cried out as he reached him.

Murt Feygor murmured something, and slumped onto the ground.

Brostin scooped his limp body up and began to run.

'SEE THAT?' BASKEVYL cried out. 'They did it!'

Wilder waited. He watched the huge, dense cone of smoke rise from the fireball engulfing the gate. He thought he might almost be ready to start smiling.

He felt the cool breeze of a pressure change sweep across him, as if a door had opened somewhere, letting in the cold. The smoke billowed and the flames seethed away as chilly air fanned through them. A line of crimson battle tanks, rusted and heavy, began to roll out of the sixth compartment gate, spilling the debris and dying flames in front of them.

They *hadn't* done it. Not even slightly.

TWENTY-SEVEN

18.11 hrs, 199.776.M41
Fifth Compartment
Sparshad Mons, Ancreon Sextus

THE TRAITOR HOSTS of the damned and the insane
vomited out of the gate mouth in a swollen tide. It
seemed to the men on the ground as if the warp itself
had torn open and scattered its contents forth. The
charging formations of war machines and troops, of
mobile guns and fluttering banners, made everything
that they had faced so far seem trivial and slight. The
forces they had struggled and fought with over the last
few days had been just an advance guard.

Night was falling, but the black filth coiling out of the
sixth compartment gate around the arriving hostiles
reached upwards and accelerated the descent of darkness. The arcane door had opened so wide this time,
weather swept through with it from the climate systems
of whatever fell world these creatures had embarked
from. Not just cold winds, but fog and moisture. Lightning discharge crackled around the tops of the

compartment walls, and covered the stone face of the Mons's towering heart like luminous ivy. Ice rain began to fall, hissing into the fires.

The Kolstec forces took immediate heavy losses and fell back in a desperate, scrabbling retreat. Then fire fell upon the Eighty-First First too. Callide and almost his entire company were cut down and destroyed. Hundreds of bodies in black battledress lay amongst the burning scrub.

Wilder drew the Eighty-First First back, through the rain, through the belts of scraggy woodland and outcropping granite. The temptation was to flee, but that would hasten yet greater disaster. The archenemy had to be slowed. They had to be harried and delayed. The Kolstec, half-breaking to the west, seemed unable to accomplish this, but the remnants of the Hauberkan treads were still operating in support of the Eighty-First First.

The sound of gunfire was constant and deafening. Wilder caught up with Keshlan at a dry watercourse.

'Signal DeBray!' Wilder yelled above the noise. 'Tell him the retiring line has got to move faster! As fast as it can. Tell him they've got to get out of the compartment! Tell him all hell is coming after them!'

Half a kilometre back, in a stretch of burning woodland, Rawne, Kolea and Baskevyl had established decent bounding cover between the men they brought with them. Two sections would sustain fire while the third fell back. It worked against the foot troops and the ranks of grotesque mutants that poured into the treeline. But there were tanks coming, heavy Brigands by the sound of their engines, perhaps something even bigger, and the sections had no rockets left.

Rawne saw men move past him in the smoke, stragglers trying to rejoin the retreat. Many were badly hurt.

He saw Meryn, covered in blood, helped along by two Belladon troopers.

He saw Brostin, trotting as fast as he could, a limp figure in his arms.

'Brostin!' Rawne ran to him. The flame-trooper was smeared in blood. He'd been hit himself several times. Feygor was just a loose bundle, blood soaking his tunic.

'Put him down,' Rawne said.

'I can carry him. I've got to get him to a medic. I've got to get him to Dorden. He'll patch him up.'

Rawne put his hand against Feygor's neck. It was impossible to tell if there was a pulse left, or any sign of respiration. Even if Feygor was still alive, he wouldn't be by the time Brostin had carried him back down the compartment.

'Put him down,' Rawne repeated.

'No!' Brostin was agitated by the idea. 'We didn't come all the way through fething Gereon to wind up dying in a place like this! I can carry him!' he moved on, blundering through the smoking trees. 'I can carry him!'

WILDER REACHED AN area of rising, open ground, and tried to take his bearings. To the east, at least four companies of the Eighty-First First, along with some Hauberkan armour, was cutting along the scrublands, moving steadily south. Directly behind him, Daur's company and parts of Obel's, along with an assortment of men from Kolosim and Varaine's commands, were caught in a brutal firefight with the leading edge of the Blood Pact units.

Wilder realised the western flank of the breakaway was yawning dangerously. If the enemy overlapped, they'd catch Daur, Obel and the others quickly and simply. What had happened to his formation?

He looked around again, calling A Company up around him into a firing line. His throat was sore from smoke. The rain was getting heavier, and the ground was turning to mire. To the south of him, the ground shelved away and rose into a significant hill. With a little surprise, Wilder realised it was Hill 56, the very site they'd been assigned to at the start of this punishing and pointless expedition. If he could retain cohesion long enough to get a force onto its back, he'd have a commanding field of fire right across the scrub. To the west of the hill, the main trackway ran wide. It was choked with a portion of the fleeing Kolstec units. He saw, to his dismay, that in the mayhem, both Domor's and Sabrese's companies had fallen back too far, right onto the track. That was where the gap had formed.

'Keshlan!' he yelled. 'Get me Sabrese, quickly! We've got to get him to move up a little.'

The vox-officer obeyed, but he looked dubious. The distance was significant. Persuading those men to turn back into the teeth of the enemy advance was going to be a tall order. Fierce shelling and heavy weapons fire was coming out of the ruined scrub to the left. Even the most loyal soldiers would falter from an effort like that.

A curious thing began to happen. Keshlan had yet to secure a clear channel, but Sabrese and Domor's men were beginning to move back anyway. They were advancing into the fight, covering the trackway. The gap was actually starting to close.

'Link up with those men!' Wilder shouted to A Company. 'Across the slope! Give them covering fire as they close up!'

Blood Pact and mutant troopers swarmed out of the scrub, but the supporting companies drove them back again with a blistering rate of shots. Wilder could hear shouts coming from Domor's men, and Sabrese's too. Battle cries. Passionate, almost eager.

He saw two figures amongst them. Two commissars, directing the steady flow of the regroup. One had a sword raised aloft.

'GHOSTS OF TANITH! Men of Belladon!' Gaunt shouted. 'Close the line! Deny the enemy!'

'First-and-Only!' the men were shouting.

'Domor! Get some men onto those rocks,' Gaunt yelled as he strode forward through the men. Eszrah came with him, reynbow raised. The men seemed as astonished at the sight of Gaunt as they were by the towering warrior at his heels.

'Yes, sir!' Domor barked. Despite the enclosing horror, there was a renewed vitality in the troops. 'Gaunt's with us!' Domor shouted. 'Gaunt's with us! Chiria, Nehn! Get men into those rocks! Raglon, section to the left, rapid fire!'

'We can do this,' Gaunt said to Domor. 'We can't win, but we can hold them back.'

'Yes, sir,' Domor said. He couldn't quite accept the sight of the man in front of him. Even with his augmetic eyes, Gaunt didn't seem real. 'Sir, are you a ghost?' he asked.

Gaunt smiled. 'Always have been.'

Ludd ran up. 'Sections are holding to the right, sir.'

'Go to them, Ludd. Keep them together and keep them strong.'

'How, commissar?'

'Improvise. Sing them a song, tell them you're my clone-son, whatever works.' Ludd nodded, and rushed away. Wounded stragglers from the rear of the break-away stumbled past. The Tanith and Verghastite amongst them blinked when they saw Gaunt. Some stopped, and despite their injuries, came to him.

'Keep moving,' Gaunt called out. 'Get onto the track and get away from here. We'll drink to this day together, later on.'

Gaunt saw Brostin amongst them, Brostin and the sad bundle he carried. He went over to the bulky flame-trooper immediately. Brostin sank down to his knees, tired, hurt and barely able to go on. He clutched Feygor's limp body tightly in his hefty arms.

'Let him go,' Gaunt said. 'Let him lie on the ground.'

'Sir…'

Eszrah knelt down and examined Feygor. He looked at Gaunt and shook his head.

'He's gone, Brostin,' said Gaunt. 'I'm too late for him, but not the rest of you.'

Brostin gently laid Feygor's body on the wet grass. Rain streamed off his beard like tears.

'Get moving, Brostin. I'll catch you up.'

Gaunt straightened up and turned back to face the fight. Eszrah touched his arm lightly and pointed. An officer was approaching.

'Commissar Gaunt?'

'Colonel Wilder?'

They stood facing each other in the rain. Gaunt put his sword in his left hand and held out his right.

'My compliments, colonel. The lord general has ordered me back to the line to assist with the rearguard.'

Wilder shook his hand. 'We don't seem to need much help dying right now,' Wilder said.

'You've executed a fine breakaway action, Wilder,' Gaunt said. 'A great number of lives have been spared by–'

'It's not over,' Wilder said bluntly. 'You have no idea of the weight of hostiles at our heels.'

'Nevertheless, I believe we should still call the day done. Move the men onto the trackway and get them out to–'

'You're not listening!' Wilder snapped. 'There is a nightmare coming and we must check it for as long as we can. I intend to get a force up onto that hill, at least a company strong. From there, they should be able to hold the scrubland long enough to allow the rest to get away.'

Gaunt regarded the hill. 'It would be possible, I suppose…'

'Look, Gaunt. I know you just want to get your men out.'

'My men? They're not my men, Wilder. They're yours. The Eighty-First First. And a fine regiment too. Give me command of a company, and I'll hold that hill for you. I'll buy you enough time to get the rest of your men clear.'

Wilder smiled and shook his head. 'I'll not order a man to die while I run for home. Nor do I expect you to do a job I wouldn't do myself. My regiment, you said. My men. My job.'

'Wilder–'

'I believe I outrank you, commissar. You don't hold a command rank. I will hold the hill with A Company. My orders to you are to take field command of the remainder of the regiment, and conduct them to a place of safety while I cover your backs.'

'Throne's sake, Wilder, don't be so awkward! This isn't some contest to see which of us is the bigger man, this–'

'Actually, it almost is. This way, we both win and we both lose.'

'Colonel, I'm not–'

'Are you disobeying direct orders, Gaunt? I'd heard you'd come back from that place with an unruly streak to you. A touch of taint, they say. A lack of proper discipline. No place for that in the Imperial Guard. I've given you your orders. Are you going to follow them?'

Gaunt glared at Wilder. 'Yes, sir,' he said, and saluted.

'Excellent. Carry on.' Wilder saluted back and turned away.

'The Emperor protects,' Gaunt said.

Wilder snorted. 'Some of us he does.'

THE ANGLE OF fire from the top of Hill 56 was as good as Wilder had hoped. He formed A Company up, and began laying fusillades down across the scrub, where the enemy formations were now in sight, toiling forward through the scorched and smoking land.

'Keep the rate up, A Company!' Wilder yelled. There seemed to be a near impossible number of targets crossing the valley below, hordes of red and black figures, machines that rolled or walked. The woods beyond burned like a blast furnace and threw smoke up the towering compartment wall. Stalkers had appeared in great numbers too, no doubt from their mysterious doorways. Many were bounding ahead of the enemy troops like gigantic attack dogs, hooting and roaring. Some were gigantic things.

Down on the trackway to the west of A Company, the last of their comrades moved away, south, into the enclosing darkness.

Genadey Novobazky strode down the A Company line, his voice firm and defiant. 'On the Shores of Marik, my friends,' he declaimed, 'the fathers of our fathers made a stand under the flag of Belladon. Did they break and run? Yes! But only in their minds. They ran to friendly places and loved ones, where they could be safe... and then, by the providence of the God-Emperor, they saw what those friendly places and loved ones would become if they did not stand fast, and so stand fast they did! How do you feel?'

There was a triumphant bellow from the ranks.

'Belladon blood is like wine on the Emperor's lips!' Novobazky stormed. 'Belladon souls have a special place at his side! If we spill our blood here today, then this is the soil He has chosen to bless and anoint! Oh, lucky land!' He took out the plasma pistol, and carefully toggled off the safety. No mistakes this time. 'Stand firm and fire, my friends, stand firm and fire! If they're going to have our precious blood, then they'll find the cost is dearer than they can afford! Fury of Belladon! Fury! Fury!'

Wilder grinned as he heard the surge of Novobazky's speech. A piece of art that, he'd always thought. And never more so than now.

'Keshlan!' The vox-officer ran to him.

'Yes, colonel!'

'Wilder beckoned for the vox horn. 'Speaker broadcast, please, Keshlan. All the volume you've got.'

'Yes, sir!'

THE FIRST OF the archenemy warriors began to charge up the slopes of Hill 56, into the hail of gunfire. Hundreds fell, but there were thousands behind them to take their places. The Blood Pact horns bellowed into the night air. Blades flashed, banners swung. Feral mutants and wrought beasts led the attack.

Crookshank Thrice-wrought was at the very front of the storming line, shrugging off the flashes of light that stung at his hide. He came up the long slope, roaring through his throat sacs. He could see and smell the meat ahead of him. The rows of little meat figures who curiously refused to flee at the sight of him.

Bounding forward, the thrice-wrought opened his mouth and engaged his teeth.

WILDER THUMBED ON the vox horn and raised it to his mouth. When he spoke, his voice boomed out from Keshlan's vox, distorted with volume.

'Stand firm, A Company! Fury of Belladon! Hold this line and deny them!'

His amplified voice echoed out across the bleak hillside, carrying his command away into the rain and the raging night.

His last command.

EPILOGUE

00.07 hrs, 200.776.M41
Ancreon Sextus

THE SUN CAME out, in the middle of the night, and the step-cities died. Even from a great distance, it was impossible for observers to look directly at the bombardment without filters or glare-shades. Devastating pillars of white light came down from the top of the sky and burned deep, black holes into the world.

It took the warships of the Imperial Navy five hours of sustained orbital bombardment to wipe the ancient and cursed stones of the monolithic cities from existence.

In the days that followed, all that remained at the sites where the step-cities had once stood were gaping wounds in the earth, some a kilometre deep. Within these slowly cooling cavities, jewelled beauty lurked. The fury of the weapons had transformed the rock and sand, fusing it into swathes of glass that glinted and swam with colour in the bright sun.

***

JUST AFTER MIDNIGHT, Gaunt was amongst the many hundreds of Imperial officers congregated on the hull-top landing pads of one of the command Leviathans to watch the distant doom of Sparshad Mons. Zweil stood by his side. He'd borrowed Eszrah's glare-shades, and winced and gasped at every flash of light.

'You did that, Ibram,' Van Voytz said, coming up to Gaunt and nodding in the direction of the fearsome lightshow. 'Hope you're proud of yourself.'

'Proud of something, sir.'

'I understand they're yours again?' Van Voytz said.

'It's a field command only,' said Gaunt. 'Just temporary.'

'We'll see,' said Van Voytz.

'He said he couldn't, but he could, you know,' Zweil said after Van Voytz had moved on.

'What?' Gaunt asked.

'He said he couldn't bring things back from the dead, but it turned out he could.'

'Who are we talking about, father?'

'Wilder,' Zweil said.

'Oh.'

'You and Rawne and the others all came back when we thought you dead. And now the unit has too.'

'I don't–'

'It's yours again. Wilder gave them back to you. Not his Ghosts. Yours again. Gaunt's Ghosts, back from the dead.'

'You know, you talk a lot of nonsense sometimes, father,' Gaunt said.

THE HATCH OF the holding cell opened and Inquisitor Welt entered the chamber. Commissar Faragut got up from the table to make room for the inquisitor.

Welt sat down beside the commissar-general. 'How are we doing?' he asked.

'I think we're getting somewhere,' Balshin said, looking across the table at the interview subject.

'Good, good,' said Welt. 'Shall we go back over the main areas, in case there's something we missed?'

'Fine with me,' said Balshin. Welt looked questioningly at the interview subject.

Sabbatine Cirk shrugged. 'Just tell me what you want to know.'

ABOUT THE AUTHOR

Dan Abnett lives and works in Maidstone, Kent, in England. Well known for his comic work, he has written everything from the *Mr Men* to the *X-Men* in the last decade, and is currently scripting *Legion of Superheroes* and *Superman* for DC Comics, and *Sinister Dexter* and *The VCs* for 2000 AD. His work for the Black Library includes the popular comic strips *Lone Wolves*, *Titan* and *Inquisitor Ascendant*, the best-selling Gaunt's Ghosts novels, and the acclaimed Inquisitor Eisenhorn trilogy.